THE END OF THE WORLD CLUB

THE JAGUAR STONES
Book Two

THE
END OF THE WORLD
CLUB

J&P VOELKEL

EGMONT
USA
New York

EGMONT

We bring stories to life

First published by Egmont USA, 2011
443 Park Avenue South, Suite 806
New York, NY 10016

1 3 5 7 9 8 6 4 2

www.egmontusa.com
www.jaguarstones.com

Library of Congress Cataloging-in-Publication Data
Voelkel, Jon.
The end of the world club / J&P Voelkel.
p. cm. — (The Jaguar Stones ; bk. 2)
Summary: With the end of the Mayan calendar fast approaching, fourteen-year-old Max Murphy and
his friend Lola, the Maya girl who saved his life in the perilous jungle, race against time to outwit the
twelve villainous Lords of Death, following the trail of the conquistadors into a forgotten land steeped
in legend and superstition.
ISBN 978-1-60684-072-6 (hardcover) — ISBN 978-1-60684-201-0 (e-book) [1. Adventure and
adventurers—Fiction. 2. Supernatural—Fiction. 3. Mayas—Fiction. 4. Indians of Central America—
Fiction.] I. Voelkel, Pamela. II. Title.
PZ7.V861En 2011
[Fic]—dc22
2010036641

Book design by Becky Terhune

Printed in the United States of America

CPSIA tracking label information
Random House Production • 1745 Broadway • New York, NY 10019

Note on the paper:
Egmont is passionate about helping to preserve the world's ancient and precious forest habitats.
The papers used in this book are made from legal and known forestry sources and the
inside pages contain 20 percent recycled material, all of which is post-consumer waste.

To Harry, Charly, and Loulou

k yahkume'ex

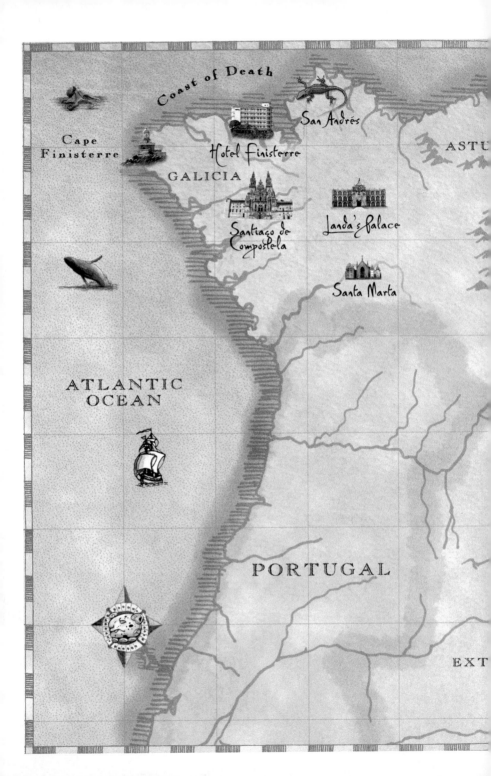

BAY OF BISCAY

CANTABRIA

RIAS

CASTILE & LEON

Madrid

Polvoredo

REMADURA

SPAIN
THE NORTHWEST

CONTENTS

CHARACTERS
In order of appearance

In Boston

MAX (Massimo Francis Sylvanus) MURPHY: fourteen years old, only child, video gamer, drummer, pizza connoisseur

FRANK and CARLA MURPHY: Max's parents, famous archaeologists

ZIA: the Murphys' mysterious housekeeper

In San Xavier

LOLA (Ix Sak Lol—*each sock loll*): Maya girl about Max's age

UNCLE TED: Max's uncle, banana exporter, and reformed smuggler

LORD 6-DOG (Ahaw Wak Ok—*uh how walk oak*): ancient Maya king

LADY COCO (Ix Kan Kakaw—*each con caw cow*): Lord 6-Dog's mother

CHULO and SERI: howler monkey siblings, currently hosting the spirits of Lord 6-Dog and Lady Coco

RAUL: Uncle Ted's butler

In Spain

NASTY (Anastasia) SMITH-JONES: music blogger

SANTINO GARCIA: law student

DOÑA CARMELA: innkeeper

PUNAK MO, aka CAPTAIN MO: Maya warrior, captain of the guard

INEZ LA LOCA: Maya princess, wife of a conquistador

OFFICER GONZALES: policeman in Polvoredo

AH PUKUH (*awe pooh coo*): Maya god of violent and unnatural death

PLAGUE RATS: punk band, comprising Ty Phoid (vocals), Vince Vermin (lead guitar), Trigger Mortis (bass), and Odd-Eye Ebola (drums)

ANTONIO DE LANDA: Spanish aristocrat

K'AWIIL (*caw wheel*): god of lightning, kingship, and lineage

FRIAR DIEGO DE LANDA: monk who burned all the Maya books

TZELEK: Lord 6-Dog's evil foster brother

In Xibalba

LORD KUY (*coo-ee*): messenger of the Lords of Death

LORDS of DEATH: twelve lords of the underworld, minions of Ah Pukuh (One Death, Seven Death, Blood Gatherer, Wing, Packstrap, Bone Scepter, Skull Scepter, Scab Stripper, Demon of Woe, Demon of Pus, Demon of Jaundice, and Demon of Filth)

HERMANJILIO (*herman-hee-leo*) BOL: Maya archaeologist, university professor

LUCKY JIM, aka Jaime Ben: Uncle Ted's foreman and bodyguard

The continuing story
of a city boy,
a jungle girl,
and, quite possibly,
the end of the world
as we know it . . .

THE TWELVE LORDS OF DEATH WERE BORED. Bored to death, in fact. For three *bak'tuns* (over a thousand years by our calendar), their power over Middleworld—the ancient Maya name for the world of mortals—had been waning.

Where had they gone wrong?

They were still doggedly tormenting humankind with famines, droughts, pain, sickness, and all manner of horrible diseases. But they no longer got the credit. Once, everyone in Middleworld had lived in fear of them. But now, no matter what hideous suffering they inflicted on the denizens of Middleworld, no one seemed to believe in them anymore.

It was de-motivating, to say the least.

Feeling forgotten and unappreciated, the Death Lords frittered away their time in the gambling halls of Xibalba, the Maya underworld, and pined for their glory days.

"Do something," they begged their boss, Ah Pukuh, the

god of violent and unnatural death, ruler of Xibalba. "The mortals don't fear us anymore."

"What can I do?" said Ah Pukuh, emitting one of his trademark bouts of flatulence. "We have been replaced by the new gods Money and Big Business."

"It's time to reassert yourself," urged the Lords of Death, holding their noses. "Remind Middleworld who's in charge."

Ah Pukuh thought about it.

A smile spread over his evil, bloated, pock-marked face.

"Yes, why not?" he said. "When the *bak'tun* changes, I will seize my chance. Those idiot mortals are already fearful that the Maya calendar is about to end—and their pathetic lives with it. I will exploit their panic and bring Middleworld to its knees. All I need are my natural talents for destruction . . . and the five Jaguar Stones."

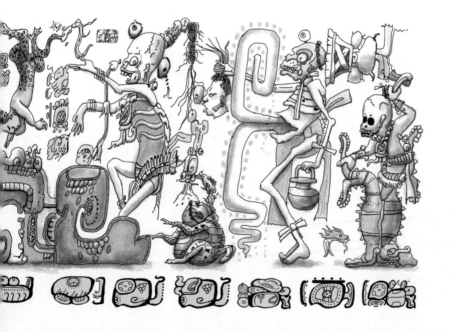

THE DREAM

Max Murphy lay in his coffin, gasping for air.

He'd been buried alive.

The wooden box was exactly the same size as his body, as if it had been tailor-made for him. It smelled of pine resin, straw, and fresh sawdust, with an undertone of cow dung.

A wave of nausea swelled the rising tide of panic in Max's brain.

He felt something crawling on his cheek.

He went to brush it away and found he couldn't move.

Everything below his neck was bound in strips of cloth, like a mummy, and his arms were pinned to his sides.

He had a sense of motion, like the rolling of a ship.

As the full meaning of his situation dawned on him, his blood ran cold.

He was wrapped in a shroud, being carried in a coffin.

It could only signify one thing.

He was on his way to his own funeral.

"Let me out!" he yelled, but his voice was muffled by the box.

He strained to work his hands free of the strips of cloth. Then, gathering his strength, he curled his fists and launched them straight upward at the lid.

To his surprise, it flew open easily.

At first, all he saw was a gray sky, and a bird of prey—a vulture?—hovering above him. He could hear whistling and screaming, raucous laughter and firecrackers.

He pulled off more of the bandages until he could move enough to peer over the edge of the coffin.

Immediately, he locked eyes with a fluorescent green devil.

All around him, hideous ghouls were thrusting their garishly painted faces at him and clicking their fat tongues.

The Grim Reaper floated by, pursued by a dancing skeleton.

There was a smell of burning. A screeching of bagpipes, like the sound of a cat having its claws pulled out one by one, filled the smoky air.

Was this some kind of hell?

Max sat up and screamed a scream to wake the dead.

The light snapped on.

"Not again! Every night since we came home from San Xavier, it is the same thing," groaned his mother, pulling a bathrobe over her nightdress as she shuffled sleepily into the bedroom. "It was a dream, just another dream."

"I was in a coffin . . . ," began Max.

"Shhhh." His mother put a finger to her lips. With her tired eyes all red and bloodshot, she looked alarmingly like one of the ghouls in his dream. "It is the middle of the night. Go back to sleep."

"But it was so real, Mom. There were skeletons and demons and—"

"Were you reading about the ancient Maya again today?" she interrupted.

Max nodded.

"That is where these nightmares come from, I am sure of it. Too much bloodletting and human sacrifice. Tomorrow, I am going to hide the books, and maybe we can all get a good night of sleep."

"No!" protested Max, sitting up in bed. "I need to know everything I can about the Maya. There's something I have to do. . . ."

His mother opened her mouth to argue, then thought better of it. "I hear you," she said, choosing her words carefully. "You have made a choice to study the Maya, and I will support it. Tomorrow, I will find you a book about corn. It was one of their staple foods."

Max sighed. His mother had just acquired a parenting manual (her first in fourteen years) and, with it, the annoying habit of talking in therapyspeak.

"I wish you'd stop saying you hear me and actually listen to me, Mom. I don't need to know about corn. I need to know about the Lords of Death and their ruler, Ah Pukuh."

His mother placed the back of her hand against her forehead, like a Victorian heroine about to have a fainting spell. (Possibly because she was Italian, she was always a little prone to dramatics.) "I understand that you are exploring your identity as a preadult, but this Lords of Death silliness has got to stop." Her voice quavered. "You are ruining the summer for everyone. . . ."

"Excuse me?" he said in disbelief. "You think *I'm* ruining the summer? It was you and Dad who got us into this mess."

"You're fourteen years of age. You cannot keep blaming your father and me for everything that happens. You make us sound like bad parents."

But that's exactly what you are, thought Max.

Ironically, his friends thought he was lucky to be the only child of the famous archaeologists Frank and Carla Murphy. But then, his friends just saw the gifts that his parents lavished on him: the video games, the laptop, the electronic drums—all peace offerings for being too busy at work to support their son at school concerts and class nights and sports meets. (After the recent events in San Xavier, he was expecting a "sorry for opening a portal to the Maya underworld and unleashing the forces of evil that almost killed you" gift any day now.)

Max had long ago accepted that his parents cared more about the ancient Maya than about their own son, but recently they'd reached a new low in the history of bad parenting.

He could still remember the shock of that afternoon, a few weeks ago, when they'd come home early from work and dropped three bombshells, one after the other.

Boom! They'd canceled the upcoming family vacation in Italy.

Boom! They were leaving there and then for a dig in San Xavier, the tiny Central American country where his father had grown up.

Boom! Max's whole summer was shot to pieces.

And that was it. They were gone.

But their irresponsible behavior didn't end there.

It turned out that his father had got his hands on a Jaguar Stone, one of five sacred carvings that supposedly gave Maya kings their special powers, and his parents had gone to San Xavier to test it out.

All too predictably—didn't adults learn anything from disaster movies?—things had spiraled out of control, and soon they'd unleashed all sorts of ancient evils into the world.

And then they'd vanished off the face of the earth.

That would have been the last anyone had heard of Frank and Carla Murphy, reflected Max, if their incredibly brave and intelligent son hadn't tracked them down to Xibalba, the Maya underworld. Which was how he now found himself in negotiations with a gang of crazies called the Lords of Death.

And that was the lite version of his visit to San Xavier.

Along the way, he'd survived numerous assassination attempts, an oath of blood, a toxic stew, snakes, scorpions, an undead army, several terrifying encounters with the forces of evil, and at least one attempt at human sacrifice.

Oh, and let's not forget that Max had been all alone in the perilous jungle until he'd run into the beautiful Lola. (Of course, she didn't know he thought she was beautiful. At least he hoped she didn't.) Lola was a modern Maya girl, which was news to Max as he thought the Maya had all died out hundreds of years ago. Anyway, Chan Kan, the Maya wise man, had said that Max and Lola made a good team—like the Hero Twins in Maya mythology. And it was true that, with Lola to teach him, Max had been starting to get the hang of life in the jungle.

It was all going so well until Hermanjilio, the eccentric local archaeologist who'd been with Max's parents on the night they disappeared, decided to try and bring back the ancient Maya king Lord 6-Dog. To Lola's dismay, the spirits of the king and his mother had ended up in the bodies of her two friendly howler monkeys. But worse still, the evil priest

Tzelek had gate-crashed the party and taken over Hermanjilio's own body.

Max shivered at the memory.

"Are you cold?" asked his mother. "Would you like some hot salami soup?"

Salami soup? Who makes soup out of salami?

He shook his head in revulsion.

Since they'd got back from San Xavier, Carla Murphy had cut back her hours at work to concentrate on her mothering skills. When she wasn't reading her new parenting manual, *Understanding Your Teen*, she now spent most of her time in the kitchen, wearing a flowery apron and trying out new culinary creations. She was convinced that a talent for cooking was in her Italian genes and saw no need to consult the recipe books. As a result, her lasagna looked like joke-shop rubber vomit, her risotto resembled boiled earwax, and her pizza brought to mind a cheese-encrusted Frisbee.

Max longed for the day when they could go back to ordering takeout.

"No soup?" His mother pursed her lips. "Then I will make you something special for breakfast. Venetian liver and onions, perhaps? It is your *nonno's* favorite."

Nonno is Italian for "grandfather," and Max's Italian grandfather ate anything—even tripe, which is the lining of a cow's stomach.

Max shuddered. "Toast is fine, mom."

Her shoulders slumped in disappointment for a moment. Then she had another idea. "I know," she said, perking up. "Tomorrow we will spend quality time together. Maybe dig out your old baby photos and do some scrapbooking. . . ."

"Scrapbooking?" Max sounded appalled. "Is that an idea

21

from your parenting book? It should be called *Misunderstanding Your Teen.*"

His mother sniffed. "It is written by experts," she said.

"If you want us to spend time together, why not sit and tell me everything you know about the Death Lords? I had to promise them a favor in return for releasing you and Dad from Xibalba. I owe them big-time and, sooner or later, they're going to collect on it. I have no idea what they're going to ask me, but I'm fairly sure that it won't be for a loan of my Xbox. There's something going on, Mom, something big, and I don't know how much time I have. Will you help me learn everything I can about the Maya?"

Carla Murphy stiffened. "I cannot be an enabler for your morbid fantasies, Massimo."

Massimo was the first name on Max's birth certificate. His full name was Massimo Francis Sylvanus Murphy:

Massimo after his *nonno* . . .

Francis after his father . . .

And the truly embarrassing *Sylvanus* after some old archaeologist.

Luckily for Max, everyone had always called him *Max* for short—except his mother when she was angry with him. And boy, was she angry now.

"Either you stop this crazy talk," she was saying, "or you see a therapist. I know you are at a difficult age, Massimo, but this behavior is not normal."

"I'll show you what's not normal," responded Max. "Look at me! I'm still covered with cuts and bruises from fighting an evil Maya priest called Tzelek on top of the Black Pyramid. . . ."

He held out his battered arms and hands.

Carla inspected his wounds.

"It was that machete you used in the jungle," she said. "Those things are lethal." She pointed accusingly at the sharp steel blade Max had hung on his wall as a souvenir of San Xavier. "I do not know what you were thinking, bringing it back to Boston with you."

"What about the marks on my neck? You can still see where Tzelek dug in his fingernails." Max remembered how he'd felt his life slipping away before Lucky Jim, a tough guy from a long line of Maya warriors, had saved him in the nick of time.

Carla regarded the line of little scabs and waved dismissively.

"Insect bites," she said. "The mosquitoes are vicious in San Xavier."

"You are *so* ungrateful!" exclaimed Max. "Your own son nearly died trying to save you and two good men are still trapped in Xibalba, thanks to you!"

"Don't be ridiculous! You're living in a fantasy world, Massimo!"

"Where are they then? Lola says no one's seen Hermanjilio since that day on the Black Pyramid and Lucky's missing, too. His family is going crazy."

"Well, I am sorry about that but, wherever they are, I can tell you that they are *not* in Xibalba. It is a mythical place. It is not real!"

"How can you say that, Mom? I saw you when you came out of Xibalba. You looked really bad . . . like a homeless person. Your hair was all matted!"

His mother, who never usually had a hair out of place, instinctively patted her shiny black bob. "It is hard to keep up standards in the jungle, with all the rain and the humidity," she said defensively.

"What about the piece of jade in Dad's tooth? I'm not imagining that!"

"Just because your father has an active interest in ancient Maya dentistry . . ."

"You and Dad were prisoners in Xibalba! It happened, you know it did—"

"Massimo! Stop this!"

"But, Mom, I'm in big trouble. We *all* are. . . ."

Shaking her head in despair, his mother got up and wrapped her robe tightly around her. "I cannot take this anymore," she said, heading for the door.

"It's not about *you*, Mom. It's about *everyone*."

His mother nodded sadly. "It says in my book that an only child often thinks he is the center of the universe."

"No, I mean it really is the end of the world. . . ."

"How many times must I say *sorry*, Massimo? I am sorry that I went back to work as soon as you were born, I am sorry I did not bake all your birthday cakes myself, I am sorry we did not take violin lessons together, but—"

"Violin lessons? What are you talking about? No, Mom, you don't understand—"

She held up a finger for silence. "I do understand. You are trying to make me feel guilty. But it is not going to work. I said I was sorry for leaving you behind and going on that dig, and that is the end of it. I am doing everything I can to be a better mother. Perhaps it is time that you tried to be a better son."

Max was outraged. "A better son? I rescued you from Xibalba! And you're only out on parole, remember. If I mess up this deal with the Death Lords, they'll drag you right back there. And this time, you won't get out."

24

His mother gave a little shudder. "As long as we stay away from San Xavier, we are safe," she whispered.

Max's ears pricked up. "What did you say?"

"I . . . er . . . *niente* . . . nothing. I was talking to myself."

"You said they can't get us if we stay away from San Xavier, didn't you? But you're wrong, Mom. Can't you feel it? They're coming here, to Boston. . . ."

"No, no, you misheard me. I said that we all had strange dreams in San Xavier, but we are safe now."

"We're not safe, Mom. No one is. We need to be ready."

"We need to sleep," she said firmly.

Max sighed in resignation. "Wait, Mom, one more thing."

"What?" She sounded weary to her bones.

"It's a Mayan word, I'm trying to remember it . . . sounds like *cocoon*."

His mother shrugged. "What does it mean?"

"It's a unit of time, like a century, but it's about four hundred years?"

"You mean a *bak'tun*. It is 144,000 days."

"That's it! There's a new *bak'tun* starting soon, and—"

"Forget it, Massimo! What you are talking about, it is the Long Count calendar. Even the Maya do not follow that anymore."

"But the new *bak'tun* will be ruled by Ah Pukuh, the god of violent and unnatural death. He's in league with the Death Lords and between them, they're going to bring about a new age of destruction and chaos. . . ."

His mother massaged her temples, as if she had a headache. "Where do you get this stuff? Maybe it is those video games you like to play?"

"No, Mom, this is real life. They're coming for me. . . ."

"Enough! We are in Boston, we are safe; go to sleep." She

switched off the light and stood looking at Max in the dark for a few moments. "*Buonanotte, bambino,*" she whispered as she left the room.

Lying there in his cozy bed, Max reflected that maybe she was right. Boston was a long way from San Xavier. Maybe he *was* safe here.

For the first time in two weeks, he allowed himself to relax slightly.

Putting the ancient Maya out of his mind, he closed his eyes and pulled up the blankets.

The blankets resisted him.

There was a weight on them.

Someone was sitting on the end of the bed.

"Mom? Is that you? Are you still there?"

Max snapped on his bedside light.

It was a snake.

A big snake.

Max recognized it immediately as a fer-de-lance—the most dangerous snake in Central America. Lola had told him it was nicknamed the three-step—because if it bit you, that's how far you got before you dropped stone dead.

The snake shifted its weight and began to make its way up the bed.

It looked at Max.

Max looked at the snake.

In one more second it would strike.

With a bloodcurdling scream, Max threw the blankets on top of his unwelcome guest and leapt out of bed. Then, before the angry reptile could wind its way out, he grabbed the machete off the wall. Grunting and screaming like a demented ninja, he started hacking blindly at the bed until he had reduced it to a pile of shredded bedclothes, pillow stuffing, and mattress springs.

Only when he was sure that the machete had done its job did he calm down enough to notice his parents standing at the door, mouths open, frozen in astonishment.

Max pointed at the remains of the bed.

"It's in there," he said. "I killed it."

His father took the machete from him and, holding it at arm's length, used it to poke gingerly through the wreckage.

His mother put her hands on Max's shoulders. "You're shaking, *bambino*. Was it a mouse?"

Max closed his eyes and he saw again the deadly snake, poised to strike. "You'll see," he whispered.

"Surely not a rat?" she asked, appalled. "Did you find it, Frank?"

"I think so," said Max's father. He skewered something with the tip of the machete and held it up. "Was this it?"

Max opened his eyes.

On the end of the blade was a dismembered teddy bear.

"No!" spluttered Max. "That's not it. It was a snake. A big snake."

His father rolled his eyes. "A snake? In Boston? You had another dream, Max," he said wearily.

"But, Dad, it was a fer-de-lance. Look under the bed, look everywhere! It must have got away."

His parents exchanged glances.

"You'd better sleep on the sofa tonight," said his mother sadly.

Chapter One

THE INVASION BEGINS

Dad," said Max, "Don't you think it's odd that it rains on our house every day, when the rest of Boston is in a drought?"

He watched the torrents of rain streaming down the kitchen windows, reducing the outside world to a watery blur. The ferocity of the downpour reminded him of the rain in San Xavier, the kind that could soak you through to your underwear in a matter of minutes.

His father was sitting across the breakfast table, reading the morning paper. *DRIEST SUMMER ON RECORD*, read the headline on the front page.

"What I think is odd," said his father, from behind the newspaper, "is the fact that my fourteen-year-old son attacked his old teddy bear with a machete last night."

"I keep telling you," said Max, "there was a snake. A fer-de-lance."

Max couldn't see his father's face, but he guessed, from the whiteness of his knuckles as he gripped the paper, that he had not forgiven his son for last night's drama.

It was extraordinary to Max that his parents thought he'd chopped up his bed as some kind of plea for attention.

"I *did* see a snake, Dad," he insisted as he loaded a piece of toast with peanut butter and embedded it with banana slices and fresh blueberries. "It must be still in the house. Don't you think we should look for it?"

His father sighed and put down the newspaper. "Your mother and I are very worried about you."

"Me, too," agreed Max.

"Well, that's a start. At least you admit you need help."

Max nodded enthusiastically. "I need all the help I can get. Any day now, the Death Lords will be coming for me and—"

"That's not what I meant—" began his father before he was interrupted by an earsplitting scream. He jumped up to investigate, and Max ran after him into the hallway. They found Carla Murphy standing halfway up the stairs, pointing down in horror.

At first, Max thought she must have found the snake.

Then he saw what she was looking at. A posse of large, fat beetles was swaggering in under the front door.

"Assassin beetles!" gasped Frank Murphy, and immediately started stamping on the intruders. Their hard shells crunched beneath his feet on the wooden floor. "These guys are lethal—they carry an incurable disease. Quick, Max, squash as many as you can, then run and get the salad dressing!"

"You're not going to eat them, are you?" asked Max.

"Of course not!" snapped his father. "I'm going to leave bowls of oil and vinegar around to catch the ones that get away. They're attracted by the smell of the vinegar, so they crawl in and the oil suffocates them."

His mother was shaking her head in puzzlement. "I've

seen assassin beetles in San Xavier," she said, "but I've never heard of them this far north."

"That's global warming for you," said his father, piling up beetle corpses with his foot.

"It is certainly warm in here," agreed his mother, picking her way downstairs. "Hotter than Mount Etna in August." Something low on the wall caught her eye. "Frank! Look at this! There's fungus on the new wallpaper . . . you can almost see it spreading!"

"Calm down, Carla," said his father. "You often get mold in these old houses when it rains. Tell Zia to wipe it down with bleach."

"Zia is busy," said his mother pointedly, "cleaning up your son's room."

"He's your son, too. Why do you always call him *my* son when you're mad at him?"

Carla Murphy pursed her lips. "It's not him that I am mad at," she said quickly, making sure that Max was listening. "It is just his behavior."

"I really don't see the difference, Carla," said his father. "I say he needs to be punished."

"No, Frank," said Max's mother. "We must not play the blame game."

"So what does your book advise us to do when our son chops up his bed with a machete?"

"I will take him to buy a new bed this morning."

"He should pay for it out of his allowance," muttered his

father. He looked at his watch. "Will you be gracing us with your presence at the college today, Carla? The fellows want a debriefing on our latest findings in San Xavier."

"Are you going to tell them about your stay in Xibalba?" asked Max.

"We will be discussing the decorative frieze on the north wall at the Temple of Ixchel," replied his father. "I will try to fend them off until you arrive, Carla."

When his father had left for work, Max helped his mother clear the table.

"About the new bed, Mom . . . ," he began.

"I won't make you pay for it, *bambino*."

"But could I have a hammock instead?"

"A hammock? In your bedroom?"

"I'd feel safer. There's nowhere for a snake to hide."

His mother wagged a finger at him. "I am warning you, do not start that game again. There was no snake." She paused, evidently reviewing her words in her mind. "I hear that you would like to sleep in a hammock," she continued, "but I feel we must establish clear boundaries on this issue."

"What does that mean?"

"It means that you will sleep in a bed like a civilized person. You are not in the jungle now."

Every moment in the bed store was torture. Max found it hard to get interested in the coil count of his new mattress when the fate of the world was at stake.

"Just as long as it doesn't have *snake* coils," he muttered.

"If coils are an issue," said the baffled salesman, "perhaps you'd like to try memory foam?"

Max shrugged. "Whatever. Let's just get the cheapest bed and get out of here, Mom. I need to get home. I've got stuff to do."

"We'll take the memory foam," Carla told the clerk, "for immediate delivery." She smiled at Max as she handed over her credit card. "Maybe a comfortable mattress will put a stop to all these nightmares."

Max pursed his lips. "Can we go now?"

"But this is our quality time, *bambino*. I thought we might pick out some new clothes for you, whatever you want."

"I don't need more clothes." Max regarded the laden shoppers all around them with disdain. "One of the things I learned in San Xavier was that consumerism is a vicious circle," he said with an air of superiority.

His mother's eyes lit up. "Who taught you that? Was it Lola?"

"No. It was a chili farmer called Eusebio. He gave us a lift from Utsal to Itzamna on his boat."

"And by *us*, you mean you and Lola?"

Max blushed. "Are we done here?"

His mother pretended to inspect a patchwork comforter. "Lola seems like a nice girl," she said.

Max said nothing.

"You know, I have always imagined us like this," continued his mother. "You and me, chatting like friends, sharing confidences. I hope you'll always feel like you can talk to me about anything."

"Anything?" asked Max.

His mother nodded encouragingly. This was the moment she'd been waiting for. She had followed all the steps in her parenting manual, she had won the trust of her moody son, and now he was on the verge of telling her all about his new girlfriend in San Xavier. This was the pinnacle of parenthood. She was about to enter the inner circle of mothering achievement. Her teen was about to confide in her.

"So . . . ," began Max.

"Yes?" said his mother eagerly.

"Can we talk about what happened in San Xavier? When you and Dad activated the White Jaguar? And your camp was attacked and you ended up trapped in Xibalba? What was it like in the Maya underworld, Mom? Did you meet the Death Lords?"

The smile on his mother's face faded. "I hear you," she said. "You do not want to talk about Lola. You are asking me to respect your privacy." She reached for his hand. "But I want you to know, *bambino*, that when you are ready for an adult-to-adult relationship, I am here for you."

"Mom!" Max spoke so sharply that several other customers, all female, turned to stare. "The Death Lords are coming. You have to help me!"

His mother smiled nervously at the curious shoppers, then reached up and ruffled Max's hair. "You and your video games!" she said. The shoppers nodded and rolled their eyes in sympathy. Evidently they had teenage boys at home, too. "So, *bambino*, how about some pizza? And you can tell me more about that boat ride with Lola."

"Sorry, Mom, I need to get home."

Max's mother studied his face in alarm. "No pizza? Why are you in such a hurry?"

Max thought quickly. He couldn't tell her the truth, which was that he wanted to get home in time to quiz Zia, the Murphys' taciturn housekeeper. It was Zia who'd first instructed him to go to San Xavier, who'd implied that his parents were waiting for him, and who'd handed him the plane ticket. But she'd never explained why she'd done these things, and since he'd come back from San Xavier, she seemed to be avoiding him.

"It's not fair that Zia's cleaning my room," he explained. "I want to get back and help her."

His mother looked at him suspiciously. "You *have* changed," she said. "By the way, I asked Zia to get rid of all those Maya books."

"What? Why?"

"They are giving you bad dreams, *bambino*."

Aware of his mother's scrutiny, Max tried to look nonchalant. But it was another reason to hurry home. "Whatever," he said as casually as he could. "Gotta go!"

She blew him a kiss. "Have fun!"

Have fun. The fiends of hell were coming for him, and his mother was telling him to have fun.

He walked home as fast as he could, planning his questions for Zia.

Now, at last, she'd have to face him.

All around him, the good people of Boston went about their business. Little did they know, as they chatted on their cell phones and sipped their skinny lattes, that their comfortable lives were about to be ripped apart by Ah Pukuh, god of violent and unnatural death, and his cohorts, the twelve Death Lords.

A little boy skipped out of a toy store brandishing a plastic space monster, and Max was startled to see that the alien had a look of Ah Pukuh about it.

Maybe his parents were right. Maybe he was going crazy.

It had been a perfect summer day, not a cloud in the sky. But as he neared his house, the weather changed dramatically.

Thunder crashed, lightning flashed, and soon it was pouring rain.

Head down, collar up, Max sprinted to the front door, not even noticing that the outside of their Boston townhouse was now verdant with jungle creepers. Once inside, he gazed around in wonder.

The walls were covered in bright green mold and lichen. Luxuriant vines twined up the stairs, and butterflies played in the Spanish moss that hung from the ceiling. There was a hum of insect life.

No doubt about it, this place was turning into a rainforest.

Let's see his parents call *this* a figment of his imagination.

He ran upstairs, taking care not to step on the small lizard that basked on the landing halfway up. The door of his room was closed and, from inside, he could hear the throb of a vacuum cleaner.

Ha! He had Zia cornered. She'd have to answer his questions this time.

"Zia!" he cried, flinging open the door. "I need to ask you—"

Max stopped dead. He had never seen his room this tidy. His new bed had already been delivered and was made up with plump pillows and his old Red Sox comforter. His gleaming machete hung back on the wall. There was no sign that the putative massacre had ever taken place. Zia had even sorted all his video games and CDs and stacked them alphabetically. For the first time in living history, there was not one crusty sock under Max's bed or one old gum wrapper on the floor.

Best of all, there was the pile of Maya books prominently displayed on his desk. Luckily for Max, the linguistically challenged housekeeper had obviously not understood the instruction to get rid of them.

Zia switched off the vacuum and turned to look at him.

This in itself was an unusual occurrence. Zia usually shuffled around, head down, eyes hidden behind dark glasses. She was always sniffing and wiping away tears—due, his mother said, to a dust-mite allergy.

Then something extraordinary happened: Zia smiled at him.

He had never, ever seen her smile before. She held out her arms to indicate the newly clean room, her long black braid swinging behind her.

"It looks great!" said Max. "Thank you!"

Zia beamed.

Perhaps he could take advantage of her good mood.

"Zia," he said, "remember when you gave me that ticket to San Xavier? You said *they* wanted me to go there. Who were *they*? Who told you to buy the ticket? Who paid for it?"

Still smiling, Zia unplugged the vacuum cleaner and carried it out of the room.

It was as if she hadn't heard a word he'd said. He knew her English wasn't great, but she must have understood something. To give no reaction at all was just weird.

Not for the first time, Max wondered if Zia was a bit simple.

Well, if she wouldn't help him, he still had work to do. The encroaching rainforest outside his door told him that the

Death Lords were on their way. If he was going to play them at their own game, he needed to learn as much as he could about their world.

With the new album from his favorite band, the Plague Rats, playing on his laptop, he checked the room for snakes, selected the thickest book on the Maya, and stretched out on his new bed.

It was comfortable.

Had they gone for the memory foam? He couldn't remember. He burrowed deeper into the welcoming folds of bedding and soon fell asleep.

He slept all afternoon.

When he opened his eyes, his room was dark.

He heard a voice—two voices—calling his name.

His parents were home.

He just had time to leap off the bed, grab all the Maya books and hide them in his closet, and throw himself innocently back onto the bed, before they walked into his room.

Their faces reminded Max of people on a home-makeover show who've just had their blindfolds removed. They oohed and aahed over every detail.

"I hope you'll keep it this way," said his mother. She was wearing her flowery apron, Max noted. She must have put it on as soon as she came home.

"No more machetes at midnight," added his father.

They both chuckled.

Max looked from one to the other in disbelief.

"That's it?" he said. "You're going to make a joke out of it and pretend everything's back to normal?"

His mother nodded happily.

37

"I wish it wasn't happening, too, Mom, but we can't just ignore it."

"Ignore what?" replied his mother.

"Oh, come on!" erupted Max. "Don't tell me you didn't notice all the vines and butterflies on your way upstairs? This house is turning into a rainforest!"

His mother's bright smile faded.

"Don't exaggerate, Max," said his father.

A toucan flew into the room and circled it, looking for food. Finding nothing, it croaked in protest and flew out again.

Max's mother stifled a sob.

"Now, now, Carla," said his father. "We're in a trough of low pressure. I'll buy a dehumidifier tomorrow."

"That's not the answer—" began Max, but his father hadn't finished.

"While I'm at the store," he continued, "why don't I get one of those big-screen TVs? If it's going to rain all summer, Max could teach me to play his video games. What was that one you've been wanting—*Hellhounds 3-D*, wasn't it?"

Max shuddered. Since he'd crashed Ah Pukuh's party in the Black Pyramid and the host had set actual hellhounds on him, he'd lost interest in that particular game.

"It's only raining on *our* house," Max pointed out. "I don't understand why you're both in denial. I know it must have been horrible in Xibalba, but you can't pretend it didn't happen. I made a deal with the Lords of Death to get you out. I did it for *you*! And now I need your help. The house is turning into a rainforest because they're coming to claim whatever it is they want in return. They're evil and vicious and untrustworthy. Lola said they'll stop at nothing to get what they want. You've got to help me!"

Max's parents looked uncomfortable but said nothing.

There was a faint clatter of saucepans downstairs, and a musty aroma, like boiling dishcloths, wafted up from the kitchen.

"Mmm," said Max's father, grateful for the distraction, "something smells good. What gastronomic delights are you cooking up for us tonight, Carla?"

Max's mother smiled, her happy-housewife persona restored. "Zia is teaching me to make something special. I should go down—*ciao*, boys!"

When she'd gone, Max's father sat down on the bed.

"Go easy on your mother, Max," he said. "She's taking this very hard. She's convinced we suffered some sort of mass hallucination in San Xavier. She just wants to forget about it. She hates it when you talk about the Lords of Death."

"But I owe them. I wish I didn't, but I do. And if I don't pay them back, they'll drag you and Mom back to Xibalba. Do you believe me?"

"Suppose I *did* believe you. What then?"

A tapping at the window made them jump.

They turned to see a green macaw rapping at the glass with its beak, as if asking to come in. Behind, in the dripping backyard, a strangler fig was squeezing the life out of an apple tree.

"Chan Kan said the legions of hell are coming for

me," said Max. "He said that me and Lola—"

"Lola and I," his father corrected him.

"—that Lola and *I* must work side by side, like the Hero Twins, to outwit the Lords of Death because the fate of the world is in our hands."

"You must admit," said his father, "it sounds a little far-fetched."

"But the Internet's obsessed with the Maya calendar and the end of the world. Search it, Dad, and you'll see. There must be a gazillion Web sites. You can't tell me that *something* isn't going to happen."

Max's father shook his head. "How many times have I told you not to believe everything you read on the Internet? It's all media hype. *The End of the World Club*, I call it. People trying to make money off other people's fears. People who say that the end of the world is inevitable while they pump their big cars full of gas and eat three times their own body weight in junk food."

"But there's a rainforest in our house. . . ."

"Between you and me, son, I agree that things are a little strange around here. But whatever else is going on, the Maya did *not* predict the end of the world. Dead ends are not their style. They believed in recurring cycles."

Max groaned. "That's what *I'm* trapped in—a recurring cycle of doom."

"It's called being a teenager."

"That's not funny, Dad. Most teenagers don't have the ancient Maya Lords of Death on their backs."

"And neither do you. Whatever happened in San Xavier is over now. To say that some allegorical characters from an ancient myth can turn up in Massachusetts is as ridiculous as saying that the Maya calendar predicted the end of the world."

"But what about the rain? The vines? The bugs?"

"There must be a rational explanation. I'll call someone to take a look at it." He patted Max's shoulder. "Now let's go downstairs and see what your mother's cooking up."

The answer, it turned out, was tamales.

Hundreds of them.

Tamales on every kitchen counter, on every shelf in the refrigerator.

Max used to hate these greasy little corn dumplings steamed in corn husks, but since his stay in San Xavier (where tamales were pretty much the national dish), he'd learned not to be so picky.

"Why so many?" asked his father cautiously. "Are we expecting company?"

Carla laughed. "I think Zia is expecting someone."

Max and his father looked at Zia, who was humming to herself as she scraped another termite nest off the back door.

You'd think a housekeeper would freak out over the current conditions, but Zia had never seemed happier.

Definitely insane, thought Max.

Chapter Two

UNREALITY TV

More volume, Dad!"

Frank Murphy jabbed happily at the remote. "Amazing, isn't it?" he marveled. "The picture's so lifelike. What did the salesman say it had again?"

"Orbital pixels," said Max, staring straight ahead at the giant screen.

"Cool," said his father.

Max shot him a sideways glance.

Cool? Since when did his ginger-bearded, shorts-wearing, archaeologist father start talking like that? He'd probably been watching too much TV.

They'd both been watching too much TV.

They'd been sitting there for hours, transfixed, hypnotized, watching anything and everything, ever since they'd brought home the new flat-screen beauty that afternoon.

The TV was like an anesthetic, numbing Max's brain, stopping him from thinking. And frankly, it was a relief. He'd had enough of worrying about the Death Lords. All he wanted to know now was who would win the cooking challenge in Las Vegas.

His mother's pleas to switch the TV off during dinner had gone unheard. His father had insisted on eating in front of it and made his wife cry by refusing her homemade pasta in favor of hot dogs and popcorn.

Now, Max noted guiltily, there was ketchup on the sofa and popcorn all over the floor.

Carla stuck her head around the living-room door.

"Good night," she said frostily.

No answer.

She stalked into the room, took the remote control out of her husband's hands, and turned off the TV.

The room seemed cold and empty without it.

"I said good night," she repeated. "It's getting late."

"Just one more show," begged Max. He clasped his hands together in supplication and gave her his sweetest smile.

She sighed. "At least, if you're watching TV, you're not reading about the Maya. One more show, *bambino*, then straight to bed. And no horror movies."

"Thanks, Mom."

Frank Murphy looked at his wife hopefully.

"Not you," she said, pulling him up off the sofa and pushing him out the door. "You have work tomorrow."

"Good night," Max called after them.

As he looked around for the remote, he heard the rain start again outside and went to close the window. In the darkness of the yard, an owl hooted, and somewhere thunder roared like a distant troop of howler monkeys.

For a moment, he had the strangest feeling that he was being watched. The hairs on his neck stood on end.

If he turned around, would the Death Lords be standing behind him?

Were they here, in this room, right now?

Was this the moment he'd been dreading?

He took a deep breath and, tingling with fear, slowly looked behind him.

No one.

Just his mother's collection of Maya figurines, lined up on the edges of their shelves, as if they'd shuffled out front and center to watch the new TV.

Out of the corner of his eye, Max saw a movement, a blur of white.

He spun around again.

It was a column of leaf-cutter ants carrying popcorn instead of leaves. Max watched them march their booty out to the hallway, where the new humidifier hummed bravely. Judging from the vine tendrils that snaked under the door and the tawny moths as big as Max's hands that danced around the lamp, the machine was not yet winning its battle against the encroaching rainforest.

Max found the remote and clicked the TV back on.

It was a news bulletin.

"Good news for chocolate lovers," the announcer was saying, "as growers in Central America report a record harvest of cocoa beans. . . ."

Max clicked through the channels.

Showbiz: "And now we preview *With All My Heart*, a zany blockbuster about human sacrifice. . . ."

Cooking: "For an easy supper, fillet your iguana, marinate in honey, and grill until crispy. . . ."

Sports: "You're joining us live for tonight's *pitz* match.

For viewers not familiar with *pitz*, otherwise known as the Mesoamerican ballgame, it was the first team sport in history. . . ."

Nature: "The jaguar, lord of the Maya jungle, is a solitary animal, who hunts at night. . . ."

Shopping: "And here's the perfect gift for all ages—a Make Your Own Chewing Gum kit containing real rainforest *chicle* from the sapodilla tree. . . ."

Makeovers: "So, Jessica, don't you just love your new facial tattoos . . . ?"

Cartoons: "Mwahahahaha," laughed the obese, bulgy-eyed villain as two small children, a red-haired boy and a black-haired girl, were thrown to a pack of razor-toothed, salivating hounds. . . .

Max quickly clicked to the next channel.

A talk show.

A weird talk show.

The studio audience was applauding wildly as the house band, dressed as skeletons and bizarre half-animal, half-human monsters, played bongo drums and long wooden trumpets.

A cheery announcer's voice declaimed off-screen: "And now, here he is, the one you've been waiting for . . ."

The screen went blank, the lights went off, and a warm, damp wind blew through the room.

Something with sharp claws and a scaly tail ran over Max's bare foot.

He drew his legs up under him.

This was feeling very wrong.

He jabbed at the remote, but the TV was dead.

Calm down, it's just a power outage, he told himself.

The high-pitched hum of the humidifier outside in the

hallway, now buzzing furiously like a swarm of insects before a storm, told him it was not a power outage.

He knew what it was.

He knew there was someone in the room with him.

And he wanted to be anywhere but here.

There was a torturous sound, like nails scratching on chalkboard, coming from inside the TV. Then a crash of lightning split the screen and thunder boomed so loud, Max thought it might blow the speakers.

He considered making a run for it, but suddenly the distance between the sofa and the door seemed as wide as the endless rainforest.

A cold yellow fog poured out of the TV and rolled across the floor, filling the room with the sulfurous odor of decay.

A massive winged figure was rising out of the smoke, its vicious curved talons reaching for Max like a raptor seizing its prey.

Max pushed himself back into the sofa, shielding his head with a pillow. He closed his eyes tight.

He vowed never to open them again.

He heard a rustling noise, followed by a rasping, like a cat trying to spit up a hair ball or—Max's stomach did a double flip—like an owl about to regurgitate a pellet of bones and fur.

He opened one eye.

Through the darkness, he looked into two unblinking round yellow orbs.

"Lord Muan?" he whispered.

Lord Muan was the messenger of the Death Lords. He had the head of an owl and the body of an old man. It was with

His vicious curved talons reached for Max
like a raptor seizing its prey.

Lord Muan on the Black Pyramid that Max had negotiated the release of his parents in return for, well, whatever the Death Lords wanted. At the time his plan had been to promise them anything and worry about it later.

Now later had arrived.

The Death Lords had sent their messenger to claim the prize.

And if what they wanted was his still-beating heart, he would have to give it to them.

"Muan's gone," said a voice. "I'm in charge of communications now. We're sharpening up our image, ready for the new *bak'tun*. Muan was old-school with his endless hooting. Focus groups tell us they want today's messengers from Xibalba to be 'less long-winded, more service-oriented, and more ruthlessly efficient.'"

As this messenger stepped out from the shadows, Max saw he was much younger than Lord Muan. His owl face was less round and more rapacious. His winged cape was glossy brown where Muan's had been silver. He wore a short feathered tunic. His human arms and legs were muscular, and on his feet he wore boots made of sewn-together rat pelts and laced with long rat tails.

"I am Lord Kuy. Shall we get down to business?"

Max nodded.

"Massimo Francis Sylvanus Murphy," proclaimed Lord Kuy. "I come from their malevolent majesties, One Death, Seven Death, Blood Gatherer, Wing, Packstrap, Bone Scepter, Skull Scepter, Scab Stripper, and their heinous highnesses, the Demons of Woe, Pus, Jaundice, and Filth, to tell you it's payback time."

The smell of half-digested rodent on the owl-man's

breath almost made Max gag. "What do they want from me?" he whispered.

"First, let us recap; what do you want from them?"

"I want my parents to be permanently released from Xibalba . . . and Hermanjilio and Lucky Jim, too . . . and me. I want to be free again."

"Five lives," observed Lord Kuy. He looked Max up and down. "And what will you give my masters, the Death Lords, in return?"

Max cast wildly around the room. "Have they got a flat-screen TV?"

Lord Kuy hooted with laughter. "They don't need one. They get their entertainment from watching human babies dying slowly in their mother's arms. That last cholera outbreak was a scream!"

Max swallowed nervously. "So what do they want from me?"

The owl-man appeared to have lost his train of thought.

His yellow eyes were fixed on something under the sofa.

Suddenly his feathered head darted forward and reappeared with a fat gopher in his beak. He ate the body in one gulp, but the hairless, little pink tail hung out for several seconds before he sucked it in like a noodle.

Max tried to hide his revulsion.

In a few more minutes, he might be a goner like the gopher.

"Do excuse me," said Lord Kuy. "I worked through lunch. Now where were we?"

"You were telling me what the Death Lords want."

"Ah, yes. They want the Stone of Truth."

"The what now?" said Max.

The messenger rotated his owl head in surprise. "Was I misinformed? I was told you were familiar with our sacred Jaguar Stones."

"They want a Jaguar Stone? But Lord Muan took them all . . . on the Black Pyramid. . . . He came back and he took them all with him to Xibalba!"

"Wrong."

"But I saw him. . . ."

"No. You saw him take the Black Jaguar of Ah Pukuh, the Red Jaguar of Chahk, the Green Jaguar of Itzamna and the White Jaguar of Ixchel. But there is one stone still lacking in the Death Lords' collection. . . ."

"The Yellow Jaguar!"

"Exactly. Just bring them the Stone of Truth, the Yellow Jaguar of K'awiil, and you'll be home and dry."

"But Hermanjilio said it's been lost for centuries. . . ."

"Ah, Lord Hermanjilio. Was he a friend of yours?"

"Why do you say *was*?" asked Max, alarmed.

The owl's eyes narrowed to slits. "Let us just say that life in Xibalba has not suited him."

"What does that mean?"

"Deliver the Stone to Xibalba and you'll find out. Any questions?"

"How will I find it? The Yellow Jaguar could be anywhere."

"My masters will help you. They'll give you a clue."

"The Death Lords know where it is?"

"They do."

"Then why don't *you* get it for them?"

"The Stone of Truth cannot be taken. It must be given freely. Do you accept the task?"

"But who will give it to me?"

"Do you accept? Yes or no?"

"At least tell me where it is?"

"Yes or no?"

Max took a deep breath. "Yes."

"Good." Lord Kuy pulled a piece of bark paper from inside his cape. "Now, if you'll sign in blood here and here . . ."

"In blood? But . . . *ouch*! What was that?"

"Just a pinprick. Now press your thumb down and we'll be done with the paperwork. That's right . . . and again—super! And now I can give you your clue." Lord Kuy produced a small, accordion-folded book. "To show you that we have our fun side in Xibalba, their Lordships got together and composed a riddle for you."

Max groaned. "Not a riddle. Riddles suck."

"We like riddles in Xibalba." Lord Kuy sounded hurt. "But if you don't want it . . ."

"No, no, I do want it," said Max. "I need all the help I can get."

Lord Kuy held out the book.

Trying to keep as much distance as possible between himself and the owl-man, Max snatched it and quickly unfolded it. He scanned its bark-paper pages.

"What does it say? I can't read it. It's all in glyphs!"

"What did you expect? The Maya are famous for their hieroglyphic writing. We had the most advanced writing system in the ancient world."

"Never mind, I'm sure my parents can translate it for me. . . ."

"Ah," said Lord Kuy, "I forgot to tell you the rules."

"Rules?"

"You're forbidden to ask your parents for help."

"But why?"

"They're meddlers. They lay bare what should stay covered."

"That's their job. They're archaeologists."

Lord Kuy shrugged. "I didn't make the rules. But I would advise you not to break them. Watch . . ."

Lord Kuy slunk into the shadows as the living-room door opened and Max's father entered in his pajamas.

"Max?" he said. "Why aren't you in bed?"

"I'm trying to read some Maya glyphs. Can you help me?"

"With pleasure!" Even as his father rubbed his hands together in anticipation, an angry rash broke out on his face.

"Are you okay, Dad?"

"I'm . . . um . . . fine," said his father, running his fingers over the welts. "It must be an allergy. So what did you want to show me?"

Max passed him the bark book, but as he did so, his father's rash exploded into huge, red lumps with pulsating yellow centers.

"Dad?"

Enthralled by the book, his father was oblivious to the war on his face. "Where did you get it, Max? It's exquisite. I've never seen anything like it. . . ."

A drop of blood splattered on the bark-paper pages.

"Sorry," said his father. "Nosebleed. Must be all the excitement." He covered his nose with his hands as he looked around for a Kleenex, but thick red blood oozed through his fingers.

"Dad?" said Max again.

His father put his head back to stanch the flow. "Sorry," he mumbled as he staggered out of the room. "Back soon."

It seemed fairly obvious that he would *not* be back soon.

"I'll come and help you." Max got up to follow his father, but Lord Kuy stepped out of the shadows and barred his way.

"Leave him be."

"What did you do to him?" asked Max angrily.

"It was a warning. Do not involve your parents."

"So how am I supposed to read the riddle?"

"One moment." Lord Kuy held one clawed hand up for silence and cupped the other over his tufted ear, like a news anchor listening to instructions from the control room through an earpiece. He was evidently communing with his masters in Xibalba, for when he lowered his hands again, he said, "The Death Lords say you can work with that old windbag in the monkey suit."

"Lord 6-Dog?"

"Yes. And to make it more entertaining for their Lordships to watch, you can also take his nagging mother . . ."

"Lady Coco?"

"And that girl you like who's out of your league."

"Lola? How do you know she's—?" began Max, then stopped himself. Secretly, *he* thought she was out of his league, too. He wasn't going to justify his love life (or lack of one) to the Death Lords.

The good news was that he'd get to see her and the monkeys very soon.

The bad news was that they were all doomed.

"So, if you have no further questions, let's just agree timings and wrap things up," said Lord Kuy. "Today is 13-Lord. You have until 6-Death to bring the Yellow Jaguar to Xibalba."

"6-Death? When's that?"

"Don't they teach you anything in school?"

"No . . . I mean yes, but not the Maya calendar."

Lord Kuy did an owlish approximation of rolling his eyes. "13-Lord, 1-Crocodile, 2-Wind, 3-Darkness, 4-Maize, 5-Snakebite, 6-Death," he chanted, as if he was talking to a small child.

"What?" protested Max. "I've got seven days? That's all? But what if I can't find the Yellow Jaguar?"

"As per the terms of our arrangement, Hermanjilio and Lucky Jim will molder in their chains, your parents will be dragged back to Xibalba, and you yourself will die on the road, vomiting blood."

"But it's not fair. You haven't explained anything. Seven days isn't enough. I don't stand a chance."

"I heard you were a whiner," said Lord Kuy. "So to keep you focused on the task, Lord Ah Pukuh, god of violent and unnatural death, is sending some old friends to touch base with you."

The messenger gave a low whistle, and a hellhound slunk out from behind the new TV. It was as tall as a Great Dane, with black leathery skin stretched tight over its lean and muscular body. A row of cartilage spikes followed the curve of its spine from its tail, along its back, to its head. As it growled menacingly at Max, its saliva dripped onto the floor like acid and burned holes into the blue hearth rug.

Max's father chose that moment to stick his head around the door. He had blood-soaked cotton balls stuffed up his nose and blobs of white cream all over his face.

"Now, about those glyphs . . . ," he began.

Before he knew what was happening, the hellhound had lunged at him and sunk its teeth into his arm. He howled in agony and fell back onto the sofa.

"Stop!" screamed Max. "Call it off!"

Lord Kuy did so, and the dog backed away, never taking its eyes off Max's father.

"Super!" said Lord Kuy. "So I think we've covered everything. Good night, Massimo Francis Sylvanus Murphy. It was a pleasure doing business with you. See you on 6-Death!"

Max felt a rush of wind, like an owl flying silently across the room, and then the lights were on and the TV was blaring. It was the end of the talk show and the house band were waving their good-byes. The music got faster and the camera work got crazier, until sound and vision melded into one cacophonous blur. An acrid smoke began to rise from the TV, then it burst into flames and dissolved into a pool of melted plastic.

There was a low moan from the sofa.

"Dad!"

"I'm okay, Max, just a bit of a cramp in my arm. I must have fallen asleep watching TV."

"It's not a cramp, Dad. You were bitten by a hellhound! Look at your sleeve."

He pulled at the dog-shredded sleeve of his father's pajama jacket.

His father winced. "I didn't realize my pj's had gotten so tattered," he said. "They're probably older than you are, Max!"

"But didn't you see what just happened? A messenger from Xibalba and a hellhound were right here in this room."

Frank Murphy smiled through his pain.

"I can't believe we waited so long to buy this TV," he said. "It makes everything look so real, doesn't it?"

Chapter Three

THE RIDDLE

H as Lord 6-Dog deciphered the riddle yet?" asked Max. "I e-mailed you the glyphs hours ago."

"Yes, and you've called every ten minutes since," answered Lola, laughing.

"Time is precious when you've only got six days to live. What's taking him so long?"

"I don't know. He's locked himself in the office. He said not to disturb him. But didn't Lord Kuy give you any clues?"

"Only that the Yellow Jaguar can't be taken, only given."

"Really? This is so exciting!"

"I'm not sure that's the word I'd use."

"Oh, come on! It's another job for the Hero Twins! Just think, you and me on the trail of the long-lost Yellow Jaguar! It must be somewhere in San Xavier, don't you think, Hoop?"

Hoop was Lola's nickname for him. It was short for *chan hiri'ich hoop,* or "little matchstick" in her native Mayan language. With his red hair and thin white body, that's what he'd looked like to her the first time she saw him.

"Yeah. It's probably hidden in some creepy temple, guarded by zombie jaguars."

"Zombie jaguars? Count me out," Lola teased him.

"You owe me, Monkey Girl"—Max's nickname for Lola, because she'd been hanging out with howler monkeys the first time he saw her. "I saved your life on the Black Pyramid."

"I could have freed myself," sniffed Lola. "I didn't need your help."

"Excuse me? You were painted blue and tied down to an altar, ready to be sacrificed."

"Well, you'd be dead already, if I hadn't saved *your* life on the underground river."

"What? You have some nerve to—"

Max's protestations were interrupted by an ear-splitting howl.

He held the receiver away from his ear. "What was that?"

Lola giggled. "That's Mr. Murphy. Your Uncle Ted."

"Is he hurt?"

"He's singing."

"Singing?" Max pictured the melancholy, wrinkled face of his father's older brother. "I can't imagine Uncle Ted singing. He always seems so sad."

"Not anymore. He sings all the time, and he's teaching me to paint. You know, I thought I'd hate living in this house, Hoop, but we're like a little family."

Family. He knew that word meant a lot to Lola.

She'd never known her parents. She'd been found in the jungle as a baby by Hermanjilio, who'd taken her straight to

Chan Kan, the Maya wise man. She'd lived with Chan Kan's family, as his adopted granddaughter, until she'd been old enough to go to Itzamna and study with Hermanjilio.

Since Max had returned from San Xavier, she'd been staying with his Uncle Ted in the big old house on the coast, which was run with clockwork precision by Raul the butler. With her were Lord 6-Dog and Lady Coco, the ancient Maya king and his mother, whose spirits had occupied the bodies of Chulo and Seri, Lola's two tame howler monkeys.

Max felt a twinge of jealousy at being excluded from this cozy picture.

"So how are Their Royal Highnesses?" he asked.

"Lady Coco's really enjoying herself, helping Raul in the kitchen and playing at keeping house. Sometimes she comes to Jaime's house with me and watches soap operas with his mother, while I play with his little brothers and sisters. They miss him so much. . . ."

Max bristled. "Who's this Jaime?"

"You know him as Lucky Jim. Remember, the guy who saved your life? His real name is Jaime Ben. It's like James Reed in English. It was your uncle who nicknamed him Lucky Jim." Lola sighed. "He's not so lucky now, is he?"

Lucky Jim had been Uncle Ted's foreman at the banana warehouse and his bodyguard during his smuggling days. Lucky was Maya, but he'd always rejected his heritage until the day he body-slammed Tzelek the evil priest (who was hiding inside Hermanjilio) all the way to Xibalba. Now Lucky and Hermanjilio were both stuck in the underworld, until someone figured out how to rescue them.

"How about Lord 6-Dog?" asked Max.

"He's as moody as ever. He hates being trapped in the

body of a howler monkey. He sits around all day staring out to sea or having deep conversations with your uncle about history and philosophy and literature. Wait . . . I hear the office door opening. Lord 6-Dog's coming out. Let me change to speakerphone."

"Good morning, young lord."

Max smiled to hear Lord 6-Dog's deep and lugubrious tones.

"Good morning, Your Majesty. Did you solve the riddle?"

"The Death Lords have set thee a complex puzzle. The text is as dense as my mother's cassava brownies."

"I heard that," came the voice of Lady Coco. Then she added sweetly, "Good morning, young lord."

"Good morning, Lady Coco," replied Max glumly. "I'm sure your brownies are delicious, but what kind of riddle is ten pages long?"

"Fear not, young lord; at least nine and a half pages can be ignored. They deal with the history of creation, the glorious exploits of the Death Lords, the astronomical portents, et cetera, et cetera. It is typical in Maya documents to set the scene in this lengthy way. Cast thine eyes halfway down the last page, and thou wilt find the glyphs that hold the clue."

Max unfolded the book.

"Aaargh!" he exclaimed. "It's fading away! It's gone all stained and moldy. It's a good thing I took pictures of it for you."

"Your pictures are fading, too," said Lola. "I only printed them this morning, and they look like they've been buried in the jungle for a hundred years. And they've vanished completely off your uncle's computer."

"The Death Lords love tricks and practical jokes," observed Lord 6-Dog. "They would find it most amusing to make thy clue disappear under thy nose."

"We better work fast then," said Max. "What have you got, Lord 6-Dog?"

"Bearing in mind that each glyph has several interpretations and the sense of the whole lies in the context, I believe I have arrived at a basic translation. It does not, however, convey the poetry of the piece nor give thee a sense of the complexity of the wordplay."

"I have six days left to live. Just give me what you've got."

"Art thou ready?"

"Ready!" replied Max, grabbing a pen and a pad of paper.

Lord 6-Dog cleared his throat.

It is hidden
The Yellow Stone, the stone of K'awiil
At his yellow dawn place
His many yellow flowered place,
The place of yellow rotting bones,
His yellow ancestor-bone place.

"That's it?" asked Max, sounding disappointed.

"I told thee it was a basic translation."

"So what does it mean?"

"It could mean many things, young lord. But"—Lord 6-Dog hesitated—"I would have to say that yellow is an important factor."

"I got that."

"And dost thou understand its significance?"

"It's the Yellow Jaguar, right?"

"Not a riddle. Riddles suck."

There was a silence as deep as a bottomless well.

"The thing is, Hoop," said Lola eventually, "for the Maya, yellow is the color of death."

"Whose death?" asked Max.

Another silence. The silence of an invisible penny dropping.

"Oh," said Max dully. "It's mine, isn't it?"

Lord 6-Dog hastily changed the subject. "I had not realized the Death Lords had such literary talents. This riddle has many layers."

"But let's not rule out the obvious," said Lola. "All this yellow must refer to K'awiil, home of the Yellow Pyramid. The Spanish razed the pyramid to the ground, but the stone could still be hidden on site somewhere—maybe buried under some yellow flowers with some yellow rotting ancestor bones."

"Out of interest, young lord," asked Lord 6-Dog, "where *do* the yellow rotting bones of thine ancestors lie?"

"Can we drop the *yellow* and the *rotting* and just say *bones?*" requested Max.

"Thou hast a problem contemplating the inevitable decay of thy skeletal remains?"

"Mortals are squeamish," Lady Coco reminded her son.

"I would advise thee to toughen up, young lord," said Lord 6-Dog. "Thou art dealing with the Lords of Death. They stink and rot and trail their diseased entrails behind them."

"Back to the riddle!" Lola commanded hastily. "Lord 6-Dog asked about your ancestors, Hoop."

Max considered the question. "They're from all over the place. My father's family is from Ireland, my mother's is from Italy. . . . Wait! This could be it! My father's parents,

Patrick and Isabella, are buried in San Xavier!"

"That's right! Raul told me your family history." Lola sounded excited. "He said they're buried in a family crypt in Puerto Muerto, not far from your uncle's house."

"Puerto Muerto is on the east coast," observed Lord 6-Dog, thinking aloud, "and east is the sunrise—"

"And Puerto Muerto is yellow because *muerto* means 'death,' and the color of death is yellow!" interrupted Lola. "We've solved the riddle! The Yellow Jaguar is in the crypt in Puerto Muerto, where the sun rises over the rotting yellow bones of Max's grandparents!"

Max rolled his eyes.

"But the color of east is red, not yellow," cautioned Lord 6-Dog.

"And what about the flowers?" added Max.

He could almost hear Lola rolling her eyes. "Details, details," she said. "The point is, Hoop, that the Yellow Jaguar is in San Xavier—so you need to get over here as fast as you can!"

"I'm not sure . . . ," said Max.

"I, too, have my doubts," agreed Lord 6-Dog. "Today is 1-Crocodile, a day to solve problems with creative thinking. It is my hunch that the answer requires a little more cunning."

"Must you drag the ritual calendar into everything?" snapped Lady Coco.

"Mortals ignore it at their peril," opined Lord 6-Dog rather pompously. "Every day has its meaning."

"What about the day of 6-Death?" said Max. "It doesn't actually mean death, does it?"

"What else should it mean?" replied Lord 6-Dog. "It is a good day to visit Xibalba."

"It's also a day of transformation, of new beginnings," added Lady Coco quickly.

Max thought about this. "Would that, by any chance, be the transformation from me living to me dead? As in, my new beginning as a dead person?"

There was another awkward silence.

"Cheer up," said Lady Coco. "Sometimes a day is what you make it."

"You can't live your life by some old calendar," agreed Lola.

"Either way," said Max, "if I don't find the Yellow Jaguar in the next six days, I'm dead, right?"

"So stop wasting time!" Lola urged him. "Jump on the next plane to San Xavier, and I'll meet you at the airport. It'll be like old times, Hoop!"

Max sighed.

What should he do? The gamer in him agreed with Lord 6-Dog—they needed to think more creatively. But Lola also had a good point. Where else would they look for the Yellow Jaguar, if not at the last known site of the Yellow Pyramid?

"You win," he said. "I'll e-mail you my flight details."

"Great! And say hi to your parents from me, Hoop!"

He could hear Lola's excited babble as he put down the phone, and Lord 6-Dog trying to reason with her.

But something didn't feel right.

He went into the kitchen, where his mother was scraping a blackened piece of toast.

"Lola says hi," he said.

"Forget it, Massimo. You're not going back to San Xavier."

"But, Mom . . ."

"No."

"Admit it, Mom. You know the Death Lords are gunning for me, and you think we can pretend it's not happening as long as we stay away from San Xavier. That's why you don't want me to go back there, isn't it?"

"Not at all," she protested, but she didn't look up. "It is just that the summer is flying by and we need to spend quality time together in Boston, just the three of us, as a family. Tell him, Frank. . . ."

They both looked at Max's father. He was sitting at the breakfast table, reading the paper as usual. His face was covered in Band-Aids, his nose dripped stalactites of dried blood, and his arm sported an oozing bandage. He looked feverishly hot, but underneath his ever-present multipocketed safari jacket, he was wearing a heavy turtleneck sweater.

"Listen to your mother," he said without looking up.

She set down a cup of thick black Italian sludge. "Drink your coffee, Frank. You must not be late for the doctor."

"Extraordinary, isn't it?" mused his father. "I was fine when I went to bed last night. . . ."

"But don't you remember, Dad?" said Max. "The owl guy, Lord Kuy, made your face break out, then the hellhound sank his teeth into your arm—"

"I think we'll leave the diagnosis to the doctor, shall we?" said his father, scratching his neck.

"What's that lump?" asked Max suspiciously.

"It's nothing," replied his father, pulling his turtleneck up higher.

Max looked more closely. "I can see it under your sweater. You've got a lump on your neck, and it's moving."

Max's mother ran over and pulled down the turtleneck. "A botfly maggot!" she squealed. "You were trying to hide it from me!"

"Now, now, Carla, it's just a harmless little parasite growing under my skin. People get them all the time in

Central America. It's nothing to fuss about."

"Stay right there," she said. "I will find the tweezers."

"No need for that," said Max's father, hastily standing up and getting ready to leave. "It'll pop out on its own in a few weeks' time. See you later!"

As the screen door slammed behind him, Max's mother threw up her arms. "What is happening to us?" she cried.

"I'm trying to tell you, Mom. Lord Kuy came here last night; he's the new messenger for the Death Lords—"

"Stop!" said Carla, bursting into tears. "No more! I have had enough of your crazy nightmares!"

"It wasn't a nightmare, and I can prove it." Grabbing his mother by the hand, Max pulled her into the living room. "I'll show you where the TV melted and the hellhound's drool burned the rug. . . ."

He flung open the living room door and pointed triumphantly.

"Look!"

Carla looked carefully at the corner where the TV had been. Then she looked at the hearth rug. Finally, she looked at Max.

"I think perhaps you should see the doctor, too."

A brand-new TV was sitting innocently in the corner. The rug showed no signs of acid burns.

"Aha!" Max spotted a brownish stain on the sofa. "Look here, Mom! It's Dad's blood, from where the hellhound bit him."

Carla scratched at the stain. "Ketchup," she said flatly, "from the hot dogs you ate in front of the TV last night."

Something caught her eye and she glanced over the back of the sofa.

"Oh, hello," she said. "I didn't see you there."

It was Zia.

She looked hot and bedraggled, like she'd been working hard.

Behind the sofa, Max glimpsed a battalion of cleaning supplies. He scrutinized Zia more carefully and saw something that could have been the instructions for a new TV peeking out of her apron pocket. She followed his eyes and tucked it out of sight.

"Zia!" Max wailed. "Did you repair the rug? Did you replace the TV?"

"Massimo!" his mother chided him. "Leave Zia alone."

Zia flicked back her braid, gathered her cleaning supplies into a bucket, and picked up a bulging black garbage bag, ready to make her exit.

"Wait!" yelled Max, grabbing at the bag. "Let's look in the trash! I bet we'll find bits of molten TV and owl pellets and—"

"I am so sorry about this, Zia," said Max's mother as she unpicked his fingers one by one from the garbage bag.

"You have gone too far this time," said his mother, sitting down heavily on the sofa. "Poor Zia, as if she did not have enough on her plate."

"What do you mean?" asked Max. "What does Zia have on her plate?"

"It is not easy for her, *bambino*."

"But she's the only one who's happy around here. She's up to something, Mom. I don't trust her."

"Massimo! Zia has lived with us since you were a baby. This silly game has got to stop."

"It's not a game and you know it, Mom. It rains on our house and nowhere else in Boston. Every room is crawling with bugs. There's a jungle in our hallway and a strangler fig in our backyard. You can't go on pretending that this is all a figment of my imagination. The Death Lords mean business."

His mother put her head in her hands.

An evil-looking spider, as furry as a kitten and about the same size, scuttled across the carpet in pursuit of a small lizard. Max threw a pillow at the spider, and the lizard made a break for freedom.

When his mother looked up, her face was fearful and tearstained.

"Why must they torment us like this?" she asked, her voice barely audible.

Max sat down next to her. "You *know* why. I owe the Death Lords a favor, and now they're calling it in. Last night, Lord Kuy gave me seven days to fulfill my side of the bargain. Make that six days now. Six days left to live. This time next week, if I haven't given them what they want, it will be over for all of us."

"Six days?" His mother looked at him with fear in her eyes.

Then she nodded slowly as if she'd made a decision.

"What did they ask for?" she whispered.

"I can't tell you."

"Why not?"

"The Death Lords will punish you, like they punished Dad."

Max's mother took his hands in hers. "It was horrible in Xibalba. I wanted to forget about it, to convince myself it never happened. But enough is enough. I cannot keep running from the truth. I am not going to live my life in fear of the Death Lords. Tell me what they want."

"I have to deliver the Yellow Jaguar to Xibalba."

"The Yellow Jaguar of K'awiil? The Stone of Truth? But no one knows where it is."

"The Death Lords do. They gave me a stupid riddle to help me find it. Lola thinks it's in San Xavier, but Lord 6-Dog isn't so sure."

"Show me the riddle."

"The Death Lords will get you for it, Mom."

"Show me."

Max pulled out the book. It had faded so much it was barely legible, but since his mother was the world's foremost authority on Maya glyphs, he trusted her to make an educated guess. She went straight to the back page. "'His yellow dawn place,'" she muttered, "'his many yellow flowered place . . . his yellow ancestor-bone place.'" A smile of triumph spread across her face, quickly followed by an angry pink rash. "I know it! I know the answer!"

"Mom, your face . . ."

"Listen to me, *bambino*! I have always suspected that the Yellow Jaguar was stolen by Diego de Landa, the Spanish monk who burned all the Maya books. We know from his journal that he was obsessed with the Jaguar Stones. He tortured whole villages to get his hands on them. . . ."

As she talked, Max watched her closely. The rash spread and darkened and congealed into lumps until she looked like she'd been dunked in a vat of plum jam.

"Your grandmother, Isabella Pizarro, was descended from the first conquistadors," she was saying. "They sailed from the east, out of the rising sun. I do not know this yellow city, but I would bet all the ham in Parma that it is in . . . *aaaaaghhhhh!*"

She had brushed her hair out of her eyes and a large hank had come off in her hand. Even as she patted her scalp to assess the damage, more strands fell away, until half her head was bald.

She stared in horror at the tresses in her lap, then jumped up and ran upstairs. He could hear her screaming as she surveyed her hideous appearance in the bathroom mirror.

What had she been about to tell him?

Round one to the Death Lords, he thought bitterly.

He was on his way to e-mail Lola about this curious development when good smells from the kitchen derailed him.

Roast chicken.

Homemade gravy.

Chocolate cake.

Since any meal right now could be his last meal, Max decided to investigate.

Zia was frosting the cake, humming to herself as she worked. Not for the first time, Max wondered why she was so happy these days. The house was falling apart, the Murphys were all acting strangely, and Zia was smiling for the first time ever. Either she'd lost her mind or maybe, as Max strongly suspected, she knew something the rest of them didn't. . . .

He thought back to the days before his trip to San Xavier. He'd surprised Zia in the middle of some creepy ritual, like a fortune-telling ceremony. He remembered that her room was crammed full of jars and potions, like a witch doctor's lair . . . like the hut of Chan Kan, the Maya wise man, in Lola's home village of Utsal. And it had been Zia who'd come up with his plane ticket.

He had to make her talk.

"Hello, Zia," he said warily. "I'm sorry about that thing with the trash bag." The housekeeper shrugged—did that mean she didn't understand or she didn't care?—and indicated that he should sit at the table. It was set for one.

Soon, he was tucking into a big plate of juicy roast chicken.

"This is so good," he said.

Zia looked up from her frosting and smiled at him.

Taking that as encouragement, he continued: "Zia, I know you don't speak much English, but I need to ask you something." She nodded. "When I went to San Xavier, where did you get the ticket from? Who told you to buy it? Who gave you the money?"

She carried on nodding.

She obviously wasn't understanding a word.

Not knowing what else to do, Max persisted. "The thing is, Zia, I need another ticket. I have to go back to San Xavier."

Zia was putting down her frosting knife.

She was wiping her hands on her apron.

She was beckoning to him.

Nervously, he got up and followed her.

She led him to her room, above the garage. It was dark in there and it smelled of incense. Even when she'd lit a candle, Max could hardly see.

"There are rules," she said. "You must follow them."

Max was so surprised at her fluent English, he just nodded mutely.

She continued, "You must be early. Three hours. No liquids."

"Did the Death Lords tell you this?" he whispered.

Zia looked at him like *he* was the crazy person.

"Transportation Safety Administration," she said, pushing a piece of paper at him.

It was a receipt for an e-ticket. American Airlines.

"Oh, thank you, thank you, thank you!" he cried, and punched the air excitedly. "San Xavier, here I come!"

"No," said Zia. She pointed at something on the paper.

And there it was, in bold uppercase.

MAD. The paper said **MAD.**

His stomach sank. He'd been right the first time: Zia was insane, and now she had a ticket to prove it.

Max tried to stay calm.

"I get it," he said. "Funny joke. You're mad. I'm mad. Ha-ha."

He crumpled up the receipt and threw it into the trash can.

"Not mad," said Zia, fishing it out again. "Airport code for *Madrid.*"

"Madrid? In Spain? But I'm going to San Xavier!" He spoke slowly and loudly, as if she were deaf.

Zia went over to a table piled high with baskets and boxes, many of them draped in gaily striped woven cloth. With a flourish, like a magician doing a trick, she whipped the cloth off the largest box to reveal a computer. She typed in a few words and waited impatiently as an image downloaded onto the screen.

Max stared at it.

For a moment, as planet Earth whirled toward him from deep space, he wondered if her computer was like a high-tech crystal ball.

Then, as the planet split into blue oceans and green landmasses with borders marked in yellow, Max saw that it was Google Earth. Closing in, the camera zoomed through continents, countries, and counties, until it rested on a battlemented castle on a hilltop. There were other buildings dotted around the hillside below the castle, but none of them were clearly visible. The picture was blurry and the resolution was poor, but one feature of the town was unmistakable: it was shrouded in a haze of yellow.

He zoomed in. They were yellow flowers, he was sure of it.

Within the space of five seconds, he had copied the coordinates, done a search, and identified the "yellow city" of the glyphs as Polvoredo in the province of Extremadura, western Spain.

Another frenzied search told him that Polvoredo was noted for the number of conquistadors who'd been born within its walls and for its abundance of flowers—all of them, thanks to a quirk in the local soil chemistry, a brilliant shade of yellow. The town contained little of touristic interest besides an unremarkable central square, a Romanesque church, and a castle (closed to the public). Population: 341. Motto: *La Verdad Sobre Todo* ("Truth Above All").

"The Yellow Jaguar is the Stone of Truth! This is the place! It's east of San Xavier and it's famous for yellow flowers. Grandma Isabella's family must be buried around there somewhere. This is what Mom was trying to tell me! The Yellow Jaguar's in Spain!" He was punching the air and dancing round Zia's room. "Oh, Zia, you're so clever! The conquistadors stole the Yellow Jaguar and brought it back to Spain with them!"

Max checked his flight information. "I leave tonight! I need to call Lola and then get to the airport!" Max went to hug Zia, thought better of it, grabbed her hands, and shook them. "Will you tell my parents where I've gone?"

She nodded and fished a thick roll of euro bills out of her apron pocket. "For you," she said.

"Where did you—?" began Max, but Zia pointed at her wristwatch. "Hurry," she said. "They are waiting."

Chapter Four

WELCOME TO MAD

From the airplane window, Max looked down on Spain. Greeny brown and browny green, plains and mountains, lots of roads, not many houses.

He remembered a jigsaw puzzle he had when he was little, a world map. Each little country in Europe had a picture, like the different lands in Disney World: Italy was a straw-hatted boatman rowing a gondola; Britain was a soldier in a red jacket and a black fur hat as tall as his head; Ireland was a green leprechaun; and Spain was a black-haired dancer in a red spotted dress.

He knew from visiting his mother's family in Venice that the puzzle had got it right about Italy: everywhere he'd looked, there were straw-hatted boatmen rowing gondolas. He wondered if the streets of Spain would be filled with whirling Spanish dancers.

But first he had to get through the airport, and there was a distinct lack of merriment in the immigration hall. Just the usual fearsome wall of officials in glass cubicles, and slow-moving lines of exhausted passengers shuffling forward with their paperwork in hand.

Eventually, Max made it to the front of his line.

The sour-looking official eyed his passport distastefully and scribbled something in a notebook.

"Reason for visit?"

Max decided against mentioning the Maya Death Lords and his quest to find the Yellow Jaguar, answering simply: "Vacation."

"Address in Spain?" barked the official, still writing busily.

"It's a town called Polvoredo. In Extremadura."

The official looked at Max with newfound respect. "You will not find many tourists there, my friend." Chuckling to himself, he stamped the passport and gave it back. "Be sure to try the blood sausage. But do not ask what's in it."

Max stumbled out into the baggage hall, to be met by a wall of noise. It was a mixture of cheers and angry shouts, and it seemed to be centered on one of the baggage carousels.

Scanning the crowd for the source of the commotion, he saw that someone was riding on the conveyor belt with the suitcases. It was a tall, skinny figure dressed all in black leather, with long black hair that whipped to and fro as its owner rocked out with an invisible guitar. The guitarist's face was daubed with white makeup, his eyes heavily accentuated with black eyeliner.

Max knew that face.

It was the one and only Vince Vermin, lead guitarist of the Plague Rats, Max's favorite band!

And wait—Max thought he might faint with pleasure—now joining Vince on his makeshift revolving stage were his bandmates: lead singer Ty Phoid, bass player Trigger Mortis, and drummer Odd-Eye Ebola. They jostled one another and fooled around as they threw off various pieces of black luggage.

Max couldn't believe his luck. What were the chances he would land in Madrid at the same time as his idols, the notoriously elusive Plague Rats?

Heart pounding with excitement, he pushed his way to the front of the crowd.

"Hey, watch it, doofy!" said an angry voice beside him.

Max turned to see a girl about his age, with punky black hair and big blue eyes. "You're blocking me," she said, and he realized that, until he'd stepped in front of her, she'd been taking photos with her cell phone.

"Sorry," he said, moving aside. "Is it really the Rats? What are they doing here?"

"Beats me. They're supposed to be touring in Japan right now." She pushed Max out of the way as she went for a close-up of Vince Vermin. "All I know is, I'm getting an exclusive for my blog. . . ."

"You're a music blogger? Cool."

"And you're a Rats fan?"

"Yeah."

As he looked into her big blue eyes, it seemed to Max that bells were ringing. Wait, they *were* ringing. Alarms were sounding on the luggage carousel, red lights were flashing, and security guards were yelling as the Plague Rats leapt into the crowd and the lines of travelers closed up behind them.

The girl was frantically tapping into her cell phone. "Come on, give me a signal," she begged it. "They won't believe this back home!"

"Where's home?" asked Max (rather suavely, he thought).

"Boston," mumbled the girl, staring at her cell phone intently, as if she could conjure up a signal by sheer force of will.

"No way! Me, too!" said Max. "I didn't see you on the airplane."

The girl looked embarrassed. "We were in first class."

Max tried to sound nonchalant. "Who's we?"

"I'm on vacation with my parents," she sighed. "Two boring weeks of museums, art galleries, and"—she made quote marks with her fingers—"'cultural activities.' I just hope I can track down the Rats somewhere."

"Maybe I'll bump into you along the way."

Her eyes met his. "Cool," she said.

A large woman in a pink suit and pearls came rushing over. "There you are, darling! I've been looking for you everywhere. Now please stay close, there are some strange people around."

This last remark was directed at Max.

"He's not a strange person, Mom; he's from Boston like us."

"I don't care where he's from, you're not to talk to him."

"But Mom, you said you hoped I'd make new friends on this trip—"

"I meant cultured Europeans: princes, counts, archdukes." She surveyed Max disapprovingly. "People with breeding."

The girl frowned at her mother, and held out her hand to Max. "Pleased to meet you. My name is Nasty—Nasty Smith-Jones."

"Your name," said her mother, "is Anastasia. Now come on, your father is waiting for us."

Max reached out to shake Nasty's hand, and their fingertips brushed for the merest nanosecond before her mother pulled her away.

"My name is Max," he called after her, but he wasn't sure she heard.

Unable to break free of her mother's armlock, Nasty twisted around, grinned at Max, gave him the finger sign for rock 'n' roll, and attempted Ty Phoid's trademark tongue waggle.

Laughing, Max watched until mother and daughter joined a middle-aged man wearing a carefully ironed safari suit and the three of them left the baggage hall. Seeing her mother's iron grip on one side and her father's protective hand on the other, Max doubted her chances of escaping her parents for long enough to track down the Plague Rats.

Still, he was definitely going to look her up when he got back to Boston.

Make that *if* he got back to Boston.

Meanwhile, he had another hour to kill before Lola's plane landed. He decided to go and buy a map of Spain. And maybe a snack.

A little later, juggling his new map, a cappuccino, a cheese pizza, a chocolate doughnut, and an apple that he'd bought by accident, Max found a table within sight of the international arrivals doors.

Trying to look like a seasoned jet-setter, he sat back and slurped his cappuccino. Then he ate his food as slowly as he could.

Finally he allowed himself to look at the airport clock.

Nearly three p.m. Lola's plane would be landing soon.

With excitement bubbling in his stomach (or maybe it

was the pizza fighting the doughnut), he wiped his fingers and spread out the map.

Extremadura was a large province mostly southwest of Madrid, on the border with Portugal. Max forgot about clock-watching as he set about finding Polvoredo. After a long time, it revealed itself as tiny cluster of buildings on a hill, overlooking the thin blue curve of a river. Max spotted a train line nearby and traced it with his finger back to Madrid. Perfect! He'd read somewhere that trains were faster in Europe—and that train travel was considered romantic.

But where was Lola?

He saw from the monitors that her flight had landed ages ago. Was it possible that she'd missed the plane?

A ripple of laughter went through the arrivals hall.

Max looked up.

What he saw made his mouth drop open.

Coming through the automatic doors were Lord 6-Dog and Lady Coco, the two ancient Maya royals whose spirits were subletting the bodies of Chulo and Seri, Lola's two friendly howler monkeys.

What took Max by surprise was the fact that they were wearing clothes. Lord 6-Dog, his expression as mournful as ever, was trying to maintain a regal bearing while sporting a little black suit with a sequined matador jacket and a jaunty red sash. His mother, the vivacious and fun-loving Lady Coco, was lapping up the attention of the crowd in a red and white spotted flamenco dress with layers of frills and ribbons. Apart from her hairy body, she looked just like the Spanish dancer off Max's jigsaw map of the world.

"Lady Coco, over here!" yelled Max.

It took her a moment to spot him in the crowd. The eyes

of the young Ix Kan Kakaw (Lady Coco's original Maya name, which translated as something like "Lady Perfect Precious Treasure of Accumulated Wealth through Judicious Trading of Ripe Cacao Beans") had been trained to cross, a sign of beauty much admired by the ancient Maya upper classes. So now she was a cross-eyed monkey, which rather impaired her vision. But as soon as she saw Max, she ran to him, whooping with pleasure, and jumped into his arms.

Lord 6-Dog, or Ahaw Wak Ok as he'd been known to his ancient Maya subjects, walked sullenly behind, his gaze fixed on the airport floor.

Lola came through the doors next. She was wearing her usual black T-shirt and cargo pants, denim jacket knotted around her waist, and she looked even prettier than Max remembered. She tucked her long, coppery black hair behind her ears as her gentle brown eyes searched him out in the crowd.

Max had been planning to wave and jump up and down like a madman as soon as he saw her. But now, intimidated by her good looks and remembering that even the Death Lords thought she was out of his league, he walked stiffly over and greeted her formally.

"Hello, Lola, it's good to see you."

"Hoop!" screamed Lola, squashing him in a bear hug. Lady Coco, caught in the middle, screeched in protest, and Max set the monkey down, laughing.

"*Bienvenido a Madrid!*" he said, reading out the sign on the wall.

Lola made a rueful face. "It's a good thing you didn't listen to me," she said, "or we'd be in San Xavier right now."

"I was beginning to think you'd stayed there," said Max.

"What took you so long? I was wondering if you'd missed your plane."

"There's a lot of paperwork when you travel with animals," said Lola ruefully. "Luckily, I got some help with it or I'd still be filling it out."

"So how was the trip?"

"Not good," admitted Lola. "Lord 6-Dog has been sulking since we left San Xavier."

Max looked over to where the monkey-king was leaning moodily against a pillar, lips pursed, arms folded, staring pointedly at the ceiling and ignoring the curious glances of passing travelers.

"What's his problem?"

"It's the clothes. He hates being dressed up like a pet monkey."

"I don't blame him."

"I thought they might be allowed to sit with me on the plane if they looked more human, but it didn't work. They were still put in cages in the hold. So it's been one humiliation after another for him. And, of course, I had to ask them not to talk until we're alone."

"I guess it's not the kind of VIP treatment he's used to," said Max. He waved at Lord 6-Dog and called over, "Lookin' fly, Your Majesty!"

If looks could kill, the story of Max Murphy would have ended right there. The monkey glared at him with the steely-eyed contempt of a mighty king who had once been the most fearsome warrior of the mighty Maya.

Lola sighed. "At least Lady Coco's happy."

Stamping her feet and rotating her paws at the wrist, Lady Coco was attempting to dance flamenco in a circle of clapping children. It was hard to imagine that she had ever been an imperious Maya queen.

"We should get going," said Max. "There's a train. . . ."

But Lola wasn't listening. She was waving to a smartly groomed young man in a business suit who'd just come through the automatic doors.

"Santino! Over here!" she called, and the young man trotted obediently over, a look of besotted love on his handsome face.

"Max Murphy, meet Santino Garcia," she said. "We sat next to each other on the plane. Santino's a law student and he helped me with all the paperwork back there. I don't know what I would have done without him." She flashed her widest smile at the young Spaniard. "I was so lucky to meet him."

"It is I who was the lucky one," said Santino, gazing at Lola with smoldering eyes.

Max surveyed Santino Garcia with loathing.

From his shiny black hair to his shiny black shoes, he was too good-looking, too clean, too *nice*. He must be clever, too, if he was a law student, and his well-cut suit suggested he was not short of funds. Handsome, smart, rich. Max had never felt so ugly and badly dressed and lacking in prospects.

Santino moved to shake hands. Max kept his hands firmly in his pockets.

"Señorita Lola has told me much about you," said Santino, in a voice as rich and smooth as a movie star's. "But she did not mention that you have the red hair. You know here in eh-Spain, we used to think that the redheads, *los pelirrojos*, were in league with the devil."

"My hair is brown," replied Max coldly.

"I am sorry, I must need eh-spectacles," said Santino, with a wink at Lola.

"You need spectacles," Max corrected him.

"You think so?" asked Santino. "You are eh-student of ophthalmology?"

"No," said Max, getting irritated. "I'm just telling you there's no *eh* sound in those words. It's just *spectacles* and *student.*"

"Eh-spectacles, eh-student."

"May I have a word with you, Hoop?" asked Lola sweetly. "Please excuse us for a moment, Santino."

The law student made an extravagant bow, and Lola pulled Max aside.

"What is wrong with you?" she hissed, once they were out of earshot. "You're being so rude. He has a little problem with pronunciation, big deal."

"He has a little problem with his brain," said Max. "Must be all that hair gel."

Lola narrowed her eyes. "For your information, Santino knows Polvoredo, and he's offered to drive us there. You could at least be polite to him."

"*What?*" howled Max.

Lola signaled to him to keep his voice down.

"What were you thinking?" he continued in a muffled snarl. "You can't trust some guy you just met on a plane. Particularly him. He has shifty eyes."

"I think he has nice eyes," stated Lola.

"What have you told him?"

"The truth."

Max stared at her in disbelief. "You do understand that I'll die a long and painful death in five very short days' time if we mess this up?"

"Have you finished?" asked Lola. "All I told him is that we're old friends meeting up for a vacation and researching

85

your family history along the way. That's pretty much true, isn't it?"

"How did you explain the howler monkeys?"

"My devoted pets who cannot be separated from me. He said he'd feel the same in their position." Lola smirked. "He said I was the girl of his dreams."

"What a slimeball. What a complete eh-slimeball. Let's just say *adiós* and get going. There's a train—"

"Don't be silly, Hoop. It's getting late and we'll be there much faster if we get a lift from Santino. Now come and be nice to him. . . ."

While they'd been gone, Santino had bought flowers for Lola—a big bouquet of red roses.

"Thank you—they're beautiful," she said.

"But not," replied Santino, "as beautiful as you."

Max scowled all the way to the airport parking lot.

As he trailed behind with the baggage cart, he saw Santino casually drape an arm around Lola's shoulders. He considered ramming the Spaniard's ankles with the cart, but he knew Lola would not approve. He could tell she really liked her new friend from the plane. But the question was, how much?

"He's not even her type," he muttered to the monkeys, who were riding on top of the bags. Lady Coco responded by squeezing his hand with her paw. "*You* don't think he's handsome, do you?" he asked her, but she was preoccupied in arranging her ruffled skirts and seemed not to hear him.

By the time they reached the parking lot and he was stowing the bags in the trunk of Santino's shiny black car, Max had worked himself up into a jealous funk.

He was vaguely aware of some shouting behind him and a crunching of gears, but was too caught up in thinking hateful things about Santino to pay it any attention.

"Mac! Mac!" came a voice.

Lola tapped him on the shoulder. "I think someone's calling you," she said.

He turned to see Nasty Smith-Jones leaning out of the window of a rental car that her father was trying and failing to back out of a tight spot on the far side of the parking lot. She was waving and waggling her tongue and making rock 'n' roll signs.

"Mac! Mac!" she called.

Max waved back enthusiastically.

"Who's that?" asked Lola.

"She's a close friend of mine from Boston," said Max smugly.

"She can't be that close. She thinks your name is *Mac*."

"That's what she calls me."

Lola pursed her lips. "What's she doing in Spain?"

"She's on vacation. We're hoping to meet up."

"There won't be time for that," said Lola firmly.

"You never know," said Max.

Lola climbed into the passenger seat and slammed her door.

With a final wave at Nasty, Max ducked into the backseat with the monkeys, and soon they were eh-speeding south down the highway.

Max's iPod had run out of juice somewhere over Ireland, so he settled down to watch the passing scenery.

As the suburbs of Madrid fell away, the apartment blocks and shopping malls were replaced by rolling expanses of tall yellow grass. Every so often a rocky hill would rise out of the plains, surmounted by a giant cutout of a black bull, silhouetted in all its magnificence against the blue sky.

Lola looked back over the seat. "See that bull? Santino says they're billboards that were put up all over Spain to advertise a brand of sherry. Everyone liked them so much they've never been taken down."

"How fascinating," said Max sarcastically.

The monkeys had long since fallen asleep, and Max considered joining them. As he rested his head against the car window, he saw another huge silhouette looming up on a hill. Another of Santino's fascinating billboards, no doubt. He regarded it without interest until, just as they drew level, he realized that it was not a bull but a hellhound, ten times larger then life.

"Look! Look!" he spluttered.

Rapt in their Spanish conversation, Lola and Santino ignored him.

By the time he'd persuaded them to look back, the car had crested the hill and the hellhound was out of sight.

It must be the jet lag, he told himself, shutting his eyes.

When he woke up, everyone was gone.

It was hot as a furnace inside the car.

And someone was banging on the window.

Chapter Five
GETTING HOTTER

She was slamming her palms on the glass, and shouting something at him.

"Lola?"

Max rubbed his eyes.

"Where are we?"

He realized she couldn't hear him and tried to wind down the window.

It was electric and didn't budge.

He tried to open the door.

That didn't budge either.

Now the sweat was running down his face, and he was scared.

What scared him was the look of terror on Lola's face. Her hair was wild and loose. Her face was tear-stained. Still she was shouting at him, maybe warning him about something, gesticulating that he should get away.

But he couldn't get out of the car.

He fiddled with the door lock. The latch popped up

and down, but the door mechanism was jammed.

"Lola! Lola! What's happening? Is it Santino? What's he done to you?"

She beat her fists violently on the window as if trying one last time to break the glass with her bare hands, then turned to run away. As she straightened up, Max was astonished to see that she was wearing a costume, a long yellow ball gown trimmed with lace.

He yanked at the door handle and kicked open the door. "Lola?"

She was gone.

He staggered to his feet in the hot sun and looked around.

The car was parked under a tree in a scrubby wasteland. There was no highway in sight. In one direction, a parched yellow plain shimmered in the heat haze. The other way was a wall of jagged rocks. The sun blazed down and the air was thick with ochre-colored dust.

"Lola!" he called again, at the top of his lungs.

"There you are!" said Santino's voice, from somewhere behind him.

Max saw a flash of steel and felt a sharp pain.

Warm blood trickled down his back as he fell to the ground.

"Hoop?" Lola came running, with Santino close behind. She was wearing her street clothes again. "Why are you shouting? Are you okay?"

"It was Santino," groaned Max. "He stabbed me."

"I did not eh-stab you," said Santino indignantly.

"Let me see," said Lola, crouching down and lifting Max's T-shirt. She sucked air through her teeth. "You've been spiked by a thornbush. Brace yourself, Hoop; I'm going to pull it out."

Actually, Max didn't feel a thing. He was too busy replay-ing what had just happened. Was he going crazy?

"Put your hand here and keep pressing," Lola instructed him. "I'll find some yarrow to stop the bleeding."

She ran over to a patch of tall weeds and pulled off a bunch of white lacy flowers. Then she lay the flowers on a flat rock, picked up a smaller rock, and began to grind the flowers between them.

As Max watched her, he wondered how she'd managed to get changed so quickly. Where had she hidden the dress? And what was Santino doing with a sword?

"You two are sick," he said.

Lola smiled over at him. "*Sick* as in *cool?*"

"No," said Max, "*sick* as in *twisted.*"

"What?" Lola slammed down her rock in outrage. "All we did was get out of the car to admire the view. You were asleep when we left you. Next thing, we heard you screaming and came to see what all the noise was about."

"Oh, yeah," said Max sarcastically, "so I suppose it wasn't you in the long yellow dress, and it wasn't your boyfriend here who stabbed me in the back with a sword?"

"Let's get one thing eh-straight," protested Santino. "I did not eh-stab you. I have no eh-sword."

"And I've never worn a long yellow dress in my life," added Lola.

Max noticed that neither of them denied Santino was her boyfriend.

"Perhaps you have sun eh-stroke," suggested Santino.

"This should help," said Lola, scooping up a handful of evil-looking paste. She wasn't particularly gentle as she rubbed it on Max's wound, but he refused to complain on principle.

"Where are the monkeys?" he asked, looking around. "Maybe *they* saw what happened."

Lola gestured vaguely. "In the trees somewhere, eating leaves."

Santino sniggered. "Even if they saw something, it's not like they can eh-speak."

Lola laughed along with him. "Talking monkeys, what an idea," she said.

Max imitated her laugh.

"That's not funny," said Lola. "Don't be so mean."

"I got stabbed."

"*No*, you didn't. Here, follow me, and I'll show you something to make you feel better. It's just over these rocks."

"Last time I followed you I got stabbed."

"No, you got pricked by a thornbush. And you *weren't* following me."

"But it seemed so real. . . ."

"Hot sun can do that. You've heard of mirages, haven't you?"

"I guess."

On shaky legs, he followed her over the rocks.

"Ta-da!" announced Lola.

Max took in the view.

On the other side of the valley, clinging to the hillside, a little town sat at the foot of a medieval castle. Climbing up the castle walls, garlanding turrets, obscuring streets and courtyards, spilling out of balconies and window boxes, covering rooftops, was a living blanket of yellow flowers—a sight made all the more extraordinary by its contrast to the dried-up riverbed below and the arid plains all around.

"It's awesome," marveled Max.

"The yellow city," whispered Lola. She passed Max a water

"It's the yellow city," whispered Lola.

bottle. "Drink," she said. "You're dehydrated. You scared me back there."

"*You* scared *me*."

The water was warm and metallic-tasting from sitting in the sun, but Max's parched mouth sucked down every drop.

"All around is dry as dust," Santino pointed out, "yet in Polvoredo, flowers grow. But only yellow flowers. If you plant red, white, purple—all of them turn to yellow. It is magic, no?"

"I read about it online," responded Max. "It's a quirk in the local soil chemistry."

"You do not believe in magic?"

"No," said Max firmly. He wasn't about to tell this guy about all the freaky things he'd seen in San Xavier.

"Does anyone live in the castle?" asked Lola.

"Yes," answered Santino, "if you believe in magic."

Max rolled his eyes. Boy, this guy was annoying.

"Will you tell me the story?" asked Lola, sitting on the rocks and patting the space next to her. Santino sat down, like a lovesick lapdog, way too close to Lola for Max's comfort.

"Excuse me," he said, squeezing himself in between them so that they had to shuffle apart. "I was wondering if either of you had any food? I'm starving."

"You're always starving," said Lola.

Santino patted his pockets and pulled out a tiny bag of peanuts. "From the plane. You are welcome to them."

"Now let Santino tell his story," said Lola.

"I hope it's a short one," said Max, tearing open the peanuts. "It must be nearly dinnertime."

"In eh-Spain, we eat dinner very late," Santino informed him.

"Great," said Max glumly, watching a gray heron circling the dry riverbed in search of nonexistent frogs. It looked like they'd both go hungry. He lay back against the rock and closed his eyes. "Go on then," he said unenthusiastically.

"And so," began Santino, "the woman who lives in the castle, they call her Inez la Loca—'Crazy Inez.' They say she is five hundred years old."

"Ah," said Lola, "a ghost story."

"No," replied Santino silkily, "a love eh-story."

Max made a retching noise. "Sorry," he mumbled. "A peanut got stuck."

"Ignore him," said Lola to Santino. "Please go on."

"It begins in the time of the conquistadors—"

"Or the invaders, as I call them," muttered Lola.

Santino looked hurt.

"I'm sorry," she said. "It's just that word *conquistadors*—it makes my blood boil. It sounds so brave and noble, but they were just a rabble—a bunch of thieves and mercenaries. They destroyed everything they touched. It was their germs that wiped us out, not their fighting skills."

Santino sighed. "I am not proud of their actions, *señorita*, but they were not all bad. Some eh-Spaniards defended the Maya."

"And some Maya betrayed their own people," admitted Lola. "But you know what they say: history is written by the winners. I've never read a history book that told the Maya point of view."

Santino nodded. "It is true. The history books show conquistadors in their shiny armor, when most could not even afford shoes. They came from here, from Extremadura, from the poorest region in all of eh-Spain. Thousands of peasants sailing to the New World, to make their fortune—"

"To steal it, you mean," Lola corrected him.

Santino shrugged. "In any case, most of them died in the jungle. And of the few who survived, most came home even poorer than before. But my eh-story is about a boy who left in rags and returned as one of the richest men in all of eh-Spain. His name was Rodrigo de Pizarro."

Max sat bolt upright.

Grandma Isabella's family name was Pizarro.

Santino noted his interest. "You know this name?"

"Why would I?" said Max. He still didn't trust the young law student and he didn't intend to tell him anything.

"He was from the same family as Francisco Pizarro, the famous conq—" Santino looked at Lola and quickly corrected himself. "The famous *invader* of Peru. But, by all accounts, Rodrigo was a good man. They say his heart was as brave as a lynx and his hair was as red as a fox." He studied Max's face intently. "You know, I have seen a painting of Rodrigo de Pizarro, and he looked like you—the eh-spitting image, as they say."

Max shifted uncomfortably on the hard rock.

"So," continued Santino, "before they sailed to the New World, the Pizarro family were eh-swineherds. But Rodrigo came home, not twenty years old, with fifty chests of treasure and a jade wedding ring on his finger. He built the castle for himself and his eh-spouse, a beautiful Maya princess."

"I bet the townsfolk loved that," said Lola drily, "an Indian in their castle."

"At first, it was a great eh-scandal. Some said that, with his red hair, Rodrigo was in league with the devil. Others said that his bride was a witch who had put some sort of eh-spell on him. It was to eh-stop all the gossip and rumors about his wife that Rodrigo gave the town its motto: *La Verdad Sobre Todo*, 'Truth Above All.' He made it a crime to tell a lie."

"Sounds like he really loved her," said Lola wonderingly.

"Her favorite color was yellow. So he gave her yellow flowers every day."

"How romantic. Did they live happily ever after?"

Santino shook his head. "Rodrigo was eh-stabbed in the back on the eve of their first wedding anniversary."

Max's wound throbbed. He remembered the girl in the yellow dress and the flash of steel. "Who did it?" he asked. "Who stabbed him?"

"It was a fellow swineherd-turned-conquistador, by the name of Landa."

Lola looked up sharply. "Friar Diego de Landa? The nut job who burned my people's books?"

"No, this was his cousin, Count Lorenzo de Landa. He was also, as you say it, a *nut job*. It seems to be a family trait. It is rumored that the present count, Antonio, murdered his own brother to inherit the estate."

"Antonio de Landa? He lives near here?" Lola looked horrified at the thought of crossing paths with the cape-twirling maniac who'd kidnapped her in San Xavier and dragged her to the Black Pyramid, apparently with plans to sacrifice her.

"Antonio lives in Galicia, a wild region in the northwest of eh-Spain," answered Santino.

"How far is that?" Lola pressed him.

"Driving? About seven hours."

Satisfied that her tormentor was not within cape-twirling distance, she relaxed slightly. "So what happened to the Maya princess?"

"Lorenzo de Landa, her husband's killer, announced his betrothal to her. Of course, all he wanted was the treasure. Every day, he brought her red roses, and every day she eh-spurned him, turning the roses yellow with the power of her love for Rodrigo. Years passed; Lorenzo grew old and died. Since then, generations of Landas have tried to claim Rodrigo's fortune; but none has ever succeeded because it is guarded eh-still by his beautiful Maya princess."

"And her name was Inez!" guessed Lola.

"That was her eh-Spanish name." Santino pulled out his cell phone and looked at the time. "We must go," he said. "It's getting late."

Across the valley, a bell began to ring. The sun was low in the sky, airbrushing the countryside with a golden glow, its rays reflecting off a window in the castle like the whirl of a yellow ball gown. The Yellow Jaguar was inside there, Max was sure of it.

"We've found what we're looking for," he whispered to Lola.

She shivered. "What we need right now is a place to stay. Are there any hotels around here, Santino?"

"I know just the place," he replied, punching a number into his phone.

"I'll call the monkeys," said Lola.

She cupped her hands around her mouth to make the sound of a howler monkey, the loudest land animal on the planet. And if Santino Garcia was surprised to hear the girl of his dreams roaring like an angry dinosaur, he was too polite to mention it.

Chapter Six

THE HOTEL OF HORROR

feel like I've been here before," said Max as Santino drove them through the narrow, cobbled streets of Polvoredo.

"Me, too," agreed Lola. "Those little houses all jammed together like they're holding each other up . . . the balconies . . . the shutters . . . the crumbling stone walls . . . even the holes in the road. . . . It all looks so familiar." They drove on in silence, until she suddenly burst out, "I know! It looks like Puerto Muerto!"

She was right. This remote village in the middle of Spain was a dead ringer for the little town where Max had first met up with Uncle Ted, half a world away in San Xavier.

"Spooky," he said.

Santino looked over his shoulder. "It is not eh-spooky at all. Puerto Muerto is a colonial town. It was built by colonists from Extremadura. What should they build but what they know?" He pulled up in front of a seedy doorway. "Welcome to Casa Carmela, the best hotel in town!"

Max surveyed the entrance of the run-down hotel, with

its broken tiles and peeling paint. "It's not exactly the Hilton, is it?"

"It is also the only hotel in town," admitted Santino, smiling. "Not many tourists eh-stay in Polvoredo overnight."

"You don't say?" replied Max, feigning surprise.

Lola shot him a warning look and turned anxiously to Santino. "Do they allow animals here?" she asked.

He nodded. "I have called ahead and pulled some eh-strings for you. Doña Carmela, who runs this place, is the second cousin of the uncle of the sister-in-law of the wife of my brother. She is expecting you all."

"Thank you for everything, Santino."

"It is my pleasure, *señorita*," he said. "And perhaps while you are in eh-Spain, you will do me the honor of visiting my home and meeting my family?"

Lola looked flustered. "Um . . . that's so kind, but we . . . um . . . we have a busy schedule. I'm not sure there's time. . . ."

"I will wait for you, *señorita*," said Santino, "for as long as it takes."

There was an awkward pause, during which Max sensed that the law student would be moving in for a kiss if he and Lola were alone in the car.

"No," said Max, "there definitely won't be time."

A red sports car roared up behind them, unable to pass in the narrow street. Its driver revved its engine impatiently and thumped on the horn.

Santino sighed. "I have to go; I have a date with my mother."

Max raised an eyebrow.

"It is her birthday," replied Santino icily.

"Oh," said Max. He got out of the car.

Santino ran around to open Lola's door for her. "Don't forget your flowers," he said.

Lola picked up the roses and stared at them in amazement. "They've turned yellow!"

"I told you! There is magic in the air in Polvoredo. Just remember everyone eh-speaks the truth here. It can seem a little eh-strange if you are not used to it. But Carmela will look after you until I can come back, tomorrow or the next day. And then I hope you will permit me to buy you dinner?"

Lola stole a glance at Max. "Um, that's so kind of you, but I'm not sure. . . ."

"Lunch?"

"It's just that we have so much to do. . . ."

"Ice cream? I know the best place in all of eh-Spain. It's not far."

Lola's resolve broke down. "Why not?" she said, laughing.

There was a furious honking from the red car.

"I will count the minutes," said Santino. He bowed. "*Hasta luego, señorita.*"

He drove off in a cloud of dust and exhaust smoke, with the red sports car on his tail.

Lord 6-Dog doubled up in a fit of coughing. "A pox on thine infernal combustion engine!"

"It's an *internal* combustion engine," Max corrected him.

Lady Coco patted her son on the back, and hopped up and down with excitement. "My first hotel!" she said. "Let's go in. I've heard they leave chocolates on your pillow!"

"Hush!" whispered Lola. "It's not safe to talk yet, Your Majesties; someone might hear you. Please wait till we get to our rooms." She looked doubtfully at Casa Carmela and pushed open the rickety front door. "Here goes."

The door opened straight into the hotel restaurant. The musty room was dark and empty, but a clattering of saucepans could be heard from somewhere in the back.

"*Hola!*" called Lola. "*Buenas tardes!*"

Max thought he saw faces peeping out of the little round windows in the kitchen doors, but when he looked again they were gone.

"*Hola!*" Lola called again. The noise of pots ceased abruptly.

Lola marched over to the kitchen door, holding the bouquet of flowers in front of her.

"*Por favor—*" she began, sticking her head around the door and offering the flowers to someone Max couldn't see. She was interrupted by a blistering torrent of Spanish, the flowers were pulled from her hands, and the door was pulled shut in her face.

She walked back to Max with a face like thunder.

"That was Doña Carmela," she said, "the rudest woman in Spain."

"What did she say to you?"

"She said she doesn't like strangers."

"So why is she running a hotel?"

"Who knows? She also said she doesn't like animals, but Santino has promised to pay her well if she lets us stay, and he has more money than sense. Then she got really personal and said she doesn't know what he sees in me, and he should marry a nice Spanish girl."

"Whoa," said Max. "Santino wasn't joking about people in this town always telling the truth. So did you tell her that you don't want to marry him?"

"It's none of her business."

"But you *don't* want to marry him, do you?"

"I don't want to marry anyone! What's got into you?"

"I'm hungry, that's all. Did she say anything about food?"

"She said they don't open for dinner for another two hours, but she'd find some old leftovers and charge us a fortune for them because we're tourists and we don't know any better."

"Telling the truth must be very bad for business," mused Max. "This place is a big enough dump as it is—"

"Shh," said Lola, "here she comes."

The kitchen door flew open and a hunchbacked old woman dressed all in black shuffled out. The expression on her wrinkled, weather-beaten face was fierce, as if someone had just stolen her false teeth.

Lady Coco whimpered and hid behind Lola.

Lord 6-Dog leapt onto the nearest table and snatched up a dinner knife, ready to fight this harridan.

"No, no, no!" screeched Carmela, stamping her foot and waving her finger at him. As she was wearing men's lace-up shoes that were several sizes too big; the effect might have been comic if she hadn't been blazing with anger.

"Get off the table!" Lola warned Lord 6-Dog.

The monkey king vaulted up to a roof beam, where he hung by his tail, still brandishing the dinner knife, while Carmela waved her fists at him.

"Tell him to behave," Max whispered. "She's going to blow a fuse."

Carmela swiveled around in the direction of his voice, took one look at him, and staggered backward, crossing herself and muttering dementedly.

"Now what's wrong with her?" asked Max.

"Quick! Put your cap on, Hoop."

"What? Why?"

"It's your hair. She says Santino didn't tell her you were a *pelirrojo*. She says she's afraid to look at you. She says you'll bring bad luck to her establishment."

"What are you talking about?"

"Don't you remember how Santino said that people with red hair were thought to be in league with the devil?"

"But this is the twenty-first century," Max pointed out. "And anyway, my hair is br– . . . br– . . . br– . . ."

Lola and Carmela looked at him curiously.

"Are you cold, Hoop?" asked Lola.

"No. Just tell her my hair is br– . . . br– . . . br– . . ."

Try as he might, Max could not form the word he was looking for.

"Are you trying to say *brown*, by any chance?" asked Lola.

Max nodded toward the old woman. "My hair. Tell her."

"It's not allowed to tell untruths in Polvoredo, remember?"

"What? You mean there's some ethereal authority on hair color in this town? I demand a second opinion–"

"Just put on your cap and stop arguing."

Max pulled his Red Sox cap out of his backpack and crammed it on.

Meanwhile, Lola spoke calmly but forcefully to Carmela.

The old lady got up quickly and, still not looking at Max, she gestured for them to sit at the nearest table. Then she hobbled back to the kitchen and shouted a stream of instructions to someone inside.

"What did you say?" asked Max. "Why did she change her mind?"

"I told her that, yes, you are working for the devil, but you would not make any trouble if she treats us well and charges fairly and brings us some decent food."

"How come you can tell a lie and I can't?"

"I didn't tell a lie. You're on a mission for Ah Pukuh and the Death Lords, aren't you? Ah Pukuh is a devil, all right."

Max went quiet. He looked shaken by this analysis of the situation.

"Cheer up, Hoop; we're still the good guys." She looked around the room. "Can you believe we made it, we're actually here in Polvoredo? Lucky we met up with Santino. We'd still be waiting for a train if it wasn't for him."

"I don't like him. He has shifty eyes. And he uses too much hair gel."

"Like that girl in the airport parking lot uses too much makeup?" retorted Lola. "Her eyes were so black she looked like a raccoon."

They glared at each other across the table as Carmela began slamming down plates and glasses, taking pains to stay as far away from Max as possible.

Lola called up to Lord 6-Dog. "It's dinnertime."

The monkey assumed an imperious air, but his twitching nose betrayed his hunger. Suddenly he leapt down and landed on the back of a chair, just as a small boy emerged from the kitchen with a loaded tray. The boy took one look at the big black howler monkey and would have dropped the tray in terror if Lola hadn't reached out a steadying hand and coaxed him forward.

Keeping his eyes fixed on the table, the boy set down several little plates of food: sausages, salami, roughly sliced morsels of ham, bread, olives, omelet, and something stringy and brown in sauce, which could have been mushrooms or possibly stewed mouse, but was the one dish that sat untouched to the end of the meal. The monkeys dived on the food without ceremony, spitting out one thing after another as they discovered it was not to their taste.

In seconds, the table had turned into a battle scene.

"Your Majesties, please!" Lola chided them. "If you behave yourselves, I'll ask for some fruit."

As she helped the boy clear up the mess, Lola noticed his shaking hands.

"*Tienes miedo?*" she asked him. "Are you scared?"

The boy whispered something to Lola and ran back to the kitchen. Max watched him go. "I guess he's never seen real live howler monkeys before."

"It's not the monkeys," Lola said. "It's you."

"What?"

"Carmela has told him you're a *fantasma.*"

Max brightened. "She thinks I'm fantastic?"

"She thinks you're a ghost."

Max's face fell again. "Why would she say that?"

"She reminds me of the old women back home. They're so superstitious. They think everything is an omen. Just ignore it."

The boy returned with a bowl of grapes for the monkeys and a plate of miniature green peppers.

Again Lola talked with him a little in Spanish. "He's Carmela's grandson," she translated. "He thinks that most of her cooking is horrible, but we should try her *pimientos fritos* because they're her specialty."

Lola took one of the peppers and nibbled it tentatively.

"They're good!" she announced to the boy, who ran off, smiling, to tell his grandmother.

Lola passed the plate to the monkeys, who each took a pawful and ate them with relish.

"Hey, save some for me!" said Max, spearing a pepper on his fork.

As he lifted the fork to his mouth, he became aware of Carmela watching him through the kitchen door. He placed the pepper on his tongue, bit into it, and screamed with pain. It was as if he'd just eaten a firecracker. His head exploded. His face blazed. His tongue throbbed. His gums burned.

He gulped down three glasses of water in quick succession. "You could have warned me those things were hot," he spluttered.

"But they're not hot," Lola protested. She took the last pepper, turning it around in her mouth to extract every bit of flavor. "Not at all."

"Very funny," croaked Max, clutching at his throat. "Water! I need more water! Water, *por favor!*"

It was Carmela herself who appeared with the earthenware pitcher. "*Dile que todo el agua en el mundo no puede apagar el fuego del infierno,*" she rasped.

"She wants you to know," said Lola, "that all the water in the world cannot put out the fires of hell."

"Charming," said Max. "I bet she tried to poison me. Ask her about the peppers."

"*Nos gustan mucho los pimientos, señora,*" began Lola sweetly.

Soon Carmela was gabbling away to Lola, her toothless mouth working at double speed. She used a lot of gesticulations and every so often she pointed in Max's direction and crossed herself again. Since he couldn't understand a word she was saying, Max amused himself by watching the hairy mole on her chin as it moved with her changing expressions.

"So?" asked Max as the old lady headed back to the kitchen.

"She said they're called *pimientos de Padrón*. Most are mild, but one or two are so spicy, they blow your head off."

"I noticed that. Why was she pointing at me?"

"She said she knew you'd get the hot pepper. She said you are cursed. She said that if Santino wasn't the brother-in-law of the sister-in-law of the uncle of her second cousin, she wouldn't allow you to sleep under her roof."

"I'm not sure that the hospitality business is her thing," observed Max. "But she *is* going to let us stay, right?"

Lola nodded. "For tonight, at least. Let's go find our rooms before she changes her mind."

Lady Coco scampered ahead, and Lord 6-Dog trailed sullenly behind as Carmela's grandson led them up a narrow staircase.

The stair carpet was dangerously threadbare, the handrail was just a greasy rope, and the old wooden treads creaked alarmingly. "What a dump. It's like the Hotel of Horror," grumbled Max.

The boy indicated two doors next to each other on the second floor and handed Lola two keys. She waited until he'd gone back down before unlocking the nearest door.

"In here, everyone," she said. "We need to talk."

"Can't it wait until morning?" Max yawned.

"No," said Lola, "it can't. Please sit down."

Max and the monkeys sat side by side on the narrow bed, while Lola stood in front of them, arms folded, looking ominously like she was going to make a speech.

"No chocolates," sighed Lady Coco, examining the pillow.

"The cockroaches probably ate them," said Max, lying back.

"Get your shoes off my bed!" snapped Lola.

Max sat bolt upright. He'd heard that tone in her voice once before, at Itzamna, when he'd made fun of her friend and mentor, Hermanjilio. She was angry with Max then and she was angry with him now.

In fact, she was angry with all of them.

She looked down the line with distaste, like a sergeant major inspecting new recruits.

"Grow up, all of you," she said. "I'm not your mother. It's not my job to look after you while you act like children. If you continue to behave like this, I'm catching the first plane back to San Xavier."

"How darest thou speak thus to a king?" asked Lord 6-Dog haughtily.

"With all due respect, Your Majesty," said Lola, "I will treat you like a king when you act like one. You're the first Maya lord in history to cross the ocean in an airplane, but instead of marveling at the wonders of aviation, you sulk like a spoiled child. And what was that about, when you swung from the rafters in the restaurant? Would you behave like that in your royal palace?"

Lord 6-Dog had the grace to look slightly ashamed.

"Lady Lola is right, son," said Lady Coco, swatting him on the head. "Your behavior was a disgrace. You could have got us ejected."

"As for you, Lady Coco," said Lola sternly, "your table manners were appalling. I cannot believe a Maya queen would grab and spit like that."

Lady Coco hung her head.

"That's a bit harsh, isn't it?" said Max to Lola. "What's got into you?"

It was the wrong thing to say.

She turned on him, eyes blazing. "I'll tell you what's got into me, Max Murphy. All you've done since we got here is whine and moan and complain. You don't like Santino, you don't like the food, you don't like the hotel. . . . Well, tough. This isn't about you. It's about rescuing Hermanjilio and Lucky Jim—"

Her voice cracked and she turned away.

Max stared at her in amazement.

So much for teamwork.

Who did she think she was?

He was about to start arguing back, when Lady Coco whispered in his ear: "I don't think this is about etiquette, young lord. I think she's got cold feet."

Max tried to look sensitive and caring. "So what's this really about?" he asked Lola. "Tell me what's wrong."

Lola looked surprised at his newfound insight. "It's just . . . well . . . I've got a headache from thinking too much. I don't know the right thing to do anymore."

"About dating Santino?" asked Max, jealously.

"No! About the mission. I don't know if we should go through with it."

"What?"

"I mean, of course, I want to rescue Hermanjilio and Lucky Jim and your parents. But I don't want the Death Lords to have the Yellow Jaguar."

"But that's the deal."

"I know. But it's bad enough that Ah Pukuh is in charge

of the next *bak'tun*. If his Death Lords have all five Jaguar Stones, there's no knowing what's going to happen. They'll have the power to do every evil thing they've ever dreamed of. They'll be like kids in a toystore. They'll send earthquakes, tsunamis, plagues, wars . . . disasters like nothing we've ever seen."

"So the End of the World Club might be right," mused Max.

"Who?"

"That's what Dad calls all the people who are freaking out about the end of the Maya calendar. The funny thing is that the end of the world might really be happening—but not for the reasons they think."

"That's not actually funny," said Lola.

"It sounds to me," said Lord 6-Dog, "as if Lady Lola is losing her resolve on the eve of the battle."

"I just want to do the right thing," she replied.

"Then stick to the plan," barked Lord 6-Dog. "We will find the Yellow Jaguar, deliver it to Xibalba, and rescue the hostages."

"Even if we're helping to bring about the end of the planet?" persisted Lola.

"The planet is not in peril," Lord 6-Dog pointed out. "Only its inhabitants."

"That's not much consolation," said Max.

"What, young lord, art thou losing heart, too?" Lord 6-Dog was getting annoyed. "Have I not told thee that, when good battles evil, good always wins? It is written in the stars."

"Was it written in the stars, the day Tzelek took the life of your father?" asked Lady Coco.

"Good *eventually* wins," Lord 6-Dog corrected himself. "The day is coming, Mother, when I will avenge my father's death. Tzelek and I will have our showdown, I promise thee. But all things are connected and the battle starts on the morrow, with the hunt for the Yellow Jaguar."

"You mean, we might be helping to *save* the world?" asked Lola.

"I am sure of it. Let us see where this quest leads us."

"Right now," said Max, yawning, "it's leading me to bed."

The others murmured in agreement.

"Good night, everybody," said Lola. "I'm sorry I got mad."

"It's been a long day," said Lady Coco sympathetically. "We'll all feel better in the morning."

The room next door was even smaller and dingier than Lola's room, but it seemed clean enough.

"I'll take the bed and you take the armchair," said Max to Lord 6-Dog.

Lord 6-Dog stretched out on the bed and instantly started snoring.

"Oh, come on!" complained Max. "You have to be faking."

No answer.

Max resigned himself to the armchair and grabbed a spare blanket and pillow. After five cramped, hot, uncomfortable minutes, he threw off the blanket and got up to open the window. A mangy ginger cat on a nearby roof hissed at him menacingly.

Max leaned out of the window and breathed in the night air. It was a little cooler than the air in the room and it carried a faint sound of Gypsy music and the scent of yellow roses.

Down below, in the little square, some teenage boys played soccer with an old tin can and some teenage girls pretended not to watch them. In a pool of light beneath a streetlamp, two small children acted out the drama of a bullfight, one swishing an imaginary cape, the other charging with imaginary horns.

At the far end of the square, a neon sign sputtered to life above a café, and a waiter came out to straighten the tables and chairs.

In ones and twos and larger groups, people came out of the side streets and drifted toward the café. A woman in a red jacket waved to catch the waiter's attention. With her long black ponytail and big sunglasses pushed back on her head, she reminded Max of a younger, more stylish version of Zia, the black-clad housekeeper who wore big black shades every waking hour, day and night.

Max felt a pang as he thought of Zia and his parents, at home in Boston. He wondered if he'd ever see them again.

"What are you thinking about?"

He turned to see Lola, leaning out of the next window.

"I was thinking about Boston," he said.

"I'd like to come to Boston one day," said Lola. "See a ballgame with your famous Red Sox."

"If we get out of this dump alive," said Max.

"You promised to stop complaining," Lola reminded him.

"Starting tomorrow," said Max.

All the tables and chairs were full now. A man strummed on a Spanish guitar. The customers stamped their feet and clapped in time and shouted their approval. Max and Lola could just make out the dark shape of a woman dancing in the moonlight. It looked like the woman in the red jacket.

"I read that Spanish towns come to life when the sun goes down. The people here are nocturnal—like jaguars."

"So long as they don't go hunting in the night," said Max.

Somewhere in the backstreets, a dog howled.

"Make sure your door's locked, Hoop!" Lola teased him. She yawned. "Well, good night. We have a busy day tomorrow."

A busy day tomorrow.

She made it sound so ordinary, like they were going sightseeing or shopping—instead of risking their lives to pay back the Lords of Death.

Max locked his door and arranged himself in the armchair to sleep.

Then he got up again, to lock the window shutters.

As he leaned forward to pull them closed, something warm and sticky dripped on his head.

He put his fingers to it and found that it was blood.

He looked up to see a hellhound sitting on the roof above his window, a ginger cat clenched in its monstrous jaws.

Chapter Seven
THE STENCH OF EVIL

A s weak sunlight filtered through the shutters, Max stretched his aching limbs. Squashed into the armchair all night, listening for the hellhound, wondering if it would dare to break into the room, he felt like he hadn't slept a wink.

Had he imagined it?

Or was it still out there, waiting for him?

He remembered his promise to Lola: no more whining or complaining. He had four days left to find the Yellow Jaguar, and from now on, he was going to be strong and brave and focused on the mission.

But first, he had to know if there was a hellhound outside his room.

Taking care not to wake Lord 6-Dog, who was still snoring on the bed, Max quietly opened the windows. Then, heart pounding, he slipped the latch on the shutters and pushed them open an inch or two.

All was silence.

He looked around for some sort of decoy and his eyes landed on a broom leaning by the door. He took off a sock, put it on the end of the broom, and poked it out of the window to see if the hellhound would pounce.

Still silence.

Feeling braver now, Max threw the shutters open and looked out of the window, still holding on to the sock-clad broom handle, just in case.

"What are you doing, Hoop?" asked Lola, still half asleep and peering blearily out of the next window.

"Just airing my socks," said Max blithely. It wasn't technically a lie.

"If you say so," she said.

Max cast a quick glance at the roof above his window. No hellhound. "You, er, haven't seen anything strange out here, have you?" he asked.

"You mean, apart from a boy with a sock on the end of a broom?"

"I'll take that as a no," said Max.

No hellhounds.

"Look!" yelled Lola, pointing at the sky.

Max shaded his eyes and looked up. All he saw was the hot Spanish sun.

"Hoop! It must be nearly noon! We've overslept!"

"What? That's crazy! Do you think Carmela drugged us?"

"I think it's jet lag, but we need to hurry! I'll wake Lady Coco, you wake Lord 6-Dog, and I'll see you downstairs!"

"Okay!" Max leaned out as far as he could and took a last look around the square. Everywhere was quiet, all the buildings shuttered tight against the noonday sun. Funny how the same scene could look sinister by night and charming by day. He had to stop thinking that every stray dog was a hellhound.

Wham! Something slid off the roof, bounced off the back of his head, and plummeted to the ground.

"What the . . . ?"

He looked down.

A dead ginger cat looked up at him, its eyes frozen in fear, its coat matted with blood.

Max slammed his window shut with a crash that made the glass rattle.

Lord 6-Dog sat up in bed.

"Has the battle begun?" he shouted, twirling an imaginary sword.

Max nodded, still too shocked to talk.

Lord 6-Dog sniffed the air. "What is that stink?"

"Sorry," mumbled Max, kicking yesterday's socks into a corner.

"Not that." Lord 6-Dog's supersensitive nostrils were working overtime.

"There's a dead cat out there, is that it?"

"It is neither thy fetid foot garments nor a fallen feline. It is the stench of evil. Mark my words, Ah Pukuh is in this place."

"But the cat . . . I think it was killed by a hellhound."

"Splendid! Let us gird our loins and join the fray!"

They arrived downstairs just as Carmela was going out. She grunted at Lola and indicated a table laden with stale breads, old pastries and rock-hard yellow cakes, a jug of not-very-hot chocolate, and a large bunch of over-ripe bananas. Then she shielded her face from Max, crossed herself, and went out the front door, dragging a wicker shopping basket on wheels behind her.

Lola tiptoed over to the kitchen and peeked inside.

"All clear," she said, coming back to the table. "Your Majesties can speak!"

"Well, isn't this nice?" said Lady Coco. She was wearing her Spanish dancer dress again and she carefully unfolded her napkin and laid it on her lap, with impressively ladylike motions. "Our first breakfast in Spain."

"I'm sorry, Lady Coco," said Lola, "but we don't have time."

"No?" The former queen looked crestfallen.

"*No!*" bellowed Lord 6-Dog. "We should be out there engaging with the enemy, not sitting around eating cake like old women."

"This old woman," said Lady Coco, reaching for a cake, "believes that an army marches on its stomach."

"Well, maybe just a quick hot chocolate, while we plan our route," said Lola quickly, before hostilities broke out in earnest.

"What a treat!" said Lady Coco, holding out her cup. "In our day, we called it *chokol ha*, which means 'hot water.' Everyone had their own recipe, but I made it with ground *kakaw* beans and chilies; it was 6-Dog's favorite."

"I hope you like the modern version," said Lola dubiously. "They make it with cows' milk and sugar."

"It looks delicious," said Lady Coco diplomatically

"It looks like dishwater," sneered Lord 6-Dog.

Lola sighed. "I think it's going to be another long day."

"Here," said Lady Coco, offering him a banana. "You'll feel better if you eat something."

"How should I feel better?" bellowed Lord 6-Dog. "I am a Maya king in the body of a howler monkey. Where once I received tributes of rare spices, jade, and quetzal feathers, thou dost offer me a banana that is older than I am?"

Lady Coco thumped on the table. "That's enough! May I remind you, Your high and mighty Majesty, that if you weren't sitting here in that fur coat, you'd still be floating around in the circles of eternity. You've been dead for a thousand years and you should grab this chance with both your hairy little hands. I have told you time and again, it is what's on the inside that counts. Here we are, at this glorious moment in history, and I, for one, intend to live every moment to its fullest."

And with that, she peeled the banana and took a defiant bite.

Lord 6-Dog stared at her. "Why, Mother," he mused, "I do believe thou wouldst have made a fine battle chief in thy day."

"*This* is my day," she declared. "*Ko'ox!*"

Lord 6-Dog smiled. "*Ko'ox!*" he repeated.

"What's *co-osh?*" asked Max.

"It's Yucatec for 'let's go'!" Lola studied Max's face. "You're very quiet this morning, Hoop. And you haven't eaten anything. That's not like you. Are you okay?"

"Last night, there was a hellhound. It killed a cat . . . a ginger cat . . . a *pelirrojo*. I think it was a warning to me. I think it's out there, waiting for me. There might be a whole pack of them."

"Or," suggested Lola, "it might have been a fight between a couple of strays. Not everything is an omen, Hoop."

Max gave her a weak smile.

"So fill up and let's go!" She pushed the water jug across to him. "*Ko'ox!*"

Max filled his water bottle from the jug and threw the

bottle, with the breakfast leftovers, into his backpack. The yellow cakes sank like stones to the bottom. "It weighs a ton," he groaned as he followed the others out into the street.

"So we're all agreed that we start at the castle?" Lola was saying.

"Indubitably," said Lord 6-Dog.

"Sounds good to me," said Lady Coco.

Max took a deep breath. This was it. He was about to go find the Yellow Jaguar. "Okay, everyone," he said in a strange, squeaky voice that betrayed his terror, "act normal. We're on vacation, just strolling around."

"That reminds me," said Lola, rooting in her day-pack and pulling out a child-size Hawaiian shirt, "I brought this for you, Lord 6-Dog, to make you look like a tourist." The shirt was brightly colored and printed with parrots, palm trees, and tropical flowers.

"It's beautiful," cooed Lady Coco. "It has all the colors of the jungle."

Lord 6-Dog tried to look disinterested, but his eyes betrayed his delight as he tried it on.

"Perfect!" said Max. "All you need now are a camera and a baseball cap."

"You're the one who needs a cap, Hoop," said Lola. "You should cover up your hair before you upset any more old ladies."

Max looked in his backpack. "It's not here; I must have left it in the room. You go on ahead. I'll run back for it and catch up to you."

Lola pointed down the street. "We're going that way, toward the Plaza Mayor, the main square. But hurry, Hoop, daylight's burning. . . ."

Max ran back into the hotel, raced up the stairs, and flung open the door to his room, only to find Carmela standing there, riffling through his passport.

"*Qué . . . qué . . . ?*" Max spluttered. His Spanish simply wasn't up to the job of questioning the old woman. For her part, Carmela made a big show of dusting the dresser, carefully replacing the passport, and moving on to make the bed. She did not meet his eyes. Not knowing what else to do, Max grabbed his passport and his Red Sox cap and ran back downstairs to find the others.

The street was deserted when he came out.

He started walking in the direction of the main square.

He heard a noise behind him and turned around.

Nothing.

He carried on walking.

Something was behind him.

He turned again, and a hellhound jumped out of the shadows and lunged at him in a frenzy of snarling teeth and gnashing jaws.

Max slipped off his backpack, heavy with food and water, and swung it at the creature. It fell back a little, giving Max time to reach into his bag for some little cakes, as dense as cannonballs. Stuffing them into his pockets, he began to run, the huge dog at his heels. He turned and lobbed a sugary missile. It bounced off the hound's nose and landed in its gaping maw, which swallowed it in one gulp. Max ran faster than he'd ever run in his life, but he could hear the hellhound growling and slavering behind him. Not sure now whether the dog wanted him or more baked goods, he threw cakes and pastries over his shoulder as he ran.

In the distance he saw Lola and the monkeys, waiting for him.

"Run!" he yelled. "Run!"

They stood there, waving at him and encouraging him on. There were no side streets or alleyways he could divert the dog into, so even if he'd been brave enough to sacrifice himself, it wasn't an option. He had to keep running toward them, hoping that one of them would realize the danger.

"Hellhound!" he screamed. "Run!"

Still Lola and the monkeys didn't move.

"Whoo-hoo!" cheered Lola. "I didn't know you could move so fast!"

"There's hellhound on my . . ." Max realized he couldn't hear the dog anymore. He glanced quickly over his shoulder. It was gone.

"There was a hellhound. . . . It was chasing me," he panted as he drew level with his friends.

"That's not funny," said Lola. "We're all on edge as it is."

"You don't believe me?" Max was outraged.

"We watched you all the way. There was no dog, not even a small one."

"Not a dog," insisted Max. "A hellhound. I think it was the same one that killed the cat outside my room last night."

Lola shook her head. "There was nothing. Get a grip, Hoop."

"You have to believe me. . . ."

Lord 6-Dog leapt onto Max's shoulder. "I believe thee," he muttered. "The stink of evil is getting stronger."

Max sniffed. "I can smell it, too," he said.

An archway at the far end of the street marked the

entrance to the Plaza Mayor. The closer they got, the more their nostrils filled with a nauseating odor.

"Halt!" whispered Lord 6-Dog. "By the bristles on my monkey chin, I know this stench—it can only be the vile emissions of Ah Pukuh, lord of Xibalba. Mark my words, evil awaits us in this plaza."

And so it begins, thought Max as they walked into the square.

What had he expected?

Definitely an orange sky in the middle of the day . . . maybe overturned trucks and burned-out buildings . . . or alien spaceships and lizardlike monsters . . . even cackling hobgoblins and smoking bonfires—all standard end-of-the-world scenarios in video games.

Or would it be something more Maya-themed? A pox-ridden death god belching fire, ominous drumming, strange animal lords, severed heads on poles, and beating hearts on wooden platters?

Yes, that sounded right.

But it was wrong.

And most wrong of all was the sight that awaited him.

He'd expected a certain amount of blood and gore and destruction, but nothing like this. . . .

This was . . .

Well, the word that leapt into his brain was *picturesque*.

It looked like the setting for a medieval tournament in a book of fairy tales.

At one end of the square, an old stone church supported a stork's nest on its precariously leaning bell tower. At the other end of the square was some sort of palace, a pennant flying from its balcony, a coat of arms emblazoned on its crumbling facade, and a knight in armor standing ready for the fray.

Between the church and the palace and all around the square, tradespeople plied their wares in an arcaded gallery. On the square itself were pitched dozens of gaily striped battle tents. Men, women, and children in medieval dress milled around excitedly, lute music filled the air, and everywhere was The Smell, although no one but Max and his friends seemed to notice it.

"It's like we've gone back in time," muttered Max.

He'd heard that medieval streets stank of unwashed bodies and household waste, but he'd never imagined how hard it would be to breathe under those circumstances. His face was clammy from the effort.

A girl in a red velvet gown stepped out in front of him, barring his way.

"*Queso?*" she asked.

She was dressed like a princess, a fairy-tale princess, but her round face was red and blotchy, and her hands were big like a man's.

He backed away.

Next thing, he was surrounded by squires and wenches, all thrusting strong-smelling plates under his nose. The odor reminded him a bit of the dentist's office. Was it chloroform perhaps? His head was swimming. . . .

Lola clutched his arm.

"I know what this is!" she said.

Max looked at her with dread. What kind of ancient ritual was being enacted? He had not expected the Death Lords to make things easy, but this odor hinted at tortures he had never dreamed of.

He swallowed nervously. "What is it?"

"It's a cheese festival!" She giggled. "It wasn't the smell of Ah Pukuh you sensed, Lord 6-Dog—just all these free samples of cheese!"

"Free samples?" said Max, suddenly interested.

"Keep walking," Lola commanded him. "We're on a mission—the fate of the world and all that, remember?"

As Max surveyed the bustling scene, he realized how wrong his first impression had been. Now that he looked more carefully, he saw that the pennant on the palace read TOURIST OFFICE and the knight in armor was posing for photographs with passersby. Aside from himself and Lord 6-Dog, no one was wearing a baseball cap or Hawaiian shirt, so he guessed that most of these visitors were local. Or at least, not American. But that was all the more reason to try and fit in.

"Tourists never say no to free food," he pointed out. "And we don't want to act out of character and draw attention to ourselves."

Lady Coco nodded in agreement, eyeing a bunch of juicy green grapes.

"Okay," said Lola, "but only while Lord 6-Dog and I go to the tourist office and see what we can find out."

Max and Lady Coco searched out the least-stinky cheese (heavy on grape garnish for Lady Coco) and stood around people-watching.

Across the square, a peal of laughter rang out. A woman in red was relating an anecdote to a table of revelers. Although he couldn't hear what she was saying (and he wouldn't have understood if he could), Max was transfixed by the way she flicked her long black ponytail as she acted out her story.

Something about her made him feel homesick.

He wished he could pull up a chair at her table and join in the laughter.

He wished he could trade places with any one of her carefree friends.

For them, history was just an exercise in photogenic costumes, an excuse for souvenir shopping, a chance to eat and drink, a mindless escape from reality.

Didn't they know that what happened a thousand years ago could still bring the world to its knees? Didn't they care that nothing is ever truly over? Didn't they understand that greed and anger and a lust for revenge can fester in the human heart long after the flesh has rotted?

He saw Lola and Lord 6-Dog making their way back across the square.

"Let's go," he said to Lady Coco. "Time to save the world."

Chapter Eight

EL CASTILLO

That tourist office was hopeless," said Lola. "They wouldn't even tell me how to get to the castle."

"Did you ask them for a map?"

"I'm telling you, Hoop, they just wanted to get rid of me. They said Polvoredo is the dullest town in Spain, there's nothing for tourists to do here, and if they were us, they would definitely go somewhere else."

"They must be the only tourist office in the world that tells the truth," mused Max. "That can't be good for business. What about all this cheese?"

"They said the locals would die of boredom if it wasn't for all the food festivals. Tomorrow they're celebrating the art of meat pies, and it's blood sausage over the weekend."

"A meat pie festival sounds pretty good."

"Max Murphy! How can you talk about saving the world one minute and meat pies the next?"

"But if we happen to be here tomorrow—"

"No."

"Do you think certain pizza pies qualify?"

"Forget it."

They were stumbling through a labyrinth of winding cobbled streets. Since the castle was the highest point, their plan had been to keep climbing upward, but the reality was not so simple. Unexpected dead ends barred their way. Streets that looked like they sloped uphill would somehow lead them back down to the cheesy ambience of the square.

"I feel like a lab rat in a maze," said Max. "You think there'd be a sign to *el castile*."

"*El castillo*," Lola corrected him. She looked around. "If only there was someone to ask." The streets were deserted, but curtains twitched at windows, and front doors slammed shut at their approach. "The people here don't seem very friendly. I hope their Their Majesties are okay," she said, suddenly concerned for the monkeys, whom she'd sent on ahead as scouts.

"Think the locals have made them into meat pies?" joked Max.

Lola cast him a stricken look and, before Max could stop her, she'd shinnied up the nearest lamppost, cupped her hands to her mouth, and let loose a series of increasingly urgent-sounding, loud, throaty barks that echoed down the narrow streets.

"Come down!" Max yelled at her. "We're not supposed to be drawing attention to ourselves!"

Reluctantly, Lola climbed down. "A real howler call carries for three miles in the jungle," she said. "I hope I was loud enough with all these buildings."

"Trust me," said Max. "You were loud enough."

After several anxious minutes with no reply, a roar came

128

back over the rooftops and Max saw Lord 6-Dog and Lady Coco bounding toward them.

"We found it!" called Lady Coco.

"The castle is both nearer and farther than it appears," confirmed Lord 6-Dog. "It would seem that *The City of Truth* is built on an illusion."

"It is an enchanted place," agreed Lady Coco dreamily. "Magic hangs over it like a morning mist."

"Good magic or bad magic?" asked Max.

Lord 6-Dog considered the question. "To the Maya, there is good and bad in all things."

Max raised an eyebrow. "Even Tzelek?"

Lord 6-Dog ignored the question. "Shall we stand and prattle or shall we march to the castle?"

"To the castle!" announced Lola, striding forward. "*Ko'ox!*"

With a heavy heart, Max followed her.

The difference between them, he reflected, was that every step brought her nearer to rescuing her beloved Hermanjilio, but every step brought him nearer to a grisly showdown with the Lords of Death. Now that they were getting close to the Yellow Jaguar, he found his courage melting like an ice cube in the sun.

But closer and closer they approached.

With the howler monkeys to guide them, Max and Lola discovered that many of the dead ends and blind alleys were optical illusions and actually quite passable. By heading downward, they gradually climbed high above the town, until they arrived at the top of the hill. Now the smell of cheese was replaced by the intense perfume of roses, thousands and thousands of yellow roses, spilling in fragrant tangles over the castle walls.

"This is it!" announced Lady Coco.

"I suggest we scale the walls under cover of all this greenery," suggested Lord 6-Dog.

Max looked up. The walls were easily twenty feet high.

"Couldn't we look for a door?" he asked.

They followed the walls around until they came to the gatehouse. It was fronted by a massive oak door, wide enough to admit a horse-drawn carriage and reinforced with metal studs the size of grapefruits. Inset into this door was a smaller door, with a square grating at eye level. Above it all, carved into the stone, was a coat of arms and the town motto LA VERDAD SOBRE TODO.

"Are those jaguars on the coat of arms?" asked Max.

"Yes! Yes!" cried Lola excitedly. She peeked through the grating and let out a whistle of surprise. "It's literally a jungle in there: ceiba trees, cacao, mahogany, sapodilla, logwood, gumbo-limbo . . ."

Lady Coco licked her lips. "Oh, for some juicy young leaves," she said.

"We are on a mission, Mother, not a picnic," Lord 6-Dog reminded her.

"But after the fighting comes the feasting," she countered with a wink.

Lola tried first the smaller door and then the big door.

"Locked. Both of them."

She stood back.

Below the grating was an iron door knocker shaped like a jaguar head. Below the knocker was a very large, official-looking sign in blocky red letters.

"What does it say?" asked Max.

"'Private property. Permanently closed. No entry. Danger.

Go away. Forbidden to tourists. Trespassers will be prosecuted. Do not knock or else,'" Lola translated.

"Whoa!" said Max, putting up his hands in mock surrender. "Or else what?"

"Let's find out," suggested Lola.

"No—!" began Max, but it was too late.

Lola lifted the knocker and let it fall against the wood. They all jumped back in horror as a deep booming sound reverberated up and down the street, bouncing off the castle walls and rolling down the hill, turning the whole valley into an echo chamber.

"A pox on it!" exclaimed Lord 6-Dog. "This din will be heard in Xibalba!"

"Make it stop," winced Lady Coco, with her paws over her ears.

A large police officer on a small motor scooter screeched to a halt in front of them. He dismounted with surprising grace and brushed the dust off his shoulders.

"*Buenos días*," he said.

They mumbled a greeting in reply.

"I am Officer Gonzales. And you? You are tourists?"

They nodded.

He looked them up and down. "So, the knocking, who did this?"

"It was me," confessed Lola. She looked slightly surprised to have volunteered this information. Max guessed it was the ethereal arbiter of truth at work.

"Why you did this?"

Lola's face twisted this way and that as her brain composed one untrue answer after another and her mouth refused to speak any of them. Eventually, her brain and her mouth reached a compromise. "I was hoping to see inside the castle." She tried to look sweet and innocent.

The officer remained unmoved. "Is not allowed."

Lola looked suitably devastated.

"Never mind, we'll find you another castle," Max said to her consolingly. "Let's go back to the cheese festival."

They turned to go.

"Not so fast," came Officer Gonzales's voice behind them.

Max's stomach lurched.

"Was there something else, Officer?" asked Lola politely.

He pointed at the monkeys with distaste. "They are with you?"

"Yes," said Lola. She held out her arms so that Lady Coco could leap into them.

Officer Gonzales curled his lip and pulled out a little notebook from his shirt pocket.

"Where do you stay?" he asked.

"Casa Carmela," answered Lola.

"Your parents, they are with you?"

"No."

"And yours?" he asked Max.

"No."

The officer made little tutting noises as he scribbled furiously in his notebook, filling several pages before looking up again. Then he put the notebook back in his pocket and held out his hand expectantly. "Passports!"

"But—" began Max.

The officer's fingers strayed toward his gun. "You want to argue with me?"

Glumly, Max handed over his passport.

"I left mine at the hotel," said Lola.

"You must carry it at all times," said Officer Gonzales, tucking Max's passport into his shirt pocket. "It is the law."

"I didn't know; I'm so sorry," said Lola, giving him her most dazzling smile. "I could go and get it right now. . . ."

He checked his watch. "I give you one hour to produce the passport and the paperwork for the beasts. Bring them to me at the police station, just off the plaza. Come, I show you where. . . ."

So they had no choice but to walk all the way back down to the square, with Officer Gonzales following them on his scooter like a sheepdog herding sheep.

"What is this, a police state?" grumbled Max.

"He's just doing his job," said Lola.

"He's a bully."

"Be nice to him, Hoop; he could ruin everything."

When they arrived at the square, Officer Gonzales pointed out the police station. "One hour," he said sternly. And with that, he puttered off down the street on his scooter.

Max groaned. "What a waste of time. By the time that guy has finished with us, the day will be over, and we haven't got anywhere yet."

"I'm so sorry, Hoop," said Lola. "I promise I'll be fast. You wait here, try some more cheese, and I'll run back to Casa Carmela. If I'm too long at the police station, go without me."

Max and the monkeys found chairs at the edge of the square.

"Wait," said Max, a few minutes after Lola had gone. "Did she mean she's coming straight back here or is she going to the police station first?"

The monkeys shrugged.

"I hope she gets back quickly. We're supposed to find the Yellow Jaguar together, like the Hero Twins in Maya legend. Do you know Chan Kan in Utsal?"

Being forbidden to talk, the monkeys looked at him blankly.

"He said we make a good team."

As he rambled on, sitting there talking to the simian equivalent of a brick wall, Max felt like he was in therapy. It was strangely relaxing. This was exactly how his mother wished he would open up to her. Why was talking to a howler monkey easier than talking to his own mother? Another mystery of adolescence that he would never understand.

Eventually, when he'd explained his favorite video game, his taste in music, the unfairness of having a name in the middle of the alphabet, and why he preferred thin-crust to deep-dish pizza, he looked around for Lola.

Still no sign of her.

The monkeys were dozing quietly in their chairs.

Some of the cheese merchants were closing up their tents for the day.

He had precisely three and a half days left to live, he was halfway through the time Lord Kuy had allotted him, and he was no closer to finding the Yellow Jaguar than when he'd stepped off the plane.

He pulled his chair up against Lord 6-Dog's. "Wake up!" he whispered urgently.

"What . . . ?" Lord 6-Dog woke with a start and clammed up the instant he remembered he was sworn to silence.

"It's okay," whispered Max, "we're sitting in the shadows here. If we keep our voices down, I think we can talk."

"Where's Lady Lola?" asked Lord 6-Dog.

"She's probably at the police station. I'm sure she'll be here soon."

"We cannot sit here all day, young lord."

Max knew Lord 6-Dog was right. But he didn't like the idea of going back to the castle without Lola. To play for time, he asked: "What day is it, anyway, in your ritual calendar?"

"In the Tzolk'in? It is 3-Ak'bal. 3-Darkness."

"Is that a good day to attack a castle?"

Lord 6-Dog chuckled. "In truth, young lord, Ak'bal is said to be a good day to declare one's love and plan a wedding."

Max pulled a face. "You don't suppose Lola has bumped into Santino, do you? Perhaps he took her for ice cream. . . ."

"The best ice cream in all of Spain!" whispered Lady Coco, waking up. The way she clutched her paws delightedly in front of her reminded Max of a bridesmaid holding a bouquet.

"Let's go," said Max, suddenly decisive.

Lord 6-Dog jumped to his feet, ready for action.

"But what about Lady Lola?" asked Lady Coco.

Max shrugged. "She knew the plan."

"But what if she comes back and we're not here?" persisted Lady Coco. "Why don't I go and find her, and bring her to the castle?"

"Okay," said Max. "But don't bring Santino."

"You're worth two of him," said Lady Coco with a wink.

Max and Lord 6-Dog set off back up the hill.

Max tried not to keep looking around to see if Lady Coco was following with Lola. "Any ideas how we're going to get in?" he asked Lord 6-Dog.

"I could scale the walls, young lord, but thy puny legs could not follow."

"I'm stronger than I look," said Max tetchily. "I could climb up the roses."

But when they reached the towering walls, Max was shocked to see how long and sharp and viciously barbed the thorns were on every stem.

"It's no use," he admitted, "I'd get ripped to shreds."

"Never fear," said Lord 6-Dog. "We will circumnavigate the perimeter. Perhaps an ingress will present itself."

"You mean, we'll walk around the outside and look for a way in?"

"Just so."

"This is pointless," complained Max as they rounded the next corner. "And all these roses are making me feel sick. It smells like an explosion in a perfume factory."

"Look," said Lord 6-Dog. They had arrived at the great oak door in the gatehouse. "Is it my perception, or does it look different to thee?"

Max studied the door. "The sign is gone! The sign that tells you not to knock?" He stepped cautiously up to the door and ran his hand lightly over the jaguar-head knocker. "If I knock, do you think someone will answer? Or will Speedy Gonzales come zooming up on his scooter and arrest me?"

"That is the question," said Lord 6-Dog.

But the question was never answered.

Because, as Max stood there looking through the grating at the rainforest beyond, the huge door creaked slowly open.

The huge door creaked slowly open.

Chapter Nine

THE SERPENT OF TRUTH

Thhat's weird," whispered Max. "Should I go in?"

"Thou hast traveled halfway around the world and summoned me through space and time to be here. The gods themselves are watching thee, and the fate of humankind depends upon what happens here today. Yes, young lord, I think thou shouldst go in."

"No need to be sarcastic about it," said Max.

He took one last look for Lola, then gingerly he stepped through the door and into the tropical rainforest.

A canopy of treetops blotted out the Spanish sky. Scarlet macaws swooped among the emerald leaves, toucans picked wild figs with their rainbow bills, tiny hummingbirds flitted in search of nectar, and a neon blue butterfly warmed its wings in a shaft of sunlight. Yellow flowers as big as teacups climbed up the tree trunks, and yellow orchids hung from the branches. The humid air was alive with the buzzing of insects and the croaking of bullfrogs.

"Are we still in Spain?" asked Max, in awe. "It feels like San Xavier."

"My forest," murmured Lord 6-Dog. "If thou wilt excuse me, young lord, I believe I am going to brachiate."

"You're not sick, are you?"

"On the contrary, young lord. To brachiate is to swing by one's arms through the trees. It is not common behavior for howlers, but in this beautiful place I am tempted to try it."

Max laughed. "Go for it!" he said. "I'll follow the old driveway and I'll see you at the castle."

He watched as the large black howler climbed the nearest tree trunk and disappeared into the foliage. Wishing that he, too, could swing through the trees instead of having to watch every timorous step for biting ants and sleeping snakes, Max began to make his own way to the castle.

But Lord 6-Dog was gone only a few minutes before he returned with a great crash of branches and landed inelegantly at Max's feet.

"What's wrong?" asked Max. "You're trembling. . . ."

"I shake with anger, young lord," said Lord 6-Dog. "Thou wilt not believe what I saw from the treetops. It is the Temple of Blood . . . the pyramid of K'awiil . . . home of the Yellow Jaguar. . . . It is here. . . ."

"Here?"

"Right here, in the center of the castle."

"It must be a copy," said Max.

"It is the real thing," insisted Lord 6-Dog. "I would stake my life on it."

"But how is that possible?"

"K'awiil was by far the smallest pyramid, little more than a ceremonial staircase leading up to a temple. I wager the conquerors dismantled it and transported it hither in their galleons."

Now it was Max who was shaking. He was about to lean

against the nearest tree when Lord 6-Dog stopped him. "It is a trumpet tree, young lord. Biting ants live in its trunk." The king guided Max to a nearby ceiba tree and cleared the leaf litter from between its huge buttress roots. "Sit here, young lord."

Max sank weakly to the ground. "What does this mean?"

"It means that some scoundrel has dared to steal the very stones of Maya kingship. It was at this temple that the Jaguar Kings held their weddings and coronations. . . ."

Max could tell from the distant look in his brown monkey eyes that Lord 6-Dog was a thousand miles and a thousand years away. "But what does it mean to *us*?" he asked impatiently. "Is it good news or bad news? Does it make our mission easier or harder?"

Lord 6-Dog thought for a moment. "Dost thou remember how the Black Jaguar slotted into the altar stone at the Black Pyramid? Here at K'awiil, there was a throne that worked in the same way. When the Yellow Jaguar and the throne made contact, a portal was opened to Xibalba. . . ."

Max considered his words. "You mean that if the Yellow Jaguar and the throne are still inside, we could take the stone to Xibalba from here?"

Lord 6-Dog nodded. "Thou couldst sup with the Death Lords this very night!"

Max gulped. "I have to find Lola first."

"There is no time for that, young lord. If we leave this place, who knows when the door will open again?"

"But Lola's supposed to come to Xibalba with me. . . . We're a team . . . like the Hero Twins. . . ."

"*I* will be with thee."

Max's stomach was churning like a washing machine. "But Chan Kan said—"

"There is no time for doubts, young lord. Come, we must enter the castle." Lord 6-Dog began to climb the ceiba tree. "I see a way in."

"Up there? You're kidding me."

"It is the way."

With a great deal of effort and pain, holding on to the thick vines that circled the trunk, Max hauled himself up to the great crook of the tree where Lord 6-Dog was waiting for him.

"Stop . . . ," wheezed Max. "I . . . have . . . to . . . get . . . my . . . breath."

"Look," said Lord 6-Dog, pointing at a broken window halfway up the castle walls. "We can enter through there. Follow me along the branches."

"I can't do it," said Max. He clutched the tree trunk, paralyzed by fear and vertigo. "We're too high. The branches won't bear my weight. . . ."

"Dost thou call this high?" scoffed Lord 6-Dog. "Imagine if thou wert a Maya king, standing on the uppermost platform of a majestic pyramid, top-heavy from the weight of thy enormous headdress, looking down at thy people like ants in the plaza below."

Max shuddered at the thought. He knew from firsthand experience how steep some of those pyramids were.

"But I'm *not* a Maya king, am I?" he said. "And I'm not a monkey, either!"

"Trust me," said Lord 6-Dog. "I will not let thee fall."

In the end, it was the thought of impressing Lola with his athleticism that drove Max on. By inching along and not looking down, he eventually reached the broken window.

"Well done, young lord."

"So we're just going to have a quick look and report back to the others, right?"

"Watch thyself on the broken glass," replied Lord 6-Dog, disappearing through the window.

Reluctantly, Max followed him.

He found himself in a once-grand room, now carpeted with dead leaves and furnished with rotting antiques, everything spackled with a white crust of bird droppings. A mouse popped out from the stuffing of a velvet cushion and scurried out of sight.

"Out here," called Lord 6-Dog from the doorway.

He was in an open hallway, like a minstrels' gallery. Max leaned over the balustrade and saw a similar gallery running around every floor below them. It seemed that the castle was built around a courtyard, but all the windows looking onto the central space had been bricked up and plastered over.

"The Yellow Pyramid must be on the other side of that wall," said Max. "Let's go find the others and come back later with flashlights."

He turned to Lord 6-Dog, but Lord 6-Dog was gone.

"Make haste, young lord!" echoed his voice from the great stone well of a spiral staircase.

"Come back!" yelled Max, but he knew he had to follow.

The long hall at the bottom of the staircase was narrow and impersonal, like a corridor in a big hotel—but in place of vending machines, laundry carts, and abstract art, it was lined with rusting suits of armor, moth-eaten tapestries, oil paintings in gilded frames, and tattered, ancient battle flags. There were doors at intervals along the outer wall, but none on the courtyard side.

The light was fading fast. A movement above his head made Max jump, and he looked up to see a flurry of bats waking from their roost in the rafters.

Lord 6-Dog nodded approvingly. "Bats are the creature of this day, Ak'bal. It is a good omen, young lord."

"I'll take your word for it." As Max was squinting up with distaste at the flying mice, he felt a dash of something land in his hair. "Aaargh!" he screamed. "It pooped! I've got bat poop in my hair!"

"I believe the correct term is *guano*," said Lord-Dog.

"Can we go?" asked Max. "We've seen enough. We need to come back with Lola and Lady Coco."

When Lord 6-Dog turned to answer him, his brown monkey eyes were glittering. "No, young lord, the time is now. Canst thou not feel it?"

Max analyzed his feelings. All he felt was fear and a deep sense of misgiving.

There was a faint sound. Max froze.

"What was that?" he whispered to Lord 6-Dog.

All was silent.

They began walking again and, no matter how lightly he trod, Max's footsteps echoed on the stone floor.

On and on the corridor stretched.

Another sound, louder this time.

They stopped in their tracks and listened.

It was the unmistakable sound of marching footsteps, like a distant army on the move. Max looked back, but could see no one behind them.

The marching ceased abruptly, and all was silent again.

Now what?

Were they watching?

Waiting?

Taking aim?

"Over here, young lord," called Lord 6-Dog from farther down the corridor. "I have found the door!"

Max ran over to him. He was standing in front of a tall black slab, set flush into the wall.

"I recognize this of old," said Lord 6-Dog. "It is the Door of Truth from the Temple of Blood at K'awiil."

In the dim light, Max made out the profile of a seated figure carved into the stone. It had sinister reptile eyes and a little anteater snout, topped by a tall, highly polished forehead, surrounded by flames of stone.

"Who's that?" asked Max.

"It is K'awiil, god of kingship and lineage."

"What's wrong with his foot?"

"It is not a foot, it is the head of a snake."

"Gross."

As Max studied the carving, he saw that this curious character had one ordinary leg and, in place of the other leg, a snake with its head resting on the ground where the foot should be.

"So how does he walk?"

"He spins like a tornado."

The marching footsteps began again, much louder now.

To Max's horror, a sea of bobbing torches rounded the far end of the corridor. Rank upon rank of steel helmets glinted in the torchlight.

"They're coming; we have to hide," whispered Max as he pulled Lord 6-Dog into an open doorway across the hall. They flattened themselves into the shadows and held their breath as the marching footsteps came nearer and nearer.

Max glanced around the room. It was a great hall with

soaring arches and a vaulted ceiling. The walls were decorated with yet more weaponry and suits of armor. The air was thick with dust.

Don't sneeze, don't sneeze, he told himself.

The footsteps drew level with the doorway.

Max sneezed.

The footsteps stopped dead.

There were a few moments of agonizing silence.

Then a voice cut through his bones like an icy wind.

"Show yourselves," it said. "Or do you hide like cowards?"

Max stayed perfectly still, not daring to breathe, but Lord 6-Dog, indignant at this insult, puffed out his chest in readiness to step out. Horrified, Max clamped a hand over the monkey's mouth and pulled him back, trying to restrain him. They scuffled in the shadows.

"I see you need persuasion," said the voice.

The castle filled with light as the moldering wall torches blazed into life. There was a clanking of metal as the suits of armor around the room stood robotically to attention. Max saw now that there were no faces beneath the helmets, nor bodies beneath the armor. The suits were empty.

Moving as one, the invisible knights drew their swords from their scabbards with a deafening metallic rasp that resounded through the castle.

"There is no blade sharper than Toledo steel," said the voice.

The ghostly army was advancing, their weapons pointing menacingly at the two interlopers.

Lord 6-Dog nipped Max's fingers.

"Ow!" he yelled, letting go of the monkey.

In one bound, Lord 6-Dog had pulled a dagger off the

wall and was out in the corridor, swaggering like a prizefighter and bellowing, "Who dares to call the mighty 6-Dog a coward? Show thyself! I cannot duel with empty air!"

Max squeezed his throbbing fingers in his armpit and assessed the enemy.

In front of them, behind them, stretching into the distance, were more massed suits of armor. A chilling array of pikes, lances, halberds, and rapiers were brandished in Lord 6-Dog's direction.

"Stand down, Your Majesty!" Max begged him. "You can't fight all of them."

"Watch me," thundered Lord 6-Dog.

He leapt onto the nearest armored shoulder and knocked off its helmet. The headless soldier thrashed around blindly. "Where is thy battle chief?" he demanded of it. "Who was it that spoke?"

"It was I," said the voice, and the army parted to allow a short, stocky figure, a soldier, evidently the captain of the guard, to step into view. The torchlight glinted off his conquistador helmet, leaving his face in shadow.

"Have at thee, varlet!" challenged Lord 6-Dog, thrusting at the newcomer with his blade. The disembodied knights instantly leapt forward to protect their leader with a barrier of swords, but the captain himself seemed only mildly surprised to be threatened by a talking monkey.

"Did you say your name is Lord 6-Dog?" he asked.

"Thou wilt not forget it when I carve it into thy heart!"

Oblivious to Lord 6-Dog's thrusts and parries, the captain stroked his chin thoughtfully. "You are Ahaw Wak Ok of the Monkey River, son of Lord Punak Ha and Lady Kan Kakaw?"

"What of it?"

"At ease, men," commanded the captain. "Return to sentry duty."

With a disappointed air, the suits of armor put down their weapons and clanked back to decorative positions in corridors and alcoves.

The soldier fell to his knees and prostrated himself at Lord 6-Dog's feet. "Thirteen blessings, mighty lord," he cried. "I am your unworthy descendant, Punak Mo."

Lord 6-Dog stared down at the captain in amazement for several seconds before his little body visibly relaxed. He laid his dagger on the floor and made a kingly flourish with his monkey hand.

"Thirteen blessings to thee, good cousin," he replied. "This is truly a strange meeting."

Lord 6-Dog gestured for the captain to rise, and he did so, shaking his head in wonder. Man and monkey regarded each other from head to toe, taking in the eccentricities of each other's appearance. Now Max could see that although the captain wore the helmet and breastplate of a Spanish conquistador, his face was distinctly Maya.

"Forgive me for asking, cousin," said Lord 6-Dog, "but why dost thou sport the armor of the oppressor?"

"My own clothes have long since worn out, Your Majesty, so I found new ones in the castle." He smoothed the yellow plume in his helmet, then polished his breastplate with his sleeve. "It pains me to admit it, but this Toledo steel serves me better than the padded cotton soaked in brine that our foot soldiers used to wear." He laughed. "But you, too, have an interesting disguise, Lord 6-Dog. I had heard rumors that my most revered ancestor had returned to Middleworld in the body of a howler, but I did not believe it until this day."

Lord 6-Dog nodded. "I have unfinished business in Middleworld, cousin. But before I tell thee more, let me present to thee my brother-in-arms." He looked around for Max and, seeing him cowering against a wall, beckoned him forward. "Come, young lord, come and meet my esteemed descendant."

As Max walked unsurely forward, before Lord 6-Dog had even introduced him, the captain dropped to the floor again, this time at Max's feet.

"Thirteen blessings, young lord," he said. "I am sorry I did not recognize you sooner. Punak Mo is honored to be at your service once again."

Baffled, Max turned to Lord 6-Dog for an explanation, but the monkey-king just nodded encouragingly. "Say, 'The honor is mine,'" he whispered.

"The honor is mine, Punak Mo," said Max obediently.

The captain got to his feet, all the while gazing at Max with the sort of dewy-eyed pride that mothers bestow on babies in diaper commercials. "Please," he said, "call me Captain Mo, like in the old days."

"The old days . . . ?"

Captain Mo looked hurt. "Don't you remember, young lord?"

"Remember what?" asked Max. "I think you've got me confused with someone else."

"What the young lord means to say," interjected Lord 6-Dog, "is that time has changed him. He may look still like a foolish adolescent, but he is not the callow youth that he once was."

Captain Mo nodded sadly. "All of us who saw those days

were old before our time. But whatever sorcery keeps him young, I am glad to see him back."

Max looked from Captain Mo to Lord 6-Dog and back again. "Would someone please tell me what's going on?"

"You are asking for my report?" asked Captain Mo eagerly.

"Uh, okay," said Max.

Captain Mo stood to attention. "As you know, young lord, I am the last high priest of K'awiil. It is my sacred duty to guard the Temple of Blood. When the invaders dismantled it and brought it here, I supervised every brick of its rebuilding, and I have guarded it ever since. Though many have challenged my dominion, none have succeeded in evicting me. I have faithfully patrolled these walls since the last *bak'tun*."

Max stared at him blankly.

"We thank thee for thy vigilance, Punak Mo," said Lord 6-Dog. He nudged Max with his hairy elbow.

"Thank you, Captain Mo," said Max.

The captain was smiling as he bowed his head humbly.

"So tell me," said Lord 6-Dog, "does the door operate as of old?"

"It does indeed. Do you remember the protocols, Your Majesty?"

"As if it were yesterday . . ."

"What protocols?" asked Max.

"You never could remember them," replied Captain Mo, with a chuckle. "Don't worry, I will help you—as always."

Max shook his head. He'd had enough. He was getting increasingly worried about Lola. What if she'd missed Lady Coco and gone back to the square? He should have waited for her. Why were they wasting time with this weirdo and his

149

magic tricks? He needed to get back and find Lola.

"Look," he said, "I don't know who you think I am, but I need to go. I have to meet someone. It's urgent. I think she's waiting for me. . . ."

"Indeed," said Captain Mo, with a wink. "She has waited long enough."

"Surely she will wait just a little longer?" ventured Lord 6-Dog.

"No," said Max. "We need to go *now*."

"Ah, the impatience of young love," sighed Captain Mo.

"She's not . . . We're not . . ."

Captain Mo smiled. "You don't have to explain to *me*, remember? I was your trusted accomplice. But you are right. We are wasting time. Let us begin."

Captain Mo handed a flaming torch to Lord 6-Dog. "It's dark out there," he said. Then, having taken off his helmet and breastplate to reveal a simple white robe, he began to sway and dance in front of the door, all the while chanting in Mayan.

Max put his head in his hands. It was like being trapped in a never-ending tourist show, and a bad one at that. "Quick," he whispered to Lord 6-Dog, "while he's not looking. Let's make a run for it."

There was a noise like the creaking of old bones.

Max peered through his fingers.

This was no tourist show.

The figure carved into the door was coming to life. Its outline was sparking and crackling with electricity. Its limbs were quivering. Its reptile eyes blinked.

Lord 6-Dog stepped forward. "Greetings to thee, Lord K'awiil, god of lineage and kingship."

The figure carved into the door was coming to life.

The creature scrutinized the howler monkey with focused intensity. Yellow flames emerged from his snout, giving him a fiery mustache. Gray smoke puffed out of his tiny ears, and thick twists of smoke grew from his head, forming serpentine curls that writhed around him.

"I am the firstborn son of Lord Punak Ha and his noble wife, Lady Kan Kakaw," continued Lord 6-Dog. "By the blood of my royal forefathers, I ask thee to grant me admittance to the temple."

The snake that was K'awiil's left leg stirred. It opened its hooded eyes. A tongue of flame darted out of its mouth. Slowly the head of the snake came out of the door, still at ground level, its body stretching behind it.

Max watched in horror as the snake wrapped itself several times around the howler monkey's furry body.

"Lord 6-Dog!" yelled Max.

"I had forgotten how much you hate snakes, young lord," whispered Captain Mo. "But don't worry. It will not hurt him."

The snake lifted Lord 6-Dog in its coils until he was level with Lord K'awiil's forehead. Now Max saw that the polished surface was a mirror, an obsidian mirror. The reflection it gave off was dull and cloudy, as if behind smoked glass, but what it showed was unmistakably the black, leathery face of a howler monkey. Then, as Max watched, the image of the monkey morphed into a handsome Maya warrior in a jaguar-pelt cloak and feathered headdress.

Gently, the snake set Lord 6-Dog down. The coils and head retracted into the door. There was a grinding of stone and a rush of night air as the slab swiveled to allow Lord 6-Dog through.

Max went to follow, but the nearest suits of armor sprang forward and blocked his way with a forest of gleaming Toledo blades.

"Have you forgotten?" asked Captain Mo. "Only the high priest and the king may pass that way."

"But I'm with Lord 6-Dog," insisted Max. "Let me through!"

Captain Mo smiled at him fondly. "You never did have much patience with our rituals."

"Can we get one thing straight?" said Max. "You don't know me."

"You're right," sighed Captain Mo. "None of us truly knows another. That's why, for all but high priests and kings, there is only one way to pass through the Door of Truth. The mighty K'awiil must see your heart."

Max swallowed nervously as Captain Mo picked up Lord 6-Dog's discarded dagger and tested its blade with his thumb. "There can be no exceptions," he was saying. "Even for you."

Max turned to run but found himself surrounded by the phantom knights.

"Here," said Captain Mo, passing him the dagger. "You will need this. It is not as sharp as obsidian, but I pray it will get the job done."

"You expect me to cut out my own heart?" whispered Max, in horror. This guy was even more twisted than he'd thought.

Captain Mo stared at him for a moment, then he laughed. "Cut out your own heart, indeed; you always were a joker! No, the blade is for hacking through the roses out there. You'll be surprised at how overgrown it is. I leave it like that for camouflage. If I had known you were coming, I would have trimmed it back."

Feeling foolish, Max tucked the dagger into his belt. "So how do I get through the door?"

"As I told you, K'awiil, the god of lineage, needs to see your heart."

"You mean, what's *in* my heart? What kind of person I am?"

"Exactly. Just tell the truth, and you will pass the test."

"But what if I was an imposter?"

"You are worried about security? Have no fear, the Lord K'awiil cannot be fooled. I pity any liars who present themselves at the Door of Truth. Shall we begin?"

Without waiting for an answer, Captain Mo launched into his swaying, dancing, chanting routine.

Once again the carving of K'awiil came to life, and once again the snake slithered forward, flicking its tongue of flames. With astonishing speed, it wrapped itself around Max's waist and raised its head until it was looking him in the eyes. It did not look impressed.

Sweat ran down Max's face as the snake's hot breath scorched his skin and waves of pungent smoke from its nostrils burned his throat and stung his eyes.

"Say after me," whispered Captain Mo. "Greetings to thee, Lord K'awiil, god of lineage. May my heart be tested by the Serpent of Truth."

Max repeated the words, and the snake licked the air as if to taste them.

"Captain Mo!" blurted Max. "I'm not who you think I am!"

"That," said the captain, "is for the Serpent of Truth to decide."

The snake opened its mouth, wide, wider, impossibly wide, until Max could see nothing but the great black hole of its gullet, ringed by row upon row of needle-sharp teeth.

"Put your left hand in the serpent's maw," Captain Mo instructed him.

"But what happens to the liars . . . ?"

With a jerk of his head, Captain Mo indicated a line of oil paintings on the wall behind him. They were all of Spanish noblemen with pointy beards and ruffled collars. Max saw, with a shock, that each one had a bloody, shriveled stump where his left hand used to be.

Max's shaking knees betrayed his terror.

"Still so afraid of snakes," clucked Captain Mo fondly. "Allow me, young lord," and he thrust Max's hand into the snake's open mouth.

"Agggggghhhhhhh," screamed Max as his left arm was sucked almost out of its socket. The pain was intense. He tried to pull back, but that made it worse. He could feel the rows of teeth penetrating his skin and the snake tongue tasting his blood. He closed his eyes, and his brain swirled in raging colors of yellow, gold, and orange.

The first questions appeared in his mind.

Friend or foe?

Toucan or tapir?

What is your treasure?

Red or black?

How many steps?

Sun or moon?

What is loyalty?

Butterfly or moth?

When is never?

Zenith or nadir?

What is all?

More and more questions crowded into his brain, like impatient commuters in a subway station. Then they were off, still pushing and shoving and jostling one another as they hurtled at top speed into his bloodstream and careened around his body, interrogating the very essence of his being. His veins throbbed and his head was pounding. No one could answer so many questions. Already his hand seemed to be paralyzed. He could feel a band tightening above his wrist as if the tourniquet were being applied before the amputation began.

No one could answer so many questions. . . .

He took a deep breath. Trying to ignore the relentless inquisition, he concentrated on convincing this cosmic lie detector that his motives were true. He thought about Lord 6-Dog and how they had worked together to defeat Tzelek on the Black Pyramid. He thought about meeting the god Itzamna in the Green Pyramid and communing with Chahk, the rain god, in the Red Pyramid. He thought about Lola's adopted family in the village of Utsal: Chan Kan the shaman, Eusebio the boatman, and Och, the little boy whose hero worship he had won and lost. Most of all, he thought about Lola. He saw her open face, her smiling brown eyes, her glossy hair. . . .

The pain began to ease.

He could move his fingers again.

He opened his eyes.

He was no longer in the corridor with Captain Mo. He was in a sinuous, pulsating, pink, fleshy tunnel that was possibly, almost certainly—but how could it be?—the snake's gullet. He was being propelled through the darkness, as if on a moving walkway at the airport but with convulsing muscle under his feet in place of hard rubber matting.

A door opened.

There was an intense smell of roses.

Max was pitched forward.

He fell.

Onto grass.

In front of two hairy feet.

He looked up.

"What kept thee?" asked Lord 6-Dog.

Chapter Ten

MISTAKEN IDENTITY

Hardly daring to look, Max lifted his left arm. It still had a hand on the end of it. The Serpent of Truth had let him pass unharmed, even though Captain Mo had clearly mistaken him for someone else.

"You could have told me," he said.

"Told thee what?" asked Lord 6-Dog.

"Oh, let me think. Maybe that I was going to be swallowed by a giant snake?"

Lord 6-Dog shrugged. "Thou didst pass the test. That is all that matters."

"But who did that guy think I was?"

"May we talk about this later, young lord? We have a mission to fulfill."

"I just think you should have warned me, that's all."

"I warn thee now, be always on thy guard."

"Why?" asked Max suspiciously. "What's next?"

"We must go up."

Lord 6-Dog lifted the flaming torch as high as he could, and Max saw that they were in a courtyard, at the foot of an ancient Maya pyramid. Its steps were completely overgrown with thickets of yellow roses.

"This is really it?" marveled Max. "I can't believe they could transport the entire Yellow Pyramid from San Xavier."

Lord 6-Dog looked sideways at him. "Of all the astonishing sights thou hast seen of late, it is the transportation of this pyramid—a mere exercise in engineering and shipping logistics—that strains thy credulity?"

"I just assumed it was a replica, that's all. I can't wait to bring Lola here."

"First we have a job to do. We must find the Yellow Jaguar and use the throne of K'awiil to open the portal to Xibalba."

"Without Lola? But we're a team."

"The jaguar hunts alone."

"But Chan Kan told me—"

"If Chan Kan were here," said Lord 6-Dog, "he would tell thee to accept thy destiny. Thou art in this place at this time for a reason. All of Middleworld is waiting for thee to climb these stairs."

Still Max hesitated.

"Just trust me," said Lord 6-Dog, losing patience. "I have a good feeling about this."

Max looked horrified. "That's what Hermanjilio said that night at Itzamna, just before he turned you and Lady Coco into howler monkeys, and Tzelek slipped through the gateway and hid out in Hermanjilio, who ended up nearly sacrificing Lola on the Black Pyramid."

"Exactly," said Lord 6-Dog, as if Max had proved his point.

"But everything went wrong that night—"

"Did it, young lord?"

Now that Max thought about it, he wasn't sure. On the one hand, he was embroiled in some hideous plan for world domination hatched by the ancient Maya Lords of Death. On the other hand, he couldn't remember life before he met Lola. He was a different person now. He had a mission.

"It's an interesting question," he mused. "If the world's going to end anyway, at least I'm having an adventure, right? But I wish Lola was here. No offense, Lord 6-Dog. I mean, I'm glad you're here, too. . . ."

He was talking to himself. Lord 6-Dog, having long since lost interest in the conversation, was now standing at the foot of the pyramid, surveying the steps from every angle. "We must clear a way to the top. These thorns are the very devil."

In the flickering torchlight, Max saw the inch-long spines that made the beautiful yellow roses as menacing as barbed wire.

"Captain Mo gave me a knife," he said.

"Then thou shouldst slash and I will burn."

Lord 6-Dog put the torch to some foliage. The leaves sizzled and charred and generated a great deal of smoke, but they refused to catch fire. The smell of roses was replaced by acrid fumes. "Not good," he observed. "Now it is thy turn."

Max made a desultory slash at a swath of roses and winced in pain. "It's impossible. These thorns—I'll get ripped to pieces."

As he inspected his wounds, a clutch of flower heads brushed their velvety petals against his bleeding hand as if to soothe it and then, to his astonishment, the vegetation curled around the dagger handle and pulled it away from him.

"Hey!" he protested. "I need that; come back with that!" But already the knife was lost in the tangled roses, which writhed like a bed of eels.

Yet there seemed to be a purpose in the collective slithering.

Feeling like the prince in *Sleeping Beauty*, Max watched openmouthed as the thorny briars untwined and peeled aside for him. Soon there was a pathway clear to the top.

"It seems thou art expected," said Lord 6-Dog. "*Ko'ox!*"

"*Ko'ox*," responded Max weakly as his monkey companion bounded up the steps, each one thinner and crumblier than the last. Eventually, wheezing and panting, Max hauled himself to the top.

"So here we are," he said. He looked around him. On top of the pyramid was a ceremonial chamber, so completely covered in yellow climbing roses that it looked like a golden dome. "Er, where are we, exactly?"

"We are outside the Temple of Blood," announced Lord 6-Dog. His voice trembled with emotion. "It was here that the kings and queens of the Monkey River were crowned."

"Do you think the Yellow Jaguar is inside?"

"That is my hope, young lord."

"I can't even see the door through all the roses."

But even as he spoke, the tangled stems that clambered over the temple and blocked the doorway sorted themselves into straight lines like a bead curtain and parted neatly in the middle.

"It's too easy," mumbled Max as he peered into the gloom. "It must be a trap."

"Or a gesture of welcome," suggested Lord 6-Dog. "Let us enter."

"Wait! Is it true that the Yellow Jaguar cannot be taken, only given?"

"It is."

"Then who will give it to me? Is someone in there?"

Lord 6-Dog shook his head despairingly. "After all that has been said and done, thou still dost not know who awaits thee?"

"Tell me, who is it?"

"Enter and meet thy destiny."

At first, Max was blinded by the reflection of Lord 6-Dog's flaming torch glaring back at them from every direction. The chamber's stone floor and walls had been polished until they shone like dark mirrors. But as his eyes grew accustomed to the light, he made out a shape in the middle of the room.

Lord 6-Dog saw it, too, and held up his torch to illuminate it.

It was a large, elaborately carved wooden armchair.

Slumped inside it, under a veil of cobwebs, was a tiny old woman in a long, tattered black dress.

Her silver hair fell in two tight braids to the floor. Her high, sloped forehead was as wrinkled as balled-up tissue paper, and the sallow skin on her delicately arched nose was so thin, Max could almost see the cartilage beneath it.

Her eyes were closed.

"It's not her," said Max.

"Who didst thou expect?" asked Lord 6-Dog.

"Inez la Loca, the girl in the yellow dress who looked like Lola. But she was young. Could this be her grandmother?"

Lord 6-Dog jumped onto an arm of the old lady's chair.

"Be careful, you'll wake her!" cautioned Max.

"I think not," said Lord 6-Dog. "This woman has long since passed over to the world beyond."

"You mean . . . she's dead?"

Lord 6-Dog nodded.

Max wasn't sure whether to be relieved that the woman presented no danger or disappointed that she would not be handing over the Yellow Jaguar anytime soon.

"It could be another trick," he mused, backing away. "Maybe she'll leap up and karate-chop us!"

"I know not this karate," said Lord 6-Dog. "But I know a corpse when I see one." He lightly brushed away the cobwebs on the woman's face.

"Come away," said Max.

"Art thou not curious?"

"No," said Max. "If the Yellow Jaguar isn't here, I want to go."

"Ah, but it *is* here. Come look at this. . . ."

It was Max's first dead body. Against his better judgment, he approached the corpse. As he leaned over her to see what Lord 6-Dog was pointing at, he was shocked to notice the depth of sadness engrained on her wizened face.

"What are you looking at?" he asked Lord 6-Dog.

At the sound of his voice, the old woman's sunken eyelids flickered open.

After centuries of silence, her voice was dry and crackly.

"I am looking at *you*, my love," she said.

Lord 6-Dog jumped off the chair arm in surprise.

"I knew it!" said Max. "Another trick!" But it was too late. The old woman's ice-cold, withered fingers closed tightly over his. He tried to pull away, but found he could not move.

"*Do* something," he called to Lord 6-Dog. "She's hurting me!"

"Rodrigo, I'm so sorry," croaked the old woman, releasing Max's hands. "Your Inez did not mean to hurt you."

"You're not Inez," said Max accusingly. "Inez is young."

She flinched.

I have been waiting for you for so long, Rodrigo . . . I am sorry if time has dealt harshly with me."

"My dear lady," Lord 6-Dog assured her hastily, "thy beauty still shines from within."

She turned her rheumy eyes on him.

"Welcome, Lord 6-Dog, revered king of the Monkey River. On behalf of the immortal K'awiil, god of lineage, I am honored to welcome you back to the Temple of Blood."

"The honor is mine, Princess Inez," said Lord 6-Dog, bowing low. "But may I ask how thou didst recognize me in this lowly disguise?"

"If there is one thing I have learned, Lord 6-Dog," she replied, her face almost cracking as it formed itself slowly into a smile, "it is not to judge by appearances. With his strange red hair and his pink skin that burned in the jungle sun, my Rodrigo was not the most handsome of men . . . but his was the truest heart."

Max felt insulted on behalf of the long-dead Rodrigo. "If you thought he was so ugly, why did you marry him?" he asked.

"Oh, Rodrigo, I do believe you are flirting with me!" She gave a girlish giggle. "You know I have loved you from the day we first met! I am so happy to see you again. Oh, this is such good news."

"Good news, indeed, dear lady," said Lord 6-Dog. "May I

have a private word with . . . er . . . with your beloved?"

She nodded her consent, her movements slow and frail. Lord 6-Dog pulled Max to one side.

"Did you see her throat, young lord?"

"What about it?"

"She is wearing the Yellow Jaguar."

"What? How?"

"As a necklet."

Max snuck a glance at the old woman's sinewy neck and saw that it was indeed encircled by dusty yellow beads.

"Is that allowed?" he whispered. "A Jaguar Stone made into jewelry?"

"Thou must persuade her to relinquish it."

"Why would she give me her bling?"

"She thinks thou art Rodrigo de Pizarro. Play along!"

"I'm not even Spanish."

"Wert thy ancestors not Pizarros?"

"Yes, but—"

"Hast a Landa not sworn to kill thee?"

"Yes, but—"

"Play along! But be careful. Remember, thou canst not tell a lie. . . ."

Max turned back to the mad old woman.

"Dear Rodrigo," she crooned. "Now, at last, our story will have a happy ending."

"Will you tell me our story again?" he asked her.

She patted the arm of her chair for him to sit next to her.

"I have relived it a thousand, thousand times," she said.

She clapped her hands almost noiselessly.

Lord 6-Dog's torch sputtered and went out.

For a few seconds they were plunged into total blackness,

165

and Max's only sensation was of her skeletal fingers entwining with his. Just when he thought he might scream, a pale yellow glow suffused the room.

"Look, my love," she said.

She was staring straight ahead.

Max followed her eyes and saw shadows moving in the mirrored walls. As she talked, the shadows became clearer, until the story was taking place in front of him, as if it were being acted out behind a thin curtain. . . .

A pretty young Maya girl was laughing with her mother as she learned to knead tortillas by an open fire and weave on a backstrap loom.

"Before I met you," Inez began, "I had no thoughts of love. My father ruled the city of K'awiil, and my destiny was to marry a stranger, a prince from another city.

"But my destiny changed when the Spanish arrived.

"They came from the sunrise, in their floating houses. Their metal helmets shone in the sun. The old folk thought they were gods. The first time we saw a man on horseback, we thought it was all one beast. Where our warriors fought hand to hand, the invaders could kill a score of men with one shot from their fire sticks. For my city, it was over quickly.

"They called our land New Spain. We took Spanish names and wore Spanish clothes, and a Spanish husband was sought for me. Lorenzo de Landa was first in line. . . ."

An effete young dandy with a pointy black beard was seen admiring himself in a full-length mirror held by two terrified Maya boys.

"Our wedding was to take place here in the Temple of Blood"—she gestured around her—"conducted by Lorenzo's brother, Friar Diego de Landa."

A hooded figure in a monk's robe greeted the dandy and they toasted each other with goblets of wine, served by another Maya boy. The boy spilled a drop of wine, and Rodrigo hit him so hard that he fell senseless to the floor.

Max shivered as Inez resumed her tale.

"I thought my fate was sealed . . . but then I saw *you*, Rodrigo. It was love at first sight for both of us."

She smiled dreamily at the reflections in the mirror.

There she was, the young Inez, the image of Lola, holding hands with Don Rodrigo, the love of her life. He was dressed in the leather doublet and woolen hose of a conquistador, and—Max did a double take—and under his metal helmet was unmistakably Max's face. . . .

"I don't understand . . . ," began Max.

"What don't you understand, my love?" asked Princess Inez. "Don't you remember how my father blessed our union and helped us escape to Spain? How he had the Yellow Jaguar made into a necklet as my dowry, and sent Captain Mo to watch over us in our new life?"

Max steeled himself not to flinch as Inez leaned over to stroke his face with her ancient fingers. "We were so happy in our castle in Spain . . . until the night Lorenzo de Landa handed me your bloodstained shirt."

The girl in the mirror screamed and fell weeping to the floor.

"He said it was a fair fight," whispered the old lady, "but I saw from your shirt that you'd been stabbed in the back. Lorenzo proposed that very night. I knew it would not be long before I, too, was sacrificed on the altar of his greed. But then his plan backfired. . . ."

"Go on . . . ," said Max, now genuinely interested.

"I was heir to the Jaguar Throne and the power of the Yellow Jaguar. But to share my fortune, Lorenzo would need to marry me in the Temple of Blood as he had originally planned. So he had the entire Yellow Pyramid of K'awiil shipped over to be rebuilt in Polvoredo. And that, my love, was his downfall."

The girl in the mirror stood at a castle window in her widow's weeds and watched the rainforest growing in the castle grounds.

"As the pyramid grew, so did my power. I used it to turn the flowers yellow, and I used it to drive away the Landa family. They called me a witch, but all they could do was withdraw and wait for me to die. They are still waiting! And now you have returned to me, Rodrigo, as I always knew you would."

The old lady clapped weakly. The pictures in the mirror began to mist over, and the last image Max saw was of the young princess turned toward him, her long hair wild and her face stained with tears, her sad eyes locked on his.

She looked so much like Lola, it gave him goose bumps.

"So where is the throne, dear lady?" asked Lord 6-Dog. "Surely it was shipped with the pyramid? For without it, the Yellow Jaguar has no power."

The old lady focused as if snapping out of a dream. "When Lorenzo de Landa understood that I would never marry him, he removed the throne to his palace in Galicia."

"Why didn't he take the Yellow Jaguar, too?" asked Max.

Then his mouth gaped open as the answer to his own question dawned on him. Suddenly he understood why the ancient Maya Lords of Death had come to find fourteen-year-old Max Murphy of Boston, Massachusetts. It was because he looked like his ancestor, the long-dead Rodrigo de Pizarro.

The Yellow Jaguar could not be taken. And, in all the world, Rodrigo was the only person who could persuade the princess to give it up.

But Max couldn't go through with it.

He took a deep breath.

"Princess Inez?"

"Yes?"

"I am not Rodrigo." He looked into her dark eyes and saw his own face reflected there, dull and hazy, like an image in an obsidian mirror. "I look like him, but I am not Rodrigo."

The old lady held his gaze for what seemed like an eternity.

Max turned to Lord 6-Dog. "I'm done. The Death Lords can find someone else to do their dirty work. Let's go."

"Wait," said Princess Inez. "I, too, am done." She reached behind her scrawny neck, untied the necklet and held it out to Max. "Take it," she said. "I give it to you freely."

"But why? I told you, I am not Rodrigo."

"You are the one I have been waiting for. Why else would K'awiil have given you free passage? Rodrigo decreed that the people of this town must never lie. Now I, too, must face the truth. My Rodrigo is dead, and I must join him. A new cycle has begun. The Yellow Jaguar is yours. Do what you have to do."

Max took the necklet.

As soon as it left the old lady's fingers, she let out a deep sigh, as if a huge weight had been lifted off her.

"Good-bye," she said. "Until we meet again."

Cracks appeared in the flagstones under his feet.

A shower of dust rained from the ceiling.

Stones fell from the temple walls.

The whole pyramid was shaking.

"We have to get out of here!" shouted Max, pulling at the old lady's arm.

She sat back in the wooden chair and closed her eyes.

Within seconds, her old body had breathed its last.

Max watched, horrified, as her wasted flesh dissolved and the fabric of her dress clung pitifully to her bones, until it, too, decayed and fell away. Soon she was nothing but a skeleton, and then a pile of glowing yellow dust.

A tear prickled Max's eyes.

"Come, young lord," said Lord 6-Dog. "The pyramid is falling down around us."

Out of the dust of Inez burst a cloud of yellow butterflies. They danced around Max's head and seemed to be shepherding him toward the doorway.

"Follow the butterflies," shouted Lord 6-Dog, as masonry crashed all around them. "It's the princess! She's leading us to safety!"

Chapter Eleven
DISASTER

Ow! No! No! No! Oh! Ah! Ow! Ow! Ow! No! Ah! Ow! No! No! No! Oh! Ah! Ow! Ow! Ow! No! Ow! No! No! No! Oh! Ah! Ow! Ow! Ow! No! Ow! No! No! No! Oh! Ow! No! Ow! No! No! No! Oh! Ah! Ow! Ow! Ow!"

Shouting in pain and terror, battered by falling stones and chunks of plaster, Max skidded and stumbled down the pyramid. He couldn't see in front of him with all the dust, and only the boom of the howler monkey, rising above the crashing of stone slabs, guided him to safety at the edge of the courtyard.

"Get down!" growled Lord 6-Dog. "Cover thy head!"

Reacting on autopilot, Max obeyed.

Lord 6-Dog crouched next to him. "Thou hast the necklet?" he asked.

"In here." Max patted his backpack.

"Good . . . Now brace thyself!"

"For what . . . ?"

Max's question died on his lips as the ground in front

of them opened up and—in eerie silence—the entire pyramid imploded, until all that was left was a rubble-filled crater.

Lord 6-Dog wiped the plaster dust from his fur. "She sleeps at last," he murmured.

Max stared into the crater. "I wish her story had a happy ending."

"She is with Rodrigo. She is happy."

"Do you think she knew that I was planning to give her necklet to the Lords of Death? She said, 'Do what you have to do.'"

"She trusted thee, young lord, as much for thy heart as for thy face."

"Odd, wasn't it," mused Max, "how *she* looked like Lola and *I* look like Rodrigo? What was that about?"

"Much as I would like to chitchat, young lord, time marches on, and we must march with it. Let us find Lady Lola and my mother, and plan our next move."

Through clouds of dust, they groped their way along the wall, looking for the Door of Truth to get back into the castle.

They quickly found it. Or, at least, they found a door-sized hole in the wall. The door itself was gone, completely vaporized, not a chip remaining of the huge stone slab.

Max and Lord 6-Dog ran back into the castle.

Everything looked the same—the suits of armor, the tapestries, the battle flags—but even in the darkness, Max could see that everything had changed. Gone was the sense of watching and waiting, the crackle of energy, the aura of menace. It was like the difference between a sleeping body and a corpse. Now it was just a museum, another dry and dusty old castle.

"Captain Mo, we're back!" shouted Max, but no one answered.

"He's gone," said Lord 6-Dog.

"But where?"

"I hope he sits under the shadiest tree in the highest heavens, for he has proved himself a great warrior in the service of his people."

"Do you think he knew I wasn't Rodrigo?"

"I think he knew thou wast the one who could release the princess. Besides, the Pizarro family are thine ancestors. Thou hast Rodrigo's blood in thy veins. In a sense, thou art Rodrigo."

Max thought about this for a moment.

"At ease, Captain Mo!" he called into the echoing, empty castle. "I will try to be worthy of your faith in me."

A night bird cried out in the guano-spattered rafters. A family of mice ran squeaking for cover as a picture fell off its nail in the wall and landed at his feet.

It was an old map of Spain.

He bent to pick it up and a moonbeam played on the glass, lighting up the northwest coast. *Galicia*, it flashed at him, *Galicia*.

Galicia. He'd heard that name before.

"Lord 6-Dog," he said calmly, "I know what we have to do." He drew himself up to his full height. "We're going to Galicia."

A yellow plume fluttered to the ground.

Max picked it up and put it in his pocket. "I won't let you down, Captain Mo," he whispered.

They left through the front door of the castle and followed the old carriage drive by moonlight to the front gate.

All around, the rainforest was dying. Tumbling yellow petals fell like autumn leaves.

"We did this," said Max sadly. "We broke the spell."

"Take heart," Lord 6-Dog told him. "Look at the sky."

High above them, over the Spanish plains, the stars were clustered in twinkling constellations.

"What am I looking at?" asked Max. And then he saw it: a shape made out of stars like a crocodile with a gaping jaw. "It's the Cosmic Crocodile!" he exclaimed. "I saw it with Lola and Hermanjilio in the Star Chamber at Itzamna! But I can't remember what it means. . . ."

"It represents the Maya heavens. It marks the path between worlds."

Max stared at the twinkling stars. The crocodile stared back at him. "But what's it doing *here?*"

"I would guess that it lights the way home for Princess Inez."

Max shivered. "*I* need to cross between worlds. Maybe it's lighting the way for *me?*"

Lord 6-Dog gestured toward the gatehouse. "Thy road lies that way, young lord."

Max peered through the grating.

As far as he could see, all was still.

He opened the gate and looked out into the street. It was deserted.

No Lola. No Lady Coco.

He'd half hoped to find them waiting out there.

"They must have gone back to the hotel," he said. "Let's go find them. Maybe get some hot chocolate. . . ."

Lord 6-Dog made a noise of disgust at this suggestion, but soon he and Max were running down the hill, glad to be out of the castle and following the faint sounds of music and merrymaking that drifted up from the square.

They passed a little fountain set into a street corner.

"I need water!" called Max. "My mouth is full of plaster dust."

"A good soldier heeds only his thirst for battle," Lord 6-Dog chided.

"I'll be quick."

He cupped his hands and took a drink. Then he held his head under the spout to wash away the dust.

"That's better," he called to Lord 6-Dog, shaking the water from his hair.

"Turn around slowly," came a voice behind him. "And put up your hands."

When Max saw who it was, his stomach sank to his sneakers.

"Good evening, Officer Gonzales," he said politely.

The police officer ignored him and jabbered urgently into his walkie-talkie. The only words Max could make out were his own name, plus *agua*, *sangre*, and *fuente*.

Eventually, Officer Gonzales turned his attention to him. "So you have washed away her blood?" he said.

Max stared at him blankly.

"Where is the girl?" demanded the officer.

"Lola? Didn't she come to the police station?"

"Do not play the innocent with me, *señor*. You are under arrest for her murder."

"What? You think I murdered Lola? That's crazy."

"We have a witness."

"Whoever they are, they're lying."

"No one lies in Polvoredo."

Max blinked in confusion. "But Lola . . . did you"—he gulped—"did you find her?"

"Not yet," replied the officer. He slammed Max face-forward into the wall and deftly handcuffed him.

A young couple, revelers from the square, walked past arm in arm.

"Help!" called Max, breaking away and running after them. "I'm a tourist! Help me!"

A door opened down the street, and the couple hurried inside without a backward glance.

"There is no one to help you," said Officer Gonzales.

With a cry like an angry dinosaur, Lord 6-Dog came hurtling out of the darkness. He landed on Max's shoulder, growling and baring his teeth.

Without blinking, the officer shot him.

Lord 6-Dog hit the ground with a dull thud and lay there motionless in a pool of blood.

"You've killed him!" shouted Max, falling to his knees.

The officer dragged him to his feet. "Walk!"

"You can't just leave him here!" cried Max.

With the tip of his toe, the officer nudged the howler monkey's body into the gutter. "The street cleaners will clear it away with the rest of the vermin."

"He's not vermin! He's a king, a warrior-king!"

"In Polvoredo, he is vermin. Now move!"

It was useless to argue.

"I'll come back for you," Max called softly to the lifeless body of his friend, as the officer pulled him away.

Lord 6-Dog was dead. Lola and Lady Coco were missing in action.

He was alone.

Still in shock, he allowed himself to be led to the police station, a low, modern building as bleak as his mood, all concrete blocks, fluorescent lights, and tiny frosted windows. It smelled of disinfectant.

At the front desk, a crowd of people milled around. The air was tense. A fight seemed to be brewing. There was a lot of finger-pointing and shouting and then suddenly everyone piled in—men, women, and children—all punching and kicking and screaming.

The officer hustled Max through the scrum and handed him over to a young policeman.

"There's been a mistake, I'm innocent," Max said to him.

The young policeman shrugged. He seemed more interested in the fracas at the desk and, after taking Max's fingerprints and confiscating his backpack, he escorted him into a side room, bare except for a table and two chairs, took off the handcuffs, and left, locking the door behind him.

After what felt like an age, the Officer Gonzales entered.

He was holding Max's passport.

"Massimo Francis Sylvanus Murphy," he said, "you are in big trouble. What is going on?"

"*You* tell me," said Max dully. "You're the murderer."

"If you are referring to that wild beast, it was a danger to the public."

"He's a *he*, not an it! And he wasn't a wild beast. He was Lola's friend, and you shot him in cold blood."

"It was self-defense. The brute was about to attack me. It was rabid."

"That's a lie," said Max.

The officer looked surprised. He flexed the muscles

around his mouth. For the first time in his life, he had told a lie. It felt strange. But good.

"It was not a lie," he said, telling another one.

Max made a little snorting noise to show his disgust.

"Tell me," said the officer, "why is a boy of"—he checked Max's passport—"fourteen years of age here on his own, in Polvoredo?"

"I wasn't on my own, was I? I came here with Lola."

"Do your parents know you are here?"

"Of course they do."

"Let us see if they can help us, shall we?"

Officer Gonzales flipped through the passport to the emergency contacts page. "*Bueno*, Frank and Carla Murphy, Boston, Massachusetts." He picked up the phone.

"No!" blurted Max, remembering how Lord Kuy had forbidden him to ask his parents for help—and how they'd suffered when he'd disobeyed.

"You don't want me to phone your parents? It seems that you have something to hide, Señor Murphy."

"I don't want to worry them. They'll think something's happened to me."

"Something *has* happened. You have been arrested for murder."

Officer Gonzales dialed the number.

"It is ringing," he said.

Don't pick up, don't pick up, don't pick up. . . .

Someone picked up.

"Señora Murphy? Señora Carla Murphy? . . . This is Polvoredo Police. . . . I am calling about your son, Massimo. . . . He needs your help to confirm—"

At the word *help*, everything changed.

"*Señora? Qué pasa?* I just want to ask you—" The officer held the phone away from his ear as Carla screamed in agony. Max could hear her shrieks from across the table. Another voice evidently came on the line. "Ah, Señor Frank Murphy, *bueno!* I have your son Massimo here, and he needs your help to—"

An anguished bellow echoed out of the phone, followed by sounds of vomiting.

The officer shook his head and put down the phone.

"It seems that you come from a disturbed family, Señor Murphy. But that is no excuse for murder. Now tell me, in your own words, how you did it."

"There's nothing to tell. I didn't do it."

"The witness says you did."

"What witness?"

There was a knock at the door.

"*Adelante!*" called the officer. "Come in!"

The young policeman entered and jabbered something in Spanish. Through the open door, Max could hear a pitched battle in full swing at the desk.

"What's going on?" he asked.

The officer shook his head in bafflement. "For the last five hundred years, the citizens of Polvoredo have told the truth. But now, tonight, an epidemic of lying has broken out." He stood up slowly. "It is as if a spell has been broken."

"But don't you see," insisted Max, "your witness is lying, too?"

"It is going to be a long night," sighed Officer Gonzales as he left the room.

The young policeman came back and took Max to a holding cell. It was empty apart from a low wooden shelf for a bed, and a bucket in the corner. Max threw himself onto the shelf and lay there, staring at the ceiling. He couldn't get the sight of Lord 6-Dog's lifeless body out of his mind.

How did things go so very wrong?

He didn't for one second believe that Lola was dead—but where was she?

And where was Lady Coco?

Max felt a flash of anger.

How could Lola be so irresponsible? She and Santino were probably looking dreamily into each other's eyes right now, while Max moldered in a jail cell, accused of her murder.

Some friend she turned out to be. They were supposed to be a team, and she'd abandoned him the first chance she got.

Well, he'd show her.

Alternating between sorrow for Lord 6-Dog, resentment at Lola, and pity for himself, Max fell asleep and dreamed about gliding with Nasty Smith-Jones through the Boston Public Garden in a swan boat pedaled by Vince Vermin.

He was woken next morning by the sound of jangling keys.

"*Tienes visita*," the young policeman called through the door. "You have a visitor."

"Lola?" Max jumped up in delight and relief, all plans of revenge forgotten.

The policeman fumbled with the keys, and Max waited impatiently for him to unlock the door. As it opened, a wave of noise rushed in from the rumpus still in progress at the front desk.

But it wasn't Lola who came through the door.

Chapter Twelve
ADIÓS, FOREVER

antino?" said Max. "What are you doing here? Where's Lola?"

The law student looked very different from the sharp-suited, clean-cut young man Max had met at the airport. Today he was unshaven, dressed in jeans and a sweatshirt, and he'd evidently forgotten his hair gel, for his bangs flopped down over his forehead.

"I will ask the questions!" shouted Santino. He seemed close to tears. "Were you jealous, is that it? You murdered her because she wanted to be with me?"

"What? No! Why do you think I murdered Lola?"

"Doña Carmela says so. She has made a eh-statement."

"But it's not true. Why would she do that?"

"Because you are a *pelirrojo*. You have the red hair."

"But why does she think Lola's been murdered?"

"When she did not turn up at the police station, Officer Gonzales sent men to the hotel. They told Doña Carmela that

Lola was missing, and she put two and two together."

"Wait—so *she's* the witness?"

"Yes."

"But she's just making it up because she hates me."

"Are you accusing the second cousin of the uncle of the sister-in-law of my brother's wife of lying? No one lies in Polvoredo."

"They do now. What do you think that racket outside is about?"

Santino opened the door slightly and listened to the insults flying at the front desk.

"They're accusing each other of lying, aren't they?" said Max. "Officer Gonzales said it's like an epidemic."

Santino shut the door. "The fact remains that the *señorita* is missing."

"That doesn't mean I murdered her."

"What is your alibi?"

"My alibi?"

"What were you doing at the time she went missing?"

"I was . . ." Max hesitated. He could hardly say that he was breaking into the castle of Polvoredo, being attacked by a phantom army, and talking to the ghost of a Maya princess. "I was sightseeing."

"Sightseeing? In Polvoredo? Now I know you are lying."

Max sat down on his hard little bed and put his head in his hands. "I don't know what's true myself anymore. Just get me out of here, Santino, so I can help you look for her."

"All I want is to find her," sighed Santino, sitting down next to him. "I have never felt like this before. I must know if she feels the same way, but now it is too late. . . ."

"It's not too late," Max pointed out. "I didn't murder her, remember?"

"Please, tell me everything. Eh-start from the beginning."

"I've been over and over it in my head. The last time I saw her was yesterday afternoon in the square."

"Why did you eh-split up?"

"She went back to Casa Carmela to get her passport. We arranged to meet later. But she never showed up."

"And you have no idea where she might have gone? Does she know anyone in eh-Spain, anyone at all? Think!"

"Um, she met Antonio de Landa in San Xavier once, but they didn't exactly hit it off."

"What about the last time you saw her? Did she seem unhappy?"

"Not at all. Why?"

"I checked her room. Everything was gone—her passport, her toothbrush, everything."

"What?" Max stared at him, openmouthed.

"You knew nothing of this?"

"No."

Santino began to pace back and forth. "Is this my fault? Did I frighten her away? I should not have asked her to meet my parents. It was too soon. She was the girl of my dreams, and I let her eh-slip through my fingers." He paused as if he'd made a decision. "Wish me luck," he said, heading for the door. "I am going to find her and win her back."

"Wait! Don't leave me here!"

"I must find the *señorita*. She needs me."

"*I* need you. Lola would want you to help me."

"She has such a big heart," sighed Santino.

"So will you speak to Officer Gonzales? Tell him I'm innocent?"

"It is not possible. I should not get involved."

"Please, Santino. Be a hero. Do it for Lola."

Santino relented. "Perhaps if I explain about Doña Carmela's eh-strange eccentricities, he will drop the charges. I will try, but I make no promises."

As Max waited for Santino to come back, he tried to think things through.

Lola and Lady Coco had packed up and left town.

Lord 6-Dog was dead.

He was on his own.

And even if he was acquitted of murder, the police would surely find the necklet in his backpack and add grand larceny to his rap sheet.

Then he realized that it didn't matter.

If he couldn't take the Yellow Jaguar to Xibalba, he had precisely three days left to live.

The door flew open and Santino ran in. "Here!" he said, producing Max's passport and backpack, "I rescued these."

"That's great," said Max. "Did you talk to Officer Gonzales?"

"He was too busy. He is arresting the whole town for eh-slander!" Santino shook his head in bafflement. "Yesterday Polvoredo was the most honest town in eh-Spain. Today it is a nest of thieves and liars."

"That's good news for you lawyers, isn't it?" asked Max, surreptitiously eyeing his backpack.

Santino focused on him in surprise. "Why, yes! I had not thought of that. I will be rich! I will be able to buy my Lola everything her heart desires. Tell me, what does she want? A big house? A fast car? Pretty clothes?"

Max slid a hand into his backpack and felt around for the Yellow Jaguar. "Um . . . she's very into saving the rainforest, that sort of thing. Or you could build eh-schools for little Maya kids. She'd like that."

"Save the rainforest? Build eh-schools?" Santino looked horrified. "But I saw us holding parties at our country estate, mixing with the cream of eh-Spanish society. Surely that would make any woman happy?"

Max's fingers found the cold yellow beads. He breathed a sigh of relief. In all the chaos of the day, the police had not yet had time to search his backpack. He became aware of Santino staring at him, waiting for an answer.

He couldn't remember the question. "Sounds good," he said.

"I thought so," said the law student happily. "Thank you for your advice. So now, if you will excuse me, I must go and make my dreams come true."

"What about me? You can't leave me here."

"You are under arrest."

"You know I'm innocent. All you have to do is get me to the airport. I'll catch the first plane out and no one except Lola will ever know you helped me."

"But I could lose everything—and for what? You are my rival for her hand, are you not?"

Max blushed. "I don't know. . . . We're good friends . . . but we've never . . . that is . . . I mean, I like her a lot—"

"Here is the deal," Santino cut in impatiently. "If I eh-smuggle you out of here, you must promise to forget any ideas about you and Lola. You will be a wanted man in eh-Spain forevermore. If you break our deal, I will turn you in."

Max crossed his fingers behind his back. "Deal," he said.

Santino took off his sweatshirt and passed it to Max. "Wear this and put up the hood. Hold your wrists together as if you are handcuffed. If anyone eh-stops us, I will say I am taking you for questioning. Now walk."

In fact, the escape was easy. It seemed like the whole

town was crammed into the front office of the police station, as five hundred years of compulsory truth-telling erupted into a free-for-all of lies, deceit, and falsehoods. There were scuffles and screaming matches in every corner, as fists and accusations flew. Officer Gonzales had his hands full and he didn't even notice the handsome young law student hustle a hooded delinquent straight out the door.

It was another hot morning in Polvoredo.

"Notice anything different?" whispered Santino as they walked quickly to his car.

Max peeked out from under his hood.

Same dusty streets. Same shabby buildings . . . but wait, there *was* something different. Where yesterday, in pots and windowboxes and cracks between cobbles, there had bloomed a riot of yellow flowers, today there were only dried-out brown stalks.

"The flowers have all died. It is eh-strange, no?" said Santino.

Max tried not to look guilty. "Don't ask *me*; I'm not a gardener."

"So you know nothing about this?"

"Lola's missing, and you're worried about flowers?" Max feigned outrage.

"I feel it is all connected in some way." Santino paused in the act of unlocking his car. "I must ask you again: is there anything you want to tell me?"

"No," answered Max, quite truthfully, getting into the passenger seat.

Santino pointed to a plastic supermarket bag at Max's feet. "Your things from Casa Carmela."

Max looked inside. A chewed toothbrush, three smelly

socks, and Lord 6-Dog's matador suit. Max's stomach lurched as he remembered the brave howler monkey who gave his life trying to protect him from a bully.

"That moron shot one of Lola's monkeys last night," he blurted out.

"Which one?" asked Santino.

"Officer Gonzales."

"No, which monkey?"

"The male, the big black one."

"The señorita will be sorry to hear that. She will need me to comfort her."

"But the body . . . it was in the gutter. . . . We have to see if it's still there. . . ."

"No! It is too risky—"

"Please," begged Max. "Lola loved him. Do it for her."

Santino sighed. "I am a fool for love," he said. "Quickly, show me the way. And keep your hood up. No one must eh-spot me with you."

They drove up the narrow streets toward the castle.

"Stop!" said Max, when he saw the drinking fountain on the corner. "It was around here somewhere. . . ." His voice trailed off as he saw the dark stain of blood on the cobbles.

Lord 6-Dog was gone.

"I have to find him," Max insisted.

"No!" Santino looked at his watch. "You have to leave eh-Spain. If we hurry, you will catch the express bus to the airport."

Max hesitated.

What would Lord 6-Dog want him to do?

Look for the body or get on with the mission?

It was no contest.

"Where's the bus stop?" he asked.

Santino drove him out of town, to a crossroads in the middle of nowhere. "That is the eh-stop," he said, pointing to a rusty metal sign with an airplane symbol. "The bus will be here any moment."

Max got out of the car. "You will find Lola, won't you?"

"I promise you, I will never, ever eh-stop looking."

"Good-bye then—and thank you."

"*Adiós* forever, Max Murphy!"

With that, Santino Garcia zoomed out of Max's life and left him sitting by the roadside, waiting for the bus.

Turned out Lola had been right, thought Max. Santino was a good guy, after all. If anyone could find her, he could.

But maybe, Max told himself, she'd be waiting at the airport.

He pictured her standing in line for the plane to San Xavier.

He smiled to himself as he imagined them running to each other in slow-motion. They'd hug; they'd laugh; perhaps they'd continue the happy reunion over pizza.

Pizza?

A growl from his stomach reminded him that he hadn't eaten since . . . when? He couldn't even remember.

His stomach growled again, more loudly.

That wasn't his stomach.

He looked behind him.

It was a hellhound.

A whole pack of slavering hellhounds was coming over the hill toward him. He tried to stay calm. He remembered how they'd attacked him once before, in the Black Pyramid. He'd survived unharmed by simply refusing to believe in them.

"To believe in something gives it power over you"—that's what Uncle Ted had told him.

These dogs were looking horribly real. And extremely powerful.

Max grabbed his backpack and started to run.

He ran for his life.

He could hear the dogs gaining on him.

Then, shimmering in the heat haze like a glorious mirage, a bus appeared in the road in front of him. He ran straight into its path, waving it down, the hellhounds snapping at his heels. The bus screeched to a halt inches in front of him, brakes squealing and tires smoking. Max banged on the glass door and it opened with a hiss, letting out a blast of cold air and a salvo of earsplitting rock music. As the door shut behind him, he turned to see the pack of hellhounds clustered at the roadside, happily wagging their tails, as if waving him off.

Still panting and shaking from his narrow escape, Max turned back to the driver.

"Is this the airport express?" he asked, shouting to make himself heard.

The driver turned down the music and gave Max an evil smile.

"This," he said, "is the fast bus to hell."

Chapter Thirteen

THE FAST BUS TO HELL

s this the bus to the airport?" Max repeated, thinking he must have misheard.

"You got cloth ears, buddy?" snapped the driver. "I just told you, it's the fast bus to *hell*! Don't they teach readin' no more? It's written on both sides of the bus." He wore a peaked cap at a rakish angle and he spoke out of the corner of his mouth like an actor in an old gangster movie.

"I . . . I . . . didn't see it. . . . I got on too fast. . . . So, um, is Hell a town near the airport?"

"Give me strength!" The driver tapped impatiently on the steering wheel. "*The Fast Bus to Hell*—it's the name of the tour bus."

"Tour bus? A bus for tourists?" babbled Max in confusion.

"Look, buddy, I ain't got all day. The boss told me to stop for you, so I did." He revved his engine. "Are you on or are you off?"

The pack of hellhounds was still sitting in line on the roadside.

"I'm on! But can you take me to the airport?"

"You'll have to ask the boss."

"Where is he—?" began Max, but the driver had lost interest in him.

Indicating with his thumb that Max should move inside, he crunched the gears, turned up the sound system even louder than before, and roared off through the Spanish countryside.

Max lurched slowly down the aisle, thanking his lucky stars that it had appeared when it did. Back in San Xavier, he'd taken the word *tourist* as an insult, but this was one tour bus he was happy to join.

Evidently, not many paying guests agreed with him, as all the seats were empty in the front part of the bus.

He kept on going toward the back.

As he passed some curtained-off bunk beds, he realized that this was no ordinary bus: it was fitted out like a luxury hotel. But the ambience that had seemed so refreshingly cool and air-conditioned when he'd first stepped aboard was becoming less and less wholesome. The farther back he made his way, the more pungent the air became.

Max hesitated before entering the next section of the bus. It was some kind of lounge area, with sofas and a huge plasma TV screen. But judging from the air of devastation, the upturned furniture, and broken lamp shades, it had recently been the scene of a minor war or possibly a wild party.

Max stepped over a pile of shredded upholstery and a discarded chain saw, then jumped out of his skin as a body flopped into the aisle. Its face was ghostly white.

Was it dead?

As he stared at the potential cadaver in horror, a loud snore whistled out of its nose.

Could it be . . . ?

No, it couldn't. . . .

It was!

Trigger Mortis, bass player for the Plague Rats.

Wait a minute. . . .

Max skirted the sleeping body and looked around the room. He spotted three more crashed-out band members festooned across the furniture.

Over there was Vince Vermin, curled up on a mattress of pizza boxes and hugging his guitar like a teddy bear; and there was Odd-Eye Ebola, half on and half off the sofa, with his drumsticks entangled in his frizzy black hair. As for the third sleeper, Max deduced that the leather-clad legs and bare feet sticking out from under the sofa could only belong to the Rats' lead singer, Ty Phoid.

How could anyone sleep through this deafening music? Max shook his head in admiration. He considered himself a pretty good drummer, but he had a lot to learn about being a rock star.

At the far end of the lounge was a bead curtain.

As Max got nearer, he saw it was made up of plastic eyeballs strung on extremely realistic-looking yellow plastic sinew. Not for the first time, he wondered if the Plague Rats' obsession with fake gore and plastic body parts wasn't getting a bit uncool.

Still looking for "the boss" and thinking he saw a movement behind the curtain, Max waited for a break between tracks and called out, "Hello?"

Immediately, all the eyeballs swiveled toward him.

Okay, *that* was cool.

"Come in!" boomed a voice.

As Max pushed aside the curtain, he was disconcerted to notice that the eyeballs felt warm and soft and not at all like plastic.

The room was thick with noxious fumes of incense, like concentrated pine disinfectant, undercut with a base of raw sewage. Max's eyes watered as the reek hit him but, at the same time, he knew he'd smelled it somewhere before.

Through the fog, on the other side of a big wooden desk piled with phones and papers and assorted Plague Rats merchandise, he could just make out the figure of an extremely large man counting piles of paper money.

The man looked up and saw him, quickly stashed the bills in a cash box, and boomed, "Max Murphy! Long time no see!"

Max's stomach did a double flip. He knew that voice.

A bloated, lumpy white face leered at him out of the smoke.

It was Ah Pukuh, the Maya god of violent and unnatural death, and ruler of the coming *bak'tun*. He and Max had last met at a hideous celebration in the Black Pyramid, where the Death Lords had impersonated his parents and, yes, now it came back to him, where he'd first smelled that aroma of acrid dung.

On that occasion, Ah Pukuh had been dressed to the nines in his ceremonial finery. Today he'd fashioned his own riff on business smart, having crammed his enormously fat body into a badly fitting pin-striped suit. His greasy hair was hidden under a black top hat, trimmed with jaguar pelt. His face was plastered in thick white makeup that tried (and failed) to conceal his plague boils, his eyes were heavily lined in black, and his lips were grotesquely daubed with red lipstick.

Credit where credit was due, thought Max. By the standards of punk rock, Ah Pukuh didn't look too bad today. But remembering his repellent behavior at their last meeting, Max had no desire to renew their acquaintance.

He turned to run back down the aisle, but two burly men stepped out of the shadows and barred his way. They had broad Maya faces, the physiques of professional wrestlers, and matching red shirts that said ROAD CREW in white letters.

"It's good to see you, man," gushed Ah Pukuh, in his most oleaginous tones. "Pull up a chair."

Max hesitated. He could see no escape route.

Ah Pukuh clapped his hands. "Bring pizza for our guest!" he barked at the roadies. "Pepperoni with extra cheese, chewy in the middle and burned at the edges!" He turned back to Max. "That's how you like it, isn't it? Am I right? How about a cold soda while you're waiting?"

Max thought back to the last time he'd experienced his corpulent host's hospitality. On that occasion, Ah Pukuh had served him a live rat for dinner.

Ah Pukuh read his mind.

"No tricks this time, I promise you," he said, leaning back and opening a small refrigerator, stacked high with cans of soda. "Help yourself."

Gingerly, Max took a can of Coke.

It looked normal.

It opened normally.

It smelled normal.

It tasted normal.

"It's good to see you, man," gushed Ah Pukuh.

Actually, it tasted better than normal. It tasted like the most refreshing, delicious, thirst-quenching, ice-cold soda Max had ever drunk. He chugged it down in one gulp.

"Have another," Ah Pukuh encouraged him, as the roadies struggled through the bead curtain with the biggest pizza box Max had ever seen. "And do help yourself to pizza."

Max took a large, juicy slice and, after sniffing it warily, stuffed the whole thing into his mouth. It was the best pizza he'd ever had. He hadn't realized how hungry he was. He took another slice. Man, this was good pizza.

The roadies retreated to the shadows.

As Max chewed, Ah Pukuh talked. He seemed like a different person from the ill-mannered, flatulent bully who'd held the party in the Black Pyramid. "I'm glad we ran into each other," he said, "because I owe you an apology, Max Murphy. I'm sorry about that thing with the rat, yeah? I realize now that it was deeply inappropriate."

Max took a third piece of pizza and said nothing. Ah Pukuh's mouth was doing a weird twisty thing that made Max suspect he was not sorry at all. In fact, he looked like he wanted to laugh.

Struggling to control his mirth, Ah Pukuh passed Max a paper napkin. "Am I forgiven? Pretty please?"

Max ignored this insincere show of penitence. "What are you doing here?"

"I'm with the band. What are *you* doing here?"

"I'm going to the airport. What do you mean, you're *with* the band?"

"I'm, like, their manager."

"What? How do you know the Plague Rats?"

"Oh, you know, we have a lot of shared interests: anarchy, nihilism, waterproof mascara. . . . It was only a matter of time before we joined forces."

"But you're the Maya god of violent and unnatural death. . . . Aren't you supposed to busy right now, getting ready to rule the new *bak'tun*?"

Ah Pukuh leaned back in his chair, with his feet up on the desk. "I'm done with all that, Max. I've changed. I mean, don't get me wrong, I'm still into senseless violence, but the whole power trip is such a bore. Imagine having to sit on a throne for the next four hundred years, wearing those heavy headdresses, making pronouncements, attending functions. . . . I'd rather be rockin' out, man!"

At this point, Ah Pukuh played a blast of accomplished air guitar to demonstrate his newfound passion.

"Cool," said Max. Then the meaning of Ah Pukuh's conversion sank in. "You mean you won't be releasing the forces of chaos and destruction in a few weeks' time?"

"Not unless that's the name of the Rats' new album!"

"Do the Death Lords know about this?"

"Yeah, they're singing backing vocals on a few tracks."

"No—I mean, do they know you've abdicated?"

"I talked it through with them last night. To be honest, it came as a big relief all round. You know when something just *feels* right? Like, the world has moved on, you know? This whole 'god of violent and unnatural death' thing, I was feeling so *labeled*. We all were. Now that they're free to be themselves, the guys are thinking about forming their own band. I mean, *The Lords of Death*—it's a gift! You have to admit it's a catchy name. I'll send you a demo if you like."

Max sensed a glimmer of hope. "What about the Yellow

Jaguar?" he asked. "Do the Death Lords still want it?"

Ah Pukuh's eyes darted to Max's backpack. He licked his fat lips. "Who knows? But I doubt it. I think they'd be more interested in a decent amp."

"Really? How can I find out for sure?" persisted Max. "I have to know."

"Relax, man," drawled Ah Pukuh. "Take a chill pill."

But Max was wired.

His heart was pounding; his throat was dry; every muscle, sinew, and nerve ending was tautly focused on the possibility that this crazy quest to deliver the Yellow Jaguar was over.

All this time, he'd been so focused on fulfilling his mission that he had never, not for one second, considered the possibility that the Death Lords might lose interest first.

But yes, now that he thought about it, it made perfect sense. Hermanjilio had told him that the Death Lords acted like delinquent children—and children had short attention spans. He could easily imagine the Death Lords being distracted by the rockstar lifestyle. And if they were dead set on entering the music business, they'd want to reinvent themselves as quickly as possible.

Ah Pukuh had done it. And if the god of violent and unnatural death could become a laidback hipster, the Death Lords could change as well.

Max smiled to himself. Already this quest was seeming a little ridiculous, a little, well, uncool.

This was the twenty-first century, after all.

Maybe it was time for ancient Maya gods to catch up with the rest of the world.

If so, this was Max's lucky day.

A sweet relief flooded over him as he imagined what life

would feel like without an ancient Maya price on his head. If only he could find out now, instantly, whether Ah Pukuh was right. Had the Lords of Death really given up on the Yellow Jaguar?

"If you were genuinely sorry about serving me rat in the Black Pyramid," he said, "*you'd* ask them for me. Right now."

"I guess I do owe you one, man." Ah Pukuh thought for a second. "Look, I'll be seeing the guys later for a poker game." He gave Max a theatrical wink. "I'll put in a good word for you, okay? See if I can get you off the hook, yeah?"

"How do I know I can trust you?"

"Oh, that's harsh, man." Ah Pukuh's many chins quivered with distress. "But hey, it's your call. But I *can* tell you that you can't move forward if you're living in the past. You have to let it go, Max."

Max squinted at him suspiciously. "That's not a very Maya thing to say. Lord 6-Dog thought time worked in cycles."

"Exactly! I'm breaking the cycle! I've been in therapy, Max, and I've done a lot of thinking. I've changed for good. Why don't you give me a chance to prove it to you? What do you have to lose?"

Max thought it over. "Okay," he agreed. A cautious optimism was welling up inside him. All he had to do now was keep on Ah Pukuh's good side.

There was a sound like distant thunder. A bad smell, elephant house times twenty, reminded Max why Ah Pukuh's Mayan nickname was Kisin—"the Flatulent One."

"So what brings the band to Spain?" squeaked Max, trying to make small talk. His eyes were watering from the smell. "Aren't they supposed to be in Japan right now?"

Ah Pukuh smirked. "That's what I wanted everyone to think. We've snuck away to play some private gigs, test out some new material, before the big world tour."

"What big world tour?"

Ah Pukuh opened his pin-striped jacket to reveal the black T-shirt underneath and pointed with a fat finger to the words printed on his chest.

"'FIN DEL . . . ,'" read Max. "Um, what does it say? I can't see the rest. . . ."

Ah Pukuh pulled out the fabric from between his rolls of stomach fat and stretched it out to reveal the lettering. "'EL FIN DEL MUNDO WORLD TOUR,'" he read. "Cool, huh?"

Even Max knew enough Spanish to translate it.

"Why's it called *The End of the World* tour? They're not splitting up, are they?"

"It's meant to be ironic—you know, a nod to all that Maya calendar hoo-ha."

"I thought you weren't interested in that anymore."

"I am if it sells tickets."

"It's a cool shirt," said Max longingly.

"It's a collectors' item, limited edition . . . ," boasted Ah Pukuh, rummaging around under his desk. He pulled out a shirt and threw it to Max. "Here, try this on for size."

Max caught it gingerly, as if he thought it might come alive and bite him. But when he held up the shirt and saw it was the genuine article, his reservations about the new, reformed Ah Pukuh melted away. "Thanks. I really like it."

"You're welcome." Ah Pukuh made a steeple with his fingers and tapped his fingertips together, as if searching for a new topic of conversation. "So," he said casually, "I heard you've parted ways with that Maya chick."

"How did you—?" began Max, and then stopped himself. He had no wish to discuss Lola with this bloated lump. He shrugged as if he didn't care.

Ah Pukuh twisted the knife. "I heard she's seeing someone else."

Max couldn't help himself. "You did? Who is it?"

Ah Pukuh laughed and tapped his bulbous nose with his pudgy forefinger. "That would be telling. But I believe you know him."

Max's face burned with anger. It was Santino. It had to be. Of all the low-down, dirty, double-crossing tricks. . . .

"That's chicks for you," said Ah Pukuh. "But there are plenty more grubs in the dungpile, right?"

"I think you mean fish in the sea," said Max.

Ah Pukuh smiled his grisly smile. His stubby yellow teeth looked like two rows of dead maggots. "So remind me, Max Murphy, where are you from?"

"Boston."

"Boston? Boston, Massachusetts? Shut up! Talk about coincidence! The End of the World tour kicks off in Boston in the fall. . . ."

"It does? It's not on the Web site. . . ."

"It's top secret, hasn't been announced yet." Ah Pukuh inspected his black-painted fingernails. "It's expected to sell out in seconds."

Max looked at him hopefully. "I don't suppose . . . ?"

Ah Pukuh reached into his desk drawer, pulled out an envelope, and tossed it across the desk.

Max looked inside. Four front-row seats and four "Access All Areas" backstage passes. He felt woozy with pleasure.

"You could bring those crazy parents of yours," suggested Ah Pukuh.

"I don't think so," laughed Max. "They're not really into the Plague Rats."

"No? Their loss! How are they these days?"

"Not so good. Mom's hair has fallen out, and Dad's got a botfly growing in his neck. It's their punishment for trying to help me."

Ah Pukuh tutted sympathetically. "Nasty business, man. You must be glad it's over."

"Technically, it *isn't* over until the Death Lords say it is."

"I told you, they're more into playing music than collecting old stones."

"But Lord Kuy said—"

"Don't take any notice of that stuffed shirt," guffawed Ah Pukuh, unleashing a wave of halitosis that almost knocked Max off his feet. "If he gives you any trouble, I'll set the hellhounds on him. Raptor meat is their favorite!"

Max laughed nervously. "Even so . . ."

"Kuy answers to me!" bellowed Ah Pukuh, thumping on the desk. Then, seeing Max's consternation, he softened his voice. "Look, this situation is a real downer for you, man. Why don't we sort it right now? I'll take the Yellow Jaguar with me to the poker game tonight and give it to the Death Lords on your behalf. End of story!"

Max thought about it. "Can I come with you?"

"No," said Ah Pukuh, "not possible. 'Gods and mortals, different portals,' as the old saying goes."

"In that case, I'll hang on to it until you speak to the Death Lords. The rules were very specific about me taking it to Xibalba in person and I don't want to mess up. My parents and Hermanjilio and Lucky Jim are all depending on me."

"Whatever you want, man," conceded Ah Pukuh. "I'll talk to them after the gig tonight."

He looked at Max pointedly, and Max took the bait.

"What gig?"

"The Rats are playing a private party to celebrate some impending nuptials."

Max looked baffled.

"A friend of mine is tying the knot," explained Ah Pukuh. "It's going to be quite a party. You're welcome to crash it."

"A wedding?" said Max dubiously.

"The wedding is tomorrow. Tonight, it's a masquerade ball."

"A ball?" said Max, even more dubiously.

"The guys will be playing their new material," wheedled Ah Pukuh.

"But I have to leave Spain tonight," said Max.

"I thought you were a free spirit, man. But if you have to get home to mommy, I suppose we could drop you at the airport. . . ."

"Well," mused Max, "I guess first thing in the morning would be okay."

"Of course it would!" Ah Pukuh encouraged him. "What's the worst that could happen?"

When he looked back at this moment, Max would realize there were many answers to that question, with each outcome worse than the last. But right then and there, blinded by the stars in his eyes, he foresaw only an easy way out.

"You'll speak to the Death Lords for me? You promise?"

"You have my word."

"It would be worth staying just for that," said Max, thinking aloud.

"That's settled, then," announced Ah Pukuh. "Tonight we party with the Rats, and tomorrow you fly home a free man!" He held out his fat hand across the table.

"Let's shake on it!"

Inexplicably, as if in a dream, Max shook on it.

Again in retrospect, he would say that he should have known better.

He would warn you that jaguars, like leopards, don't change their spots.

And he would tell you never, ever to trust the god of violent and unnatural death.

But, in that deluded moment, full of soda and pizza and the spirit of rock, he was feeling mellow.

He convinced himself that everyone deserved a second chance, even Ah Pukuh. He allowed himself to believe that the Death Lords had lost interest in claiming their favor. He told himself that, after all the fear and trouble of the last few days, he deserved time off to have some fun. For one night, he wanted to forget everything and party with the Plague Rats.

Yeah. It was really as simple as that.

Ah Pukuh came around and slapped him on the back.

"Well," he said, "it's been real, but I have work to do. No rest for the wicked and all that. Why don't you visit with the band until party time? They should be waking up any moment now."

Max nodded and turned to go hang with his idols. He was living the dream, all right.

"Oh, just one thing," said Ah Pukuh. "No cause for alarm,

but you need to watch your stuff. You'll be sleeping on the bus tonight and I can't guarantee security. You know what the fans are like—they'll take anything that isn't nailed down. If you want to give me the Yellow Jaguar, I'll put it in the safe for you, just to be sure."

Warning bells should have rung in Max's head.

Every bone in his body, every fiber of his being, should have resisted this suggestion.

Had Ah Pukuh hypnotized him in some way?

Had he spiked the soda?

Drugged the pizza?

Or was Max just so focused on the prospect of meeting the Rats that he wasn't thinking straight?

Who knows?

But the indisputable fact of the matter was that Max Murphy, in slow motion (or so it seemed when he looked back on it), unzipped his backpack, pulled out the yellow stone necklet, and willingly handed it over to Ah Pukuh, the erstwhile god of violent and unnatural death, head honcho of Xibalba, boss of the Death Lords, and cohort of every evil slimy thing in the twenty-three layers of the universe.

And that, not surprisingly, turned out to be a very big mistake.

Chapter Fourteen

HANGING WITH THE RATS

It took Max a while to get talking to the Plague Rats. He didn't want to come off like an adoring fan, so he played it cool, all the while fighting the urge to beg them all for autographs.

His polite inquiries about their travels in Spain and his ruminations on the music business were met with stony silence.

He tried again. "I saw you all at the airport; you were on the luggage carousel, remember? I was with Nasty Smith-Jones. Do you know her? She runs one of your fan sites."

"This kid can't 'alf talk," said Trigger Mortis, who was laid out on a sofa. "'Ey, kid, can you put a sock in it? I can't 'ear meself snore."

"You're British?" Max asked him, in surprise. "I thought you were from Boston, like me."

"I don't care wot you thought," snapped Trigger.

"Rock stars don't talk like 'arvard graduates," Ty Phoid sneered. "Don't you know nuffink about rock 'n' roll?"

"'E's got a cheek," agreed Vince Vermin. "Gettin' on our bus and tellin' us 'ow to talk."

As the band lapsed back into hostile silence, Max looked for another way to break the ice.

Hoping to impress the Rats' drummer, Odd-Eye Ebola, with his percussive skills, he salvaged some chopsticks from a takeout container, shook off the old noodles, and used the sticks to beat out a rhythm on a chair back.

Odd-Eye watched him for a while with interest. "'E's not bad, though, is 'e?" he said to the rest of the band.

Ty Phoid nudged Vince Vermin.

"'Ere's a good one for you, Vinnie," he said. "What do you call a geezer 'oo 'angs out wiv musicians?"

Vince Vermin shrugged.

"A drummer!" announced Ty, with a smirk.

"Oi! That's out of order!" Odd-Eye Ebola lunged at Ty, and soon they were rolling around the lounge area, pummeling each other with their fists and destroying everything in their path.

Max watched them happily, like an indulgent parent at the playground.

"Oi, kid!" yelled Odd-Eye. "Drummers' honor! Back me up 'ere!"

Looking around for a weapon, Max grabbed a can of Coke, shook it hard, and opened it over Ty's head. For a moment, everyone froze as they watched the syrupy brown fizz spray into his eyes, his nose, his mouth. It was all the time Odd-Eye needed to flip his opponent over, pin his arms behind his back, and hold his drumsticks tight across his throat like a garotte. Ty gurgled his surrender, everyone laughed, and Odd-Eye took a bow.

"Nice one, kid!" he said.

"Thanks," said Max. "It's a little trick I picked up in *Street Fight Extreme: Diner Wars.*"

Trigger Mortis sat bolt upright. "You play *Diner Wars*? Did you get past the waiter wiv the explodin' banana splits?"

"Yeah," said Max. "It took me a while to figure it out, but you have to get the banana peel out of the trash can, and throw it down, so he slips on it."

A groan went up around the lounge.

"We've been stuck on that level for days," explained Odd-Eye.

"I know all the cheats," said Max. "I'll show you, if you like."

And thus began the happiest afternoon of Max Murphy's short life, playing the latest video games with his favorite band. And at no point, not once, not ever, did he wonder how he got so lucky or question why it was happening.

On the few occasions that he dragged his eyes away from the huge plasma screen and looked out the window, he noticed that the parched scrub of Extremadura had given way to rolling green countryside. He registered a line of white windmills squatting on the crest of a hill, tractors working in neatly plowed fields, a Roman aqueduct arching high above a winding river.

By early evening, as they left the highway, the blue sky had surrendered to dark gray clouds and the landscape had changed again. Max could see little gray stone cottages and gray stone farmhouses surrounded by gray stone walls. Sky, stones, bricks, roofs—everything outside the bus window was gray except for the green of the grass and the leaves and the moss on the stones. It was the most intense green Max had ever seen, as if someone had increased the saturation on Photoshop. He guessed it must rain quite a bit around here.

As if on cue, a hard gray rain spattered the windshield like a handful of gravel.

They left the main road and headed down a narrow country lane. Branches thwacked against the bus windows, making Max instinctively duck to avoid them. He looked through the glass and jumped to see a round, red, angry-looking face staring back up at him. It was a thickset old woman, head scarf tied tightly under her chin, flattening herself against a gray stone wall to let the bus pass. In front of her was a wheelbarrow full of glistening gray fish. The lane got narrower and narrower, and the bus slowed to a crawl. More stout and ruddy women with wheelbarrows lined the route like an honor guard, until the bus finally eased itself through an ornate iron gateway and onto a long, straight driveway.

At the end of the drive sat a magnificent gray stone palace.

Max whistled in admiration. "That's quite a pile," he said to no one in particular.

Ah Pukuh stuck his head through the bead curtain. "Welcome to Galicia, boys! Time to get ready!"

Galicia?

An ominous bell rang in Max's starstruck brain.

Max turned to the nearest Plague Rat, who happened to be Trigger Mortis. "Do you know whose party it is?" he asked.

Trigger scratched his head and picked some popcorn out of his long, tangled hair. "Some rich Spanish geezer," he said.

"Doesn't *anyone* know who's getting married?" Max

asked the room at large. "Who's paying you for this gig?"

Odd-Eye Ebola pulled a crumpled card out of his back pocket and studied it. "'E's got a fancy coat of arms, 'ooever 'e is." He tossed it to Max. "'Ere, kid, 'ave a wedding invitation."

Max inspected the card.

Strangely, the name of the bride wasn't mentioned. But the name of the groom—and their host for tonight—was Count Antonio de Landa.

Chapter Fifteen

SHOWTIME

"Could *I* use some of that?" asked Max as he watched Ty Phoid cover his face with white makeup and circle his eyes with heavy black shadow.

"You wanna look like a Plague Rat—yeah, why not?" said the lead singer, passing over the cosmetics.

Odd-Eye Ebola studied Max's handiwork. "Not bad, little drummer boy, but wot about yer 'air? Want me to fix it?" And before Max could answer, he'd selected an aerosol can of hair dye from the shelf and sprayed Max's hair jet black.

"I like it," said Max, admiring his reflection.

Odd-Eye smiled. "I 'ope so, coz it won't wash out, not fer a long time."

"But it ain't finished yet," added Trigger Mortis. He squeezed a full tube of gel into Max's locks and coaxed them into rigid spikes.

"Cool," said Max, nodding his appreciation.

Vince Vermin surveyed him critically. "One last thing,"

he said, pulling out a penknife. With three deft swipes, he shredded Max's jeans just above the knee.

The transformation was complete. Max was delighted by the stranger who stared back from the mirror. His own mother wouldn't recognize him now—let alone his archenemy, Count Antonio de Landa. And that was important because his three previous meetings with Landa had not gone well.

The first time, Landa's bodyguard had threatened him in the hotel at Puerto Muerto. The second time, Landa's thugs had chased him and Lola down a raging underground river. And the third time, Landa would have shot him at point-blank range if a blowgun dart from Hermanjilio hadn't stopped him in his tracks.

So, you could say, they were not on the best of terms.

"Stop admirin' yerself," called Trigger Mortis, "and come and help us set up."

Confident in his new disguise—but still keeping a wary eye out for Landa—Max followed the band members into the palace.

It was an impressive venue, if a little incongruous for a gang of tattooed, leather-clad punks. The building had obviously been built up and enlarged over the centuries, to create an ever-more resplendent collection of towers, wings, and reception rooms. The vaulted entrance hall—a former courtyard, now roofed over—reminded Max of his uncle's home in San Xavier. There was a huge walk-in fireplace, almost as big as the Murphys' whole kitchen in Boston. Above the carved wooden mantel was painted an intricate family tree, too high to read but impressively long and old-looking. The other walls were lined with oil paintings of haughty men with pointy black beards and thin lips; gleaming suits of armor stood guard over antique side tables and stiff-backed chairs; the marble floor was spread here and there with oriental rugs.

It looked like a museum, not a home, reflected Max as he helped the roadies sort out amps and cables and mixers, while the band explored the palace. It was easy to keep track of their whereabouts from the shatter of broken china and the thuds of upturned furniture.

Now Max heard Odd-Eye Ebola calling from a nearby room, "'Ere, guys, look at me!"

"Don't do it!" yelled Trigger Mortis.

"Do it! Do it! Do it!" chanted Vince Vermin.

"Bet yer can't make it all the way to the bottom!" came Ty Phoid's voice.

"'Ow much do you bet?" called Odd-Eye.

"Ten quid!"

"Yer on!"

Max ran in to see the rest of the band staring up at Odd-Eye, who was perched at the top of a highly polished wooden banister, which swept and curled and swooped along a grand staircase from the gallery above.

In front of Max's horrified eyes, the drummer launched himself backward with a bloodcurdling cry, sliding expertly down the banister at gathering speed before becoming unseated at the first bend in the stairway and plummeting to earth with a painful crash.

"I win," said Ty Phoid. "Where's me ten quid?"

"I made it to the bottom, didn't I?" groaned Odd-Eye. "But I think I've done me back in."

Ah Pukuh came waddling into the room, as fast as his fat little legs could carry him. "What's all the noise?" he asked.

"What are you doing in here? You should be getting ready for the . . ." His voice trailed off as he took in Odd-Eye's stricken position. "What's the matter with him?"

"'E can't get up," Trigger pointed out. "'E's done 'is back in."

"Looks like 'e won't be playin' tonight," observed Ty, "but it don't matter. 'E's useless anyway."

Ah Pukuh's corpselike pallor was tinged with an angry red. His plague boils throbbed purple through his makeup, and his slicked-back hair began to spring up and bristle into snaky tufts. "We must have drums! Everything must go as planned. Get up, get up!" he bellowed, kicking Odd-Eye hard in the side.

"Steady on," said Trigger.

"Leave 'im alone," said Vince.

"'E's just a drummer, 'e don't know any better," said Ty.

"This could ruin everything!" bellowed Ah Pukuh, his eyes bulging with fury. "If he does not play tonight, I"—he searched for a suitable punishment—"I will destroy you all!"

An icy wind blew through the room, and somewhere a door slammed with a sound like a knife coming down on a butcher's block.

Now, for all their black leather and tattoos and scary makeup, the band looked like four frightened little boys. Every time Odd-Eye tried to get up, he fell back with an anguished cry.

"I can't do it," he whimpered.

"You will do it," commanded Ah Pukuh, kicking him again, and this time the band did not defend him.

This was looking bad—for Odd-Eye *and* for Max. Ah Pukuh was certainly not in the right mood to relay the all-important question to the Death Lords.

"I'll do it," said Max.

"That's it!" gasped Odd-Eye, his eyes watering with pain. "The kid can play in my place! 'E's a crackin' little drummer and 'e he knows all our songs, 'e told me."

They all swiveled their heads toward Ah Pukuh, to gauge his reaction.

Ah Pukuh stroked his multiple chins thoughtfully.

Then his blubbery face split into a hideous rictus grin. "Yes, why not? This could be perfect! I promise you an unforgettable evening, Max Murphy."

"But let's not mention the new lineup to Count de Landa," said Max hastily. "He might think he's getting shortchanged."

"Yeah," quipped Vince Vermin, "'e might smell a rat! A Plague Rat! Geddit?"

"Just clear that loser out of here," ordered Ah Pukuh, pointing at Odd-Eye, "and get ready for your sound check."

"But where's this party 'appenin'?" asked Vince. "I don't see no stage or nuffink."

"That's because Count de Landa has planned something very special!" Ah Pukuh clapped his hands together like an excited child. "Follow me. . . ."

While the roadies carried Odd-Eye back to the bus, Max and the rest of the band trooped through the palace behind Ah Pukuh, through various rooms and halls, until they came to a set of double doors embedded in the floor. The doors were open and a grand staircase, lit by flaming torches, descended underground.

"Is this a nightclub?" asked Vince, sounding impressed.

"You could say that," responded Ah Pukuh. He glanced at Max. "You could say it's the *End of the World Club*."

Max narrowed his eyes. He'd never heard anyone but

his father use that phrase. Was Ah Pukuh taunting him? He began to get a bad feeling as he followed the band down the stairs and into a cavernous space, where a small army of servants were bustling about, setting up tables, polishing glassware, and lighting incense and perfumed candles to mask the pervading smell of damp and mold. At the far end of the room was a professional-looking stage, framed by red velvet curtains. A black backdrop adorned with kitschy silver writing proclaimed CONGRATULATIONS in many different languages.

"Oi," yelled Trigger, "careful wiv me bass!" as a chain of little boys, dressed as pages in brocade coats and powdered wigs, passed the band's equipment up to the stage.

"So," said Max, "Ah Pukuh said you'd be trying out some new material."

The band exchanged mystified glances.

"Do you have a set list I could look at?" persisted Max.

"A set list?" Ty snorted. "Wot do you fink we are—a boy band?"

"But how will I know what to play?" asked Max.

Ty put an arm around him. "The fans don't care wot you play. They can't hear nuffink anyway, wot wiv all the screamin'," he explained. "Bein' a rock star is all about attitude. I don't even know the words to most of our songs."

"But you're the lead singer."

"I fink of myself more as the front man. When I forget the words, I just do me tongue waggle." He stuck out an improbably long tongue and undulated it impressively.

"It's true," said Vince. "I can only play three chords on me ax, but I can do a windmill wiv me arm, and I've got the biggest amp in the business."

Trigger nodded. "Musical talent is overrated. Wot the

fans like is when I play bass wiv me teeth."

"So what does Odd-Eye usually do?"

"'E touches 'is chin wiv 'is tongue," volunteered Ty.

"'E throws 'is drumsticks in the air and catches 'em," proposed Vince.

"And 'e takes 'is shirt off," added Trigger.

"But he's the best rock drummer in the business," said Max. "There must be more to it than that."

The remaining three Plague Rats looked at one another blankly.

"I'll call 'im," said Ty. He pulled out a cell phone and jabbed in a number. "Oi, Odd-Eye, the new kid wants to talk to you, mate. I told 'im anyone can be a drummer, but 'e wants you to give 'im some tips."

He passed to phone to Max.

"First fing, right," gasped Odd Eye, obviously still in pain, "is to ignore all the drummer jokes. They're only jealous coz you 'ave more fun than the rest of 'em. It's all about gettin' noticed. So make sure to 'old yer arms as 'igh as you can, otherwise no one will see you behind that pile of kit. Remember, yer not *playin'* the drums, you *are* the drums. Shake yer 'ed like a madman, jump in yer seat, whirl yer sticks like a dervish, bulge yer eyes, do anythin' you can to channel the beat an' steal the limelight from the guitarists. It don't matter wot rubbish yer playing, as long as you make it *look* 'ard. Got that?"

"Wow! Thanks!" said Max, giving Ty his phone back. "I better start practicing." He picked up some drumsticks.

"Give me those," said Trigger, snatching them off him. "Wot do you mean, practicin'? Do you wanna make the rest of us look bad?"

"But—"

"The 'ole point about the Plague Rats, kid, is that we're raw," said Vince.

"Raw like liver," agreed Trigger.

"Good album title," mused Ty.

"Speakin' of liver," said Trigger, "I could murder a nice steak 'n' kidney pie. Is there anythin' to eat around 'ere?"

"I'll go and have a look," offered Max, eager to get away and practice his tongue extensions.

He walked through the huge underground room, trying to guess its original function. It seemed to be dug out of the bare earth. Could it be a wine cellar? (He saw no wine bottles.) Or a dungeon? (No shackles or manacles.)

Narrow passages radiated off the central space like the spokes of a wheel. Thinking it might be a good idea to plan an escape route in case Landa recognized him, Max turned into the first passage he came to.

As soon as he stepped inside, he realized what it was.

All along both sides were deep shelves, like the rows of cramped bunk beds on a submarine. But instead of a sleeping sailor, each of these bunks housed the tomb of a dead Landa, each corpse's name engraved on its marble coffin.

In between the larger alcoves, smaller niches held neatly stacked bones and skulls. The passage was lit by hundreds of dripping yellow candles, and at the end Max could see an elaborately carved mausoleum behind a pair of iron gates. His head spinning, he peered into the next passage, and the next, and the next: more tombs, more bones, more skulls.

Max ran back to the stage, where the Plague Rats were still larking around.

"Did you find any food?" asked Ty.

"No," spluttered Max, "but guess what? This place is not a nightclub, it's a crypt!"

Trigger looked up. "A place for dead dudes?"

"Yes! They're all around us! Those passageways are full of them!"

Trigger turned to his bandmates. "Hear that, guys? We're playin' to a bunch of real-live stiffs!"

"Cool!" said Ty.

Ah Pukuh peered out from one of the velvet curtains. He was evidently in mid-toilette, as his hair was in a toweling turban and he wore a little woven cape to protect his clothes from the loose flakes of powder that rained down from his caked white face. "The guests are arriving," he trilled. "It's showtime, boys! Give it everything you've got!"

Vince Vermin strapped on his guitar.

"Let's rock!" he whooped, and Max leapt onstage to take his place behind Odd-Eye's drum kit and join the band in a full-blooded rendition of their last big hit, "Wake the Dead." The music thudded and echoed around the chamber, darkness closing in on them, flaming torches reflected in gleaming glassware like stars in the midnight sky, everything blurred by sweat and sheer exhilaration as they played on and on, crashing and screaming through the Rats' back catalog... until Max finally looked up and saw, to his surprise, a sea of party guests bobbing to the music. The masked ball was in full swing.

Vince launched into a solo and,

as he thrashed his guitar in a howl of feedback, Max took the time to study the audience.

In ball gowns, diamond jewelry, and powdered wigs, all the women looked like Marie Antoinette. Some of them also had alarmingly realistic gashes around their necks, as if they'd just come from the guillotine.

Also in powdered wigs, plus brocade vests, frock coats, frilled shirts, and knickerbockers, all the men looked like Mozart. Some of them wore so much face powder, they looked like Mozart after he'd died his untimely death.

Everyone wore an ornate mask over their eyes or carried a mask on a stick. They certainly weren't the usual Rats crowd. But to judge from the amount of screeching and braying and guzzling, they thought it a hoot to party with a punk band in an underground cemetery.

Around the edges of the room, sword-swallowers, fire-eaters, and stilt-walkers plied their trades. A group of white-painted mime artists made a living sculpture of an elephant; a headless horseman juggled a selection of large objects including his own head; a conjurer made a tray of drinks vanish from under the nose of a flustered waiter.

Just as Max was deciding that it was the best party he'd ever been to, someone pulled the plug, and all the amps and speakers lost their power.

The guitars fizzled to a halt and Max stopped with them.

As the Plague Rats looked around, confused, Ah Pukuh lumbered onto the stage. Beneath his jaguar mask of painted papier-mâché, his chubby cheeks were heavily rouged, he wore black lipstick, and his greasy hair was powdered white. But nothing could disguise his obese body. The rolls of jiggling blubber under his white ceremonial robes looked like a herd of sea cows fighting under a bedsheet.

He made a dismissive gesture to indicate that the set was finished. Max began to leave the stage with the rest of the band.

"Not so fast," said Ah Pukuh. "I'll be needing *you*."

The two Maya roadies frog-marched him back to the drumkit and pushed him roughly into his seat. He watched, glumly, as Ah Pukuh fussed with a handheld microphone—tapping it repeatedly and emitting a lot of *testing one-two-threes*—before waddling into the spotlight.

"Welcome, one and all, on this auspicious occasion, the eve of the wedding of the century—or should I say, the betrothal of the *bak'tun*."

He pointed at Max.

Ba-dum-bum-CHING. Max obediently supplied a comedy drumroll to set off Ah Pukuh's lame joke.

It was interesting, he thought, to see how completely the god of violent and unnatural death had shed the persona of a laid-back rock-band manager and become a slick, if unconventionally dressed, emcee.

"In keeping with a quaint Maya tradition," continued Ah Pukuh, "I will now begin the proceedings by inviting a genuine Maya fortune teller to tell us the meaning of these nuptial days in the ritual Maya calendar so please take your seats, ladies and gentlemen—and enjoy the show!"

A small man in a white tunic, his head wrapped in a woven scarf, entered reluctantly from the wings. He carried with him a deerskin bundle, which he placed on the stage and unwrapped with shaking hands. Max saw that it contained a variety of small objects—white crystals, yellow corn kernels, red seeds—just like he'd seen Zia set out on the Murphys' front room carpet in Boston.

"Speak!" commanded Ah Pukuh.

"Today is Kan K'an, 4-Maize," whispered the shaman.

"Louder!" barked Ah Pukuh.

"Kan K'an, a day to burn, a day of debts."

Ah Pukuh's fleshy jowls shook in fury. "What? You were supposed to say *a day of feasting and making merry.* Stick to the script I gave you or you won't get paid."

"I am a shaman, not an actor."

"It's a wedding party. Would it have hurt you to say something nice?"

"I cannot change the days, Lord Ah Pukuh. No one can change the days."

"Well, what do you have to say about tomorrow, the wedding day itself?"

The shaman regarded Ah Pukuh with dread.

"Come on now, something about happiness and many offspring, wasn't it?" prompted the god of violent and unnatural death.

"Tomorrow is Ho Chikchan, 5-Snakebite. It"—the shaman swallowed nervously—"it is a day of weeping, the day when an enemy comes."

The entire audience breathed in sharply, as one.

"Take him away!" bellowed Ah Pukuh, kicking the shaman's bundle and scattering his crystals, corn, and seeds into the audience. "I ask you, folks—is it any wonder that Maya civilization collapsed with killjoys like him around?"

He pointed at Max.

Ba-dum-bum-CHING.

The two red-shirted roadies dragged the hapless shaman off the stage.

"Tear off his fingernails and skin him alive!" Ah Pukuh called after them.

The audience laughed nervously.

Max was pretty sure that Ah Pukuh was not joking.

Speaking loudly to drown out the screams of the shaman, Ah Pukuh reverted to smarmy emcee mode. "There's nothing like a great opening act to get a party going," he said. "And that was *nothing* like a great opening act."

Ba-dum-bum-CHING.

"But don't worry, folks, we have plenty more thrills and surprises lined up for you. It's going to be an unforgettable night, and I think it's time we met the man who made it all possible." At Ah Pukuh's signal, the stage lights dimmed until he was alone in a spotlight. "And now, I am delighted to introduce your host for the evening: put your hands together, lay-deez and gentlemen, for . . . Count Antonio de Landa!"

Max watched in dread as the spotlight swung to the back of the room and picked out the loathsome Landa, looking extremely pleased with himself in a richly embroidered blue velvet doublet with a short black cape, black leather gloves, and a steel conquistador helmet.

There was a smattering of applause, and the audience parted to allow him to make his way to the stage. He pulled behind him a woman in a heavy black lace veil that made her look like a birdcage with a cloth over it. To complete her unflattering ensemble, she wore an old-fashioned yellow ball gown with a skirt so wide she had to walk slightly sideways to get through the crowd.

Max tried to hide behind his drums as the happy couple climbed the steps to the stage. Ah Pukuh handed Landa a microphone.

"*Muchas gracias,* many thanks to my best man, Lord Ah

Pukuh," began Landa in his distinctive lisp, "and thank you to all my guests for joining me on this historic evening. Tonight, my friends, we will celebrate the union of two great bloodlines. For, to the eternal glory of the house of Landa, I have at last found a vessel worthy to bear my sons."

Max studied Landa's bride-to-be.

He certainly didn't envy her fate. But what kind of person would agree to marry that creep? It was impossible to see what she looked like under that veil, but Max was sure that she must be as repellant, both physically and mentally, as the count himself. That would serve Landa right.

"Tomorrow," continued Landa, "I hope you will join us in Santiago de Compostela, the ancient city named for Saint James of the Field of Stars, as my bride and I plight our troth. How fitting that we will seal our union in the great cathedral where lies the tomb of Saint James, patron saint of Spain. For with this marriage, I will fulfill the destiny of the Landa family and bring glory to my beloved homeland—"

"Splendid, splendid," interrupted Ah Pukuh impatiently. He turned to the audience. "Now, who wants to see the bride?" At his urging, everyone shouted and whistled and stamped their feet. Ah Pukuh motioned for silence and pointed at Max. "Drumroll puh-lease."

Clumsily, Landa lifted the veil. Max ended his drumroll with a flourish as the unfortunate fiancée was revealed. From behind the drum kit, all Max could see was that she looked young and that she had dark hair twisted into a low bun. He couldn't see her face but, judging from the audience reaction, he guessed she was not the hideous monster he'd imagined.

Landa took her hand and presented her to the audience. "*Bueno*, now I give you the new Countess de Landa—a royal princess from a long and glorious dynasty."

"Kiss! Kiss!" chanted the crowd. "*Que se besan! Que se besan!*"

Landa turned the girl's chin toward him, and Max craned to see her profile.

It was Lola.

And she didn't exactly look unhappy.

Chapter Sixteen

THE KISS OF DEATH

As she stood there on the stage, awaiting Landa's kiss, Lola didn't look unhappy. She didn't look anything. Her eyes were open but her face was blank.

As Landa made his move on her, she didn't so much as flinch. But the sight of Landa's thin and bloodless lips zeroing in on Lola turned Max's stomach. He could only think that she'd been hypnotized, that she didn't know what she was doing, that he had to save her from that kiss.

Do something. . . . Do anything. . . . Make a distraction. . . .

He crashed like fury on the cymbals.

Landa jumped out of his skin.

Mission accomplished.

The romantic moment was lost.

Max was willing Lola to turn around and make eye contact so that he could give her a signal, make sure she knew it was him under the newly dyed hair and layers of face paint. But she stood stiffly facing forward, eyes cast down.

Landa cast an angry glance back at Max and his drum set.

Max froze, waiting for the shout of recognition, but his disguise held.

Ah Pukuh, roaring with laughter, slapped Landa on the back. "Never mind, Antonio," he chuckled. "There will be time for smooching later. Let us proceed with the formalities."

Landa turned back and tried to gather himself together.

He pulled a crumpled piece of paper from his pocket and began to read: "*Bueno*, before we begin, I would like to explain to my distinguished guests about the significance of the theatrical performance that they are about to witness."

"Must you?" asked Ah Pukuh. "I think your guests would rather watch the show."

"I must," snapped Landa. "My family has waited five hundred years for this day. I will have my moment."

He clapped his hands officiously, and four liveried servants staggered onto the stage with a heavy stone block. It was shaped like an anvil, but longer and flatter, and carved on all sides with jaguar heads. The servants carefully set it down and placed a couple of jaguar-pelt cushions on top.

Ah Pukuh tapped his foot impatiently. "Get on with it," he said.

Scowling at the rudeness of his best man, Landa clapped his hands, and one of the servants stepped forward with a scroll. Landa clapped again, and the servant began to read in a dull monotone:

"This is the famous throne of K'awiil, the seat of ancient Maya kingship, where the kings and queens of the Monkey River were crowned. Although some details of the ritual have been lost, we know they used the fabled Yellow Jaguar, the Stone of Truth, to release the Scepter of K'awiil that is embedded in the throne. Thus they would prove their lineage and verify their claim to rulership."

The servant rolled up the scroll and hurried off the stage.

Now Landa himself stepped up to the microphone.

"Although we do not have the Yellow Jaguar here today, I call upon my future wife to join me on the Throne of Kings."

There was a smattering of applause as Landa and Lola took their seats.

Servants lit incense bowls all around, and soon thick clouds of perfumed incense billowed onto the stage like dry ice.

Ah Pukuh came forward, applauding loudly. "And for our next surprise—"

"*Espere!* Wait!" shouted Landa. "I have not finished explaining the history—"

"Antonio, my friend," said Ah Pukuh, "your guests have come for a party, not for a history lesson. Besides, this surprise is for you. . . ."

Landa looked confused. "*Por favor*, Lord Ah Pukuh, let us stick to the script we agreed—"

"No," said Ah Pukuh, "that doesn't seem to be the way this night is going." There was a sinister edge to his voice. "Let us do this thing properly."

He snapped his fingers for another drumroll.

Landa was shaking his head.

Lola was on her feet now and looking worried.

Max suddenly knew what was coming.

He started to rise in protest, but the roadies pushed him down, their sharp fingernails squeezing his shoulders like claws.

Ah Pukuh turned to look at him, his face a mask of hate. "Drumroll!"

"You heard him," said one of the roadies. "Play it!"

Max tried to stop his arms from shaking enough to brush the snare drum.

This was bad.

This was so bad

And it was all his fault.

His worst fears were confirmed when a gasp went around the audience.

"Feast your eyes," Ah Pukuh was saying, but Max couldn't bear to look.

He took a peek.

As he suspected, Ah Pukuh was holding something up to show the crowd. "This is the authentic Yellow Jaguar of K'awiil, the mighty Stone of Truth," he proclaimed, to much oohing and aahing. "Antonio de Landa, because you love history so much, I give it to you freely, as it was given to me."

"But . . . But this is not what we rehearsed . . . ," stammered Landa.

"So live a little." Ah Pukuh turned to the crowd. "Dear Antonio is overcome with gratitude," he explained. He turned back to Landa. "There is no need to thank me," he said. "To see your happiness as you open the portal for the ancient ritual will be thanks enough."

"But . . . But . . . I can't . . ."

"Put on the necklet," boomed Ah Pukuh.

Landa shook his head.

"Do it!"

Ah Pukuh clapped his hands and led the crowd in a chant.

"DO IT! DO IT! DO IT!"

Landa was getting extremely agitated. He looked like he wanted to cry.

"Here, let me help you," said Ah Pukuh.

When Landa saw that he had no choice, he reluctantly allowed Ah Pukuh to tie the string of heavy beads around his neck. Max heard Ah Pukuh hiss into his ear: "This is a loaner. Don't get any ideas. Swear to give it back or I will destroy you."

Landa, too petrified to move, made a faint squeak.

Apparently satisfied with this response, Ah Pukuh signaled to the stagehands. "Dim the lights and start the show!"

There was a fanfare of wooden trumpets.

As the stage grew dark, a yellow light emanated from the Jaguar Throne.

Landa clutched at his neck in pain as the yellow stones in the necklet began to glow. His face was as white as the starched folds of his ruff.

The audience drew in their collective breath as a cold wind blew through the room, extinguishing candles, pulling wigs off heads, lifting tablecloths, and making the stilt walkers lose their balance.

"Be still," warned Ah Pukuh. "Nobody move." He backed away to the side of the stage. "The portal is open. Lord K'awiil is in the house."

The crowd sat in fidgety silence, sipping their drinks and exchanging apprehensive looks, their eyes darting every which way, everyone trying to be first to spot K'awiil, like children waiting for Santa Claus.

At first the noise seemed far away—a rumbling boom like a battering ram hitting a heavy oak door on some distant castle.

An expectant murmur went around the audience.

After a few seconds, there was another, closer boom.

Then one after another, the booms continued, growing louder and deeper, each one sending tremors through the floor and reverberating around the room.

The audience wasn't smiling now.

There was a crash like a giant's jackhammer striking the palace foundations. Every electrical fixture in the room—stage lights, electric guitars, amplifiers, microphones, cell phones, wall sockets—began to smoke and fizzle, exploding one by one in showers of red-hot sparks.

When the last spark died out, the terrified audience was left in darkness.

Some people stood up with the intention of finding their way to the exit, but another massive boom shook the building so violently that they were knocked off their feet.

The crowd was in chaos now, panicking and screaming, masquerade costumes ripped and torn in the rush to climb over one another and escape.

But it was too late.

They were caught at the epicenter of a furious electrical storm.

All they could do was cover their ears as the thunder crashed and jagged fingers of lightning arched in every direction, illuminating the room with retina-burning flashes of white light.

One fork lit up the base of the throne like a spotlight. All eyes that were not shut tight in terror watched as a piece of stone—thin and round like a rolling pin, maybe four foot long—tumbled free.

"Pick it up, Antonio, pick it up," Ah Pukuh ordered over the microphone.

Hesitantly, Landa obeyed.

"Behold," announced Ah Pukuh, "Count Antonio de Landa now carries the sacred scepter of K'awiil, the kingmaker. Hold it up high, dear Antonio, so everyone can see it."

Looking scared out of his wits in the yellow glow of the collar, Landa obeyed him. As Max studied the scepter, he saw that it was carved into the shape of a figure with a long head and a snake in place of one of his legs.

The scepter seemed to be glowing yellow, too.

Was Landa shrinking, or was the scepter growing?

Soon there was no doubt about it: the scepter was growing and growing, dwarfing everything around it. . . .

With an explosion of sparks, it burst out of Landa's clutch and sprang to the back of the stage, its snake leg whirling like a tornado. The head by now was twenty feet tall; the impossibly long forehead was black and polished to a dull sheen; its eyes rolled angrily from side to side; its anteater's snout emitted curls of dense gray smoke like a fire-breathing dragon. Electricity danced and popped off the surface of the creature's scaly silver-gray skin and lit up the stage around him.

Now the snake leg wound itself around, so that the body of K'awiil rested on its coils, with the great mirrored forehead shining down from the stage like a gigantic plasma-screen TV.

The audience, eyes wide in terror, sat back in their seats as if pinned there by centrifugal force.

Ah Pukuh bounded to center stage like a game-show host.

"Let's have a big hand for my friend and yours, Lord K'awiil, god of lineage and kingship," he shouted. "Welcome back to Middleworld, your lordship."

Ah Pukuh clapped loudly, encouraging the audience to do the same, but no one could move a muscle; they were all paralyzed by fear.

K'awiil exhaled through his snout and sent a ball of flame shooting out over the audience. A chorus of screams suggested that the troop of mime artists at the back had suddenly found their voices as the fireball melted their polyester costumes.

"Silence!" bellowed Ah Pukuh. He turned to Landa. "Are you ready?"

Landa shook his head. "Not this," he whimpered. "*Por favor*, not this."

Ah Pukuh cackled maniacally. "It is too late to back out now, Antonio. You wanted to be a king, didn't you? You can thank me later."

Lola seemed resigned to whatever was about to happen. Max willed her to look up, to see him, but her shoulders were slumped forward and her head hung low. She looked so tiny and fragile, like a little girl playing dress-up in a big yellow ball gown.

Ah Pukuh was addressing the great head.

"Lord K'awiil," he was saying, "I present to you Count Antonio de Landa, a noble son of Spain, who seeks to mix his bloodline with our royal lineage. I beg you to pronounce him worthy and reveal his illustrious pedigree."

K'awiil's massive forehead swiveled around until it reflected Landa in the center of its screen. For a few moments, the quivering aristocrat was bathed in a pool of sodium-yellow light. Then a single lightning bolt shot out of the mirror and blasted him to pieces, the flesh on his bones disintegrating into thousands of tiny particles until he was nothing but a glowing skeleton.

While the mirror played scenes from his life, the particles

of Landa hung in the air like glitter in a snow globe.

Max, like the rest of the audience, was transfixed in shock and awe.

He didn't know whether to watch the giant screen (which was showing scenes from Landa's life to illustrate how he'd graduated from drowning kittens as a boy to punching servants as a teenager and on to murdering his own brother when he came of age) or watch the tiny particles as they slowly floated down. When each speck landed, like a tiny seed of Landa's being, it grew into a person. Soon there were tens, then hundreds, of people crowding onto the stage. All of them—men, women, and children alike—bore an uncanny resemblance to Landa.

The first to march into the audience were several families of dirty, ragged peasants, who made straight for the buffet table and leapt on it with cries of joy. A band of swineherds traded insults with a band of goatherds, while their animals attacked each other. The audience recoiled in horror as a line of lepers wandered through, ringing their bells and looking for a place to hide themselves away. Wizened old men and hunchbacked old women accosted the elegantly dressed party guests, begging for money and trying to steal their jewelry.

The scene was bedlam. Food flew onto the stage. Tables were knocked over. People pushed and shoved in the crowd. Pigs and piglets squealed underfoot, while goats chewed on the party decorations. An aroma of manure undercut the waves of incense and caused some of the more delicate guests to faint.

A company of laughing conquistadors surveyed the chaos, ready to join the fray. As they sized up the plunder they were planning to steal and the women they intended to abduct, a hooded figure pushed through their ranks and took center stage.

An eerie silence descended.

The massed ranks of Landas froze.

The peasants dropped their chicken legs.

Even the pigs stopped squealing.

The figure lowered his hood to reveal a balding dome, a sharply pointed nose, and cold eyes like a fish.

Max recognized him straightaway from the story of Princess Inez.

It was Antonio de Landa's most notorious ancestor, Friar Diego de Landa, the rogue priest who'd burned every Maya book he could get his hands on. Three thousand years of learning destroyed by one power-crazed sadist. How many times had Max heard Lola lament Friar Diego's actions?

And now, assuming that her fiancé's flesh and bones were ever reunited—she was marrying into his family.

Max understood that you couldn't blame the entire Landa clan for the actions of one bad apple. But Antonio and Diego had the same cold-fish look about them and, from what Max had seen of Antonio, they seemed to share the same vicious and volatile nature.

Friar Diego's newly appeared relatives apparently felt the same way, cowering away from him and scrambling to get down the stairs. Even the conquistadors gave him a wide berth and leapt from the stage into the audience.

All this time, the friar's descendant, Count Antonio, was perched motionless and fleshless on the Jaguar Throne like a neon-yellow skeleton in a steel helmet. Through the jostling generations of Landas, Max could just make out Lola, sitting beside the remains of her husband-to-be, staring at the friar in shock.

Then, as he watched, she reached down, picked up a stray chicken leg that had landed on the stage, and hurled it at Diego de Landa's back. Even before the chicken bone made contact, she followed it with a fat chorizo sausage and a large orange, which exploded pleasingly on his bald head.

The food fight was on. As the friar wiped orange pulp from his eyes, an artillery of fruit, vegetables, and meat products splattered onto his head. It seemed that everyone had a grudge against him.

The Maya roadies stage-dived into the crowd to join in. Max could pick out their red shirts at the buffet table as they lobbed custard tarts at the malevolent monk.

Diego de Landa raised a bony finger and pointed into the audience.

"Repent!" he screeched.

An apple sailed toward him and lodged in his mouth, making his eyes bulge in surprise and giving him the look of a roasted pig at a medieval banquet.

More and more Landa ancestors were accumulating at the back of the stage. The ones who'd been born after the conquest were better dressed than their peasant forebears, but none of them had good manners nor an ounce of noble bearing. While the men brawled among themselves and pulled one another's beards, the women kicked one another's shins and grabbed at one another's hair.

What a rabble they were.

Ducking the missiles that were raining down, Ah Pukuh made his way over to the microphone. "Let's give it up for our surprise guest, Friar Diego de Landa!" Ah Pukuh didn't seem a bit bothered about the chaos that had broken out and he put his arm around the priest's shoulders in a chummy, old-boy-network sort of way and tried to lead him off the stage.

But the monk—who by now had so much food splattered on him that he looked like one of those make-your-own-volcano kits encrusted in luridly colored lava—was angry. He cursed and gesticulated at the crowd, his face a mask of pure hatred.

Ah Pukuh roared with laughter and clapped his hands.

At this signal, the monk's unholy language was drowned out by the wailing of conch shells and the stage lights came back on.

The great K'awiil shrank back into a stone scepter, which rolled across the stage to the base of the throne, where it slotted itself back into place.

The yellow collar stopped glowing, the yellow haze faded, and Antonio de Landa's skeleton was absorbed into the rest of his body. He gazed out uncomprehendingly at the devastation that was his engagement party.

Most of his relatives had evaporated, but a few lolled drunkenly in the shadows. A small pig snuffled around his feet.

"Welcome back, dear Antonio!" gushed Ah Pukuh into his newly restored microphone. "And thank you for introducing us to your delightful family. What a spirited bunch! It's so refreshing to meet aristocrats who have not lost their common touch!" Here he made a face at the audience to show what he really thought of Landa's lineage. "We'll round up any stray ancestors later, but you might want to count your silver . . . !"

Landa groaned and sank his head into his hands, massaging his temples as if he had a headache.

"Just joking, Antonio!" More mugging at the audience by Ah Pukuh. "Well, it's been quite a show, hasn't it, folks?" he prattled on, as servants cleared the stage of piglets and debris. "But it's not over yet!"

He gestured to a stagehand, who began to haul on a rope. The glitzy backing curtain rose jerkily out of sight to reveal a painted backdrop depicting the top platform of a Maya pyramid, blue sky above and rainforest canopy below.

"And now," boomed Ah Pukuh, "to ensure the fertility of this union, I am delighted to present the happy couple with my final gift . . . a human sacrifice!"

The stunned audience began to applaud politely and then stopped as his words sank in. *A human sacrifice?* What kind of wedding gift was that? Since when did toasters go out of style?

Ah Pukuh clapped his hands.

There was a creaking noise as the servants brought out a sacrificial altar. It looked authentic, like the stone altars Max had seen on Maya pyramids in San Xavier, but it had been mounted on wheels for ease of mobility, so that it now rolled onto the stage like a squeaky room-service cart in a fancy hotel.

But the special tonight was not lobster or steak.

Tied down and writhing on the altar stone lay a young man. He wore only a loincloth, and the rest of his body glistened with bright blue paint. Max recognized the color as surely as if it were a paint chip at Home Depot.

Sacrificial cobalt.

He'd seen it before when Lola was daubed in it, ready to be sacrificed by Tzelek on the Black Pyramid.

Was this a skit? This was going a little far even for Ah

Pukuh. That blue guy had to be an actor. Max mentally awarded him full marks for historical accuracy. He was also impressed by the Oscar-worthy howls of terror that were emanating from the "victim."

Man, this was a weird party.

He looked around for the Plague Rats in the audience and gave them a halfhearted thumbs-up sign, more of a signal between survivors than anything. They responded enthusiastically, and he guessed from their rapt expressions that they were already planning to incorporate a little mock human sacrifice into their next performance.

Ah Pukuh lumbered to a position behind the altar.

He fumbled around inside his capacious robes and pulled out a razor-edged obsidian dagger.

The audience gasped.

"For tonight's grand finale," announced Ah Pukuh, "I will pluck out the beating heart from this human body and have it served to the newlyweds for their wedding breakfast—"

A bloodcurdling scream from Lola interrupted him.

She was on her feet and yelling hysterically at her future husband. *No! You can't do this! You promised me! YOU PROMISED—!*

Without even looking at her, Antonio de Landa darted out one black-gloved hand, fast as a lizard's tongue catching a fly, and grabbed her wrist to restrain her.

With the other hand, he snapped his fingers.

A posse of guards appeared, and Landa made a gesture to indicate that Lola should be conveyed from his presence with all speed.

The guards dragged her, still screaming, off the stage.

Ah Pukuh, who seemed to think the evening was going swimmingly, waved her good-bye. "It seems the bride has a tender heart." He looked down at the blue guy. "And speaking of hearts, it's time to say *adiós, amigo*. . . ."

"Eh-stop!" screamed the blue guy. "Eh-stop!"

Santino?

Santino?

Max felt sick, confused, terrified, frozen to the spot.

His makeup running and his lipstick smeared, Ah Pukuh's eyes glittered with bloodlust as he raised the dagger high above Santino's chest.

"Prepare to die, you wretch!" he thundered.

"Eh-stop! Eh-stop!"

Bang!

The sound of gunfire somewhere in the palace broke Ah Pukuh's spell. The crowd, suddenly galvanized, began to scream and run.

Ah Pukuh looked around in irritation. This was his favorite bit of the program, and he was losing his audience.

"Prepare to die, you wretch!" he repeated, in his most menacing god-of-violent-and-unnatural-death voice.

But no one was listening.

Panic was sweeping through the room.

"*Fuego! Fuego!*"

There was an intense smell of smoke.

"*Fuego! FUEGO!*"

People were fighting to get out of the crypt.

"*FUEGO! FUEGO!*"

Now distant fire alarms could be heard in the palace above.

Count Antonio de Landa's ears pricked up. He listened

for a few moments. He sniffed the air. And then, still wearing the Yellow Jaguar necklet, he flew down the stage steps like a bat out of hell and barged through the screaming partygoers to make it to the stairs.

"Come back! Come back!" screeched Ah Pukuh, but the bridegroom was gone. The god of violent and unnatural death was furious as he looked around the crypt. No one was listening to him anymore. His big moment was lost.

As Max tried to slip away, he brushed against a cymbal.

Ah Pukuh wheeled around, incandescent with rage.

"Are you still here, you worm?" he thundered. "I have a good mind to finish you off, right now. Choose how you want to die, Max Murphy. As long as it's violent and unnatural, I will be happy to oblige."

A sprinkler system burst into action above his head.

Max watched, openmouthed, as the resulting downpour gouged streaks into Ah Pukuh's makeup, plastered his long hair to his skull, and saturated his robes, making them cling repulsively to the rolls of fat beneath. Even for a dweller of the underworld, it was not a good look.

"What are you staring at?" Ah Pukuh asked, hurling the sacrificial dagger at Max's heart. Max grabbed a cymbal to use as a shield, and the dagger bounced off it with an ominous crash.

Cowering behind the bass drum, Max decided this was probably not a good moment to confront the god about giving away the Yellow Jaguar.

"I'll get you, Max Murphy," snarled Ah Pukuh as he squelched offstage. "You and everyone you know are dead meat."

Max extricated himself from the drums, retrieved the

dagger, and ran over to the altar, where Santino appeared to have passed out.

"Wake up!" shouted Max, shaking the law student's shoulders.

Santino opened his eyes, took one look at Max, and screwed them tight shut again. "Eh-stay away from me, you devil!" he said.

"Santino!" repeated Max, more urgently. "Wake up! We've got to get out of here."

Santino opened one eye. "How do you know my name?"

"It's me, Max Murphy. You rescued me from the police station this morning. . . ."

Santino studied Max's features. "No," he said. "You have black hair. Max Murphy is a *pelirrojo*."

Max sawed at the ropes with the dagger. "I haven't got time to argue. There's a fire; we need to get out of here."

"Is it really you? But you were supposed to leave eh-Spain tonight."

"I took the wrong bus," said Max. "What are you doing here?"

"Looking for Señorita Lola, of course. You said Antonio de Landa was the only person she knew in eh-Spain, so I thought it was worth coming to eh-speak with him. Why did she not tell me that she was betrothed?"

"Let's go ask her in person," said Max, cutting through the last rope.

"No," said Santino, sitting up and rubbing his wrists and ankles. "She has made a fool of me. I never want to see her again."

"At least, let's find out what's going on . . . ?"

"All I need to know is that I was nearly eh-slaughtered tonight. I am going to the police."

"Please don't, Santino!" begged Max. "I can't explain now, but one day soon, you'll know what this was all about. The whole world is in danger, and it's up to me to save it."

Santino regarded him with pity. "Are you not a little old for such games?"

"It's not a game. Besides, do you really think the police will believe that Landa threw a party in his family crypt, and the Maya god of lineage came back and showed him his ancestors? Or that the Maya god of violent and unnatural death, who was posing as the manager of a rock band, tied you to an altar and tried to sacrifice you?"

"Doña Carmela was right about you," said Santino. "You are evil, Max Murphy."

In a flash, he had grabbed the dagger and jumped off the stage, his blue skin disappearing into the darkness of the crypt and the stairs beyond.

The smell of burning was getting stronger.

"No! Wait! I'm one of the good guys!" called Max, but Santino was gone.

Chapter Seventeen

AN UNHAPPY REUNION

A s he climbed up the stairs from the crypt, Max wondered who'd be waiting at the top. Ah Pukuh? Count de Landa? Or Santino Garcia, armed with the razor-edged sacrificial dagger?

At this point, he didn't know which one of them scared him more.

In the event, he fell over the skinny, leather-clad legs of Vince Vermin, who was lying facedown on the floor.

"Vince! Are you okay? You've got to get out of here. All this smoke—"

Vince groaned. Already too weak to stand from smoke inhalation, the lead guitarist was fading fast.

Max turned him over, grabbed him by the armpits, and pulled him backward along the corridor. Vince was surprisingly light for an adult. But then again, Max speculated, punk rockers had to be thin to look good in leather pants.

The palace was in chaos. There was much screaming and wailing and a faint smell of barbecued pork. Liveried servants ran to and fro with hoses and buckets of water.

Max found some French doors and dragged Vince out into the night air. The earlier heavy rain had given way to light drizzle, and he collapsed with his cargo onto the wet grass.

"You're safe now," he said, panting from the exertion of his rescue effort.

Gradually, Vince regained consciousness. "Wow, that was intense," he mumbled. "I owe you one, kid."

Max smiled. "That's easy. Give me a shout-out when you play Boston in the fall. Ah Pukuh gave me front-row tickets."

"Boston? In the fall?"

"Have you forgotten? You must be groggy from the smoke. It's the start of your big *End of the World* tour, remember?" Max jabbed at his own chest. Speaking slowly and loudly, he read out the words on his shirt. "El . . . Fin . . . del . . . Mundo? The End of the World?"

Vince stared at the shirt. "I wondered wot that meant," he said.

"Seriously? You've never heard of it?"

"It's news to me, man. Sounds like you've been 'ad."

He'd been had.

That figured.

Not for the first time that night, Max asked himself what he'd been thinking to trust Ah Pukuh. How was it possible that, after all he'd been through in San Xavier, he was ready to drop his guard and hand over the Yellow Jaguar in exchange for a T-shirt, some pizza, and four fake Plague Rats tickets?

Was he really that shallow?

Yeah, he was.

He must be, or he wouldn't have done it.

"'Ere, are you cryin'?" asked Vince.

"I've got smoke in my eyes," lied Max.

Next minute, Vince and Max were knocked sideways as a sweaty heap of black leather landed on top of them. It was Trigger and Ty making a reunion pig pile.

"Wotcha!" Trigger greeted Max, rolling off and slapping him on the back.

"'Ere, go easy on 'im," protested Vince. "'E just saved my life. Rescued me from the blazin' inferno, 'e did. Our Max is a regular little 'ero! An' to fink that Ah Pukuh's been 'avin' a larf at 'is expense. 'E gave Max some tickets for a gig that ain't even 'appenin'!"

Ty giggled. "Never trust yer manager, kid—first rule of rock 'n' roll!"

"He lied to me about other things as well," admitted Max.

"'E's gettin' too big for 'is boots, that Ah Pukuh. I didn't like 'is tone tonight. You should 'ave a word with 'im, Vince. Tell 'im wot's wot," said Trigger. He grabbed a bottle of water and poured it on his own head. "And next time, make sure 'e checks the fire certificate. Blimey, it was 'ot in there."

"Did you 'ear wot caused it?" asked Ty. "Some geezer let off a musket in the library. It's burnt to a crisp."

"Great party, though," said Vince.

"An' you did a good job on drums," said Ty to Max.

"Odd-Eye will be off 'is feet for weeks," observed Trigger.

The three Plague Rats exchanged meaningful glances.

"So 'ow about it, kid?" asked Ty.

The three Plague Rats looked at Max expectantly.

"How about what?" he asked.

"Wanna be our drummer?" asked Vince.

Max couldn't believe his ears. "Me? A Rat?"

"Why not? We'll fire that loser Ah Pukuh an' get ourselves a decent manager. We've got some sweet gigs comin' up: Madrid, Rome, Paris . . . ," wheedled Trigger.

"Ever kissed a French girl?" asked Ty.

"You'll be livin' the dream, kid," said Vince. "So 'ow about it?"

"It's a great offer," said Max.

"Let's get on the bus and talk about it," said Vince.

"Wot's to talk about?" asked Ty as they walked across the lawn. "Every kid wants to play in a rock band."

"I know," said Max glumly. "But Ah Pukuh—"

"I told you, we'll fire 'im. 'E's 'istory."

"Wot's yer problem, kid? You 'ad fun tonight, didn't you? I mean before fings went crazy. . . ."

"Yes, but . . ."

But what? Max asked himself.

He'd lost the Yellow Jaguar. Lord 6-Dog was dead. Lola was getting married. In the morning, he'd have two days left to live. Why not spend his last hours on earth as the drummer of his favorite band?

He climbed aboard the tour bus.

The Plague Rats cheered and clapped and stamped their feet.

Max looked around longingly at all the trappings of rockstardom, the plasma screens, the fully stocked fridges, the reclining seats.

And he heard Lola's voice in his head, saying, "*Turn around, Hoop. It's people that matter, not things.*"

And Lola mattered more than anyone.

He sighed. "I'm sorry, guys, but I can't come. Not tonight."

Before they could stop him, he jumped off the bus.

The Plague Rats stood in the door, calling to him.

"I don't get it," said Vince.

"This is yer big chance, kid!" shouted Ty.

"We should've shut the door before 'e could escape," said Trigger.

"'E's just messin' with us," pronounced Ty confidently. "No one walks away from fame and fortune and French girls. . . ."

"Get back on the bus, Max Murphy," said Vince. His tone sounded slightly threatening. "Or you'll regret this for the rest of yer life."

Yeah, all two days of it, thought Max. "I'm grateful, honestly I am," he said, "but there's someone I have to find first. I could meet you tomorrow . . . ?"

"It's now or never," said Vince.

"Then it's good-bye," said Max after only a second's hesitation. "And thank you. I'll never forget the night I was drummer for the Plague Rats."

Trigger burst out laughing, quickly followed by the other two. They were snorting and honking, the tears running down their faces.

"You actually think—" began Trigger.

"—that a band like the Plague Rats—" continued Ty.

"—would be interested in a runt like *you*?" finished Vince, wiping his eyes.

"But you just asked me . . . ," pointed out Max.

"Massimo Francis Sylvanus Murphy," said Trigger, "will you never learn?"

"The Plague Rats aren't even British," sniggered Ty.

"They're from Boston, like you!" Vince was wiping away tears of laughter.

I knew that, thought Max. *I knew that.*

"We punked 'im good, lads," cheered Vince.

"You can drop the accent now!" Trigger pointed out.

The three black-leather-clad punks exchanged high fives.

And their black leather began to grow greasy brown fur.

Their noses became more pointed, their cheeks sprouted whiskers, their teeth became longer, their hands turned into claws.

Max met Vince's pale pink eyes. "I saved you from the fire," he said accusingly.

"More fool you," squeaked the aptly named Vince Vermin.

As Max watched in horror, his bandmates shrank back into the disgusting, disease-ridden sewer rats they really were. Instinctively he threw his backpack at them, and they scurried away into the bushes, their long, scaly tails glinting in the moonlight.

As for the bus, it was nothing but a pile of rusting tin cans.

It was his own personal Cinderella story, reflected Max, with rats and cans instead of mice and a pumpkin.

But where was his fairy godmother when he needed her?

What would have happened to him if he'd joined the band?

Where would that ghoulish bus have taken him?

When the clock struck twelve, would he have found himself down in the sewers with the rest of the Rats?

Most important of all, when would he, Max Murphy, stop falling for Ah Pukuh's tricks?

Now it was clear to him that the real Plague Rats were on tour in Japan, just as Nasty had said. The band Max and Nasty had seen at the airport was the same band that had just turned into rodents. No wonder they couldn't play their instruments. Like the tour bus, and the hellhounds that had herded Max onto it, they'd been conjured up by Ah Pukuh to lull him into handing over the Yellow Jaguar.

And he'd fallen for it.

Now that he thought about it, there was something else—something even more unlikely than the Plague Rats inviting him to join them—that he'd allowed himself to believe recently.

Furious at his own stupidity, Max ran back to the palace to find Lola.

By following a human chain of servants passing along buckets of water, Max traced the source of the fire to what was left of Landa's library.

It was bad.

Smoke hung heavy in the air.

Ruined books, manuscripts, and paintings were heaped in charred and dripping piles in the center of the room. The wood paneling was scorched and peeling. Shattered glass from the windows crunched underfoot.

As Max surveyed the sorry scene, he heard someone talking in a side room. He stepped behind a pillar and listened.

First came Landa's voice, shrill and whiny: "My head aches so much! What a terrible night!"

Then Lola's voice, calm and reassuring: "It's okay, Toto, relax."

It was all Max could do not to vomit on the spot. *Toto? She called him Toto?*

"I have been planning this night all my life and that *idiota* Ah Pukuh had to ruin it! What was he thinking? To bring them back without any warning! Humiliating me like that in front of my guests . . ."

Lola tried to soothe his ego. "I'm sure no one knew it was for real. They probably all thought it was a show. They will think it was hilarious that you were pretending to be so scared."

"I was not scared! I was angry!"

"If you say so, Toto."

Landa was still ranting. "Those stinking peasants dare to come in here, into my sanctum, touching my family heirlooms—"

"But they *are* your family. Those peasants are your ancestors. They can't help being poor."

"Can they help being *stupid*? Who but a madman would let off a firearm in a library?"

"It was an accident, Toto. Just be happy that no one died in the fire—"

"Happy? *Happy?*" Landa thumped angrily on the nearest table, and its fire-damaged timbers splintered under his fist. "For five hundred years, my family has hauled itself up the social ladder, rung by rung. We have transformed ourselves from pig farmers into nobility. And all the proof was in this room. Birth certificates, title deeds, documents, oil paintings . . ." He groaned, as if he'd suddenly remembered something. "My new acquisition . . . a diary written by Friar Diego himself. And now it's gone, all gone."

"I'm sorry about your old books and things, Toto, but—"

"*Old books and things?*" he thundered. "My family history has been burned to ashes—do you not understand?"

There was a silence as charged as an electric shock and as cold as liquid nitrogen.

Then Lola's voice again: "It was Friar Diego who burned the history of *my* people to ashes."

"Then we are even, are we not?" snapped Landa.

"Oh, Toto, let's not argue on our wedding night. Tomorrow I will be a countess and you will be a Jaguar King."

A pause.

Then Landa's voice, conciliatory. "You are right. Forgive me for speaking sharply, Princess. I have such a pain in my head, I am not thinking clearly."

"But you will keep your promise?"

"My word is my bond."

"So why was poor Santino Garcia nearly sacrificed tonight?"

"He was snooping around. How was I to know he was a friend of yours? But no harm done."

"No harm done? He was painted blue and tied to an altar. Oh, Toto, I don't expect you to like all my friends, but that's just plain bad manners. Who knows what would have happened to Santino if one of your ancestors hadn't fired off that musket. . . ."

"It was not a musket," said Landa. "It was a harquebus."

There was another pause.

"You have so much to teach me, Toto," said Lola. Max was shocked to hear by her tone. It was almost flirtatious.

"Yes," said Landa, "I do." He sniffed the smoky air. "But first I must go and teach my imbecile servants how to put out a fire. . . ."

"And I need to prepare for our big day. May I try on the yellow necklet, Toto? It would go so well with my wedding dress."

"I am sorry, Princess, but it is mine, all mine, and I will never be parted from it."

"You have to give it back to Ah Pukuh."

"Never."

He's a lot braver now than the sniveling wimp from earlier tonight, thought Max. *Wearing the Yellow Jaguar has changed him.*

"But you swore to him, Toto. You swore to Ah Pukuh that you would return it. I thought your word was your bond?"

"I think we both know me better than that."

Lola let out a little scream of joy. "You mean we're keeping it?"

"I mean *I'm* keeping it."

Lola ignored this subtle distinction. "Oh, Toto! We have our very own Jaguar Stone! I *must* wear it at the wedding tomorrow. Just imagine your guests' faces as they see me walking down the aisle. They'll know that you have riches beyond their wildest dreams. And if a silly girl like me isn't scared to wear it, they'll realize that tonight's, er, *spectacle* was just a bit of fun."

"*Bueno.*" At this juncture, Max pictured Landa stroking his ludicrous goatee as he thought through Lola's vision. "But can I trust you to give it back?"

Lola laughed. "You don't *need* to trust me, silly. I have no choice. Once we're married, all that I have is yours. I'm just a woman, Toto. My job is to look pretty, make tortillas, and bear children. What would I do with a Jaguar Stone?"

Her fiancé made a high-pitched braying sound. It took a few seconds before Max realized he was laughing. "What indeed?" agreed Landa.

"So may I wear the necklet? Please! Please! Please!" Lola sounded like a little girl jumping up and down with excitement. "I want to try it on right now, so I can practice fixing my hair for the wedding."

"Very well, why not? As my bride, you may wear the Jaguar Stone. But straight after the ceremony, you will give it back."

"Your wish is my command, Toto."

There was a clanking of beads as Landa took off the necklace and retied it around Lola's neck.

"I have been a bachelor for too long," he murmured. "I look forward to having a woman about the place."

"I can still smell burning," said Lola quickly. "I hope the fire isn't spreading."

Max heard Landa's pointed black boots click on the tile floor as he rushed out of the library. Then, *No! No! No! Idiotas!* as he chided the hapless servants in the corridor.

Okay, so this was awkward.

How would he reveal himself to Lola, without her knowing he'd been eavesdropping?

"You can come out now, Hoop," she called. "By the way, I like your hair. Not sure about the makeup."

Max froze.

"Come out!" she repeated.

Bossy. Bossy. Bossy.

"How did you know I was there?"

"You never were much good at hiding," she said. "Remember the first day we met? How I snuck up on you by the clearing?"

"Yeah," said Max. He came out from behind the pillar. "I also remember that you were supposed to meet me in the square at Polvoredo. What happened?"

Lola avoided his eyes. "I'm sorry about that, Hoop. It all happened so quickly. Toto and I fell in love."

She was wearing the yellow necklet.

She looked beautiful. Like a princess.

"By *Toto*, you mean Antonio de Landa?"

"Yes! Isn't it wonderful? We're getting married tomorrow!"

"Antonio de Landa? The guy who stalked you and drugged you and held a gun to your head at the Black Pyramid?"

"Oh, that. It was all a big misunderstanding. He's explained everything. He was taking me to the top of the pyramid to *propose* to me, not to sacrifice me. He wanted the Maya gods to bless our union. He says it's written in the stars. That's why he collected all those photographs of me. He says I'm the only one for him. But now he understands that a proposal is more romantic if the bride is fully conscious at the time."

"Oh, come on, Lola! We're talking about a descendant of the guy who destroyed Maya culture!"

"That's ancient history. Let it go."

"*Let it go?* What about our mission? Have you forgotten why we came to Spain in the first place?"

"I'm sorry, Hoop, my plans have changed."

"How can you stand there and say that, wearing the Yellow Jaguar? Do you know what I went through to get that thing? I walked through a giant snake, I talked to a ghost, I survived an earthquake. . . ."

"I said I'm sorry. I'll sort it out. Ah Pukuh is our best man. I'll have a word with him tomorrow and ask him to cancel your debt. But you need to go now. Toto gets very jealous. He has this crazy idea that you and me had a thing."

"We still have a thing! We're the Hero Twins! Come with me, help me deliver the Yellow Jaguar to Xibalba—and then marry Landa if you want to."

"It's not that simple."

"Why not?"

She bit her lip. "He needs me."

"What did you mean when you asked him to keep his promise? What did he promise you?"

"He promised to love me forever and ever."

"You're lying; I know you are. Come with me, Lola. I'll help you escape, somewhere he can't find you—"

"I don't want to escape."

"What about Hermanjilio and Lucky Jim? Are you abandoning them?"

"I'll have more chance to help my people when I'm a wealthy aristocrat."

"What? You've never wanted money."

"You don't know what I want."

"What about Lady Coco? Is she here?"

"No. I haven't seen her since Polvoredo."

"Where is she?"

"The monkeys can look after themselves. They'll be fine."

"Lord 6-Dog isn't fine. He was shot."

A look of pain flashed across Lola's face. "You need to go," she said, turning her back to him. "I have a wedding to get ready for."

Max stared at her. "That's kind of selfish, isn't it?"

She faced him again. Now her eyes were hard. "You should know," she said. "You're the world expert on selfishness. Why don't you just go and leave me alone? I have a new life now."

"You can't stay here with that madman."

"That's my fiancé you're talking about."

"It's all a trick, Lola. Do you know why he calls you *Princess?*"

"He thinks I have royal blood."

"He's using you. He's pretending you're a Maya princess, so he can rewrite history. He wants to do what his ancestor Lorenzo never could and marry Princess Inez, so he can inherit the Jaguar Throne and the castle at Polvoredo and who knows what else?"

"How do you know I'm *not* a princess?"

"Because baby princesses don't get abandoned."

Lola flinched as if he'd slapped her.

"I'm sorry, I didn't mean—"

"Get out!" she snapped. "I never want to see you again!"

They heard the click of Landa's boots returning.

Lola picked up a stack of charred papers and began to sort them.

"Toto!" Lola's face lit up as her husband-to-be entered the library. Her expression changed to concern. "Are you limping? Did you hurt yourself out there? Oh, my brave firefighter! Let me find you a chair. . . ."

Landa's cold gaze fell on Max. "And who is this? He looks familiar to me."

"He should look familiar, Toto. He's one of the famous Plague Rats. They played at our party tonight!"

Landa surveyed Max with distaste. "A princess does not associate with the hired help."

"It was you I was looking for, sir," said Max. "I wanted to ask you something—"

"My fiancé is tired," said Lola. "Now is not a good time. I'm sure the rest of your band are waiting for you—"

"Actually," said Max, "they've gone without me. I was hoping I could crash here tonight."

"That's out of the question," said Lola. "It's late, we've

had a fire, and there's a small matter of a wedding tomorrow. My fiancé will arrange a car for you, señor. Are you hungry?"

Max nodded his head hopefully.

"I will go and find some leftovers for your journey."

She put down the charred papers and swept out to the kitchen.

Landa took Max by the elbow and steered him toward the library door. "My driver will take you where you want to go, señor. But tell me, what was your question?"

"It was something you said at the party, sir, about the historic union of two great bloodlines?"

"Ah," said Landa, "you are interested in genealogy?"

"You said this marriage would fulfill your family's destiny. What destiny is that?"

"It will be the final jewel in the Landa crown. I will attain the greatest prize of all. . . ."

"Which is . . . ?"

"Immortality!"

"And how does that work exactly?"

"Thanks to my wife of royal Maya lineage, I will unite old and new worlds. When my best man, Ah Pukuh, takes power in the next *bak'tun*, he has promised me the throne of Middleworld while he himself rules the cosmos!"

Max stared at him openmouthed. He was insane.

Surely Lola couldn't be in love with this raving megalomaniac.

But there she was now, at his side, face shining with admiration.

"Brrr," she said. "I love your Galicia, Toto, but I wish it was as warm as San Xavier!" She gripped a woolen shawl tightly around her and held out a brown bag of food for Max. "Safe journey, señor."

And with that she turned away to carry on sorting fire-damaged papers.

"Good night, Princess" said Max.

She didn't even look around as he said good-bye forever.

Out in the hallway, Landa was shouting orders in Spanish, and flustered servants were scurrying around at his beck and call. He screamed at a little maid who was scrubbing the floor and kicked over her bucket. Then an old man carrying a tray of wineglasses slipped in the water and fell at his employer's feet. Instead of helping him up, Landa aimed a savage kick to the old man's head.

Glad to be escaping from within reach of those pointed black boots, Max slipped outside and looked for the car that had been arranged for him. A shiny black stretch limousine with darkened windows materialized out of the gloom.

The rear door opened and Max got in.

As they rolled down the gravel driveway, he relived his meeting with Lola. How had it gone so wrong? He couldn't believe that she'd stayed behind with Landa and the Yellow Jaguar. Of all the people who might have scuppered his mission, he never thought it would be her.

He felt sick.

Sick because he had only two days left to live.

Sick because Lord 6-Dog had died in vain.

Sick because Lola wasn't the person he thought she was.

She was no better than those sewer rats.

They'd been on the road for quite a while, when he realized that the driver hadn't asked for a destination.

But where should he go?

To Polvoredo?

To San Xavier?

He made up his mind.

He was done with all of it. He'd had enough of Spain. He was finished with the Maya. He'd failed in his quest and he was going home. Let the Death Lords do their worst.

He just hoped he could get to the airport in time for the first flight to Boston.

He tried to open the sliding-glass window between himself and the driver. It was locked.

He looked around for an intercom system but couldn't find one.

He tapped on the window. "Airport! Airport!" he shouted.

The driver paid no attention.

They seemed to be going very fast. Max was thrown to one side or another every time they took a bend in the road. The world was dark outside the car, but every so often the headlights illuminated trees and hedgerows in the drizzle.

Max knocked again on the glass.

"Slow down!" he yelled.

If anything, the driver went faster.

Now Max was kneeling on the floor of the limo, rapping with both hands on the glass. "Stop! Where are we going? I want the airport. *Air-o-porto!*"

The driver didn't even turn around.

Then, in a moment that would give him icy chills for as long as he lived, Max Murphy looked in the rearview mirror. The driver met his eyes and smiled. It was the driver from the tour bus. The Fast Bus to Hell.

They were gathering speed, careening wildly down wet country lanes in the pitch-black night.

Max sat back on the seat and frantically tried his door handle.

Locked, of course.

He had a very bad feeling that this ride could only end in death.

(And he was right.)

They seemed to be entering a village now.

Little houses flashed by in the headlights. Inside those houses, good people were sleeping, unaware that a demon from hell was racing through their dreams on a shortcut home.

There was a bump, a thud, a screech of brakes, and an almighty impact as the limo crashed into a stone wall.

Max was thrown out of his seat and hit his head hard against the door.

Slightly concussed, he got to his knees and peeped out the window.

Lights were coming on in the little houses, and he could see people converging on the car from all directions.

The driver got out and started to run.

Max banged on the glass. "Help! Help!" he called.

An old man put his toothless face against the rain-spattered window.

The face disappeared, to be replaced by a shotgun.

Max pressed himself into the farthest corner of the limo.

Bang! The old man blew the lock off the limo door.

The door swung open, and Max climbed nervously out into the drizzle. An old woman with a pitchfork grabbed his arm. She was shrieking and crying and pointing at something on the wet road.

It was a flattened goose.

Max tried to look sorry for the scrawny fowl that had met its end under the wheels of his limo. But inside he was not sorry at all. There was no doubt in his mind that it had been the goose or him. He didn't know what gruesome fate the driver had planned for him. All he knew was that if that goose had not run across the road when it had, it would have been Max Murphy who was dead meat.

A group of angry farmers had caught the driver and were dragging him back to the scene of the accident. As the villagers clustered around, accusing him and prodding him and screaming at him, Max sank into the background. His head was throbbing from the accident, and all this shouting was making it worse. He wandered down the lane to find somewhere quiet and dry to sit down.

Eventually, he came to a barn.

It didn't smell too bad inside, although the floor was wet and muddy.

He listened for the sounds of cows or horses but heard nothing but the dripping rain.

He stumbled against a long box on the ground, filled with straw. Some kind of animal feeder, he supposed. The straw looked comfortable. Head aching and brain in a whirl, he decided to lie down for a moment. *Makes a pretty good single bed*, he thought as he drifted off to sleep, his backpack clutched to his chest, lulled by the patter of rain on the barn roof.

Chapter Eighteen
DAY OF THE LIVING DEAD

Max Murphy lay in his coffin, gasping for air.

He'd been buried alive.

The wooden coffin was exactly the same size as his body, as if it had been tailor-made for him. It was unbearably hot in there, and he had a sense of motion, like the rolling of a ship, which was making him feel dizzy. His arms were pinned to his sides but, gathering the last of his strength, he curled his hands into fists and began to pummel weakly on the lid.

To his surprise, it flew open easily.

At first, all he saw was a gray sky and a bird of prey—a vulture?—hovering above him. He could hear whistling and screaming and raucous laughter. He peered over the edge of the coffin and locked eyes with a fluorescent green devil. All around him, hideous ghouls were thrusting their garishly painted faces at him and clicking their fat tongues. The Grim Reaper floated by, pursued by a dancing skeleton.

There was a smell of bonfires. A wailing of bagpipes

filled the smoky air like the screeching of a cat having its claws pulled out one by one.

Was this some kind of hell?

Had he died in the car crash after all?

He lay still and did a pain check. Nope, nothing was hurting.

But did the dead feel pain?

He peered over the side again and tried to make sense of what he saw.

He was in the middle of a funeral procession.

In front of him and behind him, a crowd of sobbing people dressed in black were making their way up a steep hill. Most walked in groups of four or six, each group carrying an open coffin between them on their shoulders. From his vantage point, Max could see the corpses coming up the hill behind him: men, women, and children, lying white and silent in their Sunday best, all carried by solemn pallbearers.

Max leaned over the side to see who was carrying *his* coffin.

A phalanx of stout old ladies looked up at him disapprovingly. One of them had his backpack slung over her shoulder.

"Put me down," he shouted. "I want to get out! I'm alive!"

At his words, a cheer went up, but still the old ladies held his coffin high.

A bell was tolling as a church came into sight at the top of the hill.

They headed past the church and into a graveyard at the far side. It was lined with gray stone tombs. Some tombs were like ornately carved miniature houses with wrought-iron front doors; others were more like rows of school lockers, with empty slots waiting to receive new tenants.

Max's blood ran cold.

At some invisible signal, the pallbearers set the coffins down.

Max tried to get up, ready to run, but the old women pushed him back with surprising force. One of them brandished a spade.

Was that to dig his grave?

A hush fell over the crowd, broken only by sobs and wails.

Max's old women regarded him lovingly, while holding him down with muscles of iron. They took turns letting go of him to dab their eyes.

All he could see were their faces and the gray sky. And the vultures wheeling overhead.

Firecrackers exploded like gunfire.

People screamed and laughed.

A Gypsy band began to play.

Finally the old women released their grip, and Max scrambled out of the coffin. All around the graveyard the recently arrived corpses were sitting up and waving at one another. Then, encouraged by their mourners, the living dead leapt out of their coffins and began dancing to the band.

Max's personal pallbearers urged him to do the same.

It seemed rude not to obey after they'd lugged him up the hill.

An old lady clutched him to her and led him in a spirited tango. Feeling extremely self-conscious, he tried to channel the Gypsy in his soul and dance wildly in the churchyard, while the spectators clapped and threw flowers.

He caught a flower and tucked it behind his ear.

The old women hustled and jigged and twirled him between them, cackling like witches, until their cardigans fell off their shoulders and their woolen stockings bunched at the ankles.

Max was aware of tourist cameras clicking and flashing. At least he was still wearing stage makeup from the night before, so there was a good chance no one would recognize him if the footage turned up on YouTube.

"Mac? Is that you?"

No. It couldn't be.

Please, please, no.

Not Nasty Smith-Jones.

Not here.

Not now.

Max tried to hide behind a conga line.

"Mac! It *is* you! Don't you remember me?"

Nasty cut in on the old women and started dancing with him. She seemed genuinely happy to see him. She even took his flower and put it behind her own ear.

"Wow!" she said. "I love your black hair! And what's with the makeup? Are you wearing *guy*-liner? It's so great to see you, Mac! I haven't talked to anyone my own age since we've been in Spain!"

"It's good to see you, too," replied Max, noticing again her big blue eyes. "But my name is *Max*. It's short for *Massimo*. My mother's Italian. From Venice." (Was this too much information? Was he babbling? *Stay cool, man*, he told himself.)

"Got it! Max short for Massimo!" repeated Nasty, giggling. She noticed his shirt. "Is that a Plague Rats T-shirt? I haven't seen that one before. . . ." She studied it more closely. "You know it's a fake, right?"

Max nodded ruefully.

"Still, it's a cool souvenir," said Nasty. "I was right, though: the real Plague Rats are still in Japan. Those guys at the airport must have been some kind of tribute band. Pretty convincing, huh?"

"They sure fooled me," agreed Max. "I heard they played a private party last night and the drummer was really good."

"That's a first," said Nasty, laughing. "So what are you doing here, Max-short-for-Massimo?"

"I'm on vacation, like you."

"No, I mean, what are you doing in a graveyard, dancing with old ladies?"

"Honestly? I don't know. I fell asleep in an old wooden box full of straw and when I woke up this morning I was being carried along in this parade. I don't even know what town this is."

Nasty laughed. "You're at the Fiesta of the Near-Death Experience in Santa Marta. Anyone who's had a close call and lived to tell the tale gets to ride in a coffin."

"How do you know this?"

Nasty pulled a guidebook to northwest Spain out of her pocket. "So *did* you?" she asked.

"Did I what?"

"Have a near-death experience?"

My whole life is a near-death experience right now, Max wanted to answer. But he didn't want to frighten her away, so he answered as flippantly as he could. "Yeah, I guess so. My cab ran over a goose."

"I'm glad you're okay." She smiled at him. "I like the hair, but your makeup's a bit messed up. Want a Kleenex?"

They sat on a wall, and Max wiped away the greasepaint with tissues and bottled water.

"What have you been doing in Spain?" he asked Nasty.

She groaned. "We've visited every historic building between here and Madrid." She pulled out the guidebook and opened it at random. "'The pilgrimage city of Santiago de Compostela is famous for its Romanesque cathedral,'" she read. She looked over the top of her sunglasses and put on a schoolmarm voice. "The Romanesque style has rounded arches, whereas Gothic arches are pointed, don't you know?"

He laughed. "I'm impressed."

"Don't be," she said. "I'm hating every minute of it. What have *you* been doing?"

She wouldn't have believed him if he told her.

"Not much," he said.

"Well, I'm glad I ran into you."

"Ditto!"

They grinned at each other.

It felt great, Max realized, to be with someone from the normal world, someone who'd never heard of Jaguar Stones or hellhounds or Death Lords. It felt *so* great that he had an overwhelming urge to tell her everything—just to hear how silly it all sounded.

"You won't believe this—" he began.

"Anastasia! There you are! We've been looking everywhere for you!"

Nasty's parents trooped over, loaded down with flowers, postcards, plastic coffins, skeletons, shawls, umbrellas, soft toys, and everything else the opportunistic souvenir sellers had been able to unload on them.

"Who's this?" asked her mother, regarding Max with suspicion.

"This is . . . Massimo," said Nasty.

"He looks familiar," said Mrs. Smith-Jones.

"You've probably seen him in the society pages," said Nasty, winking at Max to warn him to play along. "He's an Italian aristocrat. . . . His family has a palace in Venice. . . ." Her eye fell on the guidebook. "We were just discussing architecture."

Nasty's parents exchanged a smirk. Max could tell from their faces that Massimo was exactly the kind of blue-blooded boy they'd been hoping their daughter would meet in Spain. So much more suitable than that red-haired punk she'd been talking to at the airport.

"Won't you join us for lunch, Massimo?" asked Mrs. Smith-Jones. "The guidebook recommends a place down the street."

He attempted a charming smile. "*Grazie, signora*," he said in his best Italian accent.

Mrs. Smith-Jones giggled and nudged her husband. "We're lunching with an Italian aristocrat," she said. "Imagine."

Nasty rolled her eyes. "My parents are driving me crazy," she whispered to Max as they walked down the street together. "They keep trying to talk to me."

"What about?"

"Anything. They want to have, like, *conversations*."

Max grimaced in sympathy.

"Here we are," said Mr. Smith-Jones, holding open the door of a restaurant. "This place is renowned for its local cuisine."

"Don't forget the Italian accent," Nasty whispered to Max as they went inside.

Before the rest of them had even looked at the menu, Mr. Smith-Jones ordered the house specialty for everyone. "Let's walk on the wild side," he said. "I always say that trying new foods is half the fun of traveling."

"He *does* always say that," sighed Nasty. "He says it everywhere we go."

The house specialty, when it came, was a foul-smelling vat of octopus, stewed in its own ink.

"Mmmm, looks good," said Mr. Smith-Jones without conviction.

"It looks disgusting," Nasty corrected him.

Mrs. Smith-Jones tucked a napkin into her husband's collar to protect his impeccably ironed designer polo shirt, then half turned her back so she wouldn't have to watch as he attacked the bowl of tentacles in front of him. "How long have you been in Spain, Massimo?" she asked, trying to ignore the slurping sounds coming from her husband.

How long *had* he been in Spain?

It felt like weeks, but it was only three days.

Three days in which everything had gone from bad to worse.

Lola was about to get married.

Lord 6-Dog was dead, and Lady Coco was missing in action.

And as for Max Murphy, who'd once thought he could outwit the Maya Lords of Death, he was on the run from the Spanish police and wanted dead or alive for murder. But as the Death Lords would be executing him in two days time, that seemed like the least of his worries.

What a mess. What a huge, stinking mess.

He groaned and put his head in his hands.

"Are you all right, Massimo?" asked Mrs. Smith-Jones. "Is something wrong?"

"You're giving him a headache with all your questions," said Nasty.

"I bet it's the sight of that octopus that's made him ill," said Mrs. Smith-Jones.

"Nonsense," said her father. "I'm sure they eat octopus all the time in Italy."

As Nasty and her parents bickered about the cause of his groans, Max took stock of his situation.

He'd blown it big-time.

There was no way he could make this okay.

It was all over. His adventure. His game plan. His life.

When he looked up, heavy rain was lashing the windows of the restaurant, and the families of the living dead were crowding inside, laughing and joking with one another.

Max wanted to see the people he loved one last time.

"I have to go home," he said, forgetting to sound Italian. "Are you going anywhere near the airport?"

"Sorry," said Mr. Smith-Jones, "but that's south, we're headed east to Bilbao." He winced as if someone had kicked him under the table.

"What my husband meant to say," explained Mrs. Smith-Jones, "is that we will be delighted to take you to the airport, Massimo. We'll drop you off at the airport and carry on to La Tomatina, the festival of overripe tomatoes in Valencia."

"But Madrid is six hours away," pointed out her husband.

"Good," she replied. "It will give Anastasia and Massimo a chance to get to know each other better."

For the first time in their vacation, Nasty gave her mother a big smile.

Chapter Nineteen

SHELL-SHOCKED

Have you noticed," said Max to Nasty, "that almost every woman we go past is pushing a wheelbarrow? Don't they have purses in Galicia?"

"Around here," said Nasty, "it's the women who work the land, while the men go out on the fishing boats."

"Don't tell me," said Max, genuinely impressed, "you read it in your guidebook."

He'd long ago dropped the Italian accent, but Nasty's parents didn't seem to have noticed. They were too busy navigating their way through the leafy, dripping lanes of Galicia, trying to find the highway to Madrid and the airport.

"Watch out for those people!" shrieked Mrs. Smith-Jones. "They're walking in the middle of the road."

Mr. Smith-Jones honked his horn, but it didn't do much good. The approaching hikers had their hoods up and their heads down. Some of them wore earphones, all of them were wet and miserable, and none of them were in a mood to huddle on the side of the road for the occupants of a dry, warm car to sweep past them.

As Mr. Smith-Jones maneuvered slowly by, Max noticed that each hiker wore a large white scallop shell on a string around his or her neck. (It was impossible to identify genders in the soggy throng of yellow rain ponchos.)

"What's with the shells?" asked Max.

Nasty waved the guidebook at him. "It's the symbol of Saint James. It shows they're pilgrims, walking to Santiago. If you're wearing a scallop shell, they feed you when you get to the cathedral."

"What do they feed you?" asked Max. He was starving. He hadn't eaten anything in that octopus restaurant.

Nasty shrugged. "I don't know. We were there yesterday, but we weren't wearing scallop shells. I'll tell you what's gross, though: they have an old statue of Saint James behind the altar, and everyone lines up to kiss it."

"Yeuch."

"I know, think of the germs," agreed Nasty. "But what's cool is the world's biggest incense burner. They fill it with burning coals, then hoist it up on ropes and swing it to and fro, like a crazy yoyo. It's supposed to disguise the smell of sweaty pilgrims. Everyone oohs and aahs because it looks totally out of control, like it's going to shoot through the window or fall on somebody's head."

"Has it ever killed anyone?" asked Max.

"Probably," said Nasty. "Here, you can read about it in the guidebook. Have it. Keep it."

"I'm flying home; I don't need a guidebook."

"Oh, yes you do," insisted Nasty, scrawling her e-mail address and phone number on the inside cover.

"Cool," said Max. He tried to shove the book into his backpack, but it wouldn't fit. Max pulled out the brown bag Lola had given him, to make room.

"What's in there?" asked Nasty.

"Food," replied Max. "I'd forgotten about it. Do you want some? It might be a bit squashed." He looked inside the bag. "There's some cookies, some bread, some cake . . . Wait, what's this . . . ?"

As Max's fingers burrowed down, he found something hard at the bottom, nestled on napkins.

What the . . . ?

He pulled it out.

It was wrapped in a piece of scorched paper.

He knew what it was before he opened it. . . .

The Yellow Jaguar.

There was a note hastily scrawled on the paper.

Hoop, go back to palace, find throne (look in bedroom), activate Yellow Jag, open portal. I'll keep Landa and AP busy in Santiago. Good luck in Xibalba! MG

Max sighed.

Bossy, bossy, bossy.

Oh, Monkey Girl, he thought, *what have you done?*

While he'd been hanging with the Rats, Lola had risked her life to put the mission back on course. She'd defied Landa and Ah Pukuh for him; they would kill her when they found out that she'd given him the Yellow Jaguar.

He remembered how she'd clutched a shawl tightly round her the last time he'd seen her. Now he knew that it was not to keep her warm, but to hide from Landa the fact that she no longer wore the necklet.

How could he ever have believed that his Monkey Girl was in love with that creepy count? He should have trusted his instincts. They were a team, and he'd abandoned her just like that in a smoking, burned-out library. Meanwhile, she was going to marry Landa, just to give Max time to get to Xibalba.

The question was, had her deception been discovered yet?

"Are you okay?" asked Nasty. "You're making strange groaning noises."

"I have to go to Santiago," he said

"Honestly, the incense burner isn't *that* exciting—"

"No, it's this necklet; I have to get it to my friend today. She's supposed to wear at her wedding. She'll die if I don't get it to her. . . ."

Nasty inspected the yellow beads. "It's a nice piece, very unusual, but she won't *die* without it. Can't she wear something else?"

"Nasty, I'm sorry; I know we've only just met and this must sound crazy, but I have to go to Santiago *now*."

"But it's in the opposite direction."

"Please help me. I promise I'll explain everything back in Boston."

Nasty looked at him. She took in his sweating brow and his shaking hands. She took a deep breath. "Okay," she said. "But I want the best pizza in Boston and a movie of my choosing, and you buy the popcorn."

"Done," said Max.

"So where's the invitation?"

Max pulled the crumpled card that Odd-Eye had given

him out of his back pocket and passed it to her.

Nasty studied it for a moment. "Mom! Listen to this!" she exclaimed, excitedly. "Massimo has just told me that a friend of his, a real live Spanish count, is getting married in the cathedral in Santiago today. Can you believe it? I've persuaded him to miss his flight and take us to the wedding! Oh, this will be the highlight of our vacation! Imagine the people we'll meet. . . ."

"I'm not going back to Santiago," said Mr. Smith-Jones, "and that's final."

"Now, dear," said his wife, "it's not every day we get invited to a society wedding in Spain! We'll be rubbing shoulders with the aristocracy! This could be the start of a whole new life for us. The bridge club will be green with envy!"

"No," said Mr. Smith-Jones.

"Not even if I throw away my list of museums and let you spend the rest of the vacation on the golf course . . . ?"

With a squeal of brakes, Mr. Smith-Jones executed a perfect U-turn. Ignoring the blue skies that beckoned them south to Madrid, they doubled back and set a course toward the black storm clouds looming over the old city of Santiago.

Chapter Twenty

LOLA'S WEDDING

espite the gathering storm, Santiago was abuzz with wedding preparations. Bells rang out from the medieval towers, their honey-colored stones shining gold in the rain. The arcaded galleries on the main square were decorated with garlands of yellow flowers that danced in the wind. Yellow petals blew through the streets like confetti and stuck on the rain-slick cobblestones. Damp white ribbons and bows fluttered from lampposts. And looking down on it all

was the great stone cathedral, immense and immovable, its three-story facade more ornate than any wedding cake.

"Shame about the weather," said Mrs. Smith-Jones as she watched the first wedding guests arrive, umbrellas blowing inside out and hats flying off across the square.

"We should go inside," said Mr. Smith-Jones, "before it starts to pour."

His wife surveyed him critically. They'd stopped at a rest area and changed into the best clothes they had in their suitcases, but she was still concerned that they looked like American tourists. Tutting to herself, she straightened her husband's tie and brushed a petal off the shoulder of his suit.

Then she turned her attention to Nasty. At her mother's insistence, Nasty had put on a white sundress and brushed her hair for the first time in weeks.

"It's nice to see you looking like a young lady for once," said Mrs. Smith-Jones. "Doesn't she look pretty, Massimo?"

Max nodded politely.

"I look stupid," Nasty whispered to him. "And so do you."

"I know," said Max miserably.

Nasty's father had forced him to borrow a white shirt, a tie, and a deeply uncool navy polyester blazer. Max particularly loathed the little anchors on the gold buttons.

"*Grazie, signor*, but eet eez not necessary," Max had protested in his terrible Italian accent.

"Yes, it most certainly *is* necessary, Massimo," countered Mrs. Smith-Jones. "If you're kind enough to take us to the wedding, the least we can do is lend you a jacket. I wouldn't dream of turning up improperly dressed for a society event, and I'm sure you feel the same. I'd rather not go than put you through that embarrassment."

Realizing that he was in danger of not getting to the wedding, Max had reluctantly surrendered to the Smith-

Joneses' sartorial ideas. But now that they stood on the streets of Santiago, one glance at his reflection in a shop window confirmed that he'd never looked less like an Italian aristocrat.

"That's where you get your boutonnieres, boys," said Mrs. Smith-Jones, pointing out a small man at the bottom of the steps who was handing out yellow flowers and pins to the male guests. To his horror, Max recognized the limo driver from the previous night among them.

He had to find another way in.

"Go with your parents and get some good seats," he said to Nasty, handing her the invitation. "I'll see you in there."

Nasty handed the invitation to her mother.

"You go with Dad and get some good seats," she said. "We'll see you in there."

When her mother hesitated, Nasty pointed to a woman in pink who was entering the cathedral. "Look! I think that's Crown Princess Valentina of Vienna! Maybe you can sit next to her if you hurry!"

"Don't be long, Anastasia," called her mother as she trotted off across the square, pulling her husband behind her.

"Go with them, Nasty," Max urged. "I have to find Lola."

"Lola's the bride, right?" asked Nasty.

"Yes. She must be in the cathedral somewhere. The wedding starts soon."

Nasty shook her head. "Don't you know anything about weddings? The bride is always last to arrive."

"She is? So where will she be?"

"Leave this to me."

Taking out her cell phone, Nasty pretended to be chatting away loudly with a friend as she walked through the square in the direction of some teenage girls who were dressed to the nines and obviously on their way to the wedding. "Yeah, no, I know, I know, I *know*. . . . No, I haven't seen her yet; hold on, I'll ask. . . ." As she passed the girls, she asked them casually, "So, have you seen the bride? What's her dress like?"

The girls started twittering and chirping like excited starlings. "We don't know, we haven't seen her yet; she's still in her room at the hotel." They pointed at a large stone building next door to the cathedral and carried on their way.

Nasty smiled triumphantly at Max.

"Impressive," he said. "Let's go."

The hotel was extremely fancy, all red carpets and gilded pillars.

"Give me the necklet," whispered Nasty.

She marched up to the reception desk. "Excuse me," she said, sounding breathless and flustered, "but Count de Landa asked me to bring this piece to Miss Lola urgently—she needs it for the wedding."

"Of course, señorita," said the girl behind the desk. "I will be happy to deliver it for you."

"*No!*" said Nasty, horrified at the suggestion. "Do you have any idea how valuable this is? It's a Landa family heirloom. The groom gave me strict instructions to deliver it in person." She leaned over to read the clerk's name tag. "Trust me, Conchita, you do *not* want to displease Count Antonio de Landa."

The groom's reputation had evidently preceded him. "This way, señorita," said the clerk. "I will take you to the room immediately."

Max followed them to the elevator, but the clerk barred his way. "Sorry, señor, but Miss Lola gave us strict instructions: no one of the male gender is to be allowed near her room today. Not even Count de Landa or the best man, no matter how much they insist. It's the custom among her people, apparently."

That figures, thought Max. *She doesn't want them to know she's given away the Yellow Jaguar.*

"See you at the wedding," said Nasty.

"Tell her it's going to be okay," said Max. "Tell her I'll think of something."

Nasty nodded and got in the elevator.

Max walked out of the hotel with a heavy heart. Would it be okay? he wondered. Would he think of something? At that moment, he had nothing. He'd even handed the necklet over to a stranger. He was fairly sure that Nasty wasn't a demon in disguise, but still . . . what did he really know about her?

He tried to focus on his next problem: how to get into the cathedral without being recognized.

Max studied the groups of overdressed, braying aristocrats who were milling around in the square. He'd never pass for one of them.

Beyond them, a long line of scruffy, shell-wearing pilgrims were making their way down some steps to the bowels of the cathedral. A priest appeared and hurried them along, trying to get them out of sight before the wedding started.

Problem solved.

Max ducked into the nearest souvenir shop and bought himself a scallop shell on a leather thong, and a long, knobbly walking stick. Then he hid in a side street and set about transforming himself into a footsore pilgrim. He scooped up some mud from the gutter and rubbed it on his face and clothes. He mussed up his hair. Then, to give himself an authentic-looking limp, he placed a little stone in each of his sneakers.

"Oh, my blisters," he groaned as he hobbled toward the end of the line outside the cathedral. "I can't believe how far I've walked today."

The waiting pilgrims welcomed him into their throng. They shook hands and hugged him and slapped him on the back and seemed completely unaware that every single one of them smelled like a skunk from their long days and nights on the road.

"Come and get some food, man," said a sunburned guy with a long beard. "You've earned it."

Down in the bowels of the cathedral, a wonderful spread had been laid out to welcome the pilgrims. There were fresh-baked breads, soft cheeses, pink hams, beef stew, cold chicken, slabs of potato omelet, golden pies, bowls of ripe tomatoes, fruit tarts, little pancakes filled with cream. . . .

For the first time in his life, Max Murphy declined the offer of free food and forced himself to keep walking.

He found a bathroom and cleaned himself up, then scurried through the passageways under the church until they narrowed and shrank into little more than ancient tunnels. This was ridiculous. Somewhere above him, Lola was getting married. And he was trapped like a rat in maze.

He turned one last corner and came face-to-face with a silver coffin. He stared at it uncomprehendingly. If only he'd paid more attention when Nasty was reading the guidebook.

The guidebook! She'd given it to him!

He pulled it out of his bag, found the page about the cathedral, and read impatiently. Okay, so this was good. This must be the casket of Saint James. From here, steps were supposed to lead up to a small chamber behind the altar, from where an old jewel-encrusted statue of the saint looked out over the faithful. Hardly daring to breathe in case anyone heard him, he found the steps and tiptoed up to the chamber. This was where pilgrims came to kiss Saint James at the end of their pilgrimage. And this was where Max Murphy peered out over the saint's left shoulder to see what was happening in the cathedral.

At least the wedding hadn't started yet.

He saw the yellow flowers decorating every pew, the priests nervously preparing the service books, and the giant incense burner, like a great golden tea urn, tied by ropes to a pillar at the side.

His eye traveled over the congregation. He recognized a few of the faces from the party last night. Near the front, sitting next to the woman in pink, were Nasty's parents. They were saving two spaces for himself and Nasty.

But where was Nasty? She should have been back from the hotel by now. All she had to do was drop off the necklet.

He was kicking himself for entrusting the Yellow Jaguar to her. Lola's life was on the line here. What if Nasty had decided to keep it? No one on earth could stop her. Or what if she'd simply lost her nerve? Or what if Landa's thugs had intercepted her?

There was an air of unease in the pews. People were craning around and looking at their watches and shaking their heads and whispering loudly among themselves. It seemed that the wedding was getting off to a late start.

The main doors of the church were thrown open and everyone turned to look.

In place of a radiant bride, in walked the repulsive figure of Ah Pukuh. He was wearing his ceremonial headdress, the exotic creation of dried human tongues and eyeballs bobbing on their optic nerves that he'd worn when Max first met him at the party in the Black Pyramid. Now as he lollopped down the aisle, the eyeballs swiveled and rolled independently, leering obscenely at the female guests. His blotchy face was daubed, as usual, in thick white makeup, and his bloated body bulged out of a traditional gray wedding suit with tailcoat and vest. As he passed each pew in turn, the occupants would start fanning themselves frantically to dissipate the foul odor he left in his wake.

A wooden side door clanked open, and Landa limped out, flanked by two bodyguards dressed in black. Landa looked ridiculous in a mustard-yellow velvet doublet and black knickerbockers, his skinny legs encased in black tights, a ceremonial sword hanging at his side. The guards took up positions on either side of the altar, while Landa paced to and fro, his hand clenching and unclenching on the handle of his sword as though he were considering killing someone.

Another side door opened to admit a band of red-robed acolytes, carrying among them a tray of burning coals. Every head in the church turned to watch as they untied the great incense burner and set the tray of coals inside.

When this sideshow was over, unrest set in again among the guests. The whispering grew to a clamor. Where was the bride? Where was the bride?

And then she was there.

Lola stood at the door of the cathedral, silhouetted by the daylight behind her.

The organist launched into a wedding march.

As Lola progressed down the aisle, the congregation fell silent and stared openmouthed. Were they stunned by Lola's beauty or horrified at the prospect of this sweet young girl being joined in matrimony to the evil Antonio de Landa?

It was impossible to say.

Lola was wearing a creamy-white, renaissance-style wedding dress, with a lace veil that fell over her shoulders and trailed behind her, its hem borne reverently by a bridesmaid. She walked slowly, almost floating like a ghost in her long silk dress, and she stared straight ahead with the unseeing eyes of a sleepwalker. Max registered, with relief, that she was wearing the Yellow Jaguar, its amber tones picked out in her bouquet of golden roses.

When Lola reached the front, the bridal party took their places at the altar steps. Even without their eccentric costumes, it made for a strange wedding photograph. The groom looked angry, the bride looked brain-dead, and the best man looked like an extra from a horror film.

Max strained to see the bridesmaid. What kind of weirdo would she be? Lola had no friends in Spain as far as he knew, so her attendant must be from the groom's family. Maybe a female version of Landa, with or without the beard. . . .

Lola turned to pass back the bouquet, and for the first time Max saw the bridesmaid clearly.

It was Nasty. In her white sundress. With yellow flowers in her hair.

As Lola handed her the bridal bouquet, Max distinctly saw her squeeze Lola's hand. A kind of "it's going to be all right because your good friend Max will think of something to stop this wedding" squeeze. And now he could see Nasty anxiously scanning the church, trying to spot him.

But it was Lola who saw him.

As the priest droned on, her gaze drifted up to the statue of Saint James behind the altar. Those jungle-sharp eyes, which could spot a brown toad on a brown log in brown mud at fifty paces, spotted Max's eye peeping over the saint's shoulder.

She looked away instantly, asking him for nothing, expecting nothing.

Max's heart lurched.

He remembered the last time they'd been alone. How he'd told her she wasn't a princess. She was looking regal at this moment, her head held high in acceptance of her fate.

She'd been ready to walk down the aisle without the Yellow Jaguar, which would surely have meant instant death. Now she was about to sacrifice her life in marriage to this creep. And Max was fairly sure that she was doing it all for him.

He couldn't let this happen.

He had to think of something.

Somehow he had to save her.

But he should have been thinking about saving himself because a big calloused hand was suddenly clamped over his mouth and he was forced down onto his knees. Max had kept an eye on the two bodyguards at the altar but, foolishly, hadn't thought to check if Landa had hired other security.

"We meet again, little drummer boy," whispered a voice in his ear.

It was one of the Maya roadies from the party.

"And this time," said the voice of the second roadie, "our orders are to finish you."

Max heard a gun being cocked. His last thought, as he braced for a bullet to his brain, was, *I'm sorry, Monkey Girl; I'm so sorry I let you down.*

He heard a faint whistling sound.

Then he was falling, falling. . . .

Max was knocked forward by the weight of the first

roadie's body collapsing on top of him. He pushed it off and saw a blowgun dart lodged in its neck. Even as the second roadie took aim, a dart whistled through the air and knocked him senseless.

Max's heart raced with pleasure. There was only one marksman in all the world who could make that shot.

"Lord 6-Dog?" he whispered.

The monkey king bounded up the steps to the chamber. He was carrying two lengths of PVC pipe.

"Lord 6-Dog! How did you—? Where did you—? I thought you were—"

The monkey's eyes twinkled, but he tried to look fierce. "I have brought thee a weapon, young lord. I hope thou canst remember thy training?"

Max nodded. He couldn't stop smiling.

Lord 6-Dog handed him the pipe. "This is thy blowgun," he whispered. "Alas, no poison dart frogs, but I have made a paste of toxic roots." He wore two small gourds at his waist and he untied one to give to Max. It was filled with wadding soaked in poison. He gave Max half his stash of darts and Max knew to dip them in the wadding before he used them. "And now, young lord, let us stop this unholy union. *Ko'ox!*"

Max tied the gourd onto his belt loop and stuffed the darts in his back pocket. "*Ko'ox!*" he replied. "It's on!"

By now, Ah Pukuh's reeking body odor had permeated every part of the cathedral, and the congregation was waiting impatiently for the gigantic incense burner to swing into air-freshener mode. There was a collective sigh of relief when the red-robed acolytes returned and began to untie the ropes.

With a clanging of pulleys, the censer shot thirty feet straight up into the air. As the acolytes pulled rhythmically on the ropes, it began to trace an arc from one side of the cathedral to the other. The wind fanned the coals into bright flames, and soon a Vesuvian cloud of perfumed smoke drowned out even the smell of Ah Pukuh.

The congregation watched in awe as the incense burner swung higher and higher, side to side, until it seemed certain to hit the ceiling. Then, as it started on its downward trajectory, they gasped to see a small, dark figure leap from a high balcony onto the rope above the censer.

It was a brown howler monkey, gripping a knife in its teeth.

"Lady Coco?" Max stared at Lord 6-Dog in incredulity.

The monkey king nodded. "It is time to attack," he whispered. "First we deal with the guards. Then, when I give the password, thy job is to escort Lady Lola far, far away from here."

"What's the password?"

Lord 6-Dog cast around wildly. "Bananas!" he announced.

They took up their sniper positions, Lord 6-Dog standing on a velvet stool, each pointing a blowgun over one of the saint's shoulders.

The incense burner was spinning wildly and careening from left to right. Everyone in the cathedral was transfixed by its progress, except for Landa—who was screaming at his remaining two guards to shoot the monkey—and Lola, who stood stock-still and expressionless in the chaos.

"Take aim . . . ," whispered Lord 6-Dog. "*Fire!*"

One guard fell.

Lord 6-Dog's dart had found its target.

Max's dart missed, and his guard spun around to retaliate.

Down, down, down the incense burner swung,
with Lady Coco riding on top of it.

Max didn't even have time to duck before a red-robed acolyte snuck up behind the guard, hit him with a candlestick, and ran off into the shadows. The guard forgot about Max and hesitated between chasing his red-robed assailant, shielding Landa, and shooting the monkey as his boss was yelling at him to do.

Nasty pulled Lola behind a pillar, out of the line of fire.

Down, down, down the incense burner swung, with Lady Coco riding on top of it to control its trajectory. As it hit the bottom of its arc and started to rise again, she grasped the rope with her tail and used her knife to cut the censer free, so that it plummeted straight toward Landa. The guard dove across and pushed him out of the way, taking the hit himself. Guard and censer crashed into the old wooden pulpit, igniting it and showering Landa in burning coals.

Smoke billowed everywhere.

The congregation erupted in panic and headed en masse for the doors, screaming and coughing.

Landa was livid, his eyes blazing like the coals from the incense burner. "This will not happen!" he screamed.

He unsheathed his sword. The Toledo steel glinted red in the light of the flames from the burning pulpit. He hadn't worked out where the darts were coming from, and he jabbed randomly into the air. Then he saw Lola and Nasty, hiding behind the pillar, and tried to pull Lola out. Nasty wouldn't let go of her, and Lola became the rope in their tug-of-war. Landa went to run Nasty through with his sword, but Lola stood between them.

By this time, Nasty's parents had fought their way to the front of the cathedral. Mrs. Smith-Jones screamed at Landa and hit him with her umbrella, while her husband dragged their reluctant daughter away to take cover in a side chapel.

Landa pulled Lola back to the altar steps. He used his sword to flush out the officiating priest from his hiding place under the altar table. "Finish what you have started!" he commanded.

His pulpit smoldering and his precious incense burner wrecked, the terrified priest began to stammer out what Max assumed was the wedding liturgy. Whether it was in Latin or Spanish or Mayan or some language of the priest's own invention, he couldn't understand a word of it.

Lord 6-Dog and Max could now get a clear shot at Landa, and they fired simultaneously. As the darts whistled through the air toward his throat, Landa smiled for the first time that day.

He held up his hand. Both darts stopped in midair and burst into flames.

Max groaned. He'd seen that trick once before, on the Black Pyramid, when Lord 6-Dog had confronted his ruthless archenemy Tzelek.

Tzelek!

"I told thee he would come, young lord," whispered Lord 6-Dog.

"But how did he get here?"

Max backtracked through the events of the last twenty-four hours to work out how Lord 6-Dog's power-crazed foster brother could have escaped from Xibalba and turned up at Lola's wedding.

He would have needed a portal . . . opened by a Jaguar Stone. . . .

And suddenly it was clear to Max why Ah Pukuh had gone

to such lengths to intercept the necklet—and why he'd forced Landa to go through with that humiliating lineage ceremony.

Ah Pukuh needed to activate the Yellow Jaguar to open the portal for his crony Tzelek. Landa's lust for power had played right into his hands. Now Tzelek was hiding in Landa, as he had once hidden in Hermanjilio.

As Max replayed the masquerade ball in his mind, he realized that the clue had been there all the time. Tzelek had a twisted foot, which he dragged behind him as he walked. Landa had walked normally before the lineage ceremony. But later, in the library, he'd been limping—just as Hermanjilio had done after he'd opened the portal at Itzamna.

While Max was working all this out, Lord 6-Dog took a flying leap off the plaster head of Saint James, all the way to the cathedral floor.

"Have at thee, Tzelek!" he challenged, waving his blowpipe like a rapier.

"6-Dog!" sneered Tzelek/Landa. "Still trapped in that moth-eaten fur coat, I see. At least I chose the body of an aristocrat."

"Aye, a cowardly, vain aristocrat. This howler has more nobility in one of its opposable thumbs than thou and thine host put together."

"Is that so? Well, let us see how nobly thy howler body dies. . . ."

Ah Pukuh, who'd been lolling in a pew eating popcorn and watching the action as if it were a movie, clapped his hands with pleasure. "Splendid! Splendid! Just before things get messy, may I be first to welcome you back to Middleworld, dear Tzelek? I told you it would be easy to arrange your passage. That vain fool Landa was putty in my hands."

He let out a loud, smelly fart of pleasure.

"Greetings, Lord Ah Pukuh," said Tzelek. "I must confess that I had planned to keep a low profile until after the nuptials, but once again 6-Dog has stuck his stinking monkey posterior into my business. With your permission, I propose to silence him once and for all, here and now."

"Proceed, by all means," said Ah Pukuh, wolfing down popcorn.

"Thou wilt have to catch me first," said Lord 6-Dog, scampering up a pillar. "Bananas to thee, Tzelek, BAN-ANAS!"

It was a strange insult, but it was the password Max had been waiting for.

"You confounded coward!" screeched Tzelek. "Get back here!"

While Lord 6-Dog lured Tzelek farther and farther away from Lola, Max tiptoed down from the chamber and made his way around to her.

"Run!" he mouthed.

She ran to him, and together they made a break for the main door of the cathedral. They could hear slashings and cursings and crashings behind them as Tzelek pursued brave Lord 6-Dog.

Only when they reached the massive golden organ halfway down the nave, did Lola and Max dare to look back.

It was clear that a howler monkey, no matter how brave, was no match for Tzelek.

As they watched, Tzelek's sword chopped Lord 6-Dog's blowgun in half, as easily as slicing a salami. For a few moments the monkey was unarmed, until a red sleeve in the shadows was seen tossing him a long metal lamplighter, which was used to light the highest candles. Lord 6-Dog's strong arms wielded it like a flamethrower, as Tzelek's blows rained down.

"Tzelek will kill him," said Lola, with tears in her eyes.

"He wants you to escape," said Max.

"But we can't just leave him."

"He's a warrior, Lola, a great warrior. You have to trust him."

Lola looked anguished.

"We have a mission, remember?" Max reminded her. "We have a planet to save."

Lola nodded. She straightened her shoulders like a soldier. "Okay," she whispered.

They turned for the door and ran straight into the rubbery body of Ah Pukuh.

"Not so fast, missy," he said. "You have something that belongs to me."

"Get out of my way, you fat pig!" said Lola, trying to push past.

It was, perhaps, an unwise mode of address to use with the god of violent and unnatural death.

"I think not!" he boomed.

Lola aimed a punch at the rolls of lard that encircled his abdomen like so many inflatable life belts. Her hand disappeared into the soft fat of his belly, and her arm followed up to her elbow.

Ah Pukuh pursed his lip-glossed lips. He raised one impeccably plucked eyebrow. All the eyes in his headdress focused on Lola.

"Big mistake!" he said.

Then he thrust out his chest, so that his wedding suit and too-tight white shirt ripped open to reveal his hairy, wobbling flesh. As Lola withdrew her hand, there was a squelching noise, and his navel unraveled to spill rotting guts on the floor in front of her. The sight of it was so disgusting that she turned away, retching.

"Works every time," crowed Ah Pukuh, sucking his innards back in like a movie in reverse. "Now give me the Yellow Jaguar. I lent it to that idiot fiancé of yours to open the portal for Tzelek, and now I want it back."

"Landa gave it to me," said Lola. "And I'm keeping it."

"You stupid child!" bellowed Ah Pukuh. He hooked his fat fingers into the necklet and tried to pull it off her. His fingers went right through it. Again and again he tried to get a grip on the beads, but they slipped through his fingers like water.

"I command you to relinquish the necklet," screamed Ah Pukuh, and the organ pipes whistled with the volume of his anger.

"Leave me alone, you bully," replied Lola. "The people of Middleworld aren't scared of *you*. The Yellow Jaguar is mine. And I'm keeping it."

In retrospect, Max described what happened next as the biggest temper tantrum he had ever seen.

First of all, the eyes in Ah Pukuh's headdress started twitching with tension, and a few popped altogether, spattering him with eye goo. Then his body began to tremble with fury, like a mountain of Jell-O sitting on a washing machine in spin cycle.

"Give it to me!"

"No."

Ah Pukuh stamped his foot, and the cathedral shook to its foundations.

A statue of Saint James riding his horse toppled from a pillar and crashed onto Tzelek, knocking him to his knees just as he was about to gain the upper hand and deal Lord 6-Dog a deathblow. He dropped his sword, and Lord 6-Dog kicked it out of his reach. In seconds, the monkey had dropped his lamplighter, grasped the sword with both hands, and held the point up to Tzelek's throat.

Tzelek spat in his direction, and the saliva sizzled and burned on the stones where it landed. "Go ahead!" he murmured. "Slit my throat. You haven't got the guts! Twice before, you've had the opportunity to kill me and twice you've lost your nerve, so—"

Tzelek's ranting dissolved into gurgles as Lord 6-Dog pressed the sword harder into his throat. A thin line of blood trickled onto his white neck ruff.

"Let us be clear," snarled Lord 6-Dog. "I could kill thee now as easily as a snake crushes a mouse. And yet . . ." He smiled and pulled back the sword a little. His voice became softer. "And yet, how can I kill my erstwhile brother on his wedding day? Tzelek in love! What a delightful notion."

"What trickery is this? You know I was marrying the wench only to unite the royal houses of Middleworld and Xibalba. I will rule on earth for Ah Pukuh."

"Come now, Tzelek, admit it!" called Lord 6-Dog. "Thou art truly in love! I see the flame of passion in thine eyes. Bring back the bride! Let us proceed with the ceremony. Perhaps a good woman can reform thee."

Tzelek stared at Lord 6-Dog in disbelief.

Max and Lola stared at Lord 6-Dog in disbelief.

Ah Pukuh broke off from his tantrum to stare at Lord 6-Dog in disbelief.

So shocked were they all that not one of them noticed a small brown figure sliding silently down the rope that had held the incense burner. Nor did they see it quickly tie the end of the rope around Tzelek's ankles and pull it tight.

"All yours, son," called Lady Coco.

Lord 6-Dog raised his sword and smashed the flat of the blade on Tzelek's skull.

"This is an outrage!" moaned Tzelek, as he lost consciousness.

"No," said Lady Coco calmly. "It is an outrage that you were ever born. It is an outrage that you killed my husband, the man who brought you up as his own. And it is an outrage that, once again, my 6-Dog has shown you mercy."

"I have merely granted him a stay of execution, Mother. If I slay him in this body, I will exterminate Landa—but Tzelek himself may escape. Our final battle draws nearer. But this is neither the time nor the place."

A creaking noise alerted Max to the movement of the pulley above his head. The red-robed acolyte who'd hit the guard was heaving on the control ropes. Max and Lola ran to help, and soon the unconscious Tzelek was hoisted off the ground and cranked high up into the roof of the cathedral, where he hung upside down like a *serrano* ham in the window of a Spanish restaurant.

"Well, this is awkward," said Ah Pukuh.

He waddled up the aisle until he stood under the swinging Tzelek.

The remaining eyeballs in his headdress copied him as he looked up at his senseless cohort and back down at Max, Lola, Lord 6-Dog, and Lady Coco. Then the eyeballs swiveled around and focused on Ah Pukuh himself, waiting to see what he would do.

"Normally," he said, "at this juncture, I would slay you all in my usual grisly manner! But I find myself somewhat stymied." He gestured around the cathedral. "This is hallowed ground. Like it or not, I am required to show professional respect."

The eyeballs looked at one another in surprise.

"Unless, of course, any of you would like to step outside?"

The eyeballs looked expectantly at Max, Lola, and the monkeys, who all shook their heads vigorously.

"Have it your way," said Ah Pukuh, "but much good it will do you." He (and the eyeballs with him) focused on Max. "Enjoy your last day of life, Max Murphy. By this time tomorrow, you will have taken the road and entered the water. And I will take great pleasure in personally devising the manner of your final demise." With that, Ah Pukuh turned on his heel. "Meanwhile, if anyone wants me," he called over his shoulder as he lumbered out of the cathedral, "I will be sucking on tentacles in that restaurant across the square. I hear they serve excellent octopus."

Max had frozen in fear at Ah Pukuh's words, and it took him a few seconds to thaw out. "What road? What water? What's he talking about?" he spluttered.

"*Taking the road* and *entering the water* are both metaphors for death," growled Lord 6-Dog.

"Don't scare the boy," Lady Coco scolded her son.

"Too late," said Max.

"That bully Ah Pukuh is all mouth. You won this round, fair and square, young lord," Lady Coco assured him. Her voice sounded weak.

"You were magnificent . . . ," agreed Lola.

"Really?" Max grinned. Perhaps it was worth receiving a personal death threat from the god of violent and unnatural death himself, if it won him praise from Lola.

"But what are you wearing, Hoop?"

He followed her eyes to his mud-spattered navy blazer with anchors on the buttons.

"It's a long story. . . ."

And before he could tell it, Nasty came over, looking stunned. "What just happened? Why is the bridegroom hanging from the ceiling? Who was that fat guy with all the eyes? And what's with the talking monkeys?"

Max took a deep breath and plunged in. "Well, we didn't know it, but Tzelek was hiding in Landa, and Ah Pukuh is like Tzelek's boss and he's taking over the world, and the monkeys aren't really monkeys because Lord 6-Dog is actually an ancient Maya king—"

"You know what?" said Nasty, shaking her head in confusion. "E-mail me when you get home."

"Thank you so much for helping me, Nasty," said Lola. "You were very brave. And you'd never even met me before."

"Well, any friend of Mac's . . ." Nasty shrugged. Max opened his mouth to protest, but she winked at him to show she was joking. "Besides," she continued, "I always wanted to be a bridesmaid."

"I don't suppose this was quite how you imagined it," said Lola.

"No," agreed Nasty. "I always thought I'd wear a *pink* dress."

Lola laughed and took Nasty's hands. "Seriously though, if you hadn't offered to keep me company out there, I don't think I could have gone through with it."

"But what were you thinking of?" Max asked her. "It was such a bad plan. If I'd have obeyed your note, you'd be dead by now."

"I had no choice about the wedding," said Lola. "Landa was going to kill you. And as I'd rather die than marry him, I figured I had nothing to lose by giving you the Yellow Jaguar and a shot at Xibalba. Besides, I knew I'd escape somehow."

"Anastasia!" Mrs. Smith-Jones's voice echoed through the cathedral. "Come away from those terrible people! We're catching the first flight back to Boston!"

"I was just congratulating the actors, Mom!" She winked at Max again. "Weren't the special effects amazing? We were so lucky to see this! Apparently it's the latest thing in performance art. Massimo knew all along it wasn't a real wedding! It's given me so many ideas for our next production at drama club. . . ."

Mrs. Smith-Jones staggered over. Her hat was adrift, her hair was bedraggled, and she was missing one shoe. "I've never been so frightened in all my life," she said. "If this is how European high society behaves, you can keep it!"

"Quite right," agreed Mr. Smith-Jones. If not for the violent shaking of his hand as he mopped his brow with a polka-dot silk handkerchief, he would have looked as dapper as ever. "I told you we should have stuck with Florida."

"If you don't need me," said Nasty to Max, "I think I better go and look after my parents. They've had quite a shock. So e-mail me—okay? Remember, you owe me pizza and a movie and a full explanation when you get back to Boston!"

"You got it," said Max. "Ciao."

"Ciao for now!" replied Nasty. She giggled. "At least I can tell my friends that I met an Italian aristocrat with a palace in Venice. They won't believe any of the rest of it!" She followed her parents demurely toward the door, turning at the last minute to give Max a wave and a Ty Phoid tongue waggle.

"She seems nice, Hoop," whispered Lola.

"She is nice," agreed Max.

He studied Lola's face. Did he detect a hint of jealousy?

No.

Sadly.

He didn't.

Not a trace.

She was looking around anxiously. "Where's Lord 6-Dog? Why did you tell me he was dead?"

"I thought he was," said Max. "The last time I saw him, he'd been shot at close range and he was lying in the road in a pool of blood."

"So how did he get here? And Lady Coco?"

"Beats me. But I'm glad they did."

They found the monkeys slumped by the altar steps.

"Thou wast invincible, Mother," Lord 6-Dog was saying. "When I saw thee riding on top of that incense burner, it was all I could do to keep from cheering!"

"Thank you, son. It was a job well done, even if I do say so myself." Lady Coco winced in pain.

Lola inspected the queen's hairy little arm. It was matted with blood. "It looks bad," she said, mopping it gently with the hem of her wedding dress. "What happened?"

"A guard shot me as I climbed the rope," explained Lady Coco. "But he didn't count on my strong monkey biceps. I could have climbed one-armed if I had to."

"How about you, Lord 6-Dog?"

"A mere flesh wound. That varlet Tzelek caught me in the leg with his sword."

"We need to get you both out of here," said Lola.

She gathered up Lady Coco, while Max bent down to give Lord 6-Dog a piggyback. "I am so glad to see you, Your

Majesty," he said as the monkey climbed on. "I thought you were—"

"Dead? I thought I was dead, too," agreed Lord 6-Dog. "Then an angel found me and nursed me back to life."

"An angel?" Max pressed. "What angel?"

"Ask my mother. She saw her, too."

"Lady Coco? What's this about an angel?" asked Lola. "I would like to meet her and thank her. When Landa kidnapped me, I thought I would never see you again. . . ."

"I walked all night trying to find you, Lady Lola. Just when all was lost, the angel found me and gave me hope."

"But who was she, this angel?"

"She's over there," said Lady Coco.

Lola and Max followed her gaze.

From out of the shadows behind a pillar stepped the red-robed acolyte.

"Hello, Max," said Zia as police sirens surrounded the cathedral.

Chapter Twenty-one
THE COAST OF DEATH

While the police stormed the front doors of the cathedral, Zia led them out a back way, down through tunnels and passageways, to a red sports car haphazardly parked across two spaces in a side street behind the cathedral.

Max had known Zia all his life as his family's morose and dowdy housekeeper. Now she had cast off her red robe to reveal a red jacket, a leopard-print T-shirt, and skintight jeans. Her thick, shiny black hair fell loose around her shoulders, and she pushed it out of her eyes with a pair of rhinestone-encrusted sunglasses worn high on her head. She replaced her flat sandals with high heels and, bending over the side mirror, applied a thick coat of red lipstick. When her transformation was complete, she looked twenty years younger than she had in Boston. Not stylish exactly, but full of life and energy.

"Is it really you, Zia?" asked Max, staring at her like she were an alien. "You look so different. . . ."

"So do you. I like your hair. Black suits you."

"Wait—*you're* Zia?" asked Lola in amazement. Standing in front of her was the most glamorous Maya woman she had ever seen. She'd heard Max's description of the old Zia, and this bedazzled jet-setter did not match it. "*Biix a beel?* How are you?" she asked, with a big smile.

"*Ma'alob. Kux teech?*" replied Zia, laughing. The old Zia hardly ever laughed. "I'm well, thank you; how are you? It's a long time since I spoke Mayan with another living person. You must be the famous Lola!"

Max noticed the strangeness of that phrase, *another living person*. Who else would she speak with, if not a living person?

"How did you learn English so quickly?" he asked her.

Zia winked at him mischievously. "It took me fourteen years."

"What? But—"

"I have a lot to tell you. But first we must get out of here."

"But what are you doing here? I mean, how did you know—?"

"Later. *Ko'ox!*"

She ripped up the wad of parking tickets that obscured half the windshield, leapt into the driver's seat, and revved up the engine. "You get in the front, Max, and make like a tourist." She threw him a camera. "Bride and monkeys, hide under a blanket in the back until we get out of the city."

She turned on some loud, thumping Eurodisco music, and they zoomed through the narrow streets of Santiago, Zia dancing in her seat and Max taking photos of everything, as if they didn't have a care in the world. They passed several policemen, and not one of them gave them a second look.

305

When they squealed to a stop at a traffic light, Zia asked Max, "How do you like my wheels?"

"Very cool," he said, surveying the convertible. "But it rains so much here, don't you get wet?"

"You sound like your father," she said disapprovingly. "Live for the moment, that's my motto. I want to feel the wind in my hair."

"You do?"

Zia had never struck Max as a wind-in-the-hair type of person. In fact, the whole time he'd known her in Boston, her hair had been twisted back in a tight braid. "So where are we headed—?" he began, but the roar of the engine drowned him out as the traffic light changed and they sped off again.

As far as Max could tell, she was headed north.

The gray skies turned to night.

Eventually they entered a wide boulevard lined with palm trees, and Zia followed it until they literally ran out of road. They pulled up outside a grand hotel overlooking the thundering ocean.

"This is the place," she said.

"Hotel Finisterre," read Lola, combing her windswept hair out of her eyes with her fingers. "It looks nice."

"Anything looks nice after Casa Carmela," snapped Max, "but what are we doing here? Where are we?"

Zia got out of the car. "Wait here while I see if they have rooms for us."

Max groaned. "She's insane. We need to get to Xibalba, and she's brought us to a seaside resort. Does she think we're on vacation or what?"

"She seemed to know what she was doing in the cathedral," Lola pointed out. "She was fantastic. Why didn't you tell me you had a Maya housekeeper?"

"I only just found out myself."

"Well, I think we should give her a chance to explain. Besides, it's late and I like the look of this place. Just think, Hoop: hot showers, clean sheets, room service. . . ."

"I thought you were more of a hammock and grilled iguana kind of girl?"

"It's been a tough couple of days."

"Yeah," agreed Max, "it has." He swallowed. "I . . . er . . . I wanted to say sorry for what I said at Landa's palace, that thing about you not being a princess."

Lola shrugged. "I know what I am, Hoop. I'm the kid that nobody wanted. I was left in the forest to be eaten by jaguars. I don't know why Landa chose me to play his Maya princess. Maybe he thought no one would miss me because I'm an orphan."

"It's because you look like Princess Inez."

"No way."

"And I look like Rodrigo."

"That's so creepy." Lola closed her eyes and took a deep breath of sea air. "It was horrible, Hoop," she whispered.

A wave washed over onto the road.

"Looks like the tide's coming in," said Max.

Leaving the monkeys to doze in the back of the car, Max and Lola walked over to the seawall. The water boiled and churned beneath them. They could see the lights of fishing boats bobbing wildly on the horizon and, far in the distance, a lighthouse flashed its warning.

"I wouldn't want to be out at sea tonight," said Lola.

"Me neither," agreed Max, shouting to make himself heard above the roar of the ocean. "I just want get out of Spain. I keep thinking the police are going to swoop in and arrest me again."

"*Again?* What do you mean, *again?* When were you arrested?"

"The same day you were kidnapped by Landa."

"What were you arrested for?"

"Murder."

Lola clapped a hand over her mouth. The wind whipped her hair into wild strands. "Hoop, what have you done? Who did you murder?"

"You."

"Me?"

"That's what Carmela told the police when you disappeared. If Santino hadn't rescued me, I'd still be in jail."

"Poor Santino," said Lola.

"Poor Santino? What about poor *me?* I was the one who was arrested and thrown in jail."

"Yes, but Santino came to declare his love for me and ended up nearly sacrificed."

"I think you've put him off Maya girls for good," said Max. "And I don't think he'll be talking to strange girls on airplanes again either."

"I'm not strange," said Lola.

At that moment the monkeys woke up and, instinctively, she called over to the car to reassure them, a rough raspy coughing sound she made through her cupped hands.

"No, not strange at all," said Max. "I bet lots of people arrive at this hotel with howler monkeys in tow, wearing a bloodstained wedding dress and a necklet of mystical ancient stones."

Lola looked down at herself. "For once, you might have a point."

She ripped away at her long skirt until she'd transformed it into a minidress. Then she struck a pose like a model on a catwalk. "What do you think?"

"Um . . . Wilma Flintstone meets Lady Gaga? Nice jewelry, though."

"It's so heavy. I can't wait to take it off."

"No! Keep wearing it! If Ah Pukuh himself couldn't take it from you, at least we know it's safe."

She nodded. "Okay then. I'll give it to you when we get to Xibalba."

When we get to Xibalba.

They both fell silent as they contemplated the prospect of a visit to that fearsome place.

"Tomorrow is 6-Death," said Max.

"Quick! Quick!" called Zia, running out of the hotel. "Back to the car!"

What was this? Had Santino tipped off the police?

"What's the matter?" asked Max.

"The car! It's starting to rain! We must put the top up!"

"That's it? I thought you'd had bad news!"

"Not at all," Zia assured him as she fiddled with switches to activate the car's folding roof. "We have the Presidential Suite with three bedrooms and a sea view from every room. The only problem is that they don't allow animals."

The monkeys, who were shivering in the cold night air and looking forward to a warm hotel room, looked crestfallen.

"Don't worry," said Zia, "I have thought about this."

She unzipped her suitcase and took out armfuls of designer clothes, many with their price tags still attached.

"Whose are those?" asked Max. He had the sudden idea that Zia had stolen a stranger's suitcase. After all, she always wore frumpy clothes in Boston, and this was a wardrobe fit for a movie star.

"I did a little shopping," said Zia.

Max took in the array of bright colors and sequins and shiny fabrics.

Zia must have seen the surprise in his eyes, because she gave a little chuckle. "What do you think? It's the new me."

Max was lost for words, so Lola quickly stepped in. "It's very glamorous," she said. "May I carry it all up to the room for you?"

Zia passed the clothes to Lola, along with several pairs of high-heeled shoes. "Okay," she said, showing the monkeys the empty case. "All aboard, and I'll wheel you to the room."

Lady Coco climbed in eagerly, admiring the leopard-print pattern of the lining. She patted the space next to her and waited for her son to follow.

"I am a king, not a piece of luggage," said Lord 6-Dog, sounding insulted. "I will climb up to the room."

"We're on the top floor," Zia warned him, "and you're wounded."

But Lord 6-Dog could not be dissuaded and, minutes later, Max and Lola were standing on the balcony of the Presidential Suite, encouraging him as he hauled himself painfully up a drainpipe. The rain was pouring down now and huge waves crashed on the rocky coast. The fishing boats were gone, pulled into port. There would surely be a storm at sea tonight.

As soon as Lord 6-Dog made it to the top, they closed the French doors and made themselves at home. While the monkeys rested their battle-weary bodies in one of the bedrooms and Zia fussed around, hanging up her new clothes,

Max and Lola inspected all the trappings of the suite.

When they'd drunk all the soft drinks in the minibar and clicked through every channel on the TV (not that many in this corner of Spain), Max put the little hotel shower cap over his beloved black hair and took the longest and hottest shower of his life. It was bliss.

"What happened to my clothes?" he asked, when he finally emerged in a fluffy white toweling robe, holding his empty backpack.

"I took them for washing," said Zia. "Your mother would have been shocked to see the state you were in."

"I was busy battling the forces of evil," Max pointed out. "Laundry wasn't at the top of my agenda."

A knock at the door made him jump out of his skin.

"Hide," said Lola, leaping up and pushing him back into the bathroom.

Heart thumping in terror that the police had tracked him down to this remote hotel on the wild and rocky coast, Max leaned on the sink and held his breath.

"Room service!" called a voice.

And relax.

All he had to do now was lie low while the waiter set out the food.

He looked in the mirror. It was all steamed up after his shower, so he wiped a little patch with his hand.

The face that stared back was not his.

It was Rodrigo.

The red-haired conquistador lifted a finger accusingly.

"I know, I know," whispered Max. "Time is running out."

Rodrigo nodded and faded away as the mirror fogged over again.

Lola knocked on the bathroom door. "All clear!"

Max splashed his face with cold water and went out.

"Are you okay?" asked Lola. "You look like you've seen a ghost."

She seemed so happy to be out of Landa's clutches and safe in a hotel that Max couldn't bear to tell her that the bathroom was, indeed, haunted.

"I'm just hungry," he answered gruffly.

Luckily, Zia had ordered enough food to feed an army.

There were bubbling cheese pizzas (scorched at the edges), fried fish, grilled steaks and juicy shrimp, fried potatoes, slabs of garlicky grilled bread rubbed with olive oil and tomatoes, little white anchovies, fat green olives, chocolate mousse, apple cake, fresh peaches, juicy grapes, and two huge bunches of bananas.

"*Hach ki' a wi'ih!* Enjoy!" said Zia.

"Aren't you going to eat with us?" asked Lola, making a picnic for the monkeys.

"Maybe later," said Zia, "but this laundry won't do itself and you'll need clean clothes for the morning."

Max had the distinct feeling that Zia was trying to avoid him.

Later, when they'd eaten as much as they could, and only the anchovies sat untouched, he stood at the window, watching the lightning over the sea.

"It sure is stormy out there," he said.

"It's always stormy out there," said Lola. She lay on the sofa, flicking through Nasty's guidebook. "It says they call this stretch La Costa de la Muerte, the Coast of Death, because so many ships have been wrecked on it."

"The Coast of Death? That sounds ominous."

"The Coast of Death? That sounds ominous."

"I'm sure it's just the tourist board trying to make things sound more exciting than they are."

"Shame they're not all as honest as the tourist office at Polvoredo," said Max.

Lola laughed.

Somewhere in the night, a pack of dogs howled.

Hellhounds?

The windows rattled, with a noise like the scratching of claws on glass.

Max felt the fear rising in the pit of his stomach. Time was running out.

He got up to look for Zia.

He found her in the other room, where she'd set up the hotel ironing board in front of a TV.

"What are you doing?" he asked. "The hotel has a laundry service. You put everything in the bag and they do it for you."

"There's no time for that," she said. "You need to look presentable tomorrow." She indicated Mr. Smith-Jones's blazer had been cleaned and neatly pressed.

"Zia," he said, "can we talk? You said you'd tell me everything when we got to the hotel."

"Did I?" said Zia vaguely, pretending to be engrossed in ironing Max's socks.

"Please," Max begged her.

"Very well," sighed Zia. She followed him into the sitting room and perched nervously on the edge of the sofa. "What do you want to know?"

"What are you doing in Spain?"

"Your parents were not allowed to help you, so I came."

"But how did you find Lord 6-Dog and Lady Coco?"

"It was not so difficult."

"But they're talking monkeys! You don't seem very surprised by any of this."

"I am Maya. Few things surprise me."

"What about the new you? You're like a different person. I've hardly ever heard you speak English before—"

"Before, I did not want to speak." Her voice was husky with emotion.

"What's changed?"

Zia looked evasive. "It's Spain," she said lamely. "I like it here. Good food, good shopping."

Max regarded her suspiciously.

Something wasn't adding up.

In fact, nothing was adding up.

Max thought back to Boston and Zia's strange behavior just before he'd left. "You knew the Yellow Jaguar was in Spain," he mused. "You bought my ticket to Madrid . . . and before that, the first time, you bought my ticket to San Xavier! How did you know to do that?" He grabbed one of her perfectly manicured hands. "Tell me, Zia. Who's behind it all?"

"I don't know what you mean."

"You have to tell me." He thought quickly. "Tell me, or I'll call my parents and make Mom's hair fall out again."

Zia said nothing, and Max reached for the hotel phone. He began to dial.

"It was the owl-man," said Zia.

Max put the phone down. "Lord Kuy? The messenger of the Death Lords?"

"Yes. And before him, the other one, the older one."

"Lord Muan? Where? When?"

"They sometimes come to the kitchen, in Boston,"

"*What?* In *our* kitchen? Why?"

"The smell of tamales seems to attract them."

"But why did they appear to *you?*"

"Perhaps they likes my tamales. A lot of people do," she said defensively. There was an edge in her voice. Max had never been a big fan of Zia's tamales, and it was evidently still a sore point with her.

"Besides liking your tamales, Zia, what did Lord Kuy say?"

Zia hesitated. "He . . . He said that if I did my job properly, he would reward me."

"And your job was . . . ?"

"To help you find the Yellow Jaguar and deliver it to Xibalba."

"Why didn't you tell me this before? Whose side are you on, Zia?"

Zia looked at him like her heart would break.

"How can you even ask that?" said Lola, coming over and putting a protective arm around Zia. "You should be thanking her, not interrogating her. If Zia wasn't here, Lord 6-Dog would be dead on the roadside, Lady Coco would be lost in Spain, and I would be married to Tzelek."

She was right.

"I'm sorry, Zia," said Max. "I don't know who to trust anymore."

"That is good," she replied. "Tomorrow, when you go to Xibalba, you must trust no one."

Max and Lola exchanged nervous glances.

"We're going to Xibalba tomorrow?" he asked.

"It is Wak Kimi, 6-Death," she said. "The day to visit the dead."

"But how will we get there?"

"The easiest way," said Zia, "is to take the bus."

Max did a double take. "What? You're telling me there's a bus from Spain to the Maya underworld?"

Zia smiled. "This place is a lot like San Xavier. The people here are superstitious; they believe in magic and ancient myths and other worlds. They even have their own sacred stones, called dolmens."

"But public transportation to Xibalba . . . ?" said Max skeptically.

"It's true," Zia insisted. "The spirits of the dead get a bus to a village called San Andrés, and from there they take a boat to the underworld."

Max stared at her. She really *was* insane. "Zia, we haven't got time for—"

"Hoop!" interrupted Lola, jabbing a finger at the guidebook. "Zia's right. It says here that if a Galician dies without visiting San Andrés, they will be reincarnated as a lizard or a frog. To avoid that happening, a relative buys two bus tickets, one for themselves and one for the spirit of the dead. When they get to San Andrés, they stroll around a bit, and then the dead guy gets in a boat and follows the setting sun to the end of the world."

"I still don't get it," said Max, shaking his head in confusion.

"*Finisterre!* The end of the world!" Lola was bouncing up and down with excitement. "Listen to this: 'According to legend, Finisterre was the place where the souls of the dead entered the sea. It gets its name from the Latin *finis terrae* or "the End of the World." The Romans referred to this stretch of the Atlantic as the Sea of the Dead, believing that the entrance to Hades was just over the horizon.'"

Max considered this information. "But Finisterre is not the end of the world for the Maya."

"But here's the thing," said Lola, reading on, "it also says that pilgrims from Santiago follow the Milky Way to take them to Finisterre."

"And?" said Max

"And it's the same for the Maya! We call the Milky Way the Road to Xibalba!"

"There is a bus tomorrow afternoon," said Zia.

Chapter Twenty-two

GHOST TOWN

The dead were a cheerful lot. Max couldn't see them or hear them, but Lola could, thanks to the Yellow Jaguar necklet she still wore. (It seemed the safest place to keep it. It also lent a certain panache to the rest of her outfit, which was a black cocktail dress, borrowed from Zia.)

She squirmed in her seat. "This dress is so itchy."

"Tell me about it," said Max. "There's so much starch in this shirt, it's like wearing cardboard."

It was Zia who had chosen their clothes for the day. "You must show the Death Lords respect," she'd said. "It is an honor for a mortal to visit Xibalba. Your names will live on in Maya legend."

"I'd rather live on by coming back alive," Max had pointed out.

"This is no time for joking," Zia chided him.

Eventually, she was satisfied with their appearance and they all said their good-byes. Zia promised to get the monkeys safely home to San Xavier, while Max and Lola took the bus to San Andrés and whatever lay beyond.

Now they were traveling along a winding road on a cliff edge high above the rocky coastline, sitting at the back of what to Max looked like a half-empty bus and to Lola looked like a full one.

When Max had first boarded, he'd noticed that every window seat was taken and every aisle seat was free. But whenever he tried to sit in an aisle seat, the window occupant would shout at him angrily.

And so on all the way down the bus.

"What's the matter with you?" whispered Lola. "Don't you remember Zia telling us that everyone buys two tickets—one for themselves and one for the spirit of their dead relative? Can't you see those seats are taken?"

"They look empty to me."

"Really? You can't see the dead people sitting in them?"

"Meaning *you* can?"

"They're kind of hazy, like faded sepia photographs, but yes."

"Oh, yeah? So what are they doing, all these dead people?"

"The usual things. Eating sandwiches, reading news-papers, playing cards. They look pretty happy."

Max peered along the aisle of the bus, trying to discern ghostly movement. "Maybe it's not so bad to be dead," he said, "if you can still eat sandwiches. Maybe I'll get pizza when my time comes."

"Don't talk that way, Hoop. You're creeping me out."

"*I'm* creeping *you* out? And you don't mind that the bus is full of dead people?"

"You know what I mean."

Max saw something out of the corner of his eye and turned to look out the back window. "Now *I'm* seeing things," he said. "I thought I saw a hellhound running after the bus."

Lola turned and looked. "I think it's gaining on us."

"You can see it, too?" Max swallowed hard. "Shouldn't we discuss strategy or something? What's the plan when we get off the bus?"

"Well, I was thinking that we'd follow the dead and see where they go. I'm hoping they might lead us to a cave."

"Why?"

"In San Xavier, they say that caves are entrances to Xibalba. This coast is so rocky, it must have hundreds of them."

"Say we find the right cave. Then what?"

"Who knows? The Death Lords are desperate for the Yellow Jaguar, so you'd think they'd make it easy for us. We'll trade the necklet for the two hostages, and get out of there as fast as we can."

"But we can't just hand it over, without a fight. Shouldn't we try to reason with them? Plead for mercy for the citizens of Middleworld? Try to pull some kind of trick once they've released Hermanjilio and Lucky Jim?"

"And risk their lives? Forget it! Jaime's mother would never forgive me. Besides, you can't reason with the Death Lords. I've thought about this a lot, Hoop. We should do whatever it takes to get the four of us out alive—and worry about the rest of it later."

"That's the thing. I don't think there is a later. Once we hand over the necklet, Ah Pukuh will have all five Jaguar Stones. End of story. End of world."

Lola shook her head. "I don't buy it. This is not the end. You have to take a longer perspective. We're not beaten yet, Hoop. I just have a feeling that the Jaguar Kings are watching over us."

"You do?"

"We're a team—like the Hero Twins, remember?"

He looked into her eyes. "You know, Nasty isn't my girlfriend or anything."

"I know that. She told me at the hotel when she brought me the Yellow Jaguar."

"She did?"

Lola raised an eyebrow. "You sound disappointed. Did you want me to think she was your girlfriend?"

"Well, you were getting married at the time."

Lola groaned.

"Just think," continued Max, "you could be Mrs. Tzelek right now."

"Stop!"

"Imagine what your children would have looked like!"

Lola hit him with the guidebook.

The bus lurched around a corner and plunged down a narrow switchback road toward the sea. "I think we're nearly there," she said. "The dead are getting very excited."

At the bottom of the hill was a little parking lot. The bus pulled over and the passengers began to disembark. Of course, it took twice as long as it looked like it should and, being at the back, Max and Lola were last off.

"You go first," said Max, "and see if there are any hellhounds. It's me they go for."

Lola stepped down and looked around the parking lot. "Just a few seagulls. You're not scared of them, are you?"

"Hey, you'd be scared of hellhounds, too, if you'd ever met one. Even their drool is lethal. One of them burned a hole in our living room carpet."

"I bet your mom loved that," said Lola as they walked along a little path to the village.

"Zia covered it up before she saw it."

"I like Zia," said Lola. "I can't believe you didn't know she was Maya. You're not very observant, are you?"

"Well, I can't see dead people, if that's what you mean. What are they doing now?"

Lola surveyed the scene. The narrow path through the village was lined with shops and stalls. "They're looking at souvenirs, eating ice cream, taking photographs . . . the usual tourist stuff. Oh, wait a minute. . . . It looks like they're going into that café. Come on!"

Max was about to follow her, when a muscular arm shot out and barred his way.

"*Cuidado!*" yelled the owner of the arm, a ruddy-faced man with bad breath and hairy ears.

"Lola! Come back! What's happening?"

He heard Lola conversing briefly in Spanish with his captor.

"It's okay, Hoop," she assured him as the man released him. "He thought you were about to step on that." Max looked to where she was pointing and saw a tiny brown lizard scuttling away down the path. "It could be the reincarnation of somebody's relative," she explained. "They're very careful about not stepping on reptiles in this village."

"That figures," said Max, picking his way extra carefully.

Lola pushed open the door to the café. "Whoa, it's busy in here!"

To Max, the café—like the bus—looked half empty. There were two chairs and one person sitting alone at every table, and every table had two glasses on it.

"Let's squeeze in at the counter," suggested Lola, raising her voice to make herself heard above the din of the merry-making dead people.

"There's no need to shout," said Max, for whom the room was silent.

They found themselves a space and tried to catch the eye of the hunchbacked old woman dressed in black who was working behind the bar. While they were waiting to be served, Max studied the shelves on the back wall. They were filled with jars of murky ingredients: pickled eggs that looked like eyes, pickled gherkins that looked like fingers, pickled cauliflower florets that looked like tiny brains. The only decorations on the walls were posters of witches in various Halloween-type poses and a set of old photographs depicting real women dressed as witches. There were even little witch trinkets—magnets and key rings in the shapes of black hats and black cats and broomsticks—for sale at the register.

"What's with all the witch stuff?" he whispered to Lola. "Do you think they're into black magic around here? I don't like it; it makes me think of Tzelek at the Black Pyramid."

"I'll ask," said Lola.

When she ordered the drinks and phrased her question, all in Spanish, Max saw the old woman freeze for a moment. Then she cackled with laughter and looked straight at him. He couldn't help but notice she had bulbous eyes, a hooked nose, jagged teeth, and a huge, hairy wart on her chin.

"She said there are no witches around here," said Lola.

They drank their sodas in silence.

Suddenly there was a scraping back of chairs, and all the lone drinkers stood up as one.

"Time to go," said Lola.

They followed the rest of the patrons out of the café, down cobbled streets, down steps, down alleyways, down, down, down, until they arrived at the beach. Like everywhere else in Galicia, the landscape was gray and green: gray with rocks and pebbles, green with glistening seaweed. The water was gray, too, interspersed with darker gray pillars of rock, and the sky was gray with just the faintest touch of watery pink where the sun was trying to call attention to its imminent setting. All down the beach, wrecked boats lay on their sides in the low tide, their wooden ribs sun-bleached to the color of old bones.

Max shivered. With no buildings to act as breakers, the full force of the wind roared in from the sea and cut like a sacrificial knife through his polyester suit.

"I'm freezing," he complained. "What happens next?"

"The dead are saying good-bye," said Lola. Her bottom lip quivered. "They're saying good-bye to the people they love. They don't know if they'll ever see them again. They're making promises they don't know if they can keep."

"I wish they'd hurry up," said Max, hugging himself to keep warm.

He watched the waves battering a skeletal galleon. With each surge of the tide, it was lifting off the sand, until it floated upright again. All along the beach, the shipwrecks were righting themselves.

"Lola, what can you see?"

"The dead souls are walking down to the sea. They're boarding the ships. . . ."

"What should we do?"

"We'll follow them," said Lola. She thought for a moment. "We'll just walk along the beach like innocent tourists, and when all the dead have boarded, we'll make a dash for the nearest boat. Stay close, Hoop, and follow my lead."

"We're going to board a ghost ship?"

"I'm sure the ghosts won't mind. They look like a friendly bunch."

"I'll take your word for it."

As the living relatives lined up to wave off the departing spirits, Lola walked nonchalantly toward the sea, stopping every so often to pick up shells and sea glass. To make sure he didn't tread on the toes of any spirits, Max stayed a few paces behind her.

"Okay," she said, "I'm going in. Follow me."

But as she waded into the shallows—"It's freezing!"—a grizzled old man in a naval cap and dark blue turtleneck came huffing and puffing up the beach

"*Turistas! Qué están haciendo?*" he shouted over the howling wind. "*Este mar es peligroso! Voy a llamar a la policía!*"

"What's he saying?" asked Max.

"He's threatening to call the police," said Lola. "He said that this sea is dangerous."

The force of the waves crashing on a nearby rock took Max's breath away. "You can see his point," he muttered.

So Max and Lola walked along the beach, trying to look like they didn't have a care in the world, as all their hopes and plans sailed away on a ship of dead souls toward the setting sun.

"What now?" said Max as the last boat slipped over the horizon.

"Let's keep walking. I think we're close to something. The necklace feels kind of warm. Maybe there's a cave. . . ."

The relatives of the dead waved their last good-byes and began to make their way back up to the village, where the bus was waiting in the parking lot and honking its horn.

Soon the beach was empty.

The waves grew bigger and angrier. Seagulls screamed. The wind was heavy with salt and menace.

Lola stopped and peered at something down the beach.

Max followed her gaze, but saw nothing.

"What are you looking at?" he asked.

"There's a boat!" she cried. "Come on!"

"Where?"

Max ran after her down the beach, trying to see what she saw. But still he saw no boats.

"Here it is!" She pointed to a pile of rotting drift-wood.

"No way," said Max.

Lola began to clear the pile of debris and seaweed, until she revealed the remains of an ancient, barnacle-encrusted rowboat. As she worked, she nodded to herself and sometimes paused as if she was listening to the wind.

"You're acting strangely," said Max.

"It's called getting the job done. Shall we launch our boat to Xibalba?"

"That thing won't float. There's nothing left of it."

"Oh, come on!" said Lola. "Where's your sense of adventure, Hoop?"

"That's exactly what you said before we went down the underground river in that raft and I nearly drowned—"

"But the point is, you didn't drown." Lola put her hands on his shoulders and looked straight into his eyes. "Trust me, Hoop."

"It's the boat I don't trust. . . ."

"Help me turn it."

They heaved it over, displacing a large colony of crabs, and pulled off most of the seaweed.

"Oars, oars . . . ," muttered Lola to herself. She looked around the beach and found two battered pieces of timber. "These will do."

"Lola, stop; this is crazy. Have you seen the state of the sea? We'll be smashed against the rocks."

"The tide's going out. If we're lucky, it will wash us clear of the rocks."

"What if we're not lucky?"

"We *are* lucky." She pointed out to sea like a conquistador pointing to El Dorado. "Your destiny awaits you, Max Murphy!"

Police sirens sounded in the distance.

"Hoop! We need to go!"

Max looked to and fro between the frail little boat and the huge, pounding waves. "It's too dangerous. They don't call it the Coast of Death for nothing. . . ."

"Okay," said Lola, looking at something over Max's shoulder. "I'll go alone. But I hope the police get here before the hellhounds."

"What do you—?" began Max, but before he could finish the question, he heard a familiar frenzied snarling.

"If I turn around now," he said, "will I see a pack of angry hellhounds thundering toward me, eyes crazed with bloodlust, fangs bared, foaming at the mouth and dripping acid saliva in anticipation of eating me?"

"Yes."

"So how do we launch this thing?"

Chapter Twenty-three
THE SEA OF STARS

For a while, the village of San Andrés was visible in the distance, lit up by the blue flashing lights of a fleet of police cars. But then the boat was pitched and tossed from wave to wave until Max lost all sense of direction, and he thought they would die for sure. He couldn't see land, he couldn't even distinguish sky from sea; all was wild, howling, sloshing grayness.

They were propelled along in the current, their little rowboat slicing through the water like Neptune's chariot towed by dolphins. They were either being transported to their date in Xibalba or swept to certain death.

Or maybe both.

The wind howled; the waves roared; there was no chance of conversation.

Max and Lola sat facing each other, holding on to the sides of the boat. It was like a demented teacups ride. Even Lola looked terrified, which Max found more scary than anything.

They covered more miles that night in their ramshackle rowboat than any mariner would ever believe. And always they headed west, into the end of the world, into the setting sun.

After what felt like hours, the waves began to calm, but the slower their little boat moved, the more ocean it let in. Soon, a modest aquarium's worth of sea creatures—crabs, rays, starfish, crayfish, and even a small octopus—swilled around their feet.

They were dangerously low in the water.

Brine oozed in at every joint.

A mist rose off the waves in the cold evening air.

It was impossible to see anything now.

They were lost in a fog in a sinking boat.

Soon it would be dark.

"Look for the lighthouse at Finisterre," called Lola. "When we see the light we're nearly home."

Max tried not to think about how this voyage was most likely to end.

A whirring noise penetrated his consciousness. He looked up.

"It sounds like a helicopter," he said. "We're saved!"

"I have come for my bride," rasped a familiar voice over a megaphone.

"It's Landa!" yelled Lola. "I mean Tzelek!"

"*Surrender or die!*" commanded the voice.

Through a gap in the mist, Max saw that Tzelek-in-Landa's body was climbing down a rope ladder. He was surprisingly agile, despite his twisted foot. Two red eyes blazed out of the fog. He was nearly level with them now.

"Hoop, stay close!" Lola shouted. "If he can pick you off,

he'll kill you! It's me and the necklet he wants . . . and he has to keep me alive for that!"

Too late. Max felt an icy grasp on his neck.

Tzelek's sharp fingernails were once again digging into his skin.

"He's got me!" Max wheezed to Lola.

"Take that!" screamed Lola, hitting Tzelek with her oar.

The boat rocked wildly, and the oar disintegrated into rotten shards.

With one hand still around Max's throat, Tzelek grabbed Lola by the hair and forced her down. "So what happened to looking pretty and making tortillas and bearing my children? I'll deal with you in a moment, wifey," he said, in a voice that sent chills down Max's spine.

Pinning Lola to the floor of the boat with his viciously pointed leather boot, Tzelek picked Max up by the neck, ready to throw him over the side.

At the exact moment Max felt himself losing the battle, felt his feet lifting from the floor, and already felt the cold salt water sucking him down, he was blinded by a bright light.

When we see the light we're nearly home.

He remembered that people who came close to dying talked in magazines about walking to the light.

He realized that this was the end.

He looked toward Lola for one last farewell.

She winked at him.

Then, as if in slow motion, she reached into the bottom of the boat, picked up the octopus, and threw it straight at him.

Wait, not at him—at Tzelek.

HA!

At Tzelek.

The octopus hung from Tzelek's nose by its beak, its tentacles thrashing wildly in his mustache as they attempted to find suction on his bony cheeks.

"Get it off me!" screeched Tzelek, losing his balance as the octopus suffocated him with its rubbery, blubbery body.

Moving as one, Max and Lola went to push his flailing body overboard.

He resisted their efforts with superhuman strength but then, as if an unseen force had kicked him from behind, he suddenly plunged into the water.

Still the bright light advanced on them.

"*Guardacostas!*" boomed a voice.

Through the drifting mist, Max saw the grizzled old sailor from the beach manning the huge searchlight on the coast guard cutter.

"*Hombre al agua!*" called Lola, waving at him furiously. "Man overboard!"

"What?" said Max incredulously. "Why are you helping Tzelek?"

"I'm helping *us*," Lola explained. "They'll be so busy rescuing him, they won't notice us sneaking away."

As the old sailor directed his beam onto Tzelek in the water, and the other crew members yelled instructions and threw in life preservers, Lola bailed out the rowboat with her hands. "We're sinking fast," she said. "We haven't got much time. Break your oar in two and let's get out of here."

The fog was dense now, and the ebb tide was strong. Using half an oar each, they rowed quickly out of the coast guard's glare.

"We're close, I know we're close," said Lola. "The entrance to Xibalba is nearby. If only this fog would lift."

The fog cleared, as if at Lola's command.

It was night. Black night. At least the wind had died down. The water lapped placidly around the boat, like a kitten drinking milk.

It didn't feel like they were moving anymore.

"We're becalmed," said Max. "We're becalmed in the Sea of the Dead."

"Stop."

"We're becalmed in the Sea of the Dead, off the Coast of Death. That can't be good."

"Stop," repeated Lola. "Look up."

It was his old friend the Cosmic Crocodile, twinkling down at him, light-years away and so close he could almost touch it.

"See where its mouth is," Lola pointed out, "the dark space of sky between its jaws?"

"Uh-huh."

"That's the Dark Rift in the Milky Way. Otherwise known as the Road to Xibalba."

"Otherwise known as . . . *we're sinking*."

"Look at the sea, Hoop."

It was glassy and still, a perfect mirror image of the night sky above them. Max couldn't see where sky ended and water began. All around were stars and reflections of stars. Stars above them, stars below them, as if they were suspended in the infinite universe.

Except that Max's feet were wet. Very wet.

And something else was bothering him, too.

"Monkey Girl?"

"Yes?"

"Do you remember what Ah Pukuh said about taking the road and entering the water?"

"Yes."

"And Lord 6-Dog said it meant I was going to die?"

"Yes."

"Well, we took the road, the pilgrim road to Finisterre. And any minute now, I think we're going to enter the water."

The moonlight played on a fin circling the boat.

"Shark!" yelled Max.

Lola tried to stay calm. "Did you know that the word *shark* comes from the Mayan word *xook*?"

"No—and I don't care! Shark! *Shark! SHARK!*"

Lola paddled them into the mouth of the reflected crocodile.

"We made it!" she said. "Good luck, Hoop!"

"Wha—?"

The little boat sank beneath the waves and took Max and Lola with it.

In the cold water, Max saw the shark. It was even bigger than he had thought. He saw its serrated teeth as it headed straight for him.

He braced himself for unimaginable pain.

But instead of biting him, the shark dived underneath him.

Am I breathing?

Am I drowning?

What?

Max felt Lola's arms around his waist as they rode down, down on the back of a shark to the Maya underworld.

Chapter Twenty-four
THE END OF THE ROAD

I t was the intense pain of the lobster bite that brought him around.

Was it a lobster? Or a jellyfish with pincers?

Max stared at the neon-orange creature that was pinching his finger. With its bulbous eyes, thick lips, and amorphous body, it looked like a child's drawing. He pulled it off and it let go without a fight, dropping with a splash into the water around Max's feet, where it instantly clamped on to his leg through its coating of wet denim.

Max sat up and detached his attacker once again.

Once again it landed in the water with a splash.

There was a smell of fish and iodine and sulfur.

He surveyed his immediate surroundings.

He was, apparently, sitting on the edge of a rock pool.

A rock pool full of strange phosphorescent sea creatures, some like miniature sharks, others like turtles and shellfish, and strange hybrids like the one that had bitten him.

The rock pool was in some sort of cave.

In front of him, a faint light illuminated the cave walls, and Max could see grotesque Maya faces carved as if by nature into the rock, their noses coaxed out of overhanging boulders, their sloping foreheads following the natural curves of the dripping walls.

"Over here!" called Lola. "This way!"

Max squinted through the gloom.

He could just make out a girl in a long black dress scrambling over some rocks. In the dim light of the cave, the Yellow Jaguar beads around her neck shone like so many little suns.

Still half dazed, Max staggered to his feet and turned to follow her.

"What happened? Where are we? All I can remember is the shark and then diving and stars and blackness. . . ."

"Don't ask me—I had my eyes shut the whole time."

"Is this Xibalba?"

"I think so."

There was no way back, so they had to go forward.

"Give me your hand," she said. "This bit is slippery."

But she didn't let go when they were back on firm ground.

As they rounded the next bend in the cave, their way was blocked by a giant skull. It was covered in a layer of pale phosphorescent moss that made it glow in the dark like a Halloween party favor, but its expression was anything but fun. Grim and terrible, it faced them like a temple wall; its mouth was the doorway, and a row of sharpened stalagmites served as jagged teeth.

Flaming torches sputtered on the wall to light the way.

"This is the place, all right," said Lola.

"Do you think we're supposed to knock?" asked Max.

"I think they're expecting us, don't you?"

Max took a deep breath. "Into the mouth of hell it is, then—"

"Wait!" said Lola. She took down a torch and passed it to Max. "Hold this," she said. Then she picked up a boulder and hurled it with both hands over the bottom teeth and into the mouth.

The second the boulder hit the ground, a large earthenware pot came crashing down from the cave roof, spilling out its contents as it fell. Soon the boulder was completely buried under a hill of rotting entrails, maggots, blood, vomit, and yellow pus.

Lola clamped her hands over her face.

Max retched.

It was quite a welcome mat and it had been intended for their heads.

Max pulled up his shirt to cover his mouth, while Lola threw in another boulder to make sure that the Death Lords had set no more traps. Then, eyes streaming and gorges rising, Max and Lola quickly skirted the stinking pile and darted through the open mouth into a cavern the size of Fenway Park.

It was cold and damp in there, lit by more sputtering torches whose joyless flames were reflected in many pools and puddles on the cavern floor. The walls ran with water, and nameless creatures scurried in the shadows, but Max and Lola were just grateful for the pervading smell of strongly perfumed incense that masked the hideous heap in the doorway.

"We made it," said Lola.

"But where are we?" asked Max.

"I don't know," she admitted. "Maybe this is the entrance hall."

"We're not dead, are we?"

"How do you feel?"

"Let me think. How about terrified, nervous, apprehensive, freaked, scared out of my wits . . . ?"

"I don't think you'd feel all those things if you were dead."

"That's comforting."

"Shh. Someone's coming."

She was right.

There were footsteps.

Getting louder.

"*Biix a beel!*" called Hermanjilio cheerily, appearing at the far end of the cavern. "Long time no see!"

Behind him was Lucky Jim.

They were both dressed in simple white shifts and they waved and cheered as they half walked, half ran to their rescuers.

Hermanjilio held his arms open to Lola. "I knew you'd come!" he said with a beaming smile.

"Get away from me, you creep!" she yelled, jumping back.

Lucky Jim winked at Max. "No hard feelings?" he said, holding out his hand.

Baffled by Lola's reaction, Max shook Lucky's hand.

It came off at the wrist.

Max dropped it in horror, and the hand scuttled away like a spider. Lucky waved his stump in mock agony and collapsed, laughing.

"That's not funny!" said Max angrily, which made them laugh even harder. "Where are the real Hermanjilio and Lucky Jim?"

"That's for us to know and for you to find out," said the fake Hermanjilio in a childish, singsong voice.

Lola stood there looking bored and pretending to inspect her fingernails.

"You're not much fun, are you?" pouted the fake Lucky Jim, before morphing into Santino Garcia, the Spanish law student. "Do you like me better now?" he asked, combing his hair with his fingers. "How do you like my eh-sexy eh-Spanish accent?"

Hermanjilio clapped his hands appreciatively. "My turn! My turn!" he said, giggling girlishly as he morphed into Nasty Smith-Jones. "Hello, Max," he said flirtatiously, batting his eyelashes, "look into my big blue eyes. I'm so much prettier than Lola. Don't forget to call me when you get back to Boston."

Lola yawned. "Is that it?" she asked.

The fake Nasty Smith-Jones finished blowing kisses at Max, and nudged the fake Santino. The two of them burst into laughter as their flesh slowly rotted away to reveal the decomposed corpses of Demon of Jaundice and Scab Stripper.

"Kiss me, Maxie!" begged Scab Stripper, in Nasty's voice. His dangling, rotting lips were covered in oozing sores.

Max wheeled around in revulsion, trying not to gag, but Lola was unmoved.

"If you guys have finished with the comedy," she said, "perhaps we could get down to business."

"Hark at her," said Demon of Jaundice. "Don't you tell me what to do, missy. You just remember where you are. . . ."

There was a rush of wind, and Lord Kuy—the half-owl, half-human messenger of the Death Lords—landed silently among them. His great brown wings settled around him like a feathered cape, but his head rotated this way and that in irritation.

"What's going on here? Do you two have permission to be ashore? If Ah Pukuh hears about this, he will eviscerate you both. Again."

The two Death Lords looked visibly alarmed.

"I'm not scared of Ah Pukuh," said Demon of Jaundice, but his jumpy demeanor told the opposite story.

"Me neither," said Scab Stripper as his eyes darted around in panic.

Lord Kuy fixed them with a stare as sharp as a raptor's talon.

"Come on, Jaundice," said Scab Stripper, trying to sound nonchalant. "It's boring here, anyway."

"Yeah," said Jaundice, "it's boring here."

Sticking out their tongues and making faces at Max and Lola, the two Death Lords sauntered backward the way they had come, before breaking into a run and disappearing into the depths of the cavern.

"I do apologize," said Lord Kuy. "Let us start again."

He cleared his throat and ejected an owl pellet.

"Greetings to you both. Welcome to Xibalba, the world-famous Maya underworld. Lord Ah Pukuh asked me to apologize that he could not be here to welcome you in person— but, as I think you know, he is currently touring Middleworld in preparation for his impending reign of terror. May I offer you some refreshments after your journey? Would you like a guided tour before we get down to business?"

"No, thank you," said Max. "If it's all the same to you, we'd like to do the deal and go."

Lord Kuy's greedy yellow eyes fastened on Lola and the necklet. "I see you have the prize."

Max took a deep breath.

This was the moment he'd been waiting for.

This was the moment he'd been rehearsing in his mind ever since he'd arrived in Spain.

He was about to hand over the Yellow Jaguar, the last stone that Ah Pukuh and his Death Lords needed to bring Middleworld to its knees. He was about to save his own life and the lives of four more human beings—and, in the process, condemn all humankind to a new age of pain, misery, and suffering.

He looked at Lola.

Her expression was inscrutable. She reminded him of Princess Inez as a young girl, before the invaders came. But he had no doubt that, underneath that innocent exterior, she was plotting some double deal to outwit the Lords of Death.

He just hoped she didn't blow everything.

He stepped forward.

"Before we go any further, Lord Kuy, I need proof that the real Hermanjilio and Lucky Jim are still alive."

"But of course," said Lord Kuy. "Please step this way. . . ."

That was easy.

The owl man led them back into the farthest reaches of the cavern, to a misty, rocky riverbank where lanterns glowed on bamboo poles and vague sounds floated in from unseen places: muffled screams, breaking pots, drums, cheers, curses, and groans. It was like waiting to board the Pirates of the Caribbean ride at Disneyland. There was even a buccaneer manning the landing stage from his little cave, but this one was a skeleton, a jaguar-patterned scarf tied jauntily around his skull, his pelvic bones draped in a skirt of roosting bats.

As they approached, the skeleton buccaneer picked up a conch shell and blew into it—a low, mournful sound that woke up the bats. They flew in lazy circles before settling back down at his waist.

"He is summoning the boat," said Lord Kuy, casually picking a bat off the buccaneer's belt and biting off its head.

"How can there be a boat," asked Lola, "when there's no water?"

It was true. Now that Max looked into the misty chasm, he saw there was nothing but a dried-up riverbed between the rocks.

"It's called technology," said Lord Kuy. "We're rather proud of it." He swallowed the rest of the bat.

A stink of disease and putrefaction filled the air as an enormous canoe rolled into view, swept along on its own river of pulsating pink slime. As the canoe drew closer, Max saw that the slime was actually a multitude of giant bloodsucking centipedes, carrying the boat on their backs. The centipedes were translucent, and Max could clearly see their digestive tracts engorged with fresh red blood, as if they'd been filled up at a ghoulish gas station before their voyage. Two boatmen, one at the stern and one at the prow, both corpses, directed the river of invertebrates with long paddles.

In the front half of the canoe, the Death Lords were engrossed in a dice game. Dice rattled, curses were spat, and skeleton fists flew as they played, bad sportsmen all.

On a platform at the back of the canoe stood Hermanjilio and Lucky Jim.

They wore the same white shifts that Scab Stripper and Jaundice had worn, but these two men were, without doubt, the real thing. They looked so haggard and weak and exhausted, so breakably, painfully human.

When the canoe drew level, the two corpse boatmen tied up at the landing stage and let down the gangplank. Then they poked and prodded the two prisoners with their paddles to encourage them to disembark.

Lucky Jim remonstrated and tried to defend himself, but Hermanjilio cowered under the blows like a stray dog beaten into submission. Moving gracefully even with bound wrists, Lucky swung for the boatman who was taunting his friend and landed a punch on his waxy corpse face, knocking him right off the canoe. He landed soundlessly on the river of centipedes and was quickly consumed—dry blood, dead flesh, and all.

Seeing this, the other boatman backed off and allowed the prisoners to walk down the gangplank at their own pace.

Lucky Jim nodded to Max and Lola, but Hermanjilio didn't see them. He looked only at the calabash gourd that he cradled like a baby and whispered sweet nothings to it.

"What's wrong with him?" Lola asked Lucky Jim.

He took a moment before answering, looking at Lola with such an intense expression that it was hard to tell if he was sad or happy. "You must be Ix Sak Lol. Hermanjilio talks about you sometimes. I'm sorry to tell you this, but when Tzelek took over his body, his mind was permanently damaged. He has never recovered. He just sits around all day whittling gourds. That one's his favorite."

"Go to sleep," cooed Hermanjilio to the gourd.

"He thinks it's his child," explained Lucky Jim. "He calls it Lola."

Max watched Hermanjilio, appalled.

This day was going horribly wrong.

If Hermanjilio had lost his mind, then nothing could ever

be as it was. It didn't matter what Max did or didn't do next; he was powerless to make things right. He felt rage boiling up inside him like a volcano about to blow.

He turned angrily to Lord Kuy. "You said he was alive and well."

"It was fifty percent true. He's alive, isn't he?" He waved a wing at the buccaneer. "Gag the prisoners. They should not be conversing with the other side."

The buccaneer did as he was told.

Max looked at Lola. There were tears in her eyes.

"Okay," he snapped at Lord Kuy, "what happens next?"

At a signal from Lord Kuy, the skeleton buccaneer blew his conch shell again, and the Death Lords, who were now engaged in a rambunctious game of cards, turned to see what was happening.

"If I could have your attention, Your Majesties," called Lord Kuy, "it is time to do the deal."

In a second, the twelve Lords of Death had scrambled to their feet and lined up, bony and ancient and cadaverous, arms slung over one another's shoulders, laughing and joking and shadowboxing.

They were a hideous sight. But all blood and gore aside, Max realized they reminded him of his father's all-time favorite rock band, the Rolling Stones.

"Presenting the twelve Lords of Death!" announced Lord Kuy. "Their lordships, One Death and Seven Death . . ."

A pair of corpses, one slightly taller than the other, their flesh blackened and moldy and crawling with maggots, broke off their scuffling to step forward.

Each wore a tall headdress of black feathers and carried an assortment of bloodstained weapons.

"Are you ready to die, Massimo?" asked the taller one.

"We will harvest his organs one by one and eat them as he watches," added the other one.

"No," argued the taller one. "We will liquefy his insides and drink them through a straw in his brain."

"We'll see about that," shouted the smaller one, choosing an obsidian battle-ax from his armory and hacking his colleague's head off. As he did so, his victim drove a lance through his stomach. For a moment, they both lay wounded, oozing old brown blood. Then their bodies reformed and they went at each other again with another set of weapons.

"Why are they talking about killing me?" Max asked Lord Kuy suspiciously.

"They are Death Lords. It's force of habit. Now let me introduce Lord Blood Gatherer. . . ."

A skinless body, looking like one of those anatomy drawings you see in doctors' offices, took center stage.

"And Lord Wing . . ."

He was half human, half vulture, with half-eaten body parts dangling from his beak.

"Stop!" called a mummified body with its bones on the outside. "Don't tell him our names, Kuy. That's how the Hero Twins got power over us, remember?"

"Good point, Lord Packstrap," responded Lord Kuy.

Packstrap groaned. "Birdbrained idiot," he muttered.

But really, even without formal introductions, it wasn't hard for Max to put names to the rest of the faces.

Demon of Jaundice and Scab Stripper he'd already met a few minutes before. Demon of Pus was covered in yellow pustules; Demon of Filth dragged his diseased purple intestines through the dirt behind him, attracting a cloud of flies; Bone Scepter and Skull Scepter were tufty-haired skeletons, with just the merest hint of old cartilage sticking to their bones; Demon of Woe was morbidly obese, with heavy black shadows under his eyes.

"So what's the delay, Kuy?" shouted One Death.

"Tell him to hand over the Yellow Jaguar!" demanded Seven Death.

"It's in the hou-ouse, it's in the hou-ouse," sang Skull Scepter, stirring an imaginary pot with two hands and rotating his pelvis.

"I called it first!" said Wing.

"Why don't we just kill him?" asked Woe.

"Look at them," whispered Max to Lola. "They're morons. They'll bring about the end of the world and they won't even care."

"I think I can stop them," said Lola. "I've had an idea."

"What is it?"

"Trust me. Just do what I say."

"Okay, but you're not going to pull any funny stuff? We have to give them the Yellow Jaguar, or the deal will be off! They'll kill Hermanjilio and Lucky Jim and my parents . . . and *me*." Max's insides felt like melted ice cream, churning around. He just wanted this scene to be over.

"Is there a problem?" asked Lord Kuy.

"No," said Max. "Ready when you are."

"Then let's do this thing," said Lord Kuy.

Max looked expectantly at Lola. "So may I have the Yellow Jaguar?"

"No," she said.

"Stop messing around, Lola! Give it to me."

"No."

"What's the matter with you?" Max asked her. "You want to get out of here, don't you?"

"Think about it, Hoop. If I give you the necklet, Lord

347

Kuy will tell you to take it to the Death Lords, as agreed. You'll notice that the Death Lords are staying on the canoe. How do you know that as soon as your feet are on board, the gangplank won't be raised and you won't sail off forever on a sea of bloodsucking centipedes, into the deepest, darkest reaches of Xibalba?"

Max turned to Lord Kuy. "Is she right? Is this a trick?"

Lord Kuy looked as guilty as an owl can look. "Don't blame me. You took the road. You entered the water. What did you expect?"

"I expected you to keep your word."

At this, the Death Lords screamed with mirth. Bone Scepter literally cracked up and Skull Scepter laughed his head off. Even the Demon of Woe was holding his corpulent belly and shaking with laughter.

"Tell him, Kuy," ordered One Death, wiping the tears from his dead eyes. "We lie. We cheat. That's what we do. It's our entire raison d'être."

"Duplicity is their brand platform." Lord Kuy's head swiveled slowly back to Max. "Didn't anyone ever tell you not to trust the Lords of Death?"

Only a gazillion times, thought Max.

Lord 6-Dog had told him every single day of their acquaintance.

Lola had tried to tell him, too.

Even his own mother had warned him of the Death Lords' duplicity.

But, for some reason, he'd thought he knew better.

Max felt sick to his stomach.

He'd been through so much. He'd actually tracked down the Yellow Jaguar that had been lost for centuries and, even more remarkably, he'd found a way to take it to the ancient Maya underworld. Now it was time for the happy ending. But instead, for his reward, the fiends of hell were threatening to drink him through a straw.

"I have a question," said Lola to the Death Lords.

"Well, keep it to yourself," sneered Wing.

"I'd be nice if I were you," said Lola, stroking the yellow beads around her neck. "As long as I am wearing it, this necklet is mine to give—and mine alone."

"What is your question?" asked Skull Scepter sulkily.

"Why must you kill this boy? He has fulfilled his quest and brought you the Yellow Jaguar. Isn't that enough?"

"We need a human trophy," Scab Stripper explained. "It's been a while since we had a decent sacrifice. We're wondering if that's why mortals fear us less. We're getting back to basics, working out a new core strategy before the new *bak'tun*."

"I see," said Lola. "So all you need is a sacrificial victim?"
Scab Stripper nodded.

"Then take me," she said. "I will bring you the necklet."
Before Max could stop her, Lola had raced up the gangplank and jumped into the canoe.

"Noooooooo!" screamed Max.

"Good-bye!" she called. "Always remember that I loved you!"

But it was too late.

Lucky Jim was making strangulated sounds under his gag.
Even Hermanjilio looked agitated.

But it happened so fast, there was nothing anyone could do.

349

The Death Lords whooped and cheered, the gangplank was raised, and a brave Maya girl sailed off forever on a sea of bloodsucking centipedes, into the deepest, darkest reaches of Xibalba.

Max watched until he could no longer see the Yellow Jaguar necklet shining through the gloom. "Oh, Monkey Girl," he whispered. "That was your worst idea ever."

Lord Kuy flapped his cape. "The matter is settled," he announced, looking at Max. "The girl gave her life for yours, and you are also freed." He sounded cold and officious, as if he was ticking off boxes on a clipboard. "Good-bye, Massimo Francis Sylvanus Murphy. And if you still want those half-wits"—he nodded toward Hermanjilio and Lucky Jim—"take them with you. Otherwise, just throw them in the riverbed, and the centipedes will finish them. I speak for all Xibalba when I say good riddance."

With that, he flew away.

And that was it.

Max Murphy's noble quest to save the world had ended in disaster. He couldn't even save his best friend. The Death Lords had all five Jaguar Stones. But even more unthinkable, they had Lola.

After a while, he mustered the presence of mind to untie Hermanjilio and Lucky Jim and take off their gags. But no one said anything.

They just sat on the rocks, staring into the darkness.

Eventually Lucky Jim spoke. "She's not coming back."

"I don't know what to do," said Max. "What would she want me to do?"

Lucky thought about it.

"Let's get Hermanjilio to a doctor," he said.

They asked the buccaneer how to get back to Middleworld.

"Follow the sun as it exits Xibalba," he said. "Should be along any minute."

Whoomph!

A fireball shot out of space like a cannonball and went hurtling down a tunnel in a sizzle of steam.

Max and Lucky Jim each took one of Hermanjilio's arms and led him into the tunnel behind the rising sun. The fireball was soon out of sight, but it was easy enough to follow its scorched trail.

Who knew where or when they would emerge?

Max didn't care.

"I smell the forest," said Lucky Jim when they'd walked in silence for what felt like hours. "We're in San Xavier."

After a few more twists and turns, they stepped out into a jungle clearing.

Max looked back at the way they'd come, trying to imprint it on his mind, wondering if it would ever lead him back to Lola. He was surprised to see that the entrance to the tunnel was a manmade building, a derelict temple, its facade carved into a monster face. Even as he looked at it, the mouth filled up with rubble until the door was blocked—like it had been when he first saw it, all those weeks ago.

"I know this place," he said. "That temple, it's called Structure Thirteen! This is where I first met Lola."

He gazed around, remembering the pretty Maya girl who'd snuck up on him in the jungle, who'd introduced him to her howler monkeys, who'd shared her last tortilla, who'd rescued him from the clutches of Antonio de Landa.

But something was different.

Something was very, very wrong.

It was early morning, but the forest was eerily silent. No birds sang. No insects buzzed. No monkeys crashed through the trees.

There were no trees.

The earth was bare and scorched and smoking.

"What's happened here?" whispered Max.

"Loggers," said Lucky Jim.

"Will it grow back?"

"No, they've cut too much. Once the topsoil's gone, that's it."

Max sat down on a tree stump.

His life had been destroyed like this forest. He felt dead inside.

No trees, no birds, no animals, no Lola.

Lucky Jim sat next to him and put his head in his hands.

"Welcome to the end of the world," he said.

Chapter Twenty-five
A SURPRISE

Another 7 hours or 420 minutes or 25,200 seconds ticked by before Max found out what had happened to Lola. First Max, Lucky Jim, and Hermanjilio had to make their way through what was left of the forest back to Villa Isabella, Uncle Ted's mansion by the sea at Puerto Muerto. They walked like zombies, heads down, putting one foot in front of the other, each one crushed by the sorrow of what had happened. Even Hermanjilio seemed to understand the situation, and his face was a blur of tears.

No one talked because there was nothing to say.

Lola was gone.

Lola was gone.

Lola was gone.

After the first six hours of silent marching through rain and sun, Max asked Lucky Jim, "When Lola said, 'Always remember that I loved you,' do you think she was she talking to Hermanjilio or to me?"

"Maybe to both of you?" Lucky Jim suggested diplomatically.

A bit later, as they walked along the beach toward Villa Isabella, Lucky Jim took deep lungfuls of sea air. "I feel guilty about saying this when Lola's in that terrible place, but it sure is good to be home."

"It's my fault you were in Xibalba," said Max. "I never had a chance to thank you for saving my life."

"Anytime. Besides, I learned a lot in Xibalba."

"Like what?"

"Like what it means to be Maya."

"So how are we going to get Lola out of there?"

"I don't know."

Lucky sighed heavily. "I'm going to be honest with you Max. You see, Hermanjilio and I were kept in a sort halfway house. They beat us a lot, especially Hermanjilio, but I heard it was nothing compared to the tortures of the lower levels. Lola sailed off with the Death Lords, so she must be going straight to Level Nine."

"Level Nine?"

"It's the lowest level. It's like the royal court of Xibalba, the high-security wing. I'm sorry, Max, but I don't think anyone can escape from Level Nine."

"Lola can do anything," insisted Max.

"I wish I'd known her," said Lucky Jim as he pushed open the door of the villa. "Sounds like she was quite a girl."

Max nodded. "Lola was the most amazing girl I've ever met."

"A bit less of the *was*, if you don't mind, Hoop," said Lola.

She was sitting in an armchair in Uncle Ted's hallway, reading a book.

"What are you doing here?"

"Waiting for you, of course."

"Are you a ghost? I mean, I'm just asking; that's fine if you are."

Lola stood up and held out her arms. "No, I'm not a ghost. And I'm sorry for what I put you through. It must have been awful. But it was the only way, Hoop. The Death Lords were never going to let us all walk out of there. Someone had to stay behind."

"But how did you get out?"

"I'll tell you everything. But first I need a hug. From all of you."

A quick embrace for Lucky Jim and a slow, sad waltz with Hermanjilio.

"My turn, my turn," demanded Max impatiently.

And it wasn't until he felt her living, breathing warmth that he finally believed she wasn't dead.

"Now tell me how you did it—"

"Ah! Splendid! You're here!" cried Uncle Ted, strolling down the hall. He looked around at everyone and beamed from ear to ear. "From what Lola tells me, you've had quite an adventure." He ruffled Max's hair. "I see you've ditched the Murphy red, Max! Maybe I'll dye mine, too! But first things first. Are you hungry?"

Max nodded.

"Raul is planning a victory feast on the terrace. Does that sound good?"

Max nodded. It sounded great.

A victory feast. It made him feel like a Viking returning home from battle. He was giddy with triumph and relief and exhaustion. Never mind that the Death Lords possessed all five Jaguar Stones. Never mind that in a few months' time, Ah Pukuh would take over the world. The world could take its chances. All that mattered was that the quest was over and that somehow Lola had escaped from under the Death Lords' noses. And that was the only victory Max cared about right now.

Uncle Ted gave a great bear hug to Lucky Jim, his foreman and trusted friend. Then he turned to Hermanjilio. "I'm so pleased to meet you at last, Professor Bol. I've heard so much about you from Lola."

Hermanjilio stared at him blankly, a fixed grin on his face.

"I think he's still in shock," said Lola.

"We all are," said Max. "Are you going to tell us what happened?"

"So—" began Lola, but Uncle Ted interrupted.

"Excuse me," he said, "but I have to ask Max to make a phone call first. I'm under strict instructions from Carla to put him on the line as soon as he walks through the door."

"I'll call her later," said Max. "I need to talk to Lola."

"No," said Uncle Ted firmly. "Your mother has been worried sick about you. Just let her hear your voice, and then we can all relax."

"But—"

"Call her."

She had good news for him. "Really, Mom? Your hair's grown back? That's great! And Dad's botfly's popped out? Cool! And the rainforest in the hallway is all gone? That's awesome! It's really over. . . ."

Uncle Ted tapped him on the shoulder and made eating motions.

"I have to go now, Mom, I'll see you soon!"

Max hung up. His arm was aching from holding the receiver and talking on the phone so long. And still he hadn't told his parents the half of it. But he'd been glad to hear that the curse, or whatever it was, was lifted, and that life in Boston had gone back to normal.

"Notice any changes since last time you were here?" asked Uncle Ted as he walked with his nephew down the hallway.

Max looked around. Villa Isabella used to be so cheerless and intimidating, more like a fortress than a house. But now there were cozy touches everywhere: woven rugs on the cold, tiled floor; brightly striped pillows on the chairs; and vases of flowers on every surface.

It was quite a transformation.

Just a few short weeks ago, Uncle Ted had been a lonely, bitter, child-hating recluse, who dealt in bananas by day and smuggling by night. Now he was a reformed character, a man who loved life and family and good company. Before they'd flown out to Spain, Lola and the monkeys had been staying with him. Lola had even inspired Uncle Ted, a former art student, to stop smuggling Maya artifacts and take up his paintbrushes again.

"It looks good," said Max.

"It's all thanks to Lola," said Uncle Ted.

Max smiled to himself as he took his seat.

Lola was safe.

Lola was safe.

Lola was safe.

Except she wasn't there.

Max looked around in panic. "Where is she? Where's Lola?"

"It's okay, Max," Uncle Ted reassured him. "The doctor came to see Hermanjilio. She's sitting with him. They won't be long. And Lucky's gone to visit his own family. So it's just you and me for the moment." He pulled out a chair. "Come, talk to me."

Still anxiously looking around for Lola, Max took a seat.

There was a jug of fresh limeade on the table, and Uncle Ted poured out two glasses. "And how are things in Boston?" he asked.

"Mom said she woke up this morning and the rain had stopped and she had a feeling that I was okay. She was very happy to hear from me, though."

"I'll bet she was."

"Yeah. And just before I called, they'd had a call from Zia. Apparently, she's in Portugal with the monkeys. She thought it was wise to get out of Spain, but Lord 6-Dog wasn't well enough to get on an airplane. So she drove over the border to give him some time to recover; she's bringing them home in a day or two."

Uncle Ted pricked up his ears. "What's that? That mad-woman who lives with you in Boston? She's coming here?" He sounded appalled.

"I thought you liked having company these days, Uncle Ted."

"It's true that you and Lola changed my mind on that score, but I draw the line at—what do you call her?—Zia."

"Well, I'm looking forward to seeing her again," said Max. "I still have so many questions for her."

Lola guided Hermanjilio out onto the terrace.

He walked with a painful shuffle and he looked like a broken man.

Lola helped him into a chair and placed a blanket around his shoulders. He was still clutching his gourd, and Lola watched sadly as he took a napkin from the table and made it into a little blanket for his beloved vegetable.

"He calls it Lola," she said, looking away and trying not to cry.

"What did the doctor say?" asked Uncle Ted.

"He gave him a vitamin shot to perk him up a bit, but he said Hermanjilio has been physically and mentally tortured. At this stage, it's impossible to tell if the damage is permanent. He said to give it time."

"Well, you must both stay here for as long as it takes," said Uncle Ted.

Raul, Uncle Ted's butler, burst through the terrace doors with a loaded tray. "I am sorry it took me so long, everyone, but I got used to Lady Coco helping me. I miss my little sous-chef so much."

Max remembered when Raul had first met the talking howler monkeys and how Lady Coco had won him over with her cashew-and-mango muffins.

"She'll be home soon, Raul," he said, his stomach rumbling in delight as the butler set out platters of grilled fish, rice, avocados, tomatoes, corn, fried plantains, scrambled eggs, home-baked bread, honey cakes, and a huge bowl of fresh fruit salad.

"So talk," Max begged Lola when they'd filled their plates. "Tell me how you escaped from Xibalba."

"I was never in Xibalba, Hoop."

"But I saw you. We were together. We rode on the shark."

"That was someone who looked like me. A Maya girl in a black dress."

"Who . . . Who was she?"

"Think, Hoop. Think hard."

"Tell me."

"You know her."

Max's eyes bugged out. "Not . . . Not . . . Princess Inez?"

Lola nodded.

"But how . . . ? Why?" asked Max.

"She wanted to help you. She guessed that the Death Lords would want a human sacrifice, so she came up with a way to trick them."

"But when did you two cook all this up?"

"On the beach. She was there. You remember how I could see and hear the spirits of the dead, and you couldn't? Well, it was Princess Inez who found the old rowboat for us. When we launched ourselves into the sea, she was in the boat with us. She helped us push Tzelek into the water. When the boat sank, I gave her the Yellow Jaguar and we swapped places. Then I swam back to the coast guard boat. They were still searching for Tzelek."

"Did they find him?"

"No."

"How did you get back to San Xavier?"

"Zia was waiting on the beach. She drove me to the airport and bought me a ticket, and here I am."

"It was terrible down there," said Max, feeling slightly betrayed.

"I'm sorry, Hoop, but Princess Inez knew what she was doing. It was the only way to get you all out alive."

"She said she loved me."

"She was probably talking to Rodrigo. She said you look just like him. Wait—you didn't think that was *me* talking to *you?*"

Max changed the subject. "Don't you think it's weird that I look like him and you look like her?"

"That's why the Death Lords brought us together. It was the only way they were ever going to get their hands on the Yellow Jaguar."

"Their plan worked."

"Maybe and maybe not. I mean, Princess Inez defended the Yellow Jaguar from the Landa family for five hundred years. Maybe she can fight off the Death Lords, too. At the very least, she'll delay Ah Pukuh's plans to destroy the world."

"But it's just a matter of time," said Max miserably.

"Yeah," said Lola.

"Cheer up," Uncle Ted told them. "You're both here; you're both safe; you're freed from that ridiculous quest—that sounds like good news to me."

"But sooner or later, the Death Lords are going to take down Middleworld just for the fun of it."

"They have all five Jaguar Stones. There's nothing we can do to stop them," added Lola.

Hermanjilio made a funny little snorting noise.

"Are you all right?" Lola asked him solicitously. "Would you like some more limeade?"

"What I'd like," said Hermanjilio, "is for you two to stop whining."

Max and Lola looked at him in surprise.

"I think the vitamin shot's kicking in," muttered Uncle Ted.

"I know I've been a little out of things," continued Hermanjilio, "but I haven't lost all my faculties yet. And from where I'm sitting, you two sound like quitters. Are you telling me that you're just going to sit back and let the Death Lords call the shots?"

"There's nothing we *can* do," said Lola, sounding annoyed.

"They have all five Jaguar Stones, remember?" said Max.

"That's where you're wrong," said Hermanjilio.

"What—?" began Lola.

"But—" began Max.

"Why—?" began Uncle Ted.

They all stopped talking, mouths gaping, eyes wide open, as Hermanjilio gently laid down his gourd, unwrapped its little blanket, unscrewed its little gourd lid, and extracted a Jaguar Stone of pure white alabaster.

"The White Jaguar of Ixchel," whispered Uncle Ted.

"Hermanjilio," said Lola, "what have you done?"

"I stole it," he said.

Her face relaxed into a smile. "How?"

"You'll remember that when I landed in Xibalba, my brain was being occupied by Tzelek. When he left, I was pretty messed up. The Death Lords threw me in with the rest of the lunatics, and I took a therapy class in gourd carving. Turned out I had a knack for it. I'd had some time to study the White Jaguar when your parents brought it to Ixchel, so I carved a replica from memory. Just before you came down to Xibalba, I was able to swap it for the real thing. As far as I know, they haven't noticed yet."

"Woo-hoo!" yelled Lola. "I've always said you're a genius!"

"This calls for a celebration!" cheered Uncle Ted. "Ice-cream sundaes all around!"

Max said nothing.

He was thinking.

"Hoop?" said Lola. "Are you okay?"

He stared at her, wild-eyed. "This changes everything."

"What are you thinking?"

"It's like a video game. You solve one quest and you go on to the next level. The quest to find the Yellow Jaguar may be over, but the game isn't finished. 6-Death was a day of new beginnings, remember? There's still everything to play for."

"The Death Lords will be angry when they discover that the White Jaguar is missing," Uncle Ted pointed out.

"And that Princess Inez is not me," added Lola.

"They're going to come looking for us," said Max, "and this time, we can make our own rules."

"Here we go again." Lola groaned. "How much time do we have?"

"Not long," said Hermanjilio. "From what I overheard in Xibalba, they're expecting Ah Pukuh to make his move pretty soon."

"So," mused Max, "the End of the World Club will be happy."

"They'll be the only ones," said Lola.

"Let's just hope they're not right," said Uncle Ted glumly.

"No chance!" yelled Max and Lola together.

They looked at one another and burst out laughing.

"We're a good team, Monkey Girl," said Max, as Raul brought out a tray of massive ice-cream sundaes, loaded with cherries, nuts, and chocolate chips.

"Yes," said Lola, "we are."

To be continued . . .

What reward did Lord Kuy promise Zia?

What will happen when the
Death Lords discover the theft
of the White Jaguar?

Will Lord 6-Dog and
Tzelek have their final battle?

Is there any way to stop
Ah Pukuh from destroying the
world as we know it?

These questions and many more
will be answered in
The Jaguar Stones: Book Three.

GLOSSARY

AH PUKUH (*awe pooh coo*): God of violent and unnatural death, depicted in Maya art as a bloated, decomposing corpse or a cigar-smoking skeleton. His constant companions are dogs and owls, both considered omens of death. Ah Pukuh wears bells to warn people of his approach (possibly an unnecessary precaution, since one of his nicknames is Kisin, or "the flatulent one," so you'd probably smell him coming, anyway).

CHAHK (*chalk*): God of storms and warfare, Chahk was one of the oldest and most revered of the ancient Maya deities. He has two tusklike breath scrolls emitting from his mouth to convey his humid nature, bulging eyes, and a long, turned-up nose. Frogs were thought to be his heralds, because they croak before it rains. Just as the Norse god Thor carries Mjolnir, his enchanted hammer, so Chahk wields the god K'AWIIL as his fiery lightning ax.

CHOCOLATE: Chemical analysis of drinking vessels has revealed that the Maya were drinking hot chocolate as far back as 500 BCE. Their version was a thick, rich, foamy drink flavored with honey, maize, or chili. They called it *chokol ha*, meaning "hot water." The word *cacao* is also from the Maya word *kakaw*, and cacao beans were used as currency throughout Mesoamerica.

CODEX (plural CODICES): Strictly speaking, any book with pages (as opposed to a scroll) is a codex, but the term is most closely associated with the books of the ancient Maya. Written and illustrated on long strips of bark paper or leather, folded accordion-style, these books painstakingly recorded Maya history, religion, mythology, astronomy, and agricultural cycles. All but three were destroyed during the SPANISH CONQUEST. (See DIEGO DE LANDA.)

COSMIC CROCODILE: The two-headed Cosmic Crocodile, or Celestial Monster as it is also called, is a Maya representation of the MILKY WAY. Its two heads represent the duality of life and death, as the sun moves through the northern sky in the life-giving rainy season and through the southern sky in the dry season.

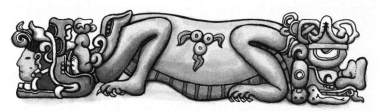

GLYPHS: Short for *hieroglyphs*, this is the name given to more than eight hundred different signs used by the Maya to write their books and stone inscriptions. The Maya writing system incorporates signs for sounds and signs for whole words. It is considered to be the most sophisticated system ever developed in MESOAMERICA and did not begin to be decoded until the 1950s. It was the teenage son of an archaeologist who cracked the last piece of the puzzle in 1987. About 80 percent of the most common glyphs have now been deciphered.

HERO TWINS: The twin brothers Xbalanke (*shh ball on kay*) and Hunahpu (*who gnaw poo*) are the main characters in the Maya creation story. Like their father and uncle before them, the twins are challenged to a ballgame in XIBALBA by the LORDS OF DEATH. But where their father and uncle died in the attempt, the twins outwit the Death Lords and take their places in the heavens as the sun and the moon. Their father is resurrected as Huun Ixim, the Maize God. The story of the Hero Twins is part of the Maya creation story, as told in the POPOL VUH.

HOWLER MONKEYS: With an extra-large voice box that makes them the loudest land animals on the planet, howlers can hear each other up to three miles away. Only the blue whale, whose whistle carries for hundreds of miles underwater, is louder.

ITZAMNA (*eats um gnaw*): Ruler of the heavens, lord of knowledge, lord of day and night, and all-around good guy. Itzamna gave his people the gifts of culture, writing, art, books, chronology, and the use of calendars. As a patron of healing and science, he can bring the dead back to life. With IXCHEL, he fathered the Bakabs. Itzamna is usually depicted as a toothless but sprightly old man.

IXCHEL (*each shell*): Like most Maya deities, Lady Rainbow had multiple personalities. As the goddess of the old moon, she is depicted as an angry old woman with a coiled snake on her head, fingernails like claws, and a skirt

decorated with human bones. In this guise, she vents her anger on mortals with floods and rainstorms. But as the goddess of the new moon, she is a beautiful young woman who reclines inside the crescent moon, holding her rabbit in her arms. Ixchel was the patroness of childbirth, medicine, and weaving.

JAGUAR: Called *bahlam* by the ancient Maya who revered it for its hunting skills, the jaguar is the largest and most ferocious  big cat in the Americas. Today, due to the fur trade and the destruction of its natural habitat, the jaguar is in danger of extinction.

JAGUAR STONES (*bahlamtuuno'ob*): A literary invention of the Jaguar Stones trilogy. Along with the five (fictional) sacred pyramids, these five stone carvings are said to embody the five pillars of ancient Maya society: agriculture, astronomy, creativity, military prowess, and kingship. As far as we know, no such stones ever existed—nor did the Maya ever relax their warlike ways enough to forge an equal alliance of five great cities.

JUNGLE/RAINFOREST: All tropical rainforests are jungles, but not all jungle is rainforest. A tropical rainforest receives at least 80 inches of rain per year. It is home to at least 50 percent of the species on Earth and more kinds of trees than any other area. The tops of the tallest trees form a canopy of leaves about 100 to 150 feet above the ground, while the smaller trees form one or two lower canopies. Between them, these canopies block most of the light from reaching the ground. As a result, little grows on the forest floor, making it relatively easy to walk through a tropical rainforest. If the canopy is destroyed, by nature or by humans, a tangle of dense fast-growing greenery springs up in the sunlight. This is jungle. Its growth provides shade for the rainforest species to reseed and grow tall enough to block out the light once more. This cycle can take one hundred years to complete.

K'AWIIL (*caw wheel*): A god of lightning and patron of lineage, kingship, and aristocracy. He has a reptilian face, with a smoking mirror emerging from his forehead and a long snout bursting into flames. Also known as Bolon Tzakab.

DIEGO DE LANDA (1524–1579): The overzealous Franciscan friar who tried to wipe out Maya culture by burning their CODICES and thousands of religious artworks in the square at Mani on July 12, 1549. Even the conquistadors thought he'd gone too far and sent him back to Spain to stand trial. Ironically, the treatise he wrote in his defense, *Relación de las Cosas de Yucatán* (1565), is now our best reference source on the ancient Maya. Landa was absolved by the Council of the Indies and returned to the New World as the bishop of Yucatán.

LORDS OF DEATH: In Maya mythology, the underworld (XIBALBA) is ruled by twelve Lords of Death: One Death,

Seven Death, Scab Stripper, Blood Gatherer, Wing, Demon of Pus, Demon of Jaundice, Bone Scepter, Skull Scepter, Demon of Filth, Demon of Woe, and Packstrap. The Lords of Death delight in human suffering. It's their job to inflict sickness, pain, starvation, fear, and death on the citizens of MIDDLEWORLD.  Fortunately, they're usually far too busy gambling and playing childish pranks on each other to get much work done.

MAYA: Most historians agree that Maya civilization began on the Yucatán peninsula sometime before 1500 BCE. It entered its Classic Period around 250 CE, when the Maya adopted a hierarchical system of government and established a series of kingdoms across what is now Mexico, Guatemala, Belize, Honduras, and El Salvador. Each of these kingdoms was an independent city-state, with its own ceremonial center, urban areas, and farming community. Building on the accomplishments of earlier civilizations such as the Olmec, the Maya developed astronomy, calendrical systems, and hieroglyphic writing. Although most famous for their soaring pyramids and palaces (built without metal tools, wheels, or beasts of burden), they were also skilled farmers, weavers, and potters, and they established extensive trade networks. The Maya saw no boundaries between heaven and earth, life and death, sleep and wakefulness. They believed that human blood was the oil that kept the wheels of the cosmos turning. Many of their rituals involved bloodletting or human sacrifice, but never on the scale practiced by the Aztecs. Wracked by overpopulation, drought, and soil erosion, Maya power began to decline around 800 CE, when the southern cities were abandoned. By the time the Spanish arrived, only a few kingdoms still thrived, and most Maya had gone back to farming their family plots. Today, there are still six million Maya living in Mexico, Guatemala, Belize, Honduras, and El Salvador.

1500 BCE		250 CE	900	1500	1800
Maya	Preclassic	Classic	Postclassic	Colonial	Modern
			Aztecs		
			Incas		

MAYAN: The family of thirty-one different languages spoken by Maya groups in Central America.

MESOAMERICA: Literally meaning "between the Americas," Mesoamerica is the name archaeologists and anthropologists use to describe a region that extends south and east from central Mexico to include parts of Guatemala, Belize, Honduras, and Nicaragua. It was home to various pre-Columbian civilizations, including the Maya (from 1500 BCE), the Olmec (1200–400 BCE), and the Aztecs (1250–1521). (The Incas of Peru in South America date from 1200 to 1533.)

MIDDLEWORLD: Like the Vikings, the Egyptians, and other ancient cultures, the Maya believed that humankind inhabited a middle world between heaven and hell. The Maya middle world (*yok'ol kab*) was sandwiched between the nine dark and watery layers of XIBALBA and the thirteen leafy layers of the heavens (*ka'anal naah*).

MILKY WAY: Seen from earth as a collection of stars against a band of hazy white light, the Milky Way is another name for the galaxy that contains our solar system. Just as the Maya called it "the road to Xibalba," so dead souls in Celtic followed the Milky Way to the underworld. In Spanish, the Milky Way is sometimes called *el camino de Santiago*, the road of St. James.

OBSIDIAN: This black volcanic glass was the closest thing the ancient Maya had to metal. An obsidian blade can be one hundred times sharper than a stainless-steel scalpel, but it is extremely brittle.

PITZ: The Maya ballgame was the first team sport in recorded history. It had elements of soccer, basketball, and volleyball, but was more difficult than any of them. The aim of the game was to gain ground while keeping the heavy rubber ball in play—using only hips, knees, or elbows. If the ball was knocked through a stone hoop high on the side wall of the ball court (a rare event), it was an automatic victory. The ballgame had great religious significance, and the losers were frequently sacrificed.

POPOL VUH (*po pole voo*): The Maya Book of the Dawn of Life, the sacred book of the K'iché (*kee chay*) Maya who lived (and still live) in the highlands of Guatemala. The title literally means "Book of the Mat" but is usually translated as "Council Book." The Popol Vuh tells the Maya creation story and explains how the HERO TWINS rescued their father from XIBALBA.

QUETZAL (*kets all*): The Maya prized the iridescent blue-green tail feathers of the resplendent quetzal bird for decorating royal headdresses. After the feathers were plucked, the birds would be set free to grow new ones. In ancient times, the penalty for killing a quetzal was death. Today, without such protection, the quetzal is almost extinct.

SAN XAVIER: A fictional country in Central America based on modern-day Belize.

SPAIN: In his search for the Yellow Jaguar, Max visits the Spanish provinces of Extremadura in the west, and Galicia in the northwest. The fictional town of Polvoredo in Extremadura is based on Trujillo, birthplace of Francisco Pizarro, conqueror of Peru, and home of the Spanish National Cheese Festival. The Castle of Polvoredo was inspired by the Palacio Moctezuma in nearby Cáceres. The *palacio* was built for Tecuichpotzin, oldest daughter of the Aztec ruler Montezuma, and her third Spanish husband, a captain in the army of Hernán Cortés. On the way north to Galicia, Max passes by the billboard bulls made famous by the Osborne sherry company. The family seat of Antonio de Landa was inspired by the Pazo de Oca, a country manor outside Santiago sometimes called the Galician Versailles. The Festival of the Near Death Experience takes place every summer in the little village of Santa Marta de Ribarteme, near

Pontevedra. The ancient city of Santiago de Compostela, the setting for Lola's wedding, has been a popular destination for pilgrims for more than a thousand years, ranking with Rome and Jerusalem in medieval times. Its great cathedral houses the *botafumeiro* (the name means "smoke belcher" in Galician), one of the largest incense censers in the world. It takes eight men to operate the pulley and it still swings giddily on its ropes on special feast days. It is said that when Catherine of Aragon stopped by for mass on her way to England to marry Henry VIII, the *botafumeiro* flew free of its ropes and crashed through the great stained-glass window. From here, Max and Lola journey to San Andrés—based on the real-life village of San Andrés de Teixido. Legend has it that any Galician who does not come here in his or her lifetime, will return after death as a lizard or a frog. San Andrés is on the *Costa de la Muerte*, the Coast of Death, so called because so many ships have been wrecked on its rocks and jagged inlets. Standing guard over this perilous coast is the magnificent lighthouse at Cape Finisterre, thought by the Celts and Romans to be the end of the world. Galicia is a wild and rainy region, famous for its seafood and, in particular, its *pulperías* or octopus restaurants.

SPANISH CONQUEST: Lured by tales of gold, thousands of Spaniards sailed to the New World in the fifteenth and six-teenth centuries, hoping to make their fortunes. Some were peasants, some were the younger sons of nobility who could not inherit the family estate and needed to fund castles of their own. Spain had just emerged from a bitter war against the Moors, so many were out-of-work soldiers. These ruthless and highly motivated fighters knew there were only two possible outcomes to their voyage: conquer or die. Their commanders (who gave one-fifth of their booty to the Spanish crown) organized and financed the expeditions, but the men had to provide their own armor and food. The three most famous commanders were Hernán Cortés, who defeated the Aztecs; Francisco Pizarro, who defeated the Inca; and Pedro de Alvarado, scourge of the Maya. The story of the conquest is as much about superstition and luck, as it is about military strategy. Cannons, muskets, and horses played their part, but the invaders' most effective weapon were the Old World germs of smallpox and measles that they unwittingly carried with them. The raggle-taggle Spanish armies marveled at the civilizations they encountered, even as they destroyed them. "We have a disease of the heart that can only be cured with gold," said Cortés to the Aztec ambassador. Most of the conquistadors endured incredible hardships and died in the jungle; only a few returned to Spain with any wealth.

XIBALBA (*she ball buh*): The K'iché Maya name for the underworld, meaning "well of fear." Only kings and those who died a violent death (battle, sacrifice, or suicide) or women who died in childbirth could look forward to the leafy shade of heaven. All other souls, good or bad, were headed across rivers of scorpions, blood, and pus to Xibalba. Unlike the Christian hell with its fire and brimstone, the Maya underworld was cold and damp—its inhabitants condemned to an eternity of bone-chilling misery and hunger.

MAYA COSMOS

This illustration (based on a painted plate from the Late Classic Period) depicts the three realms of the Maya cosmos: the heavens above, Middleworld (the world of humans), and the waters of Xibalba, the underworld. In the heavens, the two-headed Cosmic Monster (or Cosmic Crocodile, as Max calls it) contains the sun, Venus, and the Milky Way. In the middle of it all is the World Tree, which was brought into being by the king during bloodletting rituals. With its upper branches in the heavens and its roots in Xibalba, the World Tree was the doorway to the otherworlds of gods and ancestors. Communication with these spirits took place through the mysterious Vision Serpent. At the top of the World Tree sits Lord Itzamna as the bird of heaven.

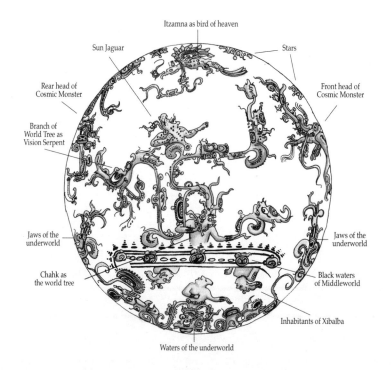

Itzamna as bird of heaven

Sun Jaguar

Stars

Rear head of
Cosmic Monster

Front head of
Cosmic Monster

Branch of
World Tree as
Vision Serpent

Jaws of the
underworld

Jaws of the
underworld

Chahk as
the world tree

Black waters
of Middleworld

Inhabitants of Xibalba

Waters of the underworld

THE MAYA CALENDAR

The Maya were fascinated by the passage of time and they developed a variety of astonishingly accurate calendars to track the movements of the sun and the stars. The Maya kings and priests used their advanced knowledge of astronomy to plan their rituals, wage their wars, and manage their agricultural cycles.

The Long Count

The Long Count counts the days (*k'in*) since the beginning of this creation. (The Maya believed there were three creations. The first two, when humans were made out of mud and wood respectively, were failures. The third creation, this one, when men were made out of corn, was deemed a success.) According to the Long Count, this third creation began, in our terms, on August 11, 3114 BCE. In the Long Count, the Maya year (*tun*) was 360 days long. Just as our 10-based counting system marks the decade (10 years) and the century (10 x 10 = 100 years), the Maya's 20-based counting system marks the *k'atun* (20 *tuns*) and the *bak'tun*, (20 x 20 = 400 *tuns*).

The Significance of 2012

There is no archaeological evidence that the Maya thought the world would judder to an end in December 2012. Quite the reverse—on King Pakal's tomb in Palenque, the Maya confidently predicted that people would be celebrating the anniversary of his coronation in 4774 CE! However, 12/23/2012 (some say 12/21/2012—the experts are divided) does have special significance in the Maya calendar. It marks the end of the thirteenth *bak'tun* (a four-hundred-year period with overtones of the mythic Maya creation date) and the beginning of the fourteenth *bak'tun*. Much like we would celebrate the dawn of a new millennium, the Maya would have marked this milestone with rituals and celebrations. Just as we don't think the world will end when our desk calendar runs out (we just buy a new calendar), the Maya also expected time cycles to continue like an odometer turning over.

The Haab

The Haab is the Maya calendar closest to our own. It tracks the solar year and is made up of 18 months, each consisting of 20 days, plus a 5-day period called the Wayeb to make a total of 365 days. The Wayeb was thought to be a time of uncertainty and bad luck, when the doors between the mortal realm and the underworld were opened and demons roamed the earth.

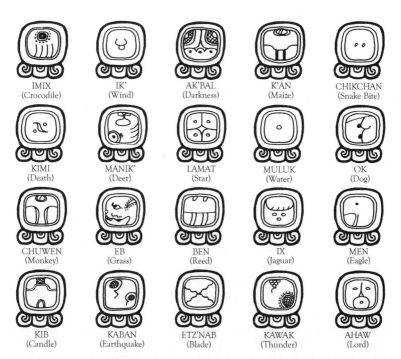

IMIX (Crocodile) IK' (Wind) AK'BAL (Darkness) K'AN (Maize) CHIKCHAN (Snake Bite)

KIMI (Death) MANIK' (Deer) LAMAT (Star) MULUK (Water) OK (Dog)

CHUWEN (Monkey) EB (Grass) BEN (Reed) IX (Jaguar) MEN (Eagle)

KIB (Candle) KABAN (Earthquake) ETZ'NAB (Blade) KAWAK (Thunder) AHAW (Lord)

The Tzolk'in

The Tzolk'in was the sacred calendar, used to predict the characteristics of each day, like a daily horoscope. It is made up of 20 day names and 13 numbers, and takes 260 days to go through the full cycle of name-and-number combinations. Each day name has a quality, some good, some bad. For example, Imix ("Crocodile") is full of complications and problems, and thus bad for journeys or business deals. The number (1–13) determines how strong the characteristic would be. So on 13-Imix, you might want to stay home.

The Calendar Round

The Calendar Round brings together the Haab and Tzolk'in calendars. It takes 18,980 days (about 52 years) to work through the 260 Tzolk'in days and the 365 Haab days. The Calendar Round is usually depicted as a series of interlocking cogs and wheels—which, in *Jaguar Stones: Middleworld*, was the inspiration for the "time machine" in the Temple of Itzamna.

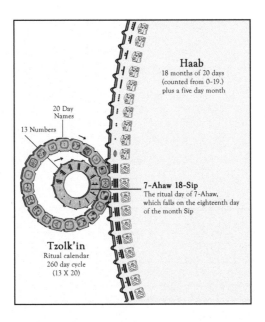

Haab
18 months of 20 days
(counted from 0–19.)
plus a five day month

20 Day Names

13 Numbers

7-Ahaw 18-Sip
The ritual day of 7-Ahaw, which falls on the eighteenth day of the month Sip

Tzolk'in
Ritual calendar
260 day cycle
(13 X 20)

PIMIENTOS DE PADRÓN

These are the tiny green peppers eaten by Max, Lola, and the monkeys on their first night in Spain. The peppers were brought back from Mexico by Franciscan monks in the sixteenth century and thrived in the fertile soil of their monastery near Padrón in Galicia. Today they are a popular *tapa* (snack) all over Spain. Most taste mild and sweet, but about one in twenty peppers is fiery hot. Hence the Galician saying "Os *pementos de Padrón, uns pican e outros non*." ("The peppers of Padrón, some are hot and some are not.")

Ingredients
Pimientos de Padrón, washed and dried well
Olive oil
Sea salt

Method
1. Heat oil in sauté pan until smoking hot.
2. Sauté peppers until they blister (around one minute), turning them to cook all sides.
3. Remove from pan and drain on paper towel.
4. Sprinkle with sea salt and serve immediately.
5. Pick up a pepper by its stem, cross your fingers, and bite.

ACKNOWLEDGMENTS

Like little orchids in the rainforest anchored by mighty trees, we're so grateful for the support of our colleagues, friends, and families, and all the amazing educators, booksellers, and librarians who've taught us so much along the way.

Thank you, *gracias*, and *dyos bo'otik* to the many, many people who've helped us, especially:

To our agent, the resplendent Daniel Lazar, at Writers House.

To our superhumanly hardworking and wonderful team at Egmont USA—especially Elizabeth Law, Mary Albi, Rob Guzman, Saint Nico Medina, Doug Pocock, Alison Weiss, and Katie Halata—for being such clever, funny, patient, encouraging, understanding, inspiring people to work with, and for leading the publishing industry in their commitment to sustainable paper sources.

To Dr. Marc Zender of the Peabody Museum at Harvard, who added immeasurably to the authentic atmosphere of this book by fact-checking our work while recovering from dengue fever in the ruins of Copan. We like to imagine him working by torchlight, in a hammock, while wearing a pith helmet, and fighting off vampire bats.

To Virginia Agagnos, Beth Garcia, and Jenny Brod at Goodman Media.

To Kathryn Hinds for her telepathic editing, Becky Terhune

for design, and Cliff Nielsen for a fantastically spooky cover.

To everyone who helped with our research, especially: in Belize, Geraldo Garcia, Franklin Choco, Karina Martinez, and Hugh Daly; in Guatemala, Jesus Antonio Madrid and José Cordoba; in Mexico, Denis Larsen, Sofi Balam Pat, and Gabino May Couoh in Valladolid, and Oscar Vera Gallegos, Vicente, and Chan Kin in Chiapas. In Spain: the Aalvik-Osuna family and José Manuel Alvarez in San Lorenzo de El Escorial, Don Mariano Zamorano, master swordsmith of Toledo, and the Lustau family in Madrid.

To our multitalented families for allowing us to exploit every one of those talents, especially: Alan, for his excellent advice on drumming, amongst other things; Christy, for blood, sweat, and tears on the lesson plan CD; Nicole, for making the Maya king costume, and Dustin, for wearing it with such panache; Andrea, for her fantastic work on the Web site; Lisa, for proofreading in English and Spanish; Jack, Mary Anne, and Trina, for looking after everyone when we're not here.

To our favorite booksellers: Liza Bernard and Penny McConnel at the Norwich Bookstore here in Vermont; the legendary Jill Moore at Square Books Junior in Oxford, Mississippi; Judith Lafitte and Tom Lowenburg at Octavia Books in New Orleans; Carol Chittenden at Eight Cousins and Vicky Uminowicz and family at Titcombs, both on Cape Cod; Emily Grossenbacher at Lemuria Books in Jackson; Brandi Stewart, Stephanie Kilgore, and Eddie Case at Changing Hands in Tempe; Lisa Sharp at Nightbird Books in Lafayette, Arkansas; Heather Herbert at Children's Book World in Haverford,

Pennsylvania; Gussie Lewis at Politics & Prose in Washington, D.C.; Summer Dawn Laurie in San Francisco; and Jennifer Stark at Barnes & Noble, New York City.

To Lucinda Walker and Beth Reynolds at the Norwich Public Library, and Zahra Baird at Chappaqua Library; and to our middle-school reader panel—Zea Eanet, Mateo Ellerson, Meredith Mackall, Tobias Reynolds, Siobhan Seigne, and Parker Thurston.

To all the teachers and librarians who've invited us into their schools, especially the inspirational Elizabeth Kahn at Patrick F. Taylor Science & Technology Academy, Jefferson Parish, Louisiana—and to all the thousands of students who've fastened their seat belts and flown to the jungle with us.

To Donald Kreis, the original Lord 6-Dog; Heather, Max, Juanga, and Julie; Cee Greene, Paul Verbinnen, and Big Guy; Jessica Carvalho; Peter and Hetty Craik; Graham Sharp; James Bowen; Andy the chef; Sarah Nasif; Stephen Barr; Brittany Czik; Grace Gartel; Peter Kraus; Tori Palmer; Maya at the Playa mastermind and educator extraordinaire, Mat Saunders.

And to Harry, Charly, and Loulou, for traveling with us.